PENGUIN CLASSICS

DANGEROUS LIAISONS

PIERRE AMBROISE FRANÇOIS CHODERLOS DE LACLOS was born in 1741, in Amiens. His family was respectable but not distinguished, and at eighteen he entered the army and spent the next twenty years in various garrison towns, and reached the rank of *capitaine-commandant* without ever seeing battle. He cut a dash in provincial society, however, and in his spare time wrote light verse, some of which was published. He wrote the libretto for *Ernestine*, a comic opera, which was produced in Paris in 1777, but was not received well. In 1779 he was sent to the island of Aix, off La Rochelle, where *Les Liaisons Dangereuses* was conceived and written. Comte Alexandre de Tilly recalls him saying: 'I resolved to write . . . a book which would continue to cause a stir and echo through the world after I have left it', which it certainly did. He went to Paris in 1781 to supervise the publishing of his book, and overstayed his leave and was promptly ordered back to his regiment. He married Marie-Solange Duperré in 1786 and proved to be an exemplary husband and father. He left the army in 1788, entering politics, and was imprisoned twice during the Reign of Terror, but returned to the army as a general under Napoleon in 1800. He died in Italy in 1803. Laclos also wrote a treatise on the education of women and on Vauban. Towards the end of his life he was considering writing another one to show that true happiness could only be attained in family life.

HELEN CONSTANTINE was born in Cornwall and educated at Truro High School and Lady Margaret Hall, Oxford, where she read French and Latin. She was Head of Languages at Bartholo-mew School, Eynsham, until 2000, when she gave up teaching and became a full-time translator. She has translated *Mademoiselle de Maupin* by Gautier, also for Penguin. She has recently published a volume of translated stories, *Paris Tales*, for Oxford University Press, and is co-editor of the magazine *Modern Poetry in Translation*. She is married to the poet David Constantine and has a daughter and son, and one grandson.

D0035931

CHODERLOS DE LACLOS

Dangerous Liaisons

Translated with an Introduction and Notes by HELEN CONSTANTINE

PENGUIN BOOKS

PENGUIN BOOKS

Published by the Penguin Group
Penguin Books Ltd, 80 Strand, London WC2R 0RL, England
Penguin Group (USA) Inc., 375 Hudson Street, New York, New York 10014, USA
Penguin Group (Canada), 90 Eglinton Avenue East, Suite 700, Toronto, Ontario, Canada M4P 2Y3
(a division of Pearson Penguin Canada Inc.)
Penguin Ireland, 25 St Stephen's Green, Dublin 2, Ireland
(a division of Penguin Books Ltd)
Penguin Group (Australia), 250 Camberwell Road, Camberwell, Victoria 3124, Australia
(a division of Pearson Australia Group Pty Ltd)
Penguin Books India Pvt Ltd, 11 Community Centre, Panchsheel Park, New Delhi – 110 017, India
Penguin Group (NZ), 67 Apollo Drive, Rosedale, North Shore 0632, New Zealand
(a division of Pearson New Zealand Ltd)
Penguin Books (South Africa) (Pty) Ltd, 24 Sturdee Avenue, Rosebank, Johannesburg 2196, South Africa

Penguin Books Ltd, Registered Offices: 80 Strand, London WC2R 0RL, England

www.penguin.com

First published in 1782
Published in Penguin Classics 2007

025

This translation and editorial material copyright © Helen Constantine, 2007
All rights reserved

The moral right of the translator has been asserted

Set in 10.25/12.25pt PostScript Adobe Sabon
Typeset by Rowland Phototypesetting Ltd, Bury St Edmunds, Suffolk
Printed and bound in Great Britain by Clays Ltd, Elcograf S.p.A.

Except in the United States of America, this book is sold subject
to the condition that it shall not, by way of trade or otherwise, be lent,
re-sold, hired out, or otherwise circulated without the publisher's
prior consent in any form of binding or cover other than that in
which it is published and without a similar condition including this
condition being imposed on the subsequent purchaser

ISBN: 978-0-140-44957-0

www.greenpenguin.co.uk

MIX
Paper from
responsible sources
FSC® C018179

Penguin Books is committed to a sustainable
future for our business, our readers and our planet.
This book is made from Forest Stewardship
Council™ certified paper.

Contents

Chronology   vii
Introduction   xi
Further Reading   xxv
Translator's Note   xxvii

Dangerous Liaisons   1

Appendix 1: Additional Letters   407
Appendix 2: Selected Adaptations
   of *Dangerous Liaisons*   410
Notes   411

Chronology

1741 18 October: born in Amiens, Pierre Ambroise François, second son of Jean Ambroise Choderlos de Laclos, secretary to the quartermaster general of Picardy, and Marie-Catherine Gallois.

1745 Crébillon *fils*'s licentious novel *Le Sopha*.

1748 Montesquieu's political treatise *L'Esprit des lois* (The Spirit of Laws).

1751 The family moves to Paris and settles in the Marais.

First volume of Diderot's *Encyclopédie*, an important organ of radical and revolutionary opinion.

1752 *Clarissa Harlowe*, Abbé Prévost's translation of *Clarissa* (1747) by Samuel Richardson.

1756 Birth of Mozart. The Seven Years War begins.

1759 Laclos becomes a cadet in the artillery at La Fère in the Aisne.

Rousseau: *Lettre à d'Alembert*. Birth of Robespierre and Danton.

Voltaire: *Candide*; Sterne: *Tristram Shandy*.

1761–2 Rousseau: *Julie ou La Nouvelle Héloïse* (1761); *Émile* and *Le Contrat Social* (both 1762).

1762 Takes up post as Second Lieutenant in La Rochelle.

1763 Posted to Toul, in the Lorraine region.

1765 The regiment is garrisoned in Strasbourg. Possible initiation into freemasonry. Becomes First Lieutenant.

1766 Birth of Madame de Staël.

1767 Publishes 'À Mademoiselle de Saint-S . . .', in *L'Almanach des Muses*.

1768 Birth of Chateaubriand. France acquires Corsica.

1769 Garrisoned in Grenoble.

Birth of Napoleon Bonaparte.

1770 Publishes some verses, 'L'Épître à Margot', in *L'Occasion et le moment*.

Birth of Hegel, Beethoven, Wordsworth and Hölderlin.

1771 Becomes a commissioned officer, rank of Captain.

1772 Promoted to Adjutant.

1774 More verses published in *L'Almanach des Muses*, which then circulate in Paris.

Death of Louis XV. Goethe: *Werther*.

1775 Garrisoned in Besançon.

Famine in Paris. Beaumarchais: *Le Barbier de Séville*.

1776 *Werther* translation published.

1777 Stages a comic opera, *Ernestine,* adapted from a novel by Madame Riccoboni.

1778 Given the overall responsibility of fortifying the island of Aix.

Begins work on *Dangerous Liaisons* and asks for leave of absence.

1781 Finishes *Dangerous Liaisons* in Paris.

1782 *Dangerous Liaisons* published by Durand in April. 2,000 copies are printed, then reprinted two weeks later. It is a resounding success. Ordered to rejoin his company in Brest.

1783 Writes an essay on women's education: *Des Femmes et de leur éducation* (published 1803). Starts a liaison in La Rochelle with Marie-Solange Duperré.

1784 Birth of their son.

1785 Elected member of the Academy at La Rochelle.

1786 Publication of his *Lettre à Messieurs de l'Académie Française sur l'Éloge de Vauban* (Letter to the Academy on the Praise of Vauban), which causes a scandal. Marriage with Marie-Solange, the mother of his child.

Mozart: *The Marriage of Figaro*.

1787 Proposes his *Projet de numérotage des rues de Paris* (Street-numbering Project for Paris), on which the present system for numbering the Paris streets is based.

Mozart: *Don Giovanni*.

1788 Enters the service of the Duke of Orleans. Birth of a daughter.

1789 Storming of the Bastille, Declaration of the Rights of Man.

October: May have been involved in the riots at Versailles. Leaves for London with the Duke of Orleans.

Mozart: *Così fan tutte*.

1790 Returns to France, active in the Club des Jacobins.

1791 Proposes the Regency of the Duke of Orleans.

1792 Reintegrated into the army.

1793 Successive arrests, incarceration and threats of execution. Execution of Louis XVI. The Terror begins.

1794 Escapes execution and is freed from prison.

1795 Writes *De la guerre et de la paix* (On War and Peace) for the government and another essay about women's education. Birth of third child. The Directoire.

De Sade: *La philosophie dans le boudoir* (Philosophy in the Bedroom).

1796 Banking projects.

1797 Possibility of his entering the diplomatic service.

De Sade: *Justine*.

1799 Unsuccessful request to be reintegrated into the artillery. Death of Beaumarchais. Birth of Balzac.

1800 Reintegrated into artillery as Brigadier General. Settles in Strasbourg. Takes part in first combats on the Rhine and then in Italy.

Beethoven's first symphony.

1802 Inspector General of the Artillery. Birth of Victor Hugo.

1803 Appointed Commander of the Artillery in Naples but falls ill with dysentery on the way there. Dies in Taranto 5 September.

Beethoven: *Eroica* symphony.

1824 The *cour royale de Paris* orders *Dangerous Liaisons* to be destroyed.

Introduction

Baudelaire noted, after reading this book in 1856: 'If this book burns, it can only be as ice burns.'[1] The fire that burns in Laclos's novel is an 'icy fire'. The poet's application of this Petrarchan idea to *Dangerous Liaisons* illustrates both the passion and the coldness we feel there is in these letters. The passion is undeniable: love, sensuality, jealousy and despair abound here; lives are played with, ruined and lost. The Vicomte de Valmont and the Marquise de Merteuil scheme and manipulate, they analyse and calculate, their language is ironic, detached, mannered, 'polite' and cool. The author's management of his characters and their deeds is as calculating, clever and ironic as Merteuil herself. Perhaps that is what Baudelaire meant: the passionate life is coldly dissected. A game is played out according to the rules and mores of a social class which Rousseau, the Romantics and many of the Revolutionaries thought incapable of real feeling and fit only for destruction. The ice Baudelaire alludes to may be not just narrative tone, language and techniques, but also the want of heart in those manipulators and their social class.

There was no doubt in Baudelaire's mind that this was a novel which had helped bring about the French Revolution. He calls it an 'historical book' and an 'essentially French book', and comments that the Revolution was created by 'des voluptueux', by which he means that it was the depraved sensuality of the aristocracy which excited the violent reaction of the people. Critics such as Michel Butor and Roger Vailland have more recently corroborated this view, calling the book a bombshell destined to serve as a weapon for the up-and-coming bourgeoisie against the privileged class, the aristocracy.[2] As a satire of an excessively wealthy and corrupt society and a moribund monarchy, which was manifestly by 1782, the year of its publication, on the point of collapsing, it is one of the very few novels which may claim, with its 'icy fire', to have contributed to a huge shift in the course of history.

Whether or not we believe Laclos's main aim in writing *Dangerous Liaisons* to have been political, it is most certainly a novel which holds the mirror up to contemporary society and shows it its ugly reflection. Not, of course, the whole of society, for the nobility were a minority, but within the parameters of that aristocracy the picture is a convincing one. Indeed when it was published most people thought it a *roman-à-clef*, and immediately tried to identify the characters. It was even rumoured that these were real letters from living persons which Laclos had stolen while on garrison in Grenoble. But such a reading is beside the point. Simply, most writers of fiction, and Laclos was no exception, do not work in that way; they may use people as models, and take from them certain traits of character or situations, real or possible, but on the whole, not just for reasons of discretion but more because of the demands of the fiction itself, they are unlikely to commit an exact portrait of any particular person to paper.

Laclos himself addresses the issue in his two tongue-in-cheek prefaces, first claiming that it is 'nothing but a novel' and saying, with heavy irony, that of course this so-called picture of the times must in fact be of a previous age, since in this century of Enlightenment we are all now honourable men and 'modest and retiring' women; and then in the second, teasing his readers and, of course, attracting more publicity in so doing, by pretending that he has 'suppressed or changed the names' of the – we are to suppose – real characters in the letters.

As is well known, all publicity is good publicity, and the inevitable happened. The first edition, as well as subsequent ones, sold out within days and the book rapidly became a *succès de scandale* in Paris. There were twenty reprintings in the first year. People soon discovered who its author was, and he himself, like his two main characters, became in the public mind, with no justification at all, a 'monster of depravity'. The reaction of most society women to Laclos's book was similar to that of his friend Madame Riccoboni, who blamed him for giving other people a damaging impression of the morals of the nation in the character of Madame de Merteuil. No doubt partly because of the book's title, it was considered dangerous and was read in secret, behind locked doors. Marie-Antoinette had a copy in her library. But it was also considered dangerous because, although Merteuil and Valmont are certainly monsters, they possess many admirable qualities and Laclos's treatment of them is certainly not wholly unsympathetic. In 1824 the *cour royale de Paris* ordered the novel to be destroyed.

Its author, meanwhile, deemed to have brought the name of the army into disrepute, was sent back to his regiment. For it may surprise us to learn that Laclos was no effete member of a dying aristocracy but a devoted husband and father and in his professional life an outstanding soldier and military engineer.

Born in 1741 in Amiens into a recently ennobled family (it was then they added the 'de Laclos'), Pierre Ambroise François Choderlos was sent to military school and joined the artillery – the preferred choice of the untitled classes. As luck would have it, he qualified for the army when the war with England ended and thirty years of peace began; and so instead of seeing action this brilliant and doubtless frustrated soldier was posted to various garrisons. These included Grenoble, for six years, and there he kept notes on various local notabilities and will certainly have used them to write the novel he began in 1778, when he was stationed on the Île d'Aix, off the coast of La Rochelle, and completed when he was on leave in Paris in 1781. After the publication of the book his leave was cut short and, back in La Rochelle, he took up the cause of the education of women in earnest and began a liaison with a woman half his age named Marie-Solange Duperré. At the relatively advanced age of forty-four he asked for her hand in marriage, and the couple, now with a small child, did indeed marry, against the wishes of her family, and remained devoted to each other for the rest of their lives.

In the same year, Laclos attacked the reputation of Vauban[3] as a builder of fortifications and soon after that proposed a new system for renumbering the streets of Paris. As the Revolution approached he appears to have become the right-hand man of the Duke of Orleans, also known as Philippe Égalité, who would become Regent if Louis XVI stepped down and then, so the intention was, make Laclos his First Minister. When this did not happen, Laclos's career took oddly different directions. He was said to have been involved in the March of the Women on Versailles in October 1789 and shortly afterwards he accompanied the Duke of Orleans to London and from there for several months conducted a vast correspondence which had as its aim the creation of a new and lasting peace in Europe. He returned to France in July 1790, joined the Jacobins[4] and became an editor of one of their newspapers. He was a constitutional monarchist until 1791, then a republican. He distanced himself from the Jacobins and lived quietly until recalled by Danton to military service in 1792 (the Duke of Orleans was guillotined in 1793). After organizing the repulse of the Coalition Forces at Valmy in September 1792, he was arrested the following year (for his moderate opinions) and threatened with execution, but survived Robespierre's Terror and was released from prison in 1794. Appointed by Napoleon as Inspector General of artillery in 1800, he carried out his duties assiduously, as well as looking after his wife and family till the end. He died of dysentery in Taranto, on his way to Naples, where he had been sent with the Napoleonic army in 1803.

Given Laclos's military background, it is not surprising that his novel is permeated with the imagery of war. The association of love and war in literature is very old indeed. Laclos continues and enlivens that tradition in his novel. The plot consists of moves and counter-moves between the two principal characters, who behave as though they were conducting a military campaign. Valmont views his seduction of Madame de Tourvel (the Présidente) in terms of tactics, rules, methods and strategies; he aims at victory and, finally, glory. Even his charm is a charm *offensive*, designed to seduce. The libertine, like the soldier, having achieved his objective, takes possession of the territory,

and then abandons it. That is what Valmont does when he
seduces both Tourvel and Cécile Volanges. In his account of
the seduction of the latter to Merteuil (Letter 96), he uses the
language of military aggression to describe their relative sexual
positions: Cécile defends herself against his kiss, which was a
'false attack', designed to leave 'all the rest' undefended; there-
upon Valmont changes his tactics and 'takes up position'. In
his account of the seduction of the Présidente to Merteuil he
refers to 'the true principles of this war, which, as we have often
observed, so closely resembles the other' (Letter 125). He urges
Merteuil to view him as a great general: 'Judge me as you would
a Turenne or a Friedrich', though his battleground is not the
Rhine or the coast of Normandy, but the drawing room, the
boudoir and the alcove. It is nevertheless Madame de Merteuil
who, after being his lover and partner in crime, becomes
Valmont's real enemy. She is the one who sends back his letter
of attempted reconciliation with the chilling words scrawled
across it: 'Very well then, war!' (Letter 153). It is she who is
in possession of the information which can lead to his downfall, and who directs and controls the campaign which will
eventually cause his demise.

'All's fair in love and war' is a phrase that may occur to us
when we read this novel, and it characterizes Merteuil's own
attitude. 'The battle of the sexes' is a concept we are all familiar
with; men and women have always struggled to assert themselves, one sex against the other, to defend themselves, attack
or outdo each other by trickery or cunning, persuasion or force.
The struggle, the fighting, is no doubt one of the aspects we
enjoy about Laclos's novel. His main characters are, despite
their reprehensible morality, intelligent and glamorous, even
sympathetic, and we may admire them without wishing to
emulate them. Readers' expectations in Laclos's day were that
the wicked would be punished and the virtuous, rewarded. But
in Laclos love is not triumphant and virtue does not win out,
and this is something that greatly shocked many of his contem-
poraries. There is very little of what we might think of as
'real' love in the book, except perhaps that of the Présidente.

Rousseau, who in *Julie ou La Nouvelle Héloïse* (1761) postu-
lated a reconciliation between passion and virtue, is completely
contradicted by Laclos. The young love of Cécile and the
Chevalier Danceny is corrupted and dismissed by Valmont and
Merteuil before it has the chance to assert its own better self.
In that debased society love is viewed as a failing, a weakness,
and something to be avoided at all costs. Valmont is ridiculed
by Merteuil when it seems he might be falling in love with the
Présidente. Despite her protestations of indifference, Merteuil
is insanely jealous of her, just as Valmont is jealous of Danceny,
and to that extent we may assume his feelings (and perhaps
even hers) are engaged to no small extent. But whatever he
feels, it certainly does not prevent him indulging his sexuality
with the prostitute Émilie or Cécile or various countesses, or
throwing the Présidente over completely as soon as he perceives
he may be the object of society's ridicule.

The epistolary novel was an obvious form for Laclos to choose.
It was by far the most popular kind of fiction in the eighteenth
century, two of whose most celebrated novels, Richardson's
Clarissa and Rousseau's *La Nouvelle Héloïse*, were composed
in this style. Laclos was writing more than thirty years after
Richardson and twenty years after Rousseau, and although he
surpasses them both in literary technique, their influence is
manifest in various contexts throughout the novel.

Each of those novels tells a fascinating story, and *Les Liaisons
dangereuses* resembles them in that respect. There are three
strands to the plot. Will the Marquise de Merteuil manage
to avenge herself by corrupting Cécile and marrying her to
Gercourt? Will the Vicomte de Valmont succeed in seducing the
Présidente, who is apparently inaccessible? Will the relationship
between Merteuil and Valmont be strong enough to withstand
the divergence of their projects and the jealousies aroused by
their relationships with other people? The structure of the novel
is strict. There are four parts. The first fifty letters end with
the apparent triumph of virtue as the Présidente escapes from
Valmont's clutches; the second section ends with the victory of
Merteuil over her would-be lover, Monsieur de Prévan; the

third seems to reproduce the movement of the first in leading us up to a scene of seduction (or, more properly, rape); and the fourth brings about the dénouement with its catastrophe for all the major characters.

The letters do not simply *tell* a story, however; each one is itself actually an incident in the plot and gives rise to the next, and we, like the characters, are drawn into the story as though into the expertly spun threads of a spider's web. As Patricia Duncker says, 'Epistolary novels ... reveal and navigate the ebb and flow of personal feelings and sentiments.'[5] Laclos excels in the genre, achieving greater variety and richness than any of his predecessors. He keeps several correspondences going simultaneously, constantly providing the reader with another point of view. Often there is a symmetry in the letters, which adds a further ironic dimension: Merteuil receives letters on two successive days (Letters 25 and 27), one from Valmont enclosing the Présidente's and one from Cécile saying she will forward Danceny's. Both women are in similar situations: how to react to a pressing suitor? Both ask for sympathy. Merteuil herself, using her literary powers, writes different accounts of the trick she has played on Prévan, according to whether she is writing to Valmont or to Madame de Volanges (Letters 86 and 87). There are four different versions of Valmont's charitable trip to the village (Letters 21, 22 and 23). We have the view of Valmont, the Présidente, Madame de Rosemonde (Valmont's aunt, and, in a later letter, Madame de Volanges; but we are the only ones who, as the novel's readers, are privy to all these accounts. The individual letter may be written to one person alone, but we are ourselves its ultimate addressee. And we see where it fits among the rest.

A letter is a chameleon-like entity. It may in turn be an auto-portrait, a weapon against an enemy, an instrument of mediation or manipulation, an internal monologue, a personal diary, an unconscious revelation of character, a threat or an instrument of ridicule; letters can be sincere, like those of the naive Cécile, Rosemonde or Madame de Volanges; or full of Machiavellian cunning and cynicism, like those of Merteuil. They can be full of double entendres, as when Valmont, while writing passionate words of love to the Présidente, uses Émilie's bottom as a desk. They can be hidden, torn up, kissed, enclosed with other letters, copied out, returned, dictated or left unread. Danceny exclaims that the letter is the portrait of the soul, and describes to Merteuil the pleasure he takes in writing to her (Letter 150). It is a way of making love to her, the visible metaphor of desire. She, however, has already told us that she is aware of the risk in committing such feelings to paper in her letters: 'so sweet, but so dangerous to write' (Letter 81). So many women, she says (and we the readers appreciate the irony of this assertion) do not see in their present lover their future enemy. Letters are the tangible proof of the liaisons which take place in the novel and they are, finally, what causes the downfall of the principal characters. They are also, of course, what constitutes the novel itself.

Laclos uses the device of the auto-portrait letter to reveal and give substance to his characters. Nowhere is this more evident than in Letter 81 where he allows the formidable Merteuil, writing to Valmont, to give us an account of her upbringing and education and a searching analysis of her own character. This remarkable letter demonstrates Merteuil's sharp intelligence, and not only gives us her assessment of the relative merits of men and women (and of course Valmont in particular, to whom she rightly believes herself superior), but also tells us how she has formed her own philosophy and created her own character since adolescence. In Laclos's time young women generally had little or no knowledge of the facts of life; girls of a certain class, like Cécile, were kept locked up in their convents, and only emerged to be married off to a husband likely to be chosen solely for his financial assets.

Against this background Merteuil stands out as an example of emancipated womanhood. She is a self-made woman, her own creation, her own masterpiece, her own *oeuvre*. At the same time she is also a woman of the Enlightenment in her desire to observe, to know, to judge for herself, and a woman of the times in her risk-taking and her denunciation of privilege. She has deliberately educated herself by studying the *philosophes*, the novelists and the thinkers of the age. She describes how she has seen the necessity of combining the talents of an actor with the talents of a writer: she is also a great reader; throughout her correspondence she refers to other works such as *Le Sopha*, by Crébillon fils (1745), and the tales of La Fontaine (1668–94), and, especially, *La Nouvelle Héloïse*, which she admires. She is indeed herself a novelist *manqué*, and we can sometimes hear the voice of Laclos in her letters. In her two or three letters about her affair with Prévan she adapts the narrative according to the person she is addressing. When she criticizes the style of other letter-writers – Valmont, Cécile, Danceny – she seems to be echoing Laclos in the Preface when he speaks of the 'over-simple style riddled with mistakes of several of these letters'. Merteuil practises a morality which is objectively revolutionary, and might justifiably be called feminist, despite the fact that her solidarity with women does not go so far as to support Cécile or the Présidente in their struggle against Valmont. Quite the opposite, in fact. She refers to Cécile and Danceny as 'our pupils', and indeed she, quite as much as Valmont, is educating them both in the arts of sexual depravity. She writes a letter to Cécile in which she lightly teases her about her lack of worldliness; she teaches her the ways of the world, how to survive in the corrupt aristocratic society of pre-revolutionary France (though this in the end causes Cécile's ruin). She refuses to be put down by any man (or any woman either). She is entirely clear-sighted about Valmont's dealings with women: 'You are never the lover or friend of a woman, but always her tyrant or slave' (Letter 141). Her independence of thought and deed is admirable. She refuses to enter the convent as is expected of her after the death of her husband. She manipulates the opposite sex mercilessly, including her father confessor, and constantly asserts her moral right and her freedom to do exactly what she wants.

Laclos was certainly fascinated by this 'monster' of a modern woman that he created. The year after the publication of *Dangerous Liaisons* he wrote the first of three treatises in which he takes up the cause of the education and emancipation of women, observing that his novel is sufficient proof that he has greatly concerned himself with the cause of women's rights and clarifying his views on women's position in society:

> Let me tell you that one cannot escape from slavery except by means of a great revolution . . . As long as your fate is ruled over by men it will be correct to assert and easy to demonstrate that there is no way that women's education will be improved.
>
> Wherever slavery exists there can be no education. In all societies women are enslaved . . . It is the role of education to develop the faculties of the mind, the role of slavery to suppress them . . . Where there is no freedom there is no morality and where there is no morality there is no education.[6]

Laclos wrote this in 1783, and it was not until 1945 that women in France were enfranchised. Many countries have been much slower to achieve even this. In many so-called democratic societies we know that women's education is still not taken as seriously as men's, girls are frequently sacrificed to the needs of society, their education cut short, and many an atrocity is committed against them.

This novel is almost classical in its attention to the unities of time and place. The letters are written between the months of August and January and mainly from one or other of the chateaux in which their aristocratic writers reside. It is a novel of interiors. Laclos is not interested in the external natural world, but in the analysis of manners and sentiments, and in most of the novel's scenes there is an interplay of these within four walls. An exception to this is Valmont's visit to a nearby village to perform his ostentatious charitable act towards the exploited peasants; but this is treated by Laclos, as it is in the film by Stephen Frears (1988), in a comic fashion, and descriptions of the natural environment play no part in it.

Valmont's battles, apart from the last one, take place in the drawing room or the bedroom and are always planned with meticulous care. Though he is not Merteuil's equal in intelligence or in his total grasp of the situation, he does possess an enormous amount of cunning and shows alarming forethought in his seduction techniques. The letter to Cécile in which he details how she may take possession of the key to the bedroom is typical of his forward planning in such matters (Letter 84). His character, as Laclos reminds us at various points – and rather overtly in Letter 107 when Valmont's valet, Azolan, reports on the Présidente's actions – is based on that of the libertine Lovelace, Richardson's hero in *Clarissa*, which was translated, and adapted, into French as *Clarissa Harlowe* by the Abbé Prévost in 1751. Prévost refined the original, converting its relative earthiness into something more moral and intellectual, in order to avoid giving offence to his public.

Questions are still asked, inevitably, about the novel's morality, although in our permissive age it may not be the sexual mores so much as other aspects of the novel which tend to shock: Valmont's callous treatment of Cécile, for example, after her miscarriage, or the whole idea of the *mariage de raison*[7] where women's feelings and interests are dismissed as unimportant. But perhaps the main reason why the novel was, and might still be, thought immoral, is that it is essentially ambivalent towards the issue of good and evil. Laclos appears to be saying that virtue will not necessarily lead to happiness, nor wicked behaviour to punishment. The Présidente dies, but Merteuil, though disfigured, goes off to Holland at the end of the novel, presumably to pursue her adventures there. So are the wicked not wicked enough? Has Laclos made them too glamorous, too sympathetic? Are we supposed to excuse Merteuil's behaviour when we know how she has reached that point in her philosophy? Do we not admire Valmont's attitude towards Danceny after the duel, and when he dies do we not have a sense, as we do at the end of Mozart's *Don Giovanni*, that life has suddenly lost its savour? The author, who surely knew that rather more of a clear moralistic viewpoint might have been expected of him, leaves us with many questions unanswered, and with a feeling of unease, a sense of danger unresolved.

This variety of possible interpretations is a part of the novel's force. Are these characters in charge of their own actions, or are they, as Camus thought, being fatally led to their inevitable

and ultimate ruin? Or we may think, when we remember the
direction taken by Laclos in later life, that he believed in
Madame de Rosemonde's pronouncement on happiness in
Letter 171 that 'if we knew what our true happiness consists
in, we should never seek it outside the limits prescribed by the
law and religion'. But we must beware of trying to match a
fiction to a biography.

Dangerous Liaisons is a truly eighteenth-century novel, very
much of its age, and yet it exceeds its age. For that reason it is
still convincing now. We may think it odd in our own electronic
society, where letter-writing as a literary art is almost extinct,
that we enjoy a novel which consists of a collection of letters.
But the large number of adaptations and versions on stage
and screen testifies to the book's continuing popularity in the
twentieth and twenty-first centuries (see Appendix 2). Frears's
film, already mentioned, was based on Christopher Hampton's
play, produced in Stratford in 1985. An opera was performed
in San Francisco in 1994; the Northern Ballet staged a pro-
duction in 2004 with music by Vivaldi; a film called *Cruel
Intentions*, in which the novel was transposed into present-day
New York society, came out in 1999; and the Korean film
Untold Scandal (2003) is proof, were any still needed, that
Laclos has the power to cross continents and centuries.

So why do we still read and need *Dangerous Liaisons*? We
may cite the universal and timeless appeal of the novel's characters: manipulative risk-takers such as Merteuil and Valmont do
still exist, as do their victims. The ideas and issues that concerned Laclos concern us too in the twenty-first century. Duel-
ling may have gone out of fashion but revenge killings still
occur. Questions of rape and seduction are raised almost daily
in our media; we debate the emancipation of women; and the
manifestations of the eternal sexual triangle never cease to
occupy us, whether in television soaps, in serious literature or
in our daily lives. But one of the main reasons for this novel's
lasting popularity must surely be its many-sidedness, the multi-
plicity of views it offers on complex issues and relations. We
can ask more of a literary work than that it should confirm us

in our way of thinking. The reading mind asks to be opened up, not shut down. This openness to different viewpoints is inherent in the epistolary form, which Laclos exploits to the full, creating something intriguing and disturbing in equal measure. The 'variety of styles', the avoidance of 'the boredom of uniformity' that he rightly prided himself on in his preface, make the book enjoyable; but in that variety lies also its seriousness. Its variety makes us think, it unsettles us. Such books live longest.

André Gide rightly points out (in his Preface to Dowson's translation in the edition of 1940) that although it may be difficult to disregard the moral viewpoint when judging this book, 'moral considerations have little or nothing to do with artistic excellence', and he notes that 'a book's qualities of form are often the last to gain recognition, for they are the qualities that are most hidden; but they are at the same time the very qualities which ensure the book's survival . . . What the author wanted to say . . . matters a good deal less than how he says it.'

Laclos was reported to have said: 'I resolved to write a work which should stand out from the ordinary and which would still cause a stir and echo through the world after I have left it.'[8] *Dangerous Liaisons* is undoubtedly still echoing.

NOTES

1. Charles Baudelaire, 'Notes sur *Les Liaisons dangereuses*', *Oeuvres complètes*, ed. Claude Pichois, Bibliothèque de la Pléiade, 1976, vol. 2, p. 639.

2. See *Pocket Classiques*, ed. Francis Marmande, 1989, pp. x and xxv.

3. Sébastien Le Prestre de Vauban (1633–1707) was a French military engineer who revolutionized the art of siege craft and defensive fortifications, and whose systems became the focus of military studies across Europe.

4. The Jacobins were the most famous political group of the French Revolution, became identified with extreme egalitarianism and violence, and led the revolutionary government from mid 1793 to mid 1794. Danton (1759–94) and Robespierre (1758–94),

who both belonged to this group, became leading figures in the new regime. Danton became Minister of Justice and Robespierre was in charge of the Revolutionary Tribunal. Both were executed.

5. Introduction to *Mademoiselle de Maupin*, Théophile Gautier, trans. H. Constantine, Penguin, 2005, p. xvi.

6. *Discours sur la question proposée par l'Académie de Châlons-sur-Marne*, in *Des Femmes et de leur éducation* (1803). Edition des Mille et Une Nuits, Librairie Arthème Fayard, 2000, p. 10.

7. Marriages at the time were generally arranged for the financial benefit of both parties: they were marriages of convenience.

8. Laclos's words as reported by the Comte Alexandre de Tilly (1764–1816) in his historical memoir of morals at the end of the eighteenth century. *Mémoires du comte Alexandre de Tilly: pour servir à l'histoire des Moeurs de la fin du 18e. siècle* (1830), edited and introduced by Christian Melchior-Bonnet, Mercure de France, Paris, 1986, p. 246.

Further Reading

Aldington, Richard, *Les Liaisons Dangereuses (Dangerous Acquaintances)*, translated with an Introduction, with wood engravings by Raymond Hawthorn, The Folio Society, London, 1962. Aldington's introduction to Laclos and his interpretation of the novel in its eighteenth-century context are particularly enlightening.

Baudelaire, Charles, 'Notes sur *Les Liaisons dangereuses*', *Oeuvres complètes*, ed. Claude Pichois, Bibliothèque de la Pléiade, Paris, 1976, vol. 2, pp. 638–40.

Bertaud, Michel, *Choderlos de Laclos*, Fayard, Paris, 2003. (At the time of writing, there are no biographies of Laclos in English.)

Byrne, Patrick W., *Les Liaisons Dangereuses: A Study of Motive and Moral*, Glasgow University French and German Publications, 1989. This study focuses on the psychological and social aspects of the novel.

Coward, David, *Laclos Studies, 1968–82*, in *Studies on Voltaire and the Eighteenth Century*, No. 219, Oxford, 1983, pp. 289–328. An assessement of critical works on Laclos up to today.

Davies, Simon, *Les Liaisons Dangereuses, Critical Guides to French Texts*, Grant and Cutler, London, 1987. A useful introduction to the novel.

Sol, Antoinette Marie, *Textual Promiscuities*, Bucknell University and London Associated University Presses, 2002. Examines the relationship between *Dangerous Liaisons* and women's writing.

Thelander, Dorothy R., *Laclos and the Epistolary Novel*,

Librairie Droz, Geneva, 1963. A competent general survey of the letter-writing genre.

Thody, Philip, *Les Liaisons Dangereuses*, Glasgow Introductory Guides to French Literature 19, 1991. Makes interesting comparisons with the film and play adaptations (see Appendix 2).

Translator's Note

Les Liaisons dangereuses, published in French in 1782, was almost immediately translated into German (1783) and English (1784). To Laclos's text in English, translated (anonymously) as *Dangerous Connections, or Letters collected in a Society and published for the Instruction of other Societies*, was appended an *Extract from the Correspondence of what concerns the Happiness of Man and Society. The Utility of Novels: The Novel of Dangerous Connections*, by the Abbé Kentzinger. There was a Russian translation in 1804 by A. I. Evand, but the novel was later banned by the Czar. It was not published in Spanish until 1822. In Italy it was read in the original French but not published in Italian until 1914. It was on the Vatican's list of proscribed books until that list was discontinued in 1966.

Laclos's novel has appeared in English as *Dangerous Connections* (1784), *Dangerous Acquaintances* (Ernest Dowson, 360 copies privately printed in 1898, with illustrations by Monnet, Fragonard and Gérard; also Richard Aldington, 1924), or simply with its original title: *Les Liaisons Dangereuses* (Douglas Parmée, 1995; P. W. K. Stone, 1961). *Dangerous Liaisons*, which we might think an obvious translation, given the sexual connotations of the words and the sexual nature of the many liaisons in the book, seems not to have been used until now for a book title.

One of the most interesting things about this novel is that after its enormous success in France in 1782 and the first translations it was banned in many countries as well as in France, and so was virtually unknown until the twentieth century. Sir Edmund Gosse, reviewing it in the *Sunday Times* on 4 January

1925, said Aldington had introduced it to a British public for the first time, which indicates how little it was known before then. The nineteenth-century *Biographie Universelle* had spoken of it as 'a picture of the most odious immorality', and a reviewer in the *Weekly Westminster*, writing about an edition privately printed in New York as recently as 1933, calls it 'a profoundly immoral book'. This remained the usual view; but Gosse's verdict indicated a shift in public opinion: 'An age which has tolerated the brutality of *La garçonne*[1] and the foul chaos of *Ulysses* must not make itself ridiculous by throwing stones at *Les Liaisons dangereuses*.' In his preface to the re-issue of Dowson (by Nonesuch 1940, printed, interestingly enough, in France), André Gide says it 'has but very recently gained the freedom of respectable bookshops' and that its renown has remained clandestine, like the course of an underground river'. It may be a sign of the times that I am, as far as I know, the first female translator of this 'dangerous' novel.

I am indebted to P. W. K. Stone, who translated Laclos for Penguin in 1961; also to Richard Aldington. The text I have used for my translation is that of the *Livres de Poche 'Classiques'*, edited by Michel Delon, based on Laurent Versini's edition of Laclos's *Oeuvres complètes*, Paris, Bibliothèque de la Pléiade, 1979.

I was fortunate to be able to spend some time in Paris while working on my translation and am most grateful to the Institut Français and the Centre du Livre for making this possible. I am grateful, too, to friends and relatives for their encouragement and, most of all, to my husband, David Constantine, for his generous and invaluable help and advice.

All notes with an asterisk are in Laclos's original text. All numbered notes are the translator's.

Helen Constantine, Oxford, February 2006

NOTE

1. A scandalous novel by Victor Marguerite (1866–1922) about the exploits of a young woman, first published in 1922.

Dangerous Liaisons

Or a Collection of Letters from One Social Class and Published for the Instruction of Others

'I have seen the mores of my times and have published these letters'

J.-J. Rousseau, Preface to *Julie to La Nouvelle Héloïse*[1]

PUBLISHER'S NOTE

We believe it is our duty to warn the public that despite the title of this work and what the editor says about it in his preface, we do not guarantee its authenticity as a collection of letters, and in fact have compelling reasons to believe it is simply a novel.

Moreover, it seems to us that the author, despite his attempts at verisimilitude, has himself most clumsily destroyed every semblance of truth by setting the events he is describing in the present day. In fact, several characters he puts on his stage have such vicious habits that it is impossible to imagine they can have lived in our age, in this age of philosophy, in which the light of reason has spread everywhere and made us all, as we know, into honourable men, and modest and retiring women.

Our opinion, then, is that if the adventures related in this work have any basis in truth, they can only have happened in another time and place. And we attach much blame to the author who, apparently beguiled by the hope of attracting more interest in his story by locating it more exactly in his own age and his own country, has dared to represent in our own costume and customs a way of life which is alien to us.

To preserve, as far as possible, the over-credulous reader from being taken unawares in this respect, we shall sustain our opinion with an argument that we offer with confidence, since it seems to us incontrovertible and unassailable. It is that, though undoubtedly the same causes would not fail to produce the same effects, we never see young girls today with an income of sixty thousand *livres*[2] taking the veil, nor any Présidente who is young and pretty dying of a broken heart.

EDITOR'S PREFACE

This work, or rather, collection of letters, which may perhaps still be thought too weighty, contains nevertheless only a very small portion of the correspondence which made up their total number. Charged with putting them in order by the people with whom they were deposited, and who, I knew, intended them to be made public, I asked nothing for my pains except permission to cut anything which in my opinion might not be to the purpose. And in fact I have tried to conserve only those letters which seemed necessary either to the understanding of the events or to the development of the characters. If one adds to this not very arduous task that of placing such letters as I have allowed to survive in the right order – and I have almost always arranged them chronologically – and finally some short and occasional notes, whose sole purpose, for the most part, is to indicate the origin of a few quotations or explain the cuts that I have taken the liberty of making, my entire contribution to this work will be known. My aims did not go beyond that.*

I had proposed more significant changes, almost all relating to the purity of the diction or style, with which one will often find fault. I should also have liked to be authorized to abridge certain letters that were too long; in several of them matters that have nothing to do with one another are discussed separately and almost without any transition between them. This idea was not approved. Of course, it probably would not have

---

* I should also indicate here that I have suppressed or changed the names of all persons mentioned in these letters, and that if among the names I have invented are found any belonging to any living person that would only be an error on my part from which no consequence should be drawn.

in itself sufficed to confer any merit upon the work, but it would at least have removed some of its faults.

Objections were raised that the intention was to publish the letters themselves and not a literary work based upon these letters; that it would have been as much contrary to all probability as truth if all of the eight or ten people who contributed to this correspondence had written with equal correctness. And upon my contention that that was very far from being the case, and there was not a single one who had not made serious mistakes, which would be certain to meet with criticism, I was told that all reasonable readers would surely expect to find mistakes in a collection of letters exchanged between private individuals, since in all those published up till now by various esteemed writers, and even by some members of the Academy, not one could be found that was totally without mistakes. These arguments did not convince me, and I found them, as I still do, easier to expound than to accept. But I did not have the final say, and accordingly I submitted. I have reserved the right to protest about it and declare, as I do now, that I was not of that view.

As to whether the work has any merit, perhaps it is not up to me to offer an opinion, since it neither can nor should influence anyone else's. However, those who, before beginning to read, prefer to know more or less what to expect would do well, in my view, to read on. Others will do better to move straight on to the text itself; they know enough about it already.

What I can say first and foremost is that if, as I concede, I am convinced I should publish these letters, I am none the less far from hopeful of success. And please do not suppose this sincerity to be false modesty on my part. For I declare with the same frankness that if this collection had not seemed worthy of being offered to the public, I should not have concerned myself with it. Let us try to reconcile this apparent contradiction.

The merit of a work lies in its usefulness or in its capacity for giving pleasure, sometimes both, when it has both to offer. But its success, which is not always proof of its merit, often derives more from the choice of subject than from its execution, from the totality of the material presented rather than the manner in which it is treated. Now in this collection, which contains, as its title proclaims, the letters of a whole class of society, this makes for a diversity of interests which weakens the reader's own. Moreover, since nearly all the feelings expressed in it are false or feigned, the only interest they excite is that of curiosity, which is always far inferior to that of sentiment and which disposes the reader to be far less indulgent and far more attentive to errors of detail, so thwarting the author in his one real objective.

These faults are perhaps to some extent redeemed by a quality inherent in the nature of the work: the variety of styles. This is a quality which an author achieves only with difficulty, but which came about quite naturally in this case and at least spares the reader the boredom of uniformity. Some might also take into account the fair number of observations, either new or not well-known, which are scattered throughout these letters. I think these too are all one may expect in the way of pleasure, even from the most sympathetic standpoint.

The usefulness of the work, which will be perhaps even more disputed, seems to me to be easier to establish. It seems to me at least that it is doing a service to society to unveil the strategies used by the immoral to corrupt the moral, and I believe these letters will make an effective contribution to this end. In them are also to be found the proof and the example of two important truths which one might suppose to be unacknowledged, seeing how little they are practised. One, that any woman who consents to receive into her circle of friends an unprincipled man ends up by becoming his victim; the other, that any mother who allows her daughter to confide in anyone but herself is at the very least lacking in prudence. Young people of both sexes might also learn from it that the friendship that immoral persons seem to grant them so easily is only ever a dangerous trap, and as fatal to their happiness as to their virtue. Morever, it seems to me that the harm which may so often follow closely upon the benefits is greatly to be feared in this case and, far from advising young people to read this book, I believe it is important to keep all such books out of their way. The age when this one may cease to be dangerous, and become useful, seems to me to have been very well understood, for her own sex, by a good mother who is not only intelligent but also sensible. 'I should believe,' she told me, after reading the manuscript of this correspondence, 'I was doing my daughter a great service if I gave it to her on her wedding day.' If all mothers thought like that, I should congratulate myself on publishing it for ever more.

But even supposing we were to accept this favourable opinion, it still seems to me that this collection must please few people. Depraved men and women will have an interest in condemning a literary work which may harm them. And as they are not lacking in cunning, perhaps they will be clever enough to win over to their side the puritans, who will be alarmed by this picture of corruption so fearlessly presented.

Those who consider themselves intellectuals will not be interested in a devout woman, whom they will regard as lacking in wit because of her devoutness; whereas the religious will be angry at the fall of a virtuous woman and will complain that religion is portrayed in a very feeble light.

From another point of view, people of fastidious taste will be disgusted by the over-simple style riddled with errors in several of these letters; whereas the majority of readers, mistakenly supposing that everything that appears in print has been laboured over, will think they detect in other letters the exertions of an author visible through the characters to whom he gives a voice.

Finally it will be said, in general perhaps, that everything is only of value in its proper place. And if ordinarily letters in society are deprived of all grace by the authors' overly cautious style, the smallest omission becomes a real mistake and is insupportable when they are put into print.

I freely admit that all of these criticisms may be well-founded. I also believe that it would be possible to answer them, even without exceeding the length of a preface. But it has to be realized that if it were necessary to answer for everything, the book itself would be unable to answer for anything. And if I had judged that to be the case, I should have suppressed both book and preface.

PART ONE

PART ONE

Cécile Volanges to Sophie Carnay at the Ursuline convent of . . .

As you see, my dear Sophie, I am as good as my word, and not spending all my time on frills and furbelows; I shall always have time for you. All the same, I have seen more finery in one single day than in the whole of the four years we spent together; and I do believe the high-and-mighty Tanville* will be more humiliated at my first visit to the convent – for I shall be sure to ask for her – than she doubtless supposed we were by all those visits she used to pay us, *en grande toilette*.[1] Mamma asks my opinion about everything; she treats me less like a little schoolgirl than she used to. I have my own maid; I have a room and closet at my disposal, and I am writing this at the prettiest little *secrétaire*;[2] I have a key to it and can lock away whatever I wish. Mamma has said that I should go and see her every day when she rises; that I do not need to have my hair dressed until dinner, because we shall always be alone; and that she will tell me each day what time I must join her in the afternoon. The remainder of the time is my own and I have my harp, my drawing and my books, just as I had in the convent; except Mother Perpétue is not there to scold me and if I choose to fritter my time away, that is my affair: but as my Sophie is not there to giggle and chatter with, I may as well keep busy.

It is not yet five o'clock; I am not to see Mamma until seven: there is plenty of time to write, if I only had something to tell! But they have not yet breathed a word. And were it not for all the obvious preparations and all the women who keep coming in to do things for me, I should believe no one had the least notion of marrying me, and that it was simply another piece of our dear Joséphine's nonsense.† But Mamma has told me so often that a young lady should stay in the convent until she marries that, now she has taken me out, I think Joséphine must be right.

A carriage has just pulled up outside the door and Mamma

---

* A pupil at the same convent.　　　† A *tourière*[3] in the convent.

has sent word for me to come to her rooms immediately. Could it be *him*? I am not dressed, my hand is shaking and my heart is thumping. I have asked my maid if she knows who is with my mother. She said: 'It's Monsieur C—, for certain,' and laughed. Oh! I think it must be him! I promise to come back and tell you what happens. That is his name, anyway. I must not keep him waiting. Farewell, for a little while.

Oh, how you'll laugh at your poor Cécile! I was so embarrassed! But you would have fallen into the same trap. When I went in to Mamma's room I saw a gentleman in black standing beside her. I curtsied to him as prettily as I could, and stood there, unable to move. You can imagine how I studied him! 'Madame,' he said to my mother, and with a bow in my direction, 'she is a charming young lady, and I am more than ever sensible of the honour you have done me.' I was overcome by such a fit of the shakes at this boldness, my knees gave way; I found an armchair and sat down, flushed and taken aback. No sooner had I sat down than suddenly the man was kneeling in front of me. At that point your poor friend Cécile lost her head; as Mamma said, I was absolutely panic-stricken. I got up and gave a loud shriek ... just like that day when there was the thunderstorm. Mamma burst out laughing, saying: 'Whatever is the matter with you? Sit down and give Monsieur your foot.' My dear, the gentleman was actually a shoemaker. I cannot tell you how embarrassed I was! Luckily there was no one there except Mamma. I think when I am married I shall not employ that shoemaker any more.

We are very worldly-wise now, don't you think? Goodbye! It's nearly six and my maid says I have to dress. Goodbye, dear Sophie; I love you just as much as if we were still in the convent.

P.S. I don't know by whom to send this letter so I shall wait for Joséphine to arrive.

Paris, 3 August 17**

LETTER 2

The Marquise de Merteuil to the Vicomte de Valmont at the Chateau de —

Come back, my dear Vicomte, come back! What are you doing, what can you possibly be doing at the house of an old aunt who has already left her whole estate to you? Leave immediately; I need you. I have had a wonderful idea, and I want to entrust you with carrying it out. These few words should be enough; you ought to be more than honoured by my decision and hasten here to receive my orders on your knees. You abuse my kindness, even though you have no further use for it. And when faced with the alternatives of eternal hatred or excessive indulgence, your happiness requires my goodness to prevail. I want to acquaint you closely with my plans: but swear to me as my faithful chevalier you will not engage in any other affair until you have brought this one to a conclusion. It is worthy of a hero: you will serve both love and revenge; and, finally, it will be one more *rouerie**⁴ to put in your Memoirs: yes, in your Memoirs, for I want them to be published one day, and I shall take it upon myself to write them. But let us leave that aside and come back to what I have in mind.

Madame de Volanges is marrying her daughter. It is still a secret, but she told me yesterday. And whom do you think she has decided upon for a son-in-law? The Comte de Gercourt! Who would ever have thought I should become Gercourt's cousin?⁵ I am in such a rage . . . Well, have you not yet guessed? You slowcoach! Do you mean to say you have forgiven him for his affair with the Intendante? And I, do I not have still more to complain about on his account than you do, you monster?† But I am calming down and my soul is quiet once more, in the expectation of exacting my revenge.

---

* The words *roué* and *rouerie*, now happily falling into disuse in polite society, were very much in vogue at the time these letters were written.

† To understand this passage one needs to know that the Comte de Gercourt had left the Marquise de Merteuil for the Intendante de — who, in her turn, had given up the Vicomte de Valmont for him. It was after this that the

You have been irritated as many times as I have, by the importance Gercourt attaches to what kind of wife he will have, and the stupid presumption which convinces him that he will escape his inevitable fate. You know his ridiculous predilection for girls educated at convents and his even more ridiculous *penchant* for blondes. As a matter of fact, I wager that in spite of the sixty thousand *livres* the little Volanges girl will bring him, he would never have thought of marriage if her hair was dark or if she had not been to the convent. So let us make a fool of him: he certainly will be one day; I have not the slightest doubt about that. But what would be amusing would be that he should be a fool right from the start. What fun we should have next day hearing him brag about it! For brag he will; and then once you have succeeded in educating the girl, we shall be extremely unlucky if Gercourt, like any other man, does not become the laughing-stock of Paris.

Besides, the heroine of this new romance[6] deserves all your attentions: she is really pretty; only fifteen, a rosebud; truly, impossibly gauche, and lacking in style: but you men are not worried about such things; moreover, she has a certain look of languor that I must admit is rather fetching. Added to that, she comes to you on my recommendation; all you have to do is thank me and do as I bid you.

You will receive this letter tomorrow morning. I insist that you be here tomorrow evening at seven. I shall receive no one until eight, not even the reigning Chevalier: he does not have the head for so large an undertaking. As you can see I have not been blinded by love. At eight o'clock I shall give you back your freedom, and at ten you shall return and have supper with the beautiful creature; for both mother and daughter will sup with me. Adieu, it is midday gone. Soon my thoughts will no longer be of you.

Paris, 4 August 17**

---

attachment between the Marquise and the Vicomte began. As that affair took place long before the events related in these letters I thought it best to suppress all correspondence related to it.

LETTER 3

Cécile Volanges to Sophie Carnay

My dear friend, I am still completely in the dark. Yesterday Mamma had a great many people to supper. I was very bored, in spite of it being in my interest to study the men especially. Both the men and the women all looked at me a great deal, and they were whispering; I could tell they were talking about me: it made me blush, I could not help it. I wished I could have prevented it, for I noticed that when the other women were looked at, they did not blush. Or else it is the rouge they wear, which means you cannot see their colour when they are embarrassed. It must be very difficult not to blush when a man stares at you.

What bothered me most was not knowing their opinion of me. I did think I heard the word *pretty* two or three times: but I heard the word *gauche* very plainly; and that must be what they think, for the woman who said it is a relative and a friend of my mother and even appears to have taken an immediate liking to me. She was the only person who spoke a few words to me in the course of the evening. We shall sup tomorrow at her house.

I also heard a man, who I am certain was talking about me, say to somebody after supper: 'We must let her ripen; next winter we shall see.' Perhaps he is the one who is to marry me; but then it would be within the next four months! I should dearly love to know what is going on.

Here comes Joséphine and she says she is in a hurry. But I want to tell you about yet another of my faux pas. Oh, I do believe that friend of my mother's is right!

After supper they started playing cards. I went and sat next to Mamma. I don't know how it came about but I fell asleep almost immediately. I was woken by a great guffaw of laughter. I could not tell if they were laughing at me but I think they must have been. I was extremely relieved when Mamma gave me permission to go to bed. It was after eleven, can you believe!

Goodbye, my dear Sophie; be true to your friend Cécile. The world is not so amusing as we once imagined, I can tell you.

Paris, 4 August 17**

LETTER 4

The Vicomte de Valmont to the Marquise de Merteuil in Paris

Your orders are charming; and your manner of issuing them even more delightful. You make despotism itself seem something to be cherished. Not for the first time, as you know, do I regret I am no longer your slave. And *monster* though I may be, I can never recall without a pleasurable feeling the days when you bestowed sweeter names upon me. Indeed, I often long to merit them anew and, with you, hold up to the world an example of perfect constancy. But larger matters beckon. It is our destiny to make conquests; we have to follow it. Perhaps we shall meet again at the end of the course; for I have to say, my most beautiful Marquise, without wishing to anger you, that at the very least you follow hard at my heels. Since we separated for the good of society and we both preach the gospel in our different ways, it seems to me that in this mission of love you have made more converts than I have. I know your zeal, your ardent fervour. And if God were to judge us by our works, you would be the patron of a great city some day, whereas your friend would be at most a village saint. This parlance surprises you, does it not? But for the last week I have understood and spoken none other; and it is in order to improve in this respect that I see I am obliged to disobey you.

Do not be angry. Listen to me. I shall confide to you, keeper of all my heart's secrets, the most ambitious plan I have ever conceived. What are you proposing? That I seduce a young girl who has seen nothing, knows nothing; who would be delivered up to me defenceless, so to speak; who would be certain to be bowled over at my first compliment and who would be swayed perhaps more rapidly by curiosity than by love. Twenty other men would have as much success as I. Not so with the business which occupies my thoughts. Its successful outcome assures me of glory as much as pleasure. The god of love himself, preparing my crown, cannot decide between the myrtle and the laurel, or rather he will weave them together to honour my triumph.[7] You yourself, my love, will be struck with holy awe, and will say with enthusiasm: 'There goes a man after my own heart.'

You know the Présidente de Tourvel: her devotion, her love for her husband, her strict principles? She is the object of my attack. She is the enemy worthy of me. She is the goal I am aiming to reach;

> And though I fail to carry off the prize
> Still there is honour in the enterprise.*

One may quote bad verse when it written by a great poet.[8]

You will know that the Président is in Burgundy as a result of an important trial: I hope to make him lose a more important one. His inconsolable better half has to spend the whole of her time during this distressing grass-widowhood here. Mass each day, a few visits to the poor in the canton, prayers morning and evening, solitary walks, pious conversations with my old aunt, and the occasional dreary game of whist. These were to be her only pleasures. I am preparing some more effective ones for her. My guardian angel has led me here for her happiness and for mine. What a fool I was, regretting the twenty-four hours that I was sacrificing out of respect for the conventions. I should be well and truly punished now if I were obliged to return to Paris! Happily four people are needed to play whist; and since there is no one here beside the local curate, my immortal aunt has been very pressing that I should give up a few days to her. I said I would, as you can guess. You cannot imagine how nice she has been to me ever since, and especially how edified she is

* La Fontaine.

at seeing me regularly at prayers and Mass. She does not suspect what divinity it is I adore.

So here am I, for the last four days victim of a powerful passion. You know how keen my desire is, how I thrive on obstacles; but what you do not know is how greatly solitude adds to the ardour of desire. I have now but one thought. I think about it by day; I dream of it by night. I really need to have this woman, to save me from the stupidity of being in love with her. For where does frustrated desire lead a man? O delicious pleasure! Come to me, I implore you, make me a happy man and above all bring me peace. How fortunate we are that women defend themselves so badly, or we should be nothing but their timid slaves. At this moment I have feelings of gratitude towards women of easy virtue, which brings me naturally to your feet. I prostrate myself before them to obtain my pardon, and there conclude this too lengthy epistle.

Adieu, my darling: no hard feelings.

From the Chateau de —, 5 August 17**

LETTER 5

The Marquise de Merteuil to the Vicomte de Valmont

Do you know, Vicomte, your letter is uncommonly rude, and I might very well be angered by it. But it is a clear proof to me that you have taken leave of your senses, and that alone has saved you from my indignation. As your generous, sensitive friend, I shall forget the wrong you are doing to me so that I can think about the danger you are in; and however tedious it might be to reason with you, I concede your need of this at present.

You, have the Présidente de Tourvel! What a stupid fantasy! I recognize here your characteristic perverseness in wanting only what you believe to be unobtainable. What does this woman have to recommend her, then? Regular features, I suppose, but quite without expression; a fairly good figure, but she does not move well. And always dressed up in that silly fashion! With all those kerchiefs tied around her bosom and her bodice buttoned right up to her chin! I am telling you this as a friend: two women like that and you would lose all the reputation you have. Just remember that day when she was collecting alms at Saint-Roch, and you thanked me so profusely for affording you that spectacle? I can see her now, about to sink down at every step, her hand held out to that long-haired beanpole of a man, blushing at every bow and always overwhelming someone with her yards of skirt. Who would have thought then that you would one day desire this woman? Really, Vicomte, you should blush yourself and come to your senses. I shall keep your secret.

And besides, look what unpleasant things are in store for you! What rival are you up against? A husband! Don't you feel humiliated by that word? What shame if you fail! And how little glory in success! I would say more. Do not expect to derive any pleasure from this. Does one ever with prudes? I mean the real prudes. They hold back at the very heart of rapture and offer nothing but half-pleasures. That entire abandonment of the self, that delirious ecstasy where pleasure becomes purified by excess, all this wealth of love is unknown to them. I predict this: at very best your Présidente will believe she has given you her all by treating you as she does her husband, and even the tenderest conjugal intimacy is not so very intimate. In this case it is far worse. Your prude is religious, with a simple piety which means she is condemned to being a child for ever. Perhaps you will overcome that obstacle, but do not flatter yourself that you will remove it; you may be able to conquer her love of God but you will not overcome her fear of the Devil; and when you hold your mistress in your arms and feel her heart beating, it will be in fear, not love. Perhaps, had you come to know this woman earlier, you could have made something of her; but she is twenty-two, and she has been married for almost two years. Believe me, Vicomte, when prejudice has become so ingrained in a woman, it is best to leave her to her fate. She will never be anything but a nobody.

Yet it is because of this beauty that you refuse to obey me, that you are burying yourself in your aunt's mausoleum, and renouncing the most delicious adventure, the one best designed to add to your repute! Are you fated to have Gercourt always retain some advantage over you? I am speaking quite neutrally; but at this moment I am tempted to believe you do not deserve your reputation. I am even tempted to withdraw my trust in you. I should never be able to accustom myself to telling my secrets to the lover of Madame de Tourvel.

But you should know the little Volanges girl has already turned one head. Young Danceny is mad about her. He has sung with her. And it must be said that she sings better than schoolgirls normally do. They practise a great many duets and I fancy she is very inclined to try singing in harmony with him; but this Danceny is like a child – he will pay court to someone and not get anywhere. The girl, for her part, is quite timid; but in any case it will be much less amusing than if you had anything to do with it. I am cross and shall pick a quarrel with my Chevalier when he arrives; he would be well-advised to treat me with care. At the moment, for two pins, I would break it off. I am sure if I had the good sense to leave him now he would be in despair, and nothing is so amusing as a despairing lover. He would call me false and I've always liked the word *false*. Next to the word *cruel*, which one has to go to more trouble to deserve, it is the one that sounds sweetest to a woman's ears. Seriously, I shall think about breaking it off. See what you have done! So I leave it to your conscience. Adieu. Ask your Présidente to remember me in her prayers.

Paris, 7 August 17**

LETTER 6

The Vicomte de Valmont to the Marquise de Merteuil

So there is not a woman in the whole world who does not abuse the influence she has acquired! Even you, whom I was wont to call my kind friend, you have ceased to be one, and do not

shrink from attacking me concerning the object of my affections! How dare you portray Madame de Tourvel like that! ...
Any man would pay for such outrageous insolence with his life!
Any other woman but you would have deserved punishment at
the very least! I beg you not to try me so sorely; I cannot answer
for my ability to withstand it. In the name of friendship, wait
until I have possessed the woman if you wish to insult her. Do
you not know that only pleasure has the right to untie the
blindfold from love's eyes?

But what am I saying? Does Madame de Tourvel need to put
on an act? No. In order to be adorable, all she has to do is be
herself. You say she is plainly dressed; and so she is: all ornament spoils her; everything that hides her detracts from her
beauty; in the abandonment of *déshabillé* she is truly ravishing.
Thanks to the exhaustingly hot weather we are having, I can
see her supple curves through her simple linen gown. A single
muslin kerchief covers her breasts, and my eyes, covert but
penetrating, have already taken the measure of their enchanting
contours. Her face, you say, is without expression. But what
should it express in the moments when nothing speaks to her
heart? No, it is quite true that she does not have, unlike our
coquettes, that falseness which sometimes seduces, but invariably deceives. She does not know how to disguise an empty
phrase with a studied smile. And though she has the most
beautiful teeth in the world, she only laughs at what she finds
truly amusing. But you should see what a picture of naive and
frank gaiety she presents when we play games; her look of pure
joy, goodness and compassion when she is near some poor
wretch she is anxious to help. You should see how, especially
at the slightest word of praise or flattery, her heavenly face
takes on a touching embarrassment, which is quite unaffected!
... She is chaste and religious, and you therefore judge her to
be cold and lifeless? I think the opposite ... What astonishing
sensitivity must she have to extend those feelings even to her
husband, and carry on loving a person who is never there?
What stronger proof could you ask for? And yet I have been
able to discover more.

I contrived a walk so that we would need to cross a large

ditch. Although she is very nimble, she is yet more timid: you can well understand that a prude would be afraid to take a tumble!* She had to entrust herself to me. I held this modest woman in my arms. Our preparations and the carrying-over of my old aunt had made the merry devotee laugh out loud; but the moment I grasped her, with a deliberate awkwardness, our arms entwined around each other. I pressed her bosom against mine; and in that brief interval I felt her heart beating ever more rapidly. A lovely blush came over her face and her embarrassed modesty told me straight away that *her heart had palpitated with love and not with fear*. However, my aunt made the same mistake as you and started to say: 'The child is afraid'; but the *child*'s charming candour did not allow her to tell a lie, and she naively replied: 'Oh no, but . . .' That one word told me everything. From that moment on, sweet hope replaced cruel anguish. I shall have this woman. I shall take her away from the husband who defiles her. I shall dare to ravish her even from the God she adores. How delicious to be both object and conqueror of her remorse! Far be it from me to destroy the prejudices which beset her! They will only add to my happiness and my triumph. Let her believe in virtue, but let her sacrifice it for my sake; let her be terrified by her sins but unable to prevent herself committing them; and, agitated by a thousand terrors, let her be able to forget and overcome them only in my arms. May she say, with my consent: I adore you. She alone of all women will be worthy to utter those words. I shall indeed be the god she worships before all others.

Let us be frank: in our own relationship, unemotional as it is uncomplicated, what we call happiness is scarcely a pleasure. Shall I tell you plainly? I thought my heart had withered away, and with nothing but sensualities left to me I was bemoaning my premature old age. Madame de Tourvel has given me back the charming illusions of my youth. When I am with her I have no need to pretend to be happy. The only thing which frightens me is the time this affair will take me; for I cannot risk leaving

---

* Evidence of the deplorable taste for punning beginning to be in fashion at that time and since become so widespread.

anything to chance. It is no use reminding myself of bold strategies that have succeeded in the past; I cannot make up my mind to use them. If I am to be truly happy she must give herself to me. And it is no small matter.

I am certain you will admire my prudence. The word 'love' has not yet been uttered, but we already talk about 'confidence' and 'interest'. So in order to deceive her as little as possible, and especially to forestall what might happen if she were to hear rumours about me, I have myself told her, as though admitting my faults, some of my more famous traits. You would laugh to see how solemnly she preaches at me. She says she wishes to convert me. She does not yet suspect what it will cost her to try. She is a long way from supposing that *by pleading for the unfortunate women I have deceived*, in her parlance, she is pleading her own cause in advance. This idea struck me yesterday in the middle of one of her sermons, and I could not resist interrupting, to assure her that she spoke like one of the prophets. Farewell, my dearest. As you see, I am not quite a lost cause.

P.S. By the way, has that poor Chevalier killed himself yet in desperation? Truly you are a hundred times worse than I am, and if I had any self-respect you would put me to shame.

From the Chateau de —, 9 August 17**

LETTER 7

*Cécile Volanges to Sophie Carnay**

If I have not mentioned my marriage, it is because I know no more than I did at the outset. I have got into the habit of not thinking about it, and I am finding this life rather to my liking.

* So as not to try the reader's patience a large part of the daily correspondence between these two young ladies has been suppressed. Only the letters deemed necessary to an understanding of events appear. For the same reason all of Sophie Carnay's letters and several written by other characters have also been suppressed.

I study singing and the harp a great deal; it seems to me that I like them better since I no longer have a music master, or rather it is because I have a better one. Monsieur le Chevalier Danceny, the gentleman I told you about whom I sang with at Madame de Merteuil's, is good enough to come here every day and sing with me for hours at a time. He is extremely nice. He sings like an angel and composes very pretty tunes, for which he also writes the words. What a shame he is a Knight of Malta![9] It seems to me that were he to marry, he would make his wife very happy ... He is gentle and charming. He never seems to be paying me a compliment and yet everything he says is flattering. He corrects me constantly, in music and in other things; but there is so much enthusiasm and good humour mingled with his criticism that it is impossible not to be grateful. He has only to look at you and you think he is saying something agreeable. On top of all that he is most obliging. For example yesterday he was invited to an important concert but he chose to stay the whole evening at Mamma's. I was exceedingly pleased; for when he is not there nobody talks to me and I am bored. But when he is there we sing and chat to one another. He always has something to tell me. He and Madame de Merteuil are the only two people I really like. But farewell, my dear friend. I have promised to get by heart a little aria whose accompaniment is very difficult, and I don't wish to break my word. I shall go back to my work until he arrives.

From —, 7 August 17**

LETTER 8
The Présidente de Tourvel to Madame de Volanges

I could not be more sensible of the confidence you place in me, Madame, nor could anyone be more anxious than I to establish Mademoiselle de Volanges in society. It is indeed with all my heart that I wish her a happiness which I am sure she deserves, and which I am certain may be safely entrusted to your wisdom. I am not acquainted with Monsieur le Comte de Gercourt; but since you have honoured him by your choice I can only form a most advantageous opinion of him. I shall simply send my best wishes, Madame, for a marriage as happy and successful as my own, which is also your doing, and for which my gratitude increases every day. May the happiness of your daughter be your reward for the happiness you have obtained for me; and may the best of friends be also the most blessed of mothers!

I am truly sorry I may not offer you the expression of my sincere good wishes in person and make the acquaintance of Mademoiselle de Volanges as soon as I would wish. Since your kindness to me has been truly that of a mother, I may surely expect from her the tender affection of a sister. Would you kindly beg her, Madame, to extend those feelings to me, until such time as I am in a position to deserve them.

I intend to stay in the country for the whole period of Monsieur de Tourvel's absence. I am spending this time enjoying and benefiting from the company of the estimable Madame de Rosemonde. This woman is always charming; her great age takes nothing away from her; she has not lost her memory or her sense of fun. Only in body is she eighty-four years old; in spirit she is but twenty.

Our retirement here is enlivened by her nephew the Vicomte de Valmont, who has consented to give up a few days of his time for us. I only knew him by reputation, and that gave me very little desire to get to know him better; but he seems to me to be worthier than people think. Here, where he is not affected adversely by the social whirl, he shows a surprising capacity for serious conversation, and blames himself for his misdemeanours with unusual candour. He confides in me most freely, and I lecture him very severely. You, who know him, will agree it would be wonderful to make a convert of him. But despite his promises, I am well aware that a week in Paris will make him forget all my sermons. At least his stay here will somewhat restrict the way he normally behaves; and I think that, judging from how he generally conducts his life, the best thing he could do is to do nothing at all. He knows that I am engaged in writing to you, and has asked me to send you his regards. Be so good as to accept mine also and do not doubt that I remain your sincere friend, etc.

From the Chateau de —, 9 August 17**

LETTER 9

Madame de Volanges to the Présidente de Tourvel

I have never been in any doubt, my dear young friend, about your friendship, nor the sincere interest you take in all of my concerns. But it is not to clarify this point, which is, I trust, henceforth understood between us, that I am sending you this reply: I believe it is imperative that I should have a few words with you about the Vicomte de Valmont.

I confess I never expected to come across that name in your letters. Indeed, what can you two have in common? You do not know this man; where could you have learned about the soul of a libertine? You talk about his *unusual candour*: ah yes! Valmont's candour really must be very unusual. He is even more duplicitous and dangerous than he is charming and seductive, and never from his most tender years has he taken one step or spoken one word without having some scheme or other; never has he had a scheme which was not dishonourable or wicked. My dear, you know me; you know that, among the virtues I try to acquire, tolerance is the one I most cherish. So, if Valmont were carried along by the fire of his passion, or if, like a thousand others, he were led astray into errors common to the age, then, while blaming him for his conduct, I should sympathize with him; I should hold my tongue and wait for him to turn over a new leaf and once again earn the esteem of respectable people. But that is not Valmont. His conduct is the result of his principles. He can calculate how far a man may permit himself to do dreadful deeds without compromising himself; and so that he may be wicked and cruel with impunity he has chosen women to be his victims. I shall not stop to count all the women he has seduced; but how many of them has he not ruined? These scandalous stories do not reach your ears in the modest seclusion you live in. I could tell you some which would make you shudder; but your sight, as pure as your soul, would be sullied by such images. You are certain that Valmont will never pose a danger for you, and that you have no need of such weapons to defend yourself. All I will say to you is that, among all the women he has pursued, whether or not he has had any success with them, there is not one who has not had reason to regret it. Madame de Merteuil is the sole exception to this rule. She is the only one to have been able to resist and control his wicked behaviour. I must admit that this aspect of her life is the one which does her most credit to my way of thinking; and it was sufficient to vindicate her completely in the eyes of society, whatever reckless behaviour she may have been blamed for at the beginning of her widowhood.*

In any case, my dear, what age, experience and most of all friendship give me the right to say to you is that people are starting to notice that Valmont is not around; and if they get to know that he has stayed alone with you and his aunt, your reputation will be in his hands. And that is the worst misfortune that can befall any woman. I advise you then to persuade his aunt not to keep him any longer; and if he insists on staying, I think you should not hesitate to leave yourself. Why should he stay? What can he be doing in the country? If you were to have his movements watched, I am certain you would discover that he has only been placing himself in a more convenient position to carry out some blackguardly deed in the neighbourhood. But though we may not remedy the evil, let us make sure it does not happen to us.

Farewell, my dear friend; the marriage of my daughter has been delayed a little. The Comte de Gercourt, whom we were daily expecting, writes to say that his regiment is in Corsica.[10] And as there are still war manoeuvres in progress it will be

---

* Madame de Volanges's mistake shows that, in common with other rogues, Valmont never betrayed his accomplices.

impossible for him to get away before the winter. It is most inconvenient. But it gives me hope that we shall now have the pleasure of seeing you at the wedding; I should have been disappointed if it had taken place without you. Goodbye; I am unreservedly and sincerely yours.

P.S. Remember me to Madame de Rosemonde who, as ever, has my loving regard, as she well deserves.

From —, 11 August 17**

LETTER 10

The Marquise de Merteuil to the Vicomte de Valmont

Are you sulking, Vicomte? Or dead? Or are you living only for your Présidente, which comes to very much the same thing? This woman who has given you back *the illusions of your youth* will also give you back its silly prejudices before very long. There you are, in a state of timid servitude already. You might as well be in love. You renounce your *bold strategies that have succeeded in the past*. So you are behaving in an unprincipled fashion, leaving everything to chance, or rather the whim of the moment. Do you not remember that love is, like medicine, *only the art of giving Nature a hand*? You see I am attacking you with your own weapons. But I shall not take any pride in it, or I should be beating a man who is down. *She must give herself*, you tell me. Ha! No doubt she must; so she will give herself, as the others have done, except that she will give herself with a bad grace. But so that she may end by giving herself, the proper thing to do is to take her at the outset. What a silly distinction – and typical of the illogicality of love. Yes, love; for you are in love. Were I to call it by any other name, I should be deceiving you; I should be hiding your malady from you. So tell me then, my languorous lover, do you believe you have *raped* the women you have had? However much a woman wants to give herself, however eager she is to do it, she must still have a pretext; and is there a more convenient one than that which makes it seem she is yielding to force? I confess that, as far as I am concerned, one of the things which flatters me most is a vigorous and skilful attack, where everything happens in an ordered fashion, though rapidly; it never puts us in the painful or embarrassing position of needing to make amends for some *gaucherie* which we should have profited from instead; it keeps up the semblance of violence even in the granting of our favours, and cleverly flatters our two favourite passions: the glory of defence and the pleasure of defeat. I acknowledge that this talent, rarer than one might think, has always given me pleasure, even when it has not prevailed, and I have on occasion capitulated, solely as a reward. It is just as it was in the jousting matches of old, when Beauty bestowed the prize for skill and valour.

But you, no longer yourself, are behaving as if you were afraid of success. Why? Since when have you travelled in short stages and by the side roads? My friend, when you wish to reach your destination, travel by the post-chaise and the high road! But let us leave this subject, which makes me crosser and crosser the more it deprives me of the pleasure of your company. At least write to me more often than you do, and tell me what progress you are making. Do you realize this silly affair has been taking up almost two weeks of your time, and that you are neglecting everyone?

Speaking of neglect, you are like those people who regularly send for news of their friends who are ill, but who never wait for an answer. You ended your last letter by asking me if the Chevalier was dead. I did not reply, and you did not trouble to ask again. Have you forgotten that my lover is your bosom friend? But rest assured, he is not dead; or if he were it would be because he had expired from joy. How tender-hearted he is, this poor Chevalier! Just made for loving! How acutely he feels things! My head is whirling. Seriously, the perfect happiness he finds in being loved by me has made me form a real attachment to him.

How happy I made him on the very day I wrote to you that

I had in mind to break it off! Just as I was occupied in finding a way to make him despair, he was announced. Whether it was fancy or reason on my part, never had he seemed more handsome. However, I received him coldly. He was hoping to spend a couple of hours with me before it was time for my doors to be opened to everyone. I told him I was about to go out. He asked me where I was going; I refused to tell him. He insisted. *Away from you*, I answered sharply. Fortunately for him he was struck dumb by my rejoinder. For had he said anything a scene would most certainly have ensued, which would have brought about the rift I had intended. Surprised by his silence, I looked at him with no other intention, I swear, than to see his expression. On his charming face I discovered a sadness, at once profound and touching, which you yourself have acknowledged is very difficult to resist. The same cause produced the same effect. For a second time I was overcome. From that moment on, my only concern was to find ways of preventing him finding fault with me. 'I am going out on business,' I said, rather more gently, 'and it has something to do with you; but do not ask questions. I shall sup at home; come back and you shall know the truth.' So he started to speak again, but I did not permit him to go on. 'I am in a great hurry,' I continued. 'Leave me. Until tonight.' He kissed my hand and left.

To make it up to him, and perhaps to myself as well, I decided to introduce him to my *petite maison*[11] whose existence he did not suspect. I called my faithful Victoire: 'I have a migraine. I am in bed if anyone calls.' And alone with my trusty confidante, while she dressed up as a lackey, I put on the clothes of a chambermaid. Then she called a cab to come to the garden gate and off we went. Once arrived in the temple of love, I chose the most elegant *négligé*. This one was delightful, and of my own invention: it reveals nothing and leaves everything to the imagination. I promise you a pattern for your Présidente, when you have rendered her fit to wear it.

After these preparations, while Victoire busied herself with other details, I read a chapter of *Le Sopha*, a letter of *Héloïse* and two tales of La Fontaine,[12] to establish in my mind the various tones I wished to adopt. Meanwhile, keen as ever, my

Chevalier arrives at my door. My footman refuses him entry, telling him I am ill. That was the first thing. At the same time he gives him a note from me, not in my handwriting, as is my prudent custom. My Chevalier opens it and finds, in Victoire's handwriting: 'At nine o'clock sharp, on the boulevard,[13] outside the cafés.' He goes there, and a little lackey he doesn't know, or at least thinks he does not, for it is in fact Victoire, comes to tell him to send his cab away and follow him. These romantic procedures excite him inordinately, but excitement does nobody any harm. He finally arrives, and is spellbound with amazement and love. To give him time to collect himself we walk a while in the shrubbery. Then I bring him back to the house. The first thing he sees is two places laid at a table; the next, a bed all prepared. Then we go into the boudoir, which is very beautifully decorated. There, half deliberately and half on impulse, I put my arms around him and allow myself to fall down at his knees. 'Oh, my friend,' I say, 'I am sorry that in order to spring this little surprise on you I distressed you by seeming annoyed, and by hiding my true feelings for a moment from your eyes. Forgive me my wrongdoing. I wish to expiate it with my love.' You may judge the effect of these sentimental words. The happy Chevalier raised me to my feet, and my forgiveness was sealed upon the same ottoman where you and I so gaily, and in the same manner, sealed our eternal rupture.

As we had six hours to spend together and I had resolved that all this time should be just as delightful for him, I curbed his passion and moved from tenderness to a pleasant flirtatiousness. I do not believe I ever took so much care to please anyone, nor do I think I was ever so satisfied with myself before. After supper, childish and reasonable by turns, gay and sensitive, sometimes even libertine, I enjoyed thinking of him as a sultan in the middle of his harem, and myself by turns a different favourite. In fact, each time his attentions were paid they were always received by the same woman, yet always by a different mistress.

Finally, at dawn, we were obliged to go our separate ways. And whatever he said, whatever he did, even, to prove the contrary, his need to go was as great as his disinclination to do so. The moment we were leaving, as a last farewell, I took the key of that happy abode and, putting it into his hands, said: 'I only took it for your sake. It is only right that you should be master of it. It is for the High Priest to do as he likes with the Temple.'[14] In this adept fashion I forestalled the thoughts which might have been provoked in him by the ever suspect ownership of a *petite maison*. I know him well enough to be certain he will use it for me alone; and, in any case, if the fancy took me to go there without him, I have another key. He was very eager to make a date to return, but I still like him too much to wish to exhaust him so quickly. One should permit oneself excess only with people one intends to leave shortly. He does not know that; but happily I know it for both of us.

I see that it is three in the morning, and I have written a book when I planned to write one line. Such are the joys of a trusting friendship, and that is why you are still the one I like the best; but the truth is, the Chevalier is the one I find the more attractive.

From —, 12 August 17**

LETTER 11

The Présidente de Tourvel to Madame de Volanges

The severe tone of your letter would have made me very apprehensive, Madame, if, happily, I had not discovered more cause to feel safe here than you have given me for alarm. The redoubtable Monsieur Valmont, that terror of our sex, seems to have laid down his deadly weapons before coming to the chateau. He has not been in the least scheming, nor has he given any appearance of doing so; and his power to charm, which even his enemies concede he has, is here almost non-existent, for he is just like a child. Apparently it is the country air which has worked this miracle. But I do assure you that, though constantly in my company and even, apparently, enjoying it, he has not

uttered one single word of anything resembling love, not one
of those phrases that every man allows himself, with far less
reason than he has. He never forces that reticence upon me that
all respectable women are obliged to adopt nowadays to keep
the men around them at a proper distance. He never abuses the
gaiety he provokes. Perhaps he is something of a flatterer; but
he is so tactful that he would accustom modesty itself to being
praised. In brief, if I had a brother, I should wish him to be like
Monsieur de Valmont as he has proved himself to be here.
Perhaps many women would prefer him to be more overtly
gallant; but I admit that I am infinitely grateful to him for being
able to judge my character well enough not to count me among
their number.

This portrait is no doubt very different from the one you
have painted. And yet both of them have perhaps been true at
different periods in his life. He himself admits he has often done
wrong, and no doubt people accuse him of more besides. But I
have come across very few men who speak more respectfully,
I might even say enthusiastically, about respectable women. At
least on that subject, as you say, he is to be believed. His
conduct with Madame de Merteuil is proof of that. He talks to
us a great deal about her and always speaks so highly of her,
and seems to have such a true attachment for her, that until I
received your letter I had the impression that what he called
friendship between the two of them was most certainly love.
I blame myself for this hasty judgement, and all the more so
because he has himself often been careful to justify her character. I admit I thought he was only being chivalrous when it was
honest sincerity on his part. I am not sure, but it seems to me
that a man who is capable of such loyal friendship with so
estimable a woman is not an irredeemable libertine. I do not
know either whether we owe his present good conduct to any
plans he has hereabouts, as you suppose. Certainly there are
some attractive women in the neighbourhood. But he seldom
goes out, except in the mornings and then he says he is going
hunting. It is true he hardly ever brings back any game, but he
insists that he is not skilled at this activity. In any case, what
he does with himself when he is out is none of my business, and

if I tried to find out it would only be in order to come round to your view or to bring you round to mine.

As to your suggestion that I work towards cutting short Monsieur de Valmont's intended stay here: it would seem to me very difficult to dare ask his aunt to do without her nephew's company, especially since she has such a great affection for him. But I do promise I shall take the opportunity of making this request, either to her or to him; but only through deference to you and not because there is any real need to do so. As far as I am concerned, Monsieur de Tourvel knows of my intention to stay here until he returns, and he would be quite understandably surprised were I to change my mind for a trifle.

These explanations are laborious, Madame: but I felt it was only my honest duty to give a good account of Monsieur de Valmont, for in your eyes he would seem to have much need of this. I am no less sensible of the friendly concern which dictates your advice. It is also to this that I owe your charming compliment about the delay in the wedding of Mademoiselle, your daughter. I am so very sincerely obliged to you. But, whatever pleasure I promise myself in spending this time with you, I should willingly sacrifice it to the wish to see Mademoiselle de Volanges settled happily sooner, if indeed it were possible for her to be happier than with a mother so worthy of all her love and respect – two sentiments which I assure you I share with her in my profound affection for your good self.

I have the honour to be, etc.

From —, 13 August 17**

LETTER 12

Cécile Volanges to the Marquise de Merteuil

Mamma is unwell, Madame; she cannot go out and I must keep her company. So I shall not have the honour of accompanying you to the Opera. I assure you I am more sorry not to be with you than I am to miss the performance. I beg you to believe me. I do like you so very much! Would you be kind enough to inform the Chevalier Danceny that I do not have the songbook he mentioned, and that if he can bring it tomorrow I shall be truly delighted? If he comes today he will be told we are not at home; but that is because Mamma does not wish to receive anybody. I hope she will be better tomorrow.

I have the honour to be, etc.

From —, 13 August 17**

LETTER 13

The Marquise de Merteuil to Cécile Volanges

I am very sorry to hear, my dear, that I am to be deprived of the pleasure of your company as well as to hear the reason for it. I hope the occasion will present itself again. I will fulfil your charge with respect to the Chevalier Danceny, who will no doubt be extremely sorry to hear of your Mamma's indisposition. If she wishes to receive me tomorrow, I shall go and keep her company. We shall together challenge the Chevalier de Belleroche* to piquet;[15] and, while we are winning money from him, we shall have the even greater pleasure of hearing you sing with your charming teacher, to whom I shall propose it. If this is agreeable to your Mamma and to yourself, I can answer for myself and my two chevaliers. Farewell, my dear: my compliments to dear Madame de Volanges. With all my love,

From —, 13 Aug 17**

---

* The Chevalier already mentioned in Madame de Merteuil's letters.

LETTER 14

Cécile Volanges to Sophie Carnay

My dear Sophie, I did not write yesterday, but not because I was out enjoying myself, I can tell you. Mamma was indisposed, and I did not leave her side all day. When I went up to my room in the evening I had no energy for anything; I went to bed straight away, to convince myself the day was really over. I had never known such a long one. It is not that I am not fond of Mamma; I don't know what it is. I was supposed to go to the Opera with Madame de Merteuil; the Chevalier Danceny was to be there and as you know they are the two people I like best in the world. When the time came that I should have been there, I could not help feeling a terrible pang. I took no pleasure in anything and I wept and wept, and could not stop. Fortunately Mamma was in bed and could not see me. I am certain the Chevalier Danceny will have been vexed as well. But he will have been distracted by the performance and the company; so it was not at all the same.

Fortunately Mamma is better today, and Madame de Merteuil will arrive with the Chevalier Danceny and someone else; but she always arrives very late, Madame de Merteuil; and it is extremely tiresome to be on one's own for such a long time. It is only eleven o'clock. It is true that I have to practise my harp; and it will take me some time to get ready, for I wish my hair to be dressed nicely today. I believe that Mother Perpétue is right and that one becomes very conscious of one's appearance when one is in society. I have never desired to be pretty so much as in these last few days, and I have discovered that I am not so pretty as I once thought. One does not look well next to women who wear rouge. Madame de Merteuil, for instance: it is plain to see that all the men consider her to be prettier than me. It does not vex me greatly, for she is very fond of me, and besides she assures me that the Chevalier Danceny thinks I am prettier than her. It is really nice of her to tell me that! She even seems to be very happy about it. Now I cannot understand why. Because she likes me so much? And as for him . . . Oh, I was so pleased! It seems to me that just looking at him makes me more beautiful. I could go on looking at him for ever if I were not afraid of meeting his gaze. For every time it happens I am obliged to lower my eyes and it is almost painful to me. But it is of no consequence.

Farewell, my dear friend. I shall begin my *toilette*. My love to you, as ever.

Paris, 14 August 17**

LETTER 15

The Vicomte de Valmont to the Marquise de Merteuil

It is very good of you not to abandon me to my unhappy fate. The life I am leading here is truly wearing, because of the surfeit of leisure and its tedious lack of variety. Reading your letter with all the details of your delightful day, I was tempted twenty times to pretend I had business to attend to, rush to your side and beg you for an infidelity to your Chevalier, who, when all is said and done, does not deserve his good fortune. Do you know, you have made me jealous of him? And what do you mean by our *eternal rupture*? I renounce those vows, uttered in a moment of madness. If they were intended to be kept, we cannot have been worthy of making them. Oh, that I might one day take my revenge in your arms on the unintentional offence to me occasioned by the Chevalier's good fortune! I am indignant, I admit, when I think that this man, without thinking it through or putting himself out in the slightest, but simply obeying his instincts, should achieve a felicity which I cannot possibly attain. Oh, I shall blight his happiness . . . Promise me I shall! Are you not yourself humiliated by it? You put yourself to the trouble of deceiving him and yet he is happier than you are. You think you have him in thrall! But you are in thrall to him. He sleeps soundly whilst you stay awake for his pleasure. Would his slave do more?

Listen, my love, as long as you share yourself out among several, I am not in the least jealous: I simply see in your lovers the successors of Alexander; they are incapable, the whole lot of them put together, of holding on to an empire where I reigned alone. But that you should give yourself entirely to just one! That there should be another man as happy as I! I shall not tolerate it; do not expect me to. Either take me back or at least take a second lover; and do not betray, for the sake of a single whim, the inviolable friendship we swore to one another.

It is quite enough that I am tormented by love. You see I am inclined to your view and I admit my mistake. In fact, if not being able to live without possessing what one desires is to be in love, to sacrifice one's time, one's pleasures, one's life, then I truly am in love. And I have made scarcely any progress at all. I might even have nothing to report, were it not for one event which gives me much food for thought, and I do not yet know if I have grounds for hope or fear.

You know my manservant: a master of intrigue and the very model of a valet in a comedy. As you may imagine, he has been instructed to fall in love with the chambermaid and ply all the servants with drink. The rogue is happier than I am; he has already had some success. He has just discovered that Madame de Tourvel has charged one of her servants to find out about my movements, and even to follow me about on my morning excursions, inasmuch as he can without being seen. What is the woman trying to do? The most modest of them all, yet daring to risk things we should scarcely permit ourselves! I swear to you ... But before I plan to avenge this feminine ruse, let us think up a way of turning it to our advantage. Until now these suspicious excursions had no motive; I must give them one. That deserves my whole attention, and I am leaving you in order to give it my consideration. Farewell, my love.

Still from the Chateau de —, 15 August 17**

LETTER 16

Cécile Volanges to Sophie Carnay

Sophie dear, I have some news for you! Perhaps I ought not to tell you: but I have to tell somebody; I cannot help it. Chevalier Danceny ... I am in such a state, I can't describe it: I do not know where to begin. After I had told you all about the lovely evening* here at Mamma's with him and Madame de Merteuil, I did not speak about it to you any more, because I did not wish to tell a soul; but it was still on my mind. After that, he became very dejected, so dejected that it troubled me greatly. When I asked him why, he denied it, but I could see that he was. Well, yesterday he was even sadder than usual. It did not prevent him being kind enough to sing with me as normal; but each time he looked at me I felt a dreadful pang. After we had finished our singing he went to close up my harp in its case and when he brought the key back he particularly asked me to practise again in the evening as soon as I was on my own. I did not suspect a thing. I did not really want to, but he entreated me so much that I agreed. He had his reasons. So then, when I had gone to my room and my maid had left, I took out my harp. Among the strings I found a letter, just folded, not sealed – and it was from him! Oh, if you only knew the things he asked! Ever since I read the letter I feel so happy I cannot think of anything else. I read it four times over straight off, and then I locked it away in my desk. I knew it by heart, and when I was in bed, I recited it so often I could not get to sleep. As soon as I closed my eyes I could see him there saying all those things I had just read. It was very late when I went to sleep; and as soon as I woke (it was still really early) I took out his letter again and read it through again slowly. I took it into bed with me and kissed it as if ... Perhaps it is wicked to kiss a letter in that way, but I could not stop myself.

* The letter has not been discovered. There is some reason to believe the evening referred to is the one proposed in Madame de Merteuil's note and mentioned in Cécile Volanges's preceding letter.

My dear friend, I am now very happy but very troubled as well, for it is certain I must not answer his letter. I know I must not, yet he asks me to. And if I do not, I know he will be so sad. But how dreadful for him! What do you advise? Well, of course you do not know any more than I do. I should like to talk to Madame de Merteuil, who is so fond of me. I should love to console him, but I should not want to do anything wicked. People are always telling us to be kind-hearted! But when it involves a man they forbid us to follow our instincts! That is not fair either. Is a man not our neighbour just as a woman is, and even more so? For do we not have a father as well as a mother, a brother as well as a sister? And then there are husbands too. However, if I were going to do something which was not right, perhaps Monsieur Danceny himself would not think well of me! Oh, if that were the case I should prefer him to remain sad. Anyway, I still have plenty of time. Simply because he wrote yesterday does not mean I have to reply today. So I will see Madame de Merteuil tonight and if I am brave enough I shall tell her everything. If I do exactly what she says, I shall have nothing to be ashamed of. And she might say I can send him a little reply to console him! Oh! What a state I am in.

Farewell, my dear friend. Tell me anyway what you think.

From —, 19 August 17**

LETTER 17

The Chevalier Danceny to Cécile Volanges

Before giving in to the pleasure or the necessity of writing to you, Mademoiselle, first, I beg you will hear me out. I feel that I must have your kind indulgence if I am to declare my feelings to you. If I only wished to justify them, I should not need that indulgence. For after all, what am I about to do, but make plain what you yourself have brought about? And what can I say, except what my looks, discomfiture, actions and even my silence have already told you? Ah! Why should you be vexed by a feeling which you yourself have inspired? Coming from you, it must be worthy of being given back to you. If it burns, like my soul, then it is pure, like yours. Is it a crime to admire your charming face, your enchanting talent, your captivating grace, and that touching candour that renders such qualities precious beyond price? Indeed it is not; but though one may not be guilty, one may still be unhappy. And that is the fate which awaits me if you refuse to accept my homage, the first my heart has offered. Had we never met I should still be, not happy, but calm. But I have met you. Peace has fled far from me and my happiness hangs in the balance. Yet you are surprised at my despondency and you ask me the reason for it. Sometimes I have even felt you found it distressing. Oh, say the word and my happiness will be your doing. But before you speak, remember that one word could also throw me into the depths of despair. So be the mistress of my fate. It is through you that I shall be eternally happy or in everlasting misery. Could I place a more serious matter into more beloved hands?

I shall end as I began, by imploring your indulgence. I have asked you to hear me out. I shall go further; I shall beg you to answer me. If you refuse, I shall have to believe you are offended, and my heart is the guarantee that my respect for you is as strong as my love.

P.S. To reply, you can use the same method I am using to send you this letter. It seems to me to be both safe and convenient.

From —, 18 August 17**

LETTER 18

Cécile Volanges to Sophie Carnay

Sophie, you blame me for what I am about to do before I have done it! I was already worried enough, but now you have added to my worries. You say it is clear I must not answer the letter. That is all very well for you, but you do not rightly know what the position is. You are not here to see. I'm sure that in my place you would do the same. Obviously as a general rule one should not reply. And as you saw from my letter yesterday, I did not wish to either. But the fact is that I do not believe anyone has ever found themselves in this situation before.

What is more, I am obliged to come to a decision all by myself! Madame de Merteuil, whom I was counting on seeing last night, did not come. Everything conspires against me. She is the reason I met him. It is almost always with her that I have seen him, that I have spoken with him. It is not that I am angry with her for that; but she has abandoned me in my hour of need. Alas! Poor me!

Just imagine, he came yesterday as usual. I was in such a state I did not dare look at him. He could not speak to me because Mamma was there. I was sure he would be vexed when he saw I had not written. I was so embarrassed. A moment later he asked me if I wished him to go and fetch my harp. My heart was thumping so much it was all that I could do to answer yes. When he returned it was much worse. I only gave him the briefest of glances. He did not look at me at all. But from his expression you would have thought he had taken ill. It made me feel dreadful. He began to tune the harp and when he had done that, as he was bringing it for me he said: 'Oh Mademoiselle! . . .' Those are the only two words he said; but he said them in such a tone of voice that I was completely overwhelmed. I started to play a few notes on my harp without knowing what I was doing. Mamma asked whether we were going to sing or not. He made his excuses, saying he did not feel very well. But I had to sing because I had no excuse. I could have wished I had never had a voice. On purpose I chose a tune I did not know, for I was very sure I should not be able to sing at all and people would notice something was wrong. Fortunately another visitor arrived. And as soon as I heard a carriage enter, I stopped and asked him to put away my harp. I was really afraid he would take his leave at the same time; but he came back.

While Mamma and the lady who had arrived were chatting together I thought I would risk another little glance at him. Our eyes met and it was impossible for me to turn away. A moment later I saw his eyes welling with tears, and he was obliged to turn round so as not to be seen. At that moment it was more than I could bear; I knew I was about to weep as well, so I left the room and straight away I wrote with a pencil on a scrap of paper: 'Do not be so sad, I beg you. I promise to answer you.' You surely cannot say there is any harm in that? And anyway I could not help myself. I slipped my piece of paper between the strings of my harp, where his letter had been, and went back into the salon. I felt calmer, but I could not wait for the lady to leave. Fortunately she had to make another visit and left soon after. As soon as she had gone I said I wished to play my harp again, and asked him to fetch it. I could tell from his expression that he did not suspect a thing. But when he came back, oh, how happy he was! As he placed my harp in front of me he positioned himself so that Mamma could not see him and took my hand and squeezed it ... How he squeezed it! It was just for one moment, yet I cannot tell you how much pleasure it gave me. But I withdrew it and so have nothing to feel guilty about.

So presently, my dearest friend, as you can see, it is not possible for me not to write to him, since I have promised. And I shall not cause him such sorrow again, for I suffer more than he does. If it were wicked, I certainly would not do it. But what can be wicked about writing a letter, especially when it is to prevent someone from being miserable? What will be difficult will be that I shall not know how to write it very well. But he will understand it is not my fault. And besides, I am sure that as long as it is from me it will always give him pleasure.

Farewell, my dear friend. If you believe I am doing wrong, tell me. But I do not think so. The nearer it gets to the time I write to him, the faster my heart beats. But do it, I must, because I promised. Farewell.

From —, 20 August 17**

LETTER 19

Cécile Volanges to the Chevalier Danceny

You were so sad yesterday, Monsieur, and that caused me such pain that I am permitting myself to reply to your letter. None the less today I still feel I should not. But as I have made a promise, I do not wish to break my word, and that must indeed be proof of the friendship I have for you. Now that you know this, I trust you will not ask me to write again. I also hope you will tell nobody I have written. For I should surely be blamed for it and might well get into a great deal of trouble. Above all, I hope that you yourself will not form a bad opinion of me, for this would cause me more pain than anything. I can assure you that I would certainly not have agreed to do it for anyone else. I should like you to be good enough not to be so despondent as you were. For that takes away all the pleasure I have in seeing you. You see, Monsieur, I am speaking very frankly to you. My greatest wish is that our friendship should last for ever, but I beg you will not write to me any more.

Yours sincerely,
Cécile Volanges

From —, 20 August 17**

LETTER 20

The Marquise de Merteuil to the Vicomte de Valmont

You are flattering me, you old rogue, because you are afraid I shall make fun of you! All right, I shall have mercy on you: you write such absurd things that I have to forgive you for the good behaviour imposed on you by your Présidente. I do not believe my Chevalier would be as indulgent as I am. He would be just the sort not to sanction the renewal of our little contract and would not find your mad schemes in the least amusing. I laughed heartily about it, and I was really put out that I had to laugh alone. Had you been there, who knows what this merriment might have led to! However, I have had time to consider the matter and to grow more strict with you. It is not that I refuse for ever, but I am deferring it, and I am right to do so. My vanity would perhaps be too much involved, and once I had got a taste for it, there is no knowing to what lengths I might go. I would be woman enough to shackle you to me again, make you forget your Présidente, and if I, all unworthy, made you feel disgust for virtuous behaviour, what a scandal it would be! To avert this danger, here are my conditions.

As soon as you have had your fair devotee, and can send me proof of that, come to me and I shall be yours. For you do realize that in important matters like this one can only accept written proof. By this arrangement I shall become, on the one hand, your reward instead of your consolation; and I prefer it that way. On the other hand, your success will be all the more exciting because it will itself become the path to infidelity. Come then, come as soon as you can, bringing me the evidence of your triumph, like the worthy knights of old who used to deposit the brilliant spoils of their victory at their ladies' feet! Seriously I am curious to know what a prude will find to write after such a moment and what veil she could put over her words when she has none left to cover her person. It is for you to judge whether I am placing too high a price on myself. But I warn you that no reduction will be made. Until that time, my dear Vicomte, you will quite understand that I shall remain faithful to my Chevalier, and that I shall amuse myself by keeping him happy, in spite of the slight annoyance this may cause you.

However, if I were less concerned about morals, I believe he would have a dangerous rival at this time: the little Volanges girl! I dote on her; it's a veritable passion.[16] I may be mistaken, but I think she will turn out to be one of our most celebrated women. I see her little heart opening out and it is a captivating spectacle. She already adores Danceny; but she does not realize it yet. He himself, though very much in love, is shy, in the way young men often are, and does not dare to admit it to her. Both of them worship me. Cécile is longing to tell me her secret; in the last few days I see she is particularly oppressed by it and I would have done her a great service by helping her out a little. However, I do not forget she is just a child and I do not wish to compromise myself. Danceny has spoken rather more plainly to me. But as far as he is concerned my mind is made up and I turn a deaf ear. As for the girl, I am often tempted to make her my pupil; it is a service I wish to do for Gercourt. He leaves me plenty of time, since he is in Corsica until October. I have a mind to use that time to present him with a woman of the world instead of his innocent convent girl. And anyway, how can this man have the insolence to sleep soundly in his bed while a woman who has every reason to complain of him has not yet taken her revenge on him? If the girl was here right now, there is no knowing what I might not say to her.

Farewell, Vicomte; goodnight and good luck: but for Heaven's sake, make a move. Remember that if you do not possess this woman, there are others who will blush to have been possessed by you.

From —, 20 August 17**

LETTER 21

The Vicomte de Valmont to the Marquise de Merteuil

My love, I have finally made some progress, nay, considerable progress, which, though it has not yet brought me to my destination, has at least made me aware that I am on the right track and has dispelled my fears that I had lost my way. At long last I have declared my love. And though I have been met with the most obdurate silence, I have perhaps obtained the least equivocal and most flattering of responses: but I must not leap ahead! Let us go back to where I left off.

You will remember that my comings and goings were to be spied upon? Well, I wanted to make use of this scandalous behaviour for the edification of all, so this is what I did. I charged my valet to seek out in the neighbourhood some unfortunate fellow who was in need of help. This task was not difficult to accomplish. Yesterday afternoon he reported to me that in the course of this morning the furniture belonging to an entire family unable to pay their taxes was to be seized. I first ascertained that there was no young girl or woman in the house who might render my actions suspect. And when in possession of all necessary information, at supper, I declared my intention to go hunting the following day. Here I have to give my Présidente her due. No doubt she was a little sorry for the orders she had given, and though unable to conquer her curiosity, she at least attempted to dissuade me from my plans: it was going to be extremely hot; I ran the risk of becoming ill; I should not kill anything, but should fatigue myself to no purpose. And during our exchanges her eyes, which expressed rather more perhaps than she intended, gave me to understand that she wanted me to take these bad arguments for good ones. I took care not to give in to her, as you may imagine, and I also stood firm against her little diatribe on hunting and hunters, as well as a small cloud of annoyance which darkened that heavenly face all evening. For one minute I was afraid her orders were going to be revoked and that her better feelings might harm my plans. I did not allow for the curiosity of a woman; so I was wrong. My manservant reassured me on the point that very same evening, and I went to bed satisfied.

Up I got at dawn and off I went. Hardly was I twenty yards away from the castle when I caught sight of my spy tailing me. I began my hunting, crossing the fields to the village I wished to reach with the sole purpose of giving the fellow following me a run for his money. He often had to cover, at full tilt, a distance three times that of my own, because he did not dare leave the paths! As a result of this exercise I became extremely hot myself and sat down underneath a tree. And do you know he had the insolence to slip behind a bush not twenty feet away and sit down too? For a moment I was tempted to fire at him, which, though it would only have been small shot, would have been enough to teach him a lesson about the dangers of curiosity. Luckily for him I remembered once more that he was useful and even necessary to my plans. This thought saved him.

Anyway, I arrive at the village. I see there is something up. I go into the village. I ask some questions. I am told what is going on. I summon the tax-collector. And, giving in to my generous compassion, I nobly part with fifty-six *livres,* for which paltry sum five human beings were being reduced to straw and poverty. After this simple little action you may imagine what a chorus of blessings echoed all around me. What tears of gratitude flowed from the eyes of the aged head of the family and embellished the face of the patriarch, who only a moment before had been rendered hideous by fear and despair. I was just studying this spectacle when another peasant, a younger one, leading a woman and two children by the hand, and advancing towards me at great speed, said to them: 'Let us all fall down before this image of God'; and at the same instant I was surrounded by this family, prostrated before me. I shall admit to a momentary weakness. My eyes filled with tears and I felt within me an involuntary but delightful emotion. I am astonished at the pleasure one feels at doing good. And I should be tempted to believe that those whom we call virtuous do not have so much merit as we are led to believe. Whatever the case, I thought it only fair to repay these poor folk for the pleasure they had just given me. I had ten *louis*[17] on me which I gave to them. At that point the thanks began again, but they did not have the same degree of power to move. Necessity had produced the important, the true effect. The rest was a simple expression of gratitude and surprise for gifts, over and above what was necessary.

However, in the midst of the garrulous blessings from this family, I looked not unlike a hero in the final act of a drama. You will not forget that my faithful spy was there in the crowd. My aim was accomplished. I extricated myself and returned to the chateau. All in all, I am very pleased with my idea. I have no doubt this woman is worth making a great effort for. One day this will count for something in her eyes. And having, so to speak, paid for her in advance, I shall have the right to use her as I please with a clear conscience.

I was forgetting to tell you that to capitalize on all this I asked these good people to ask God to bless my plans with success. You will see that already their prayers have been to some extent granted ... But they tell me supper is ready, and it will be too late to send this letter if I do not finish it before I retire to my room. So *the rest in my next*. I am cross, for the rest is the best. Farewell, my love. You are already stealing from me a moment of the pleasure of her company.

From —, 20 August 17**

LETTER 22

The Présidente de Tourvel to Madame de Volanges

No doubt you will be most happy to learn, Madame, of one of Monsieur de Valmont's qualities which to my mind contrasts most markedly with all those which you have heard attributed to him. It is so distressing that one should think ill of any living soul, so unpleasant to see only viciousness in those who may possess all the qualities necessary to cause a person to love virtue! But as you are so inclined to indulgence, I shall oblige you by giving you reasons to reverse the harsh judgement you had reached. Monsieur de Valmont seems to me to have grounds for deserving this favour, or, dare I say, justice. And here is why I believe this to be so.

This morning he went out on business which might have made you think he had some important project in the neighbourhood, as you had supposed he might; an idea that I am sorry to say I perhaps seized upon too eagerly. Fortunately for him, and most fortunately for us, since it has saved us from doing him an injustice, one of my household was obliged to take the same road;* and that is how my reprehensible but fortunate curiosity has been satisfied. He came back and told us that Monsieur de Valmont, having found in the village of — a poor family whose furniture was being sold because they

---

* Does Madame de Tourvel not then dare say this was on her own orders?

lacked the means to pay their taxes, not only hastened to pay these poor people's debt, but gave them in addition a quite considerable sum of money. My servant witnessed this good deed; and told me moreover that the village people, in the course of conversation, said that a servant, whom they named, and who my own servant thinks is one of Monsieur de Valmont's, had been sent yesterday to ascertain who, from among those living in the village, might be needy. If this is indeed the case, it is not even just a passing feeling of compassion brought about by circumstance. It is the intent to do good; it is the anxiety to perform an act of kindness. It is the rarest of virtues in the loveliest of souls. But whether it be by chance or design it is still an honest and praiseworthy deed, and merely recounting it has moved me to tears. I should add, moreover, in all fairness, that when I spoke to him about what he had done, about which he had not breathed a word, he protested and seemed to place so little store upon it after admitting to it that his modesty rendered it twice as worthy in my eyes.

So tell me, my worthy friend, if you still think Monsieur de Valmont an out and out libertine? If that is all he is and yet he conducts himself in this fashion, what is left for us respectable citizens? Are the wicked to share the sacred pleasure of kindness with the good? Would God allow a virtuous family to receive from the hands of a rogue the help for which they will thank divine Providence? And would He take pleasure in hearing pure mouths bless the name of a reprobate? No. I prefer to think rather that errors, even if they are of long standing, do not last for ever. And I cannot believe that a man who does good can be the enemy of virtue. Monsieur de Valmont is perhaps only one more example of the danger of liaisons. I leave you with this pleasing thought. If on the one hand it serves to justify him in your mind, on the other it renders ever more precious to me that tender friendship by which I shall be bound to you for as long as I live.

I have the honour to be, etc.

P.S. Madame de Rosemonde and I, though rather late in the day, are just about to visit this honest, unfortunate family

and join with Monsieur de Valmont in offering help. He shall
accompany us. Thus we shall at least give these good people
the pleasure of seeing their benefactor again. I believe that is all
he has left us to do.

From —, 20 August 17**

LETTER 23

The Vicomte de Valmont to the Marquise de Merteuil

I left off last time with my return to the château. I shall continue
my story.

I had time only for a brief *toilette* before going to the drawing
room where my beauty was occupied with her tapestry, while
the local curate read the gazette[18] aloud to my elderly aunt. I
went to sit beside the work in progress. Glances that were even
sweeter than usual, almost caressing, soon led me to guess that
the servant had already reported on his mission. And in the
event, my inquisitive lady could no longer keep silent about the
secret she had uncovered. And, without fearing to interrupt
the venerable priest, whose manner of reading in any case
resembled that of a preacher giving a sermon, she said: 'I, too,
have some news for you.' And immediately she gave an account
of my adventure, in such precise detail as to do great credit to
the intelligence of her researcher. You may imagine with what
modesty I countered all this. But who can stop a woman who
is praising the man she loves (although she does not realize it)?
I therefore decided to let her continue. You would have said
she was delivering the eulogy of a saint. Meanwhile I was
observing, not unhopefully, what part of love there was in her
animated look, her gestures, which had become less constrained, and especially in her tone of voice, which had already
altered noticeably and betrayed the turmoil in her heart.
Scarcely had she ceased speaking when Madame de Rosemonde
said: 'Come, nephew, come here and let me embrace you.' I

knew immediately that our pretty preacher would be unable to avoid being embraced in her turn. She made as if to escape, but was soon in my arms; and, far from having the strength to resist, she scarcely had enough to sustain herself upright. The more I know of this woman, the more desirable she seems. She made haste to return to her work and looked for all the world as if she was beginning to do her tapestry again. But I could see that her trembling hand did not permit her to go on with it.

After luncheon the ladies wished to go and see the poor unfortunate creatures whom I had so dutifully helped; I accompanied them. I shall spare you the boredom of this second scene of gratitude and flattery. The delicious memory makes me impatient to return to the moment we reached the chateau again. On the way back my beautiful Présidente, more pensive than usual, said not a word. I, preoccupied with thinking up ways of taking advantage of the effect brought about by the day's events, kept silence as well. Madame de Rosemonde was the only one to speak, and she obtained from us nothing but few and brief replies. She must have found us irksome. That was what I intended, and my plan succeeded. When she got out of her carriage she went to her rooms and left me alone with my beauty in the dimly lit drawing room. Sweet darkness makes the timid lover bolder!

I was spared the trouble of steering the conversation in the direction I wished it to take. The fervour of my beautiful preacher served me better than any of my skill could have done. 'When a man is so worthy of doing good,' said she, allowing her sweet gaze to dwell upon me, 'how can he spend his time behaving badly?' 'I do not merit either this praise or blame,' I answered, 'and I fail to comprehend that a woman of your intelligence has not yet understood me. Even though by taking you into my confidence you may think the worse of me, you are too worthy of it for me to refuse. You will find my conduct is explained by a character which is unfortunately too easy-going. Surrounded by immoral people, I copied their vices; perhaps in my pride I have even tried to outdo them. In the same way, here, won over by the example of your virtue, though without any hope of achieving it, I have at least attempted to emulate

it. So perhaps the action which you praise me for today would
lose all value in your eyes, were you to learn the true motive!'
(See, my dearest, how close to the truth I was!) 'It is not to me,'
I continued, 'that these poor people owe the help I gave them.
What you see as a praiseworthy action was for me simply a
means of pleasing you. I was only, I have to confess, the humble
agent of the goddess I adore.' (Here she tried to interrupt me,
but I did not give her time.) 'At this very moment,' I added, 'my
secret is out only because I am so weak. I had promised myself
not to reveal it to you; I was happy to render to your virtue, as
to your charms, an innocent homage of which you would be
for ever ignorant. But as I am incapable of deceit when I have
before my eyes the very paragon of honesty, I shall not have to
feel ashamed of guilty dissimulation. Do not imagine I am
insulting you with improper aspirations on my part. I know I
shall be unhappy, but I shall cherish my sufferings. They will
prove the strength of my love. It is at your feet, in your bosom,
that I shall lay my burden down. I shall find there the strength
to suffer anew. I shall find there compassion and goodness and
think myself consoled, since you have pitied me. O you whom
I adore, listen to me, pity me, succour me!' By this time I was
on my knees and clasping her hands in mine. But, suddenly
pulling them free, and covering her eyes with an expression of
despair, she exclaimed: 'Oh, woe is me!' and burst into tears.
Luckily I was also so carried away that I was weeping too and,
taking her hands once more in mine, I bathed them in tears.
This was a most necessary precaution, for she was so occupied
with her own grief she would not have noticed mine if I had
not hit upon this way of making her aware of it. I had a
further advantage in that I could contemplate at my leisure that
charming face, made still more attractive by the power of tears.
My head was spinning and I was so little in control of my
emotions that I was tempted to take advantage of the moment.

So how could I be so weak? How powerful the force of circumstance if, forgetting all my designs in a premature triumph, I
had risked losing the delights of a prolonged struggle and the
fascination of a painful defeat? If, seduced by my youthful
ardour, I had thought to lay the conqueror of Madame de

Tourvel open to taking as the fruit of his labours nothing but the tame distinction of having had one more woman! Oh yes, let her give herself to me, but let her struggle with herself; may she, without having the strength to conquer, have the strength to resist; may she savour at leisure the feeling of her weakness and be obliged to admit her defeat. We shall allow the humble poacher to kill the stag he has surprised in its hiding-place; the true hunter will rather prolong the chase. This project is sublime, is it not? But perhaps I should now be regretting that I had pursued this course if chance had not come to the aid of my prudence.

We heard a noise. Someone was coming into the drawing room. Madame de Tourvel, alarmed, got up in great haste, seized one of the candlesticks and left the room. I had to let her escape, but it was only a servant. As soon as I was reassured of this, I went after her. Scarcely had I gone a few steps when either she realized it was me or she had a vague sense of apprehension, but I heard her step quicken and she flung herself, rather than walked, into her room, and locked the door behind her. I tried it; but the key was inside. I did not want to knock; that would have provided her with too easy an opportunity to resist. I had the fortunate and simple idea of trying to spy at her through the keyhole, and in fact I saw this adorable woman, in floods of tears, on her knees and praying fervently. What god was she daring to call upon? Is there a god strong enough against the power of love? She is now searching in vain for help from others, but I am the one who will decide her fate.

In the belief that I had done enough for one day I retired to my rooms and started a letter to you. I was hoping to see her at supper. But she sent word that she was indisposed and had retired to bed. Madame de Rosemonde wanted to go up to her, but the crafty invalid claimed to have a headache which allowed her to see no one. As you may imagine, after supper I did not stay up long but had a headache too. In my room I wrote a long letter to complain about this harsh treatment and went to bed, intending to have it delivered to her in the morning. I slept badly, as you can see from the date of this letter. I got up and read my epistle again. I realized that I had not been cautious enough, that I had displayed more desire than love, and appeared more irritated than dejected. I shall have to write it again. But I must be more calm.

I see daylight breaking and hope that the coolness which it brings will allow me to sleep. I shall go back to bed. And whatever power this woman has over me, I promise you I shall not be so preoccupied with her that I do not have time to think of you a great deal. Farewell, my love.

From —, 21 August 17**, 4 o'clock in the morning

LETTER 24

The Vicomte de Valmont to the Présidente de Tourvel

Oh Madame, take pity on me and quieten, I beg you, the torments of my soul. Tell me what I may have cause to hope – or dread! Suspended between the excess of happiness and the excess of misery as I am, uncertainty is a cruel torment for me. Why did I tell you anything? Why did I not resist the imperious charm which made me express my feelings to you? Content as I was to worship you in silence, at least I could take pleasure in my loving. And this pure feeling, untroubled by the image of your pain, was enough to make me perfectly happy. But since I have seen your tears flow, my fount of happiness has become one of despair. Once having heard that cruel 'Oh, woe is me', Madame, those words echo and re-echo in my heart. Why must it be that the sweetest of feelings only give you cause for alarm? What is the nature of your fear? Ah! It cannot be that you fear to share my feeling: your heart, which has been so little known to me, is not made for loving. Mine, which you never cease to vilify, is the one which is touched, whereas yours lacks even compassion. If this were not so, you would not have refused a word of consolation to the poor wretch who recounted his suffering to you. You would not have removed yourself from his gaze, when his only pleasure was in seeing you. You would not have played so cruelly upon his anxiety by sending to say you were indisposed, without allowing him to go and acquaint himself with your state. You would have realized that this very night, which for you was twelve hours in which to rest, would be for him a century of pain.

Tell me, why do I deserve this harsh treatment? I am not afraid to take you as my judge: so what have I done? Except yield unwillingly to a feeling inspired by beauty and justified by virtue; always held in check by respect, my innocent avowal was prompted by trust and not by hope. Will you betray it, this trust that you yourself have seemed to allow me to place in you, and to which I have delivered myself up without reserve? No, I cannot believe it. It would be to suppose you capable of wrongdoing, and my heart cries out at the very idea. I retract my reproach; I can set it down on paper but I cannot think it. Ah, let me believe in your perfection, that is the only pleasure I have left. Prove to me that you are perfect by granting me your generous attention. What poor unfortunate have you helped who had as much need of it as me? Do not abandon me in the turmoil into which you have plunged me. Lend me your reason, since you have taken away mine; and after you have set me on the right path, enlighten me and complete your work.

I do not wish to mislead you – you will not succeed in vanquishing my love. But you will teach me to manage it. By guiding me in what I do, by telling me what I should say, you will at least save me from the terrible misfortune of displeasing you. Above all, banish my desperate fear. Tell me you forgive me, that you are sorry for me; assure me of your indulgence. You could never grant all the indulgence I crave from you; I lay claim to what I need. Will you refuse?

Farewell, Madame; I beg you will receive this homage of my feelings which in no way lessens the homage of my respect.

From —, 20 August 17**

LETTER 25

The Vicomte de Valmont to the Marquise de Merteuil

Here is yesterday's bulletin.

At eleven I went to Madame de Rosemonde's, and under her auspices was introduced into the rooms of my so-called invalid, who was still in bed. Her eyes were very heavy. I hope she slept as badly as I did. I seized the chance when Madame de Rosemonde withdrew a little to pass my letter to her. She refused to accept it, but I left it on the bed, and very properly made to pull up an armchair for my elderly aunt who wished to be near *her dear child*: she had to quickly conceal the letter to avoid any scandal. The invalid said guilelessly that she thought she had a slight fever. Madame de Rosemonde bade me feel her pulse, all the while boasting of my knowledge of medical matters. So my beauty was doubly put out in that she was obliged to give me her arm and knew that her little lie would be found out. In fact, I took her hand and held it in mine while I ran my other hand up and down her soft, dimpled arm. The crafty young woman would not respond in any way, which made me say as I left her: 'There is no sign of any agitation at all.' I guessed that she would be looking daggers at me, and so in order to punish her I did not meet her eyes. A moment later she announced that she wished to get up and we left her alone. She appeared at dinner, which was a dismal affair. She announced she would not go for a walk, which was a way of telling me that I should not have any occasion to speak with her. I felt that it would be just the moment to give her a sigh and a pained look. Undoubtedly she was expecting this, for it was the only occasion in the day that our eyes met. She may be a good girl, but like every other woman she has her little tricks. I found a moment to ask her if *she had had the kindness to let me know my fate* and was somewhat surprised to hear her say: 'Yes, Monsieur, I have written you a letter.' I was in a great hurry to have this letter; but whether it was another trick, or lack of skill, or shyness, she did not give it to me until evening at the moment when she retired to her room. I am sending it to you with the rough copy of my own. Read it and judge for yourself. See with what supreme hypocrisy she declares that she is not in love with me, when I am sure the opposite is the case. And then she will complain if I lie to her later when she does not hesitate to lie to me now! My dear, even the cleverest of men cannot hope to keep up with the truest of women. But I shall have to pretend to believe all this nonsense, and wear myself out with despair, because it pleases Madame to play at being cruel! How can one not take revenge on such villainy? Ah! Patience . . . But adieu. I still have much to write.

By the way, send me back the monster's letter. It is possible that in time she might want to put a price on these wretched things, and I must ensure that all is in order.

I have not written to you about the little Volanges girl; we will talk soon about her.

Chateau de —, 22 August 17**

LETTER 26

The Présidente de Tourvel to the Vicomte de Valmont

You would certainly, Monsieur, receive no letter from me did not my stupid behaviour of yesterday evening oblige me to give you some explanation today. Yes, I admit I wept; perhaps also the three words which you are at pains to quote did escape me: tears and words, you notice everything; therefore I must account for everything.

Accustomed as I am to inspire nothing but honourable feelings, to hear only words which I can listen to without blushing, and consequently to enjoy a security which I venture to say I deserve, I am unable to hide or combat what I am presently going through. The surprise and embarrassment your actions have thrown me into; an indefinable fear inspired by a situation which ought never to have come about; perhaps the revulsion of seeing myself taken for one of those women you despise, and being treated as lightly: all of these things contrived to provoke my tears, and caused me to say, with reason, I believe, that I was wretched. This expression, which you find so violent, would surely be no means violent enough if, like my tears, it had been prompted by something else; if, instead of disapproving of those sentiments which cause me offence, I feared that I might share them.

No, Monsieur, I do not have that fear. If I had, I should run a hundred miles from you. I should go to some solitary place and lament my misfortune in having met you. Even perhaps in spite of the certainty I have that I do not, and never shall, love you, perhaps I should have done better to follow the counsels of my friends and not allow you near me.

I believed, and that was my one mistake, that you would respect an honest woman whose only wish was to find you honest too and to see that justice was done to you; who was already coming to your defence, when you were violating her with your wicked intentions. You do not know me. No, Monsieur, you do not know me, or you would not have believed you could make your wrongdoing seem righteous, or spoken words to me that I should not hear, or believed you were authorized to write a letter I ought not to have read. And you ask me to *guide you in what you do, tell you what you should say!* Well then, Monsieur, say nothing, forget everything: this is the advice it is fitting for me to give you; this is the advice it is fitting for you to follow. And then you will indeed have a right to my indulgence. It will be up to you whether, beyond that, you win the right to my gratitude ... But no, I shall ask nothing from a person who has shown me no respect; I shall not bestow a mark of trust upon someone who has abused my confidence. You force me to fear you, perhaps to hate you. I did not wish it. I only wanted to see in you the nephew of my most honoured friend. I set the voice of friendship against the accusatory voice of public opinion. You have ruined everything. And I foresee you will not wish to make amends.

I confine myself to saying, Monsieur, that your sentiments offend me, that your admitting them affronts me and, above

all, that, far from coming one day to share in them, you will
oblige me never to set eyes upon you again, unless you impose
upon this matter a silence it seems to me I have the right to
expect and even demand from you. I am enclosing with this
letter the one you wrote and I hope you will have the goodness
to send this one back as well. I should be truly troubled if there
remained the least trace of an incident that never should have
occurred.[19] I have the honour to be, etc.

From —, 21 August 17**

LETTER 27

Cécile Volanges to the Marquise de Merteuil

Heavens, how kind you are to me, Madame! How well you
understand that it is easier for me to write than speak to you!
For what I have to say is very difficult. But you are my friend,
are you not? Oh yes, my very good friend! I am going to try
not to be shy. Besides, I need you and your advice so much! I
have such troubles. It seems to me that the whole world knows
what I am thinking, especially when he is there; I blush as soon
as people look at me. Yesterday when you saw me weeping, it
was because I wanted to talk to you and then, I don't know
what it was, but something prevented me. And when you asked
me what the matter was, my tears started up again in spite of
myself. I was unable to say a word. If it had not been for you,
Mamma would have noticed, and then what should I have
done? Yet that is what my life has been like, especially these
last four days!

That was the day, Madame – yes, I am going to tell you
everything – that was the day Monsieur le Chevalier Danceny
wrote to me. Oh, I do assure you that when I found his letter I
had no idea at all what it was. But I cannot lie to you, I cannot
say that it did not give me a great deal of pleasure when I read
it. Do you know that I would rather be miserable for the rest

of my life than that he had not written it. Yet I knew perfectly well I must not tell him so, and I can even assure you that I gave him to understand I was offended by it. But he says it is stronger than him, and I can well believe it. For I had resolved not to reply, and yet I could not help it. Oh, I only wrote to him once, and partly only to tell him not to write to me again. But in spite of that he still writes. And when I do not reply I can see that it hurts him, and that hurts me even more. So I no longer know what to do, or where to turn, and I am greatly to be pitied.

Tell me, I beg you, Madame, would it be very bad of me to reply now and again? Just to give him time to take it upon himself to stop writing, and to be as we were before. For, as far as I am concerned, if it carries on much longer, I don't know what will become of me. When I was reading his last letter, you know, I thought I should never stop weeping, and I am quite sure that if I still do not reply, we shall both be very miserable.

I'm going to send you his letter too or a copy of it and you shall be the judge. You will see that he is not asking anything wicked of me. However, if you think that I must not write, I promise you I will not do so. But I think you will share my feeling that there is nothing wrong in it.

While I am on the subject, Madame, may I ask you something else? I have been told that it is wicked to fall in love with someone. But why? What makes me ask is that Monsieur le Chevalier Danceny claims that it is not in the least bit wrong, and that almost everyone is in love with somebody. If that is the case, I do not know why I should be the sole exception. Or is it only wicked if you are a young girl? For I have heard Mamma herself say that Madame D— loved Monsieur M—, and she did not seem to be suggesting that it was so very bad. Yet I am sure she would be cross with me if she had any inkling of my friendship with Monsieur Danceny. She still treats me like a child, does Mamma. And she never tells me anything. When she took me out of the convent, I thought it was to arrange a marriage for me. But at the moment it seems that this is not the case. It is not that I am fretting over it, I assure you, but you, who are such a good friend to her, perhaps you know about it, and if you do, I hope you will tell me.

This is a very long letter, Madame. But since you have allowed me to write to you I have taken the opportunity to tell you everything, and I count on your friendship.

I have the honour to be, etc.

Paris, 23 August 17**

LETTER 28

The Chevalier Danceny to Cécile Volanges

Can it be, Mademoiselle, that you still refuse to answer my letter? You cannot be swayed; and each day bears away with it the hope it brought! So what kind of friendship – for you acknowledge it as such – is it that is not even strong enough to make you aware of my pain; that leaves you cold and unmoved, while I suffer the torments of a passion I cannot quell; that, far from giving you confidence in me, is not even strong enough to excite your pity? Your friend is suffering and you do nothing to help him! How can that be? He asks but one word from you and you refuse it! You expect him to make do with so feeble a sentiment, and yet fear to assure him even of that!

You would not wish to be ungrateful, you said yesterday. Ah, believe me, Mademoiselle, wishing to pay back love with friendship is not the same as fearing to be ungrateful but only fearing to *seem* so. However, I no longer dare to talk about feelings which can be only burdensome to you if they are not reciprocated. At the very least I must keep them to myself until I manage to conquer them. I am aware of the great cost to me; I do not hide from myself the fact that I shall need all my strength. I shall try every means; but there is one that will be more painful than the rest, and that is to tell myself over and over that you have no feelings for me. I shall even try to see you less, and I am already busy thinking up a plausible excuse.

Am I then to give up the sweet habit of seeing you every day? Ah, at least I shall never cease to regret it. Eternal unhappiness will be the price of my most tender love. And that is your will, it will be your doing! I feel I shall never recapture the happiness I am losing today. You alone were made for me. What a joy it would be to swear to live for you alone! But you do not wish to accept my vows. Your silence tells me only too eloquently that your heart feels nothing for me. It is at one and the same time the surest proof of your indifference and the cruellest manner of announcing it. Farewell, Mademoiselle.

I no longer dare hope for a reply. Love would have written with urgency, friendship with pleasure, even pity with indulgence. But pity, friendship and love are all equal strangers to your heart.

Paris, 23 Aug 17**

LETTER 29

Cécile Volanges to Sophie Carnay

I told you, Sophie, there are after all times when it is quite acceptable to write. And I assure you I am extremely sorry I heeded your advice, which has caused the Chevalier Danceny and myself so much pain. What proves I was right is that Madame de Merteuil, who certainly knows about these matters, has finally come round to my way of thinking. I have confessed all to her. She said the same as you at first; but after I explained everything, she agreed that this was quite different. All she asks is that I show her all my letters and all of Danceny's, in order to be sure that I only say what is right and proper; so for the moment I have peace of mind. I am so very fond of Madame de Merteuil! She is so good to me! And such a respectable woman! So everything will be fine.

I shall write such letters to Monsieur Danceny and they are going to make him so happy! He will be happier than he expects to be, for until now I only spoke about my friendship for him and he always wanted me to call it love. In my opinion it is really the same thing; but anyway I hesitated and he insisted

upon it. I told Madame de Merteuil, and she told me I was
right, and that you should only admit you love someone when
you cannot help it. Now I know I shall not be able to help it
for very much longer. After all, it comes to much the same
thing, and this will please him more.

Madame de Merteuil has also told me that she will lend me
books about all this which will teach me how to conduct myself,
and also how to write better than I do at present: for, you
know, she tells me all the things I do wrong, which proves how
much she cares about me. Only she has suggested to me that I
say nothing to Mamma about those books, because that would
seem as if we thought she had neglected my education, and she
might be annoyed. Oh, I shan't breathe a word!

But how unusual it is that a woman who is scarcely related
to me should care more about me than my own mother! I am
so lucky to know her!

She has also asked Mamma if she may take me to the Opera
the day after tomorrow, to her box; she has told me we shall
be alone there, and we can have a long talk without fear of
anyone overhearing. I much prefer that to the Opera. We shall
also talk of my wedding, for she has told me that it is indeed
true that I am going to be married, though we were not able to
discuss this further. But is it not rather amazing that Mamma
has still not said anything to me about it?

Adieu, my Sophie, I am going to write to the Chevalier
Danceny. Oh, I am so happy!

From —, 24 August 17**

LETTER 30

Cécile Volanges to the Chevalier Danceny

I have finally made up my mind to write to you, Monsieur, to
assure you of my friendship, of my *love*, since, without it, you
will be so unhappy. You say I am unkind. I do earnestly assure

you that you are wrong and I hope you no longer believe that. My not writing to you may have caused you some distress, but do you suppose it did not also make me suffer? It is because I should not want, for all the world, to do anything wicked; and I should not have confessed my love for you even, had I been able to prevent myself. Yet your sadness caused me too much pain. I hope now you will no longer be despondent and that we shall both be very happy.

I also hope I shall have the pleasure of seeing you this evening, and that you will come early. It will never be too early for me. Mamma is having supper at home, and I think she is going to ask you to stay. I hope you will not be engaged as you were the day before yesterday. You must have had a very pleasant supper party. You left here very early. But let us not talk of that. Now you know I love you, I hope you will stay with me as long as you can. For I am only happy when I am with you and I should like it to be the same for you.

I am very sorry that you are still in low spirits at present, but I am not to blame. I shall ask to play the harp as soon as you arrive, so that you shall have my letter straight away. I cannot do more.

Adieu, Monsieur. I love you with all my heart. The more I say it, the happier I am. I hope you will be happy too.

From —, 24 August 17**

LETTER 31

The Chevalier Danceny to Cécile Volanges

Yes, we shall be happy, of that there can be no doubt. My happiness is assured, since I am loved by you; yours, if it lasts as long as the love you have inspired in me, will never end. So you love me, you no longer fear to confess your *love* for me! *The more you say it the happier you are!* After reading that charming *I love you*, written in your own hand, I could hear

your beautiful lips say those words again. I could see those
lovely eyes gazing into mine, their look of tenderness making
them even more beautiful. I have received your vow that you
will live always for me. Ah! Let me give you mine, that my
whole life shall be devoted to your happiness. Pray, accept it
and be assured that I shall not break that vow.

What a happy day we spent yesterday! Oh, why does
Madame de Merteuil not have secrets to confide to your
Mamma every day? Why is it that those delightful memories
must be accompanied by the thought of the constraints we are
under? Why may I not forever hold that pretty little hand that
wrote *I love you*; cover it with kisses and thus avenge myself
for the refusal to grant me a greater favour!

Tell me, my Cécile, when your Mamma returned and we
were obliged, by her presence, to look at each other with indifference and you could no longer console me by assuring me of
your love for your refusal to give me a proof of it, did you not
have any regrets? Did you not say to yourself: a kiss would
have made him happier, and I am the one who has taken away
that happiness from him? Promise me, my darling, that at the
first opportunity you will not be so strict with me. With the
help of that promise I shall find the strength to bear the advers-
ities that circumstances have in store for us. And our cruel
privations will at least be made more bearable by the knowledge
that you are sharing my sorrow.

Adieu, my charming Cécile. It is time for me to come and see
you. It would be impossible to say goodbye were it not that I
am coming to see you again. Adieu, I love you so much! I shall
love you more and more each day!

From —, 25 August 17**

LETTER 32

Madame de Volanges to the Présidente de Tourvel

So would you have me believe, then, that Monsieur de Valmont
is an honest gentleman? I confess I cannot bring myself to do
that; I should have as much difficulty in believing him to be
honest on the strength of that one single action as I should in
thinking a man of acknowledged virtue to be evil, if I heard
that he had done one thing wrong. Human beings are not
perfect in any way, no more perfectly evil than perfectly good.
The wicked man has his virtues, the good man his weaknesses.
It seems to me to be all the more important to accept this truth
since it implies the need for tolerance for the wicked, as well as
for the good; it preserves the latter from pride and saves the
others from discouragement. You will no doubt think I am not
practising the indulgence which I am preaching very conscien-
tiously at this moment. But I see tolerance as only a dangerous
weakness, when it leads us to treat the wicked man and the
good in a like fashion.

I shall not permit myself to scrutinize Monsieur de Valmont's
motives for his action. I would prefer to believe they are as
praiseworthy as the action itself. But has he none the less not
spent his life bringing trouble, dishonour and scandal to many
households? Listen, if you will, to the words of the poor fellow
he has helped. But do not let it make you deaf to the cries of
the hundred victims he has sacrificed. If he is only, as you say,
an example of the danger of liaisons, would he be any the less
himself a dangerous liaison? You suppose him to be capable of
a change of heart? Let us go even further; let us suppose this
miracle has occurred. Would public opinion not still be against
him, and is that not enough to decide your actions? God alone
can absolve, at the moment of repentance; He alone can look
into our hearts. But men can only judge thoughts by actions,
and no one who has lost the respect of others has the right to
complain of the inevitable mistrust which renders his loss so
difficult to regain. Above all, my dear young friend, remember

that sometimes the respect of others may be lost if we appear to be placing too little value upon it. And let us not call this severe judgement unjust. For aside from there being every reason to believe we should never renounce such a precious thing as the good opinion of others (assuming we had any right to expect it), a person not held back by this powerful constraint is the one most likely to do wrong. An intimate relationship with Monsieur de Valmont would be sure to cast you in this light, however innocent it might be.

I am shocked at how swiftly you spring to his defence and I hasten to forestall the objections I can see coming. You will cite Madame de Merteuil, who has been forgiven for her liaison with him. You will ask me why I receive him at my house; you will tell me that, far from being rejected by respectable people, he is admitted, even sought after, in what is called polite society. I think I can answer all these points.

Firstly, Madame de Merteuil, who is indeed very respectable, has perhaps no other fault than that she has too much confidence in her own abilities. She is like a skilful driver who delights in steering her carriage between mountainside and precipice, and justifies her conduct solely by its success. We are right to admire her, but it would be imprudent to follow her. She herself acknowledges this, and blames herself for it. The more she sees of the world, the stricter her principles become. And I do not hesitate to say to you that in this matter she would agree with me.

As far as I am concerned, I shall not try to find excuses for myself any more than for anyone else. It is true that I receive Monsieur de Valmont, and that he is received everywhere. It is just one more inconsequentiality to add to the thousand others which govern society. You know as well as I do that one spends one's life observing them, complaining about them and then indulging in them. Monsieur de Valmont, with his name, large fortune and his many delightful attributes, realized a long time ago that to have any influence in society it was enough to become equally adept at approbation and ridicule. Nobody possesses that twofold talent to the same degree. He charms people with the one and intimidates them with the other. They do not respect him, but they flatter him. That is how he survives in a world which, being more prudent than courageous, prefers to humour rather than confront him.

But it is certain that not Madame de Merteuil herself, nor any other woman, would dare to go and shut herself up in the country, almost alone, with such a man. It was reserved to the wisest, the most modest among us to provide an example of such inconsequential behaviour! Forgive me for using that word. It slipped out because of my friendship for you. Your very integrity lets you down, my dear, because of the sense of security it gives you. So remember you will have sitting in judgement upon you, on the one hand, frivolous people who do not believe in a virtue they see no examples of in their society; and on the other, wicked people who pretend they do not believe in it, to punish you for having been virtuous. Consider that at this moment you are doing what some men would not dare risk doing. In fact, I have seen among many young men, who have only too often treated Monsieur de Valmont as an oracle, that the most prudent fear too close an association with him. And yet you do not fear this! Ah, come back, come back, I implore you ... If these arguments are not enough to persuade you, yield to my friendship. That is what makes me renew my pleas, that is the justification for them. You think me a demanding friend and I would that all this were unnecessary. But I had rather you should have reason to complain of my solicitude than of my negligence.

From —, 24 August 17**

LETTER 33

The Marquise de Merteuil to the Vicomte de Valmont

As long as you are afraid of succeeding, my dear Vicomte, or if your plan is to provide weapons against yourself, or you are less eager to win a victory than to be engaged in a struggle, I have nothing more to say. Your conduct is a masterpiece of prudence. It would be utterly foolish to suppose the opposite. And, to tell you the truth, I fear you may be deluding yourself.

What I am criticizing you for is not for failing to seize the moment. On the one hand, I do not quite see that this moment has arrived. On the other hand, I am very well aware, despite what people say, that a missed opportunity often recurs, whereas one can never retract a hasty action.

But your real mistake is to have allowed yourself to enter into correspondence with her. I defy you now to predict where this will lead. Are you by any chance hoping to prove to this woman by logic that she must give herself to you? It seems to me this can only be a sentimental and not a demonstrable truth, and that, in order to make it acceptable, you have to move her, not argue with her. What good would it do you to move her by writing letters, seeing you will not be there to take advantage of it? Even though your fine words may have an intoxicating effect, do you flatter yourself that that state will last long enough not to allow her time for reflection and so prevent her confessing it? Remember how long it takes to write a letter, and the time it takes before you send it. And tell me whether a woman, especially a principled woman like your devotee, can sustain for all that time a desire she is struggling never to entertain? This procedure may work with the young, who, when they write 'I love you', do not realize they are saying 'I am yours'. But Madame de Tourvel, who is so conscious of her virtue, seems to me to know perfectly well what value attaches to these expressions. So, in spite of the advantage that you gained in conversation with her, she defeats you in her letter. And you know what happens then? The simple fact that one is in dispute means one does not want to give in. By dint of seeking out valid reasons, you find them, you state them; and afterwards you cling to them, not particularly because they are good but because you do not want to climb down from that position.

Moreover, one thing you have failed to notice, much to my astonishment, is that there is nothing so difficult in the matter of love as to write what one does not feel – write convincingly, I mean. You may use the same words, but you do not put them in the same order, or rather, you do arrange them in a certain order and that is sufficient to damn you. Re-read your letter. There is an order in it which exposes you at every sentence. I am sure your Présidente is unsophisticated enough not to notice. But what of that? The effect is none the less a failure. That is the problem with novels. The author works himself up into a passion but it leaves the reader cold. *Héloïse* is the only one I should make an exception of. And, however talented the author, I still maintain that there is a basis of truth in this observation. It is not the same when one speaks. Simply opening one's mouth and uttering may excite a certain feeling. Add to that the ease with which one may dissolve into weeping. The expression of desire in the eyes mingles with the look of tenderness. And halting speech facilitates that air of troubled disorder which is the true eloquence of love. Most of all, the presence of the beloved object prevents long periods of reflection and fills us with the desire to be conquered.

Believe me, Vicomte: she has asked you not to write any more. Take advantage of this to correct your error and wait for the opportunity to speak. Do you know, this woman has more strength than I should have thought? Her defence is good. And were it not for the length of her letter, and the pretext she gives you in her sentence about gratitude to talk about the subject, she would not have betrayed herself in the very least.

What ought also to reassure you of a successful outcome, in my opinion, is that she uses too many resources at once; I foresee that she will exhaust them in argument and that she will have none left when it comes to the thing itself.

I am sending you back your two letters, and, if you are wise, those will be the last until after the happy day. If it were not so late, I should tell you about the little Volanges girl, who is making rather rapid progress; I am very pleased with her. I believe my work will be complete before yours. Shame on you! Farewell for now.

From —, 24 August 17**

LETTER 34

The Vicomte de Valmont to the Marquise de Merteuil

You are wonderfully eloquent, my darling. But why do you go
to such lengths to prove something that everybody knows? To
make rapid progress in the affairs of the heart, it is better to
talk than to write. That is the whole substance of your letter,
as I see it. But of course! These are elementary lessons in the
art of seduction. I shall only remark that you make just one
exception to this rule, whereas there are two: young people,
who take this line through shyness and yield through ignorance,
and intellectual women, who allow themselves to be drawn into
it through *amour propre*, and are led into the trap through
vanity. For instance, I am positive that the Comtesse de B—,
who did not hesitate to answer my first letter, had not at that
time any more love for me than I for her, and that she saw only
an opportunity to discuss a subject at which she could shine.

Be that as it may, a lawyer would tell you that the principle
is not relevant in this case. You are assuming I have the choice
between writing and talking, which is not so. Ever since the
incident of the nineteenth, the monster, still on the defensive,
has applied such ingenuity in avoiding any encounter that it
has thrown my own skills into disarray. We have reached the
point where, if it goes on like this, she will oblige me to concern
myself seriously with how to regain the upper hand. For I
certainly do not wish to be outdone by her in any wise. Even
my letters are the subject of a small war between us; not content
with leaving them unanswered, she refuses even to receive them.
I have to resort to a different trick each time I write, and it is
not invariably successful.

You will recall the simple method I used to convey the first
one to her. The second was no more difficult. She had asked me
to give her back her letter. I gave her mine instead, without her
suspecting a thing. But whether through pique at having been
caught out, or by caprice, or because she is indeed virtuous – for
I shall be forced to believe this in the end – she has obstinately

refused my third. But I hope the problems she is likely to face as a consequence of this refusal will teach her a lesson in future.

I was not very surprised that she did not wish to accept this letter, which I gave her directly. That would have been to grant me some concession, and I am expecting a much longer defence. After this attempt, which was only a gamble, I put my letter in an envelope and, at the time when I knew she would be at her *toilette*, when Madame de Rosemonde and the maid were present, I sent it to her via my manservant, with orders to say that it was the papers she had asked me for. I had rightly calculated that she would be afraid to give the scandalous explanation that a refusal would have necessitated. So indeed, she took the letter. And my ambassador, who had orders to observe her face – and he is quite observant – only perceived a slight reddening and more embarrassment than anger.

I flattered myself then, of course, that either she would keep the letter or, if she wished to return it to me, she would have to be alone with me, which would give me an opportunity to speak to her. About an hour later one of her servants entered my room and gave me, from his mistress, a differently shaped packet from mine, and on its envelope I recognized the longed-for handwriting. I tore it open ... It was my own letter, only folded in two with the seal still unbroken. I suspect that her fear that I would not be as scrupulous as she is in the matter of scandal made her resort to that diabolical trick.

You know me; I do not need to describe my fury. But I had to regain my composure and try some other means. This is the only one I have come up with.

Every morning people go out from here to collect the post, which is about a mile or so away. For this purpose a box with a slit in it, a little like an offertory box, is used; the postmaster has one key and Madame de Rosemonde the other. Everyone puts their letters in during the day, as they please. In the evening they are taken to the post, and in the morning the ones that have arrived are collected. All the servants perform this service, whether they are of the household or not. It was not my man's turn, but he took it upon himself to go, on the pretext that he had business in that quarter.

Meanwhile I wrote my letter. I disguised my writing as to the address, and I faked a stamp from Dijon, quite successfully. I chose this town because I decided it would be more droll to write from the same place as the husband did, seeing that I was asking for the same rights; and also because my beloved had talked all day long of how much she wished to receive letters from Dijon. It seemed only fair to procure her this pleasure.

Once I had taken these precautions, it was easy to put this letter in with the others. Another advantage of this expedient was that I could be there to witness how it was received. For it is the custom here to assemble for lunch and wait for the letters to arrive before dispersing. Finally they arrived.

Madame de Rosemonde opened the box. 'From Dijon,' she said, handing the letter to Madame de Tourvel. 'That is not my husband's writing,' says she, in an anxious voice, hurriedly breaking open the seal. She realized at first glance what had happened, and such a change came over her face that Madame de Rosemonde noticed and said: 'Is anything the matter?' I went over to her as well, saying: 'Is this letter then so very terrifying?' The shy devotee did not dare raise her eyes, did not utter a word, and, to save face, pretended to read through my epistle, which she was in no state to do. I was enjoying her discomfiture and, not at all averse to teasing her a little, I added: 'You are looking a little calmer, so let us hope the letter has caused you more surprise than pain.' Her anger then afforded her more inspiration than prudence was able to. 'It contains,' she replied, 'things which I find offensive, and I am astonished that anyone would dare to write to me in this manner.' 'So who is it from?' interrupted Madame de Rosemonde. 'It is not signed,' said my beautiful Fury, 'but the letter and its author both fill me with disgust. You will oblige me by not speaking of it any more.' With these words she tore up my bold missive, put the pieces in her pocket, got up and left the room.

In spite of this anger she nevertheless has my letter. And I trust to her curiosity that she has taken good care to read it in its entirety.

If I go into greater detail I shall run on too long. I include the rough copy of my two letters with this account. Then you will know as much as I do. If you wish to be *au courant* with my correspondence you must accustom yourself to deciphering my notes. For nothing in the world will make me copy them out again; I should find it exceedingly boring. Adieu, my love.

From —, 25 August 17**

LETTER 35

The Vicomte de Valmont to the Présidente de Tourvel

I must obey you, Madame. I have to prove to you that with all the wrongs you are pleased to impute to me at least I still have enough tact not to permit myself to reproach you, and enough courage to impose the most painful of sacrifices upon myself. You command me to be silent and to forget! Well then, I shall force my love to be silent and I shall forget, if at all possible, the cruel fashion in which you have received it. Certainly my desire to please you did not give me any right to expect that I would. And I admit that my need for your indulgence was no reason why I should obtain it. But you look upon my love as an outrage. You forget that if it were wrong you would be both the cause and the justification. You also forget that, having learned to open my heart to you, even when such confidences might do me harm, I have no longer found it possible to hide the feelings which engulf me. And what I have done in good faith you regard as a mark of boldness. The reward for my most tender, most respectful, truest love is that you cast me away from you. And finally you talk about your hatred ... Where is the man who would not complain of being treated thus? I alone submit to it. I suffer in silence. You persecute me and I adore you. The unimaginable power you exercise over me renders you absolute mistress of my feelings. And if my love alone endures, if you cannot destroy it, it is because it is your doing and none of mine.

I am not asking you to return my feelings; I have never

flattered myself that you might. I do not even expect pity, though the interest you have sometimes shown in me might have led me to hope for this. But I admit I do believe I have the right to ask for justice from you.

You tell me, Madame, that people have tried to lower me in your estimation; that if you had taken the advice of your friends you would not have allowed me anywhere near you. Those were your words. So who, then, are these officious friends? No doubt these people with such strict principles, with such high moral standards, will consent to be named. No doubt they would not wish to be clouded in an obscurity where they might be confused with vile slanderers. So I should not be ignorant either of their names or of what they are saying. Surely, Madame, I have the right to know the one and the other, since you judge me accordingly. One does not condemn a guilty man without telling him what his crime is, without naming his accusers. I do not ask for any other favour, and I undertake in advance to justify myself and oblige them to retract.

If I have perhaps been too dismissive of the vain approbation of a society for which I have scant regard, the same is not true of your good opinion of me. And now that I have devoted my life to deserving that, I shall not allow it to be snatched away with impunity. It has become so much more precious to me, in that I am sure I owe to it this request you are afraid to make, which might have given me, you say, *the right to your gratitude.* Ah! Far from claiming such rights, I shall think my gratitude due to you if you vouchsafe me a chance to please you. Begin then by acting more justly towards me, and do not leave me in ignorance of what it is you desire from me. If I could guess, I should not put you to the trouble of telling me. Add to my pleasure in seeing you the happiness of obliging you and I shall consider myself a fortunate man. What can stop you? Not, I hope, the fear of a refusal? I feel I should not be able to forgive you for that. If I do not return your letter, that is not a refusal. I wish, even more than you do, that it might not be necessary: but, accustomed to thinking of you as the gentlest of souls, it is only in this letter that I may perceive you as you wish to appear. Whenever I dare hope you may have some feeling for me, I read in your letter that, rather than consent to it, you would put a hundred leagues between us. When I feel that everything about you increases and excuses my love, it is this letter which tells me again that my love offends you. And as, whenever I see you, my love for you seems to me the supreme good, I am compelled to return to your letter to find that it is a terrible torment. You understand, then, at present that my greatest joy would be to be able to give you back this dreadful letter. To ask me for it again would be to authorize me not to believe what it contains any more. I trust you do not doubt my eagerness to put it into your hands.

From —, 21 August 17**

LETTER 36

The Vicomte de Valmont to the Présidente de Tourvel
(With a Dijon postmark)

You grow stricter each day, Madame, and I venture to say that you appear to be less worried about being unjust than of being too kind. After condemning me without a hearing, I suppose you must have felt that it would be easier not to read my reasons than to respond to them. You obstinately refuse my letters; you send them back to me with contempt. You force me to have recourse to trickery, when my sole aim is to convince you of my good faith. But the necessity you have imposed on me of defending myself will no doubt suffice to excuse the means. Moreover, the sincerity of my feelings convinces me that, in order to justify them in your eyes, all I need do is explain them to you, and so I think I may permit myself this little subterfuge. I venture to believe, too, that you will forgive me for it. And that you will not be too surprised to find that love is more ingenious in making itself manifest than indifference is in sweeping it aside.

Allow me then, Madame, to open my heart to you entirely. It is yours and it is only right that you should know what it contains.

I was very far from seeing the fate which awaited me when I first arrived at Madame de Rosemonde's house. I was unaware that you were there. And I may add, with my accustomed sincerity, that, had I known it, I should not have felt myself to be in any danger. Not that I should have failed to render to your beauty its just deserts; but, being used only to experiencing desire and of giving in to it only when I received encouragement, I was ignorant of the torments of love.

You were a witness to Madame de Rosemonde's repeated requests to me to stay longer. I had already spent one day with you. However, I only allowed myself, or believed that I was enjoying, a most natural and legitimate pleasure in paying my respects to a respected relative. The way of life here was very different, no doubt, from the one to which I was accustomed, yet it was no hardship for me to conform to it. And, without seeking the reason for the change which was taking place in me, I put it down entirely to that pliability of character of which I believe I have already spoken.[20]

By misfortune (but why should we call it a misfortune?), as I became more closely acquainted with you, I soon realized that your bewitching face, which was what had struck me, was the least of your qualities. Your angelic soul astonished and enchanted me. I admired your beauty, I adored your virtue. Without the slightest hope of winning you, I passed my days in trying to be worthy of you. In asking your indulgence for what had happened in the past, my aim was to merit your approval in the future. I sought it in your words, I studied it in your looks – in those looks from which there flowed a poison so much more dangerous in that it was poured forth without intent and received without mistrust.

At last I knew what love was. But how far I was from lamenting my condition! I resolved to bury my feelings in eternal silence, and give myself up fearlessly, unreservedly, to this delicious sensation. Every day it increased. Soon the pleasure I took in seeing you changed into a need. If you were away from me for only one moment, my heart ached. It throbbed with joy when I heard you return. I existed only through you and for you. And yet I call upon your judgement: did there ever once, during the jollity of some foolish game or in the seriousness of our conversations – did there ever escape from me one word which betrayed the secret of my heart?

Finally the day arrived when my misfortunes were to begin. And by an unimaginable twist of fate, it was signalled by a virtuous act. Yes, Madame, it was in the midst of those poor unfortunates whom I helped that you succeeded, by manifesting that precious sensibility which enhances beauty itself and makes virtue truly worthy, in leading astray a heart already intoxicated by too much love. You remember perhaps how wholly preoccupied I was as we returned? I was, alas, struggling to fight an inclination that was becoming stronger than I was.

It was after exhausting all my strength in this unequal struggle that a chance, which I could not have foreseen, left us alone together. At that point, I admit, I succumbed. My heart was overflowing, I could not hold back my words or my tears. But is that a crime? And if it is, has it not been punished enough by the dreadful torments to which I am being subjected?

I am consumed by a hopeless love. I implore your pity but receive only your hatred. Having no other happiness than that of seeing you, my eyes seek you out despite myself, while I tremble to meet your gaze. In the cruel state to which you have reduced me I spend my days hiding my pain and my nights in yielding to it. While you, calm and at peace, are ignorant of these torments except inasmuch as you are the cause of them, and commend yourself on them. Yet you are the one complaining about them and I the one begging your forgiveness.

So this then, Madame, is the faithful account of what you call my wrongdoing, and which it would perhaps be more accurate to call my misfortune. Pure and sincere love, unwavering respect, total subjugation to your will: such are the feelings you inspire in me, feelings that I would not have feared to offer in homage to God Himself. Oh, you who are His fairest handiwork, imitate His graciousness! Think of my cruel suffering. Above all, be aware that, in that state between despair and

supreme happiness where you have left me, the first word you
utter will decide my fate for ever.

                                  From —, 23 August 17**

LETTER 37

The Présidente de Tourvel to Madame de Volanges

I bow, Madame, to the friendly advice you have given me. I am
accustomed to deferring to your opinion in all things, and do
believe it is always rational and well-founded. I shall even
concede that Monsieur de Valmont is indeed infinitely dangerous if he can at one and the same time pretend to be as he
appears here, and still be the man you describe. Whatever the
case, since you say I must, I shall put a distance between myself
and him. At least I shall do my best. For often things which
ought to be the simplest become extremely difficult when you
try to put them into practice.

It seems to me impracticable to ask this of his aunt. It would
be equally disobliging both for her and for him. And I am
reluctant to take the decision to go away myself. For apart from
the reasons I have already given you concerning Monsieur de
Tourvel, if my departure annoyed Monsieur de Valmont, as is
quite possible, would he not easily be able to follow me to
Paris? And his returning there, for which I shall be, or at least
seem to be, responsible, would surely appear stranger than
meeting in the country house of someone known to be his
relative and my friend.

So no other solution remains except to persuade Monsieur
de Valmont himself to be good enough to leave. I know this is
a difficult suggestion to make. However, since apparently he is
bent on proving to me that he is in fact more honourable than
people suppose, I have not given up all hope of succeeding. I
shall not even be sorry to attempt this, and to have the opportunity to see whether, as he so frequently asserts, truly virtuous

women have never had, and never will have, cause to complain of his behaviour. If he leaves in accordance with my wishes, it will certainly be out of respect for me. For I do not doubt that he plans to spend a good part of the autumn here. If he were to refuse my request and insist on remaining, there would be nothing to prevent me leaving myself, and I promise you that is what I should do.

I think that is all your friendship requires of me, Madame. I hasten to satisfy these demands and prove to you that despite my somewhat *heated* defence of Monsieur de Valmont I am still disposed not only to listen to but even to follow the advice of my friends.

I have the honour of being, etc.

From —, 25 August 17**

LETTER 38

The Marquise de Merteuil to the Vicomte de Valmont

Your enormous packet has just this minute arrived, my dear Vicomte. If the date is correct I should have received it twenty-four hours ago. However, if I took the time to read it, I should have none left to write my answer, so I had rather simply let you know it has arrived and talk about other matters. Not that I have any news about myself; in autumn there are scarcely any males left in Paris fit to be looked at, so for the last month I have been so well-behaved I could die, and every other man except my Chevalier would be bored to tears by the proofs of my fidelity. With nothing else to engage my attention, I am passing the time with the little Volanges girl. And that is what I wish to talk to you about.

Do you realize that you have lost more than you might think by not taking this girl under your wing? She is truly delightful! No character, no principles either. You can see how easy and agreeable her company will be. I do not think she will ever shine in matters of sentiment, but she certainly looks as if she will be an ardent little creature. She has no intellect, no finesse, and yet she has a certain natural duplicity, if one may call it that, which sometimes surprises even me, and with which she will have all the more success since her face is the very image of candour and artlessness. She is by nature very demonstrative and I am sometimes amused by that. She gets excited incredibly quickly, and when that happens she is all the more amusing since she knows nothing, but nothing, about what she so much desires to know. She has very funny little bouts of impatience. She laughs, she gets cross, she cries and then, in the most beguiling way, she earnestly begs me to tell her things. In truth I am almost jealous of the man for whom such pleasures are reserved.

I don't know whether I told you, but for the last four or five days I have had the honour of being her confidante. As you can guess, at first I pretended to be very strict. But as soon as I saw she thought she had won me over by her dubious arguments I pretended to think they were valid. And she is firmly persuaded she owes this success to her own eloquence. I had to take this precaution in order not to compromise myself. I have allowed her to say and to write 'I love'; and the same day, without her suspecting anything, I engineered a meeting for her with Danceny. But just imagine! He is such a fool, he did not even kiss her. And yet the lad writes such pretty verses! Lord, how stupid these clever people can be! He is so stupid that I find him embarrassing. After all, I cannot be expected to be his guide!

It is just at present that you could be extremely useful to me. You are friendly enough with Danceny to win his confidence, and if he were once to confide in you, we should make great headway. Hurry your Présidente along a little, for I do not want Gercourt to escape. Anyway, I talked about him yesterday to our young friend, and I painted such a picture of him that if she had been his wife of ten years she could not have hated him more. Yet I have preached to her a good deal about marital fidelity; nothing equals my firmness on this subject. And so on the one hand I have re-established in her eyes my virtuous reputation, which too much complaisance might have destroyed; and on the other I am increasing the hatred which I wish her to bestow upon her husband. And finally I hope that by my convincing her it is only permissible to fall in love during the short time she has left before her marriage, she will decide more quickly not to waste a moment of it.

Farewell, Vicomte. I am about to begin my *toilette*, and shall read your epistle the while.

From —, 27 August 17**

LETTER 39

Cécile Volanges to Sophie Carnay

I am sad and anxious, my dear Sophie. I cried almost the whole night long. Not that I am not essentially very happy at present. But I foresee that it cannot last.

I was at the Opera yesterday with Madame de Merteuil. We talked a great deal about my wedding, and I have not learned any good news. It is Monsieur le Comte de Gercourt I am to marry, and it is to be in the month of October. He is rich, he is aristocratic, colonel of the regiment of —. So far so good. But he is *old*: just imagine, he is at least thirty-six years old! And then Madame de Merteuil says that he is stern and gloomy, and that she fears I shall not be happy with him. I could even tell that she was quite certain of that, but did not wish to say so in case it distressed me. All she talked about almost the whole evening was the duties of wives to their husbands. She admits that Monsieur de Gercourt is not at all amiable, and yet she says I shall have to love him. She has also told me that once I am married I should not love the Chevalier Danceny. As though there were the remotest chance of that! Oh, I assure you I shall love him for ever. I would prefer not to marry at all. This Monsieur de Gercourt can look after himself; I did not go looking for him. He is in Corsica at the moment, a long way away. I wish he would stay there for ten years. If I were not afraid to be sent back to the convent I should be sure to say to Mamma that I do not wish to be married to him. But that would make matters even worse. Oh, it's so difficult. I feel I have never loved Monsieur Danceny so much as I do at the moment. And when I think that I have only one month of freedom left, I start crying straight away. My one consolation is the company of Madame de Merteuil. She is so kind! She shares all my problems as though they were her own. And she is so amiable that when I am with her I hardly think about them any more. She is, moreover, very useful to me, for what little I know, she has taught me, and she is so good that I tell her all my thoughts without being the least bit embarrassed. When she thinks I am in the wrong, she sometimes scolds me. But she does it very gently, and then I put my arms around her and kiss her until she is not cross any more. At least I may love her as much as I want without it being wicked, and I enjoy that very much. But we have agreed that when we are in company I should not make it apparent how much I love her, and especially not in front of Mamma, so that she does not suspect anything where the Chevalier Danceny is concerned. I assure you that if I could always live as I do at present, I think I should be very happy. If only it were not for this wretched Monsieur de Gercourt! But I do not wish to speak of him further, for I shall become depressed once more. Instead, I am going to write to Danceny. I shall speak to him only of my love, not of my anxieties, because I do not wish to upset him.

Farewell, dear friend. You see that you were wrong to complain, and that though I am so *busy*, as you call it – I still have time to think about you and write to you.*

From —, 27 August 17**

---

* Letters between Cécile Volanges and the Chevalier Danceny continue to be omitted because they are of little interest and throw no light on events.

LETTER 40

The Vicomte de Valmont to the Marquise de Merteuil

The monster does not content herself with leaving my letters unanswered, or refusing to receive them. She wants to deprive me of the very sight of her, insisting that I remove myself from her presence. And what you will find even more surprising is that I put up with all this harsh conduct. You will disapprove. But I thought I had better not throw away this chance of receiving her orders. I am convinced, on the one hand, that whosoever commands, assumes responsibility. And, on the other, that the illusory authority which we apparently allow women to exercise over us is one of the pitfalls they only avoid with the greatest difficulty. Moreover, the skill which she is exercising in not being left alone with me has placed me in a dangerous situation from which I must escape at all costs. In her company the whole time and yet unable to pursue my affair, I have reason to fear she might become accustomed to seeing me without being troubled; and that state, as you well know, is very difficult to reverse.

As to the rest, you may guess I have not submitted to her without imposing my conditions. I have even taken care to stipulate one that is impossible to grant; as much to remain at liberty to keep my promise or not as to engage in a verbal or written discussion at a time when my beauty is better pleased with me, and needs me to be better pleased with her. And, for another thing, I should be behaving very ineptly if I did not find a way of receiving some compensation for renouncing my claim, however untenable it may be.

Having set out my reasons to you in this lengthy preamble, I shall begin telling you about these last two days. I shall include as evidence the letter from my beauty and my reply. You must admit that few historians are so exact as I am.

You will recall the effect my letter from Dijon had the morning of the day before yesterday. The remainder of the day was very stormy. Our pretty prude arrived only when lunch was about to be served, saying she had a bad migraine, a pretext which she wanted to use to cover up one of the blackest moods any woman could ever have. Her face was much altered. That sweet expression you are familiar with had changed into a look of defiance which bestowed a new kind of beauty upon her. I promise myself I shall make use of this discovery henceforth, and occasionally exchange my loving mistress for a rebellious one.

I could see that after lunch it was going to be rather gloomy. And so, to avoid the boredom, I pretended I had letters to write and withdrew to my rooms. I returned to the drawing room at six. Madame de Rosemonde proposed a drive, and the suggestion was taken up. But at the very moment of getting into the carriage the so-called invalid, with a devilish piece of trickery, pleaded in turn, and perhaps to take revenge on me for my having absented myself, that her pain was much worse, and I was mercilessly condemned to a tête-à-tête with my elderly aunt. I do not know if the curses I brought down on this female devil were granted but when we returned we found her lying down.

The next day at breakfast she was a changed woman. Her gentle nature was again in evidence and I had reason to suppose I had been forgiven. We had just finished when the sweet girl got up with an indolent air and went out into the grounds. I followed her, as you may guess. Addressing her, I enquired: 'Why this urge to go walking?'

'I have been writing a great deal this morning,' she replied, 'and my head is rather tired.'

'Could I perhaps be the fortunate man responsible for this fatigue?' I continued.

'I have indeed written to you,' she rejoined, 'but I hesitate to give you my letter. It contains a request, and you have given me no reason to hope it will be granted.'

'Ah! I swear that if there is anything I can do . . .'

'Nothing could be easier,' she interrupted, 'and though you ought perhaps to grant it out of fairness to me I should not mind obtaining it as a favour.' So saying, she presented me with her letter. As I took it I also took her hand, which she withdrew, but without anger and more with embarrassment than temper.

'It is warmer than I supposed,' she said. 'I must go inside.'
And she set off back to the chateau. I made vain efforts to
persuade her to continue her walk. But I had to remember that
we were able to be seen, so I could only use my eloquence to
persuade her. She went in without saying a word and I could
see quite clearly that this pretence of a walk had no other motive
than to give me her letter. She went up to her room as soon as
she got back and I retired to mine to read her epistle. Which
you too would do well to read, as you should my response,
before proceeding further . . .

LETTER 41

The Présidente de Tourvel to the Vicomte de Valmont

It seems to me, Monsieur, from your conduct towards me, that
you are only seeking each day to add to my reasons to complain
about you. You persist in trying to engage me in discussion
about sentiments which I would not, must not, hear. The way
in which you do not hesitate to insult my honesty and modesty
by sending me your letters; and especially the manner, the
indelicate manner, I might say, which you used to convey the
last one to me, not caring that my reaction to a surprise like
that might compromise me; all of this would constitute a good
reason for a sharp and well-deserved reproach on my part. But
instead of reiterating these complaints I will make do with
asking something of you which is as simple as it is just. And if
you grant it, then I consent that all shall be forgotten.

You yourself have told me, Monsieur, that I need not fear a
refusal from you. And although, with characteristic inconsist-
ency, this sentence was followed by the only refusal you could
give me,* I should like to think that today you will still honour
your promise of but a few days ago.

My wish then is that you be good enough to go away from
me. Leave this chateau, where a longer stay on your part could

* See Letter 35.

only expose me more to the criticism of a society always ready to think the worst of others and, because of your conduct, only too used to fixing its attention on any women who have anything to do with you.

I have been warned of this danger by my friends for some time now and have neglected their advice. I have even argued with them, since I was so convinced by your behaviour towards me that you wished to set me apart from the multitude of women who have had cause to complain about you. Now that you treat me the same as you do them, I can no longer be in any doubt of the danger, and I owe it to society, to my friends as well as myself, to take this necessary course of action. I might add that you will gain nothing by refusing my request, since I am resolved to leave of my own accord should you insist on remaining. But I do not wish to lessen the obligation I should feel to you were you to do as I ask, and I want you to know that were you to make my departure necessary, you would greatly inconvenience my arrangements. So prove to me, Monsieur, that, as you have professed so many times, respectable women will never have cause to complain of you. Or at least prove to me that when you do them wrong you are able to make amends.

If I thought I needed to justify my request to you, I should only have to tell you that you have spent your life in rendering it necessary, and yet it is one that I should never have needed to make. But let us not bring to mind events which I prefer to forget and which would oblige me to judge you harshly at a moment when I am offering you the opportunity to earn my wholehearted gratitude. Adieu, Monsieur; the manner in which you conduct yourself will tell me with what feelings I shall be, for ever, your very humble, etc.

From —, 25 August 17**

LETTER 42

The Vicomte de Valmont to the Présidente de Tourvel

However hard the conditions you impose upon me, Madame, I do not refuse to fulfil them. I feel quite unable to go against any of your wishes. That said, I venture to hope that you will allow me to make some requests in return; they are much easier to grant than yours, and yet I wish to obtain them only by an utter submission to your will.

One, which I hope will appeal to your sense of justice, is that you should name those who have been accusing me. It seems to me they are doing me so much wrong that I should have the right to know who they are. The other, which I might expect you to grant out of the kindness of your heart, is that you might allow me sometimes to renew the homage of my love which now, more than ever, will merit your compassion.

I hasten to do your will, Madame, as you see, even when I can do so only at the expense of my happiness; even though, I shall go so far as to say, I am convinced that you only desire my departure to spare yourself the painful spectacle you have always before you of the object of your injustice.

You must agree, Madame, that it is not so much that you are concerned about the opinion of a public so accustomed to respect you that it dare not hold you in low esteem, as that you are embarrassed by the presence of a man whom it is easier to punish than to blame. You distance me from you as one turns one's eyes away from a poor man to whom one does not want to give alms.

But when absence from you redoubles my suffering, to whom, if not you, can I address my complaint? From whom, if not you, may I expect the consolation so essential to me? Will you refuse it, when it is you and only you who have caused me this suffering?

You will surely not be surprised either that, before leaving, I am anxious to give you an explanation for the feelings you have inspired in me; nor that I shall only find the strength to distance myself from you upon receiving the order from your very own lips.

For these two reasons, I beg a brief conversation with you. It would be no use to write letters instead. We could write volumes and still not understand one another half as much as we should with a quarter of an hour's conversation. It will not be hard for you to find the time to grant me this. For, however much I hasten to obey you, you know that I have informed Madame de Rosemonde about my plans to spend part of the autumn with her, and I shall at least have to wait for a letter to have a pretext of business which obliges me to leave.

Adieu, Madame. This word has never cost me so much to write as at this moment when it recalls to me the idea of our separation. If only you could imagine how it makes me suffer, I dare believe you would be a little grateful for my willingness to please you. At least be kind enough to receive the assurance and homage of my most tender and respectful love.

From —, 26 August 17**

LETTER 40 (*CONTINUED*)

The Vicomte de Valmont to the Marquise de Merteuil

Now let us consider, my dear. You feel as I do that the scrupulously honourable Madame de Tourvel could not grant me the first of my demands, and thus betray the trust of her friends by disclosing who her accusers are to me. So by making all my promises depend on this condition, I am not holding myself to anything. But you will also realize that her refusal of this request will be a way of my obtaining the other things; when I leave, I win out by entering into a correspondence with her that she has herself legitimized; I scarcely count the rendez-vous I have begged of her, which actually has no other motive than to prepare her to consent to others when I really need them.

The one thing that remains for me to do before I go is to find out who these people are who are so busy damaging me in my dealings with her. I presume it is her pedant of a husband. I hope so. Apart from the fact that conjugal prohibition is a spur to desire, I could be sure that from the moment my beauty consents to write to me I should have nothing more to fear from her husband, since she would already necessarily be deceiving him.

But if she has a friend intimate enough to be in her confidence, and that friend is against me, I believe it will be necessary to stir up a quarrel between them, and I hope I shall be able to do this. But first I need some information.

I really thought I was about to learn something yesterday. But this woman never behaves like other people. We were in her room at the time when it was announced that dinner was served. She was only just finishing her *toilette*, and I noticed that in her haste and confusion she had left the key in her writing-desk. And I knew she never removed the key to her room. I was thinking about it during dinner when I heard her maid come downstairs. I took a swift decision. I pretended I had a nosebleed and went out. I rushed upstairs to her desk, but I found all the drawers unlocked and not the slightest sign of a letter. And yet at this time of the year we have no fires in which to burn them. Whatever does she do with the letters she receives? For she receives a great many! I neglected nothing, I looked everywhere. But all I acquired was the conviction that she must still have this precious treasure in her pockets.

How can I get hold of them? Since yesterday I have been vainly trying to think how. I am determined to do so. I regret not having the skills of a pickpocket. Should this, indeed, not form part of the education of a man of intrigue? Would it not be amusing to steal the letter or the portrait of a rival, or pull something from a prude's pockets that would lay bare her hypocrisy? But our parents do not consider these things. And though I think of everything, all I can do is realize my ineptitude, and I am incapable of doing anything about it.

Whatever the case, I came back to the table extremely put out. However, I was somewhat mollified by my beauty's air of concern about my feigned condition and I took advantage of it to assure her that for some time I had been excessively agitated, and it had been damaging my health. Convinced as she is that she is the cause of it, should she not in all conscience behave in a way that would calm my anxieties? But though so religious, she is not very charitable. She refuses to give alms in the name of love and this refusal is quite enough, in my opinion, to warrant me stealing them. But adieu, for here I am chattering away and all I can think of is those accursed letters.

From —, 27 August 17**

LETTER 43

The Présidente de Tourvel to the Vicomte de Valmont

Why seek to lessen my feelings of gratitude, Monsieur? Why should you wish to accede to only half of what I demand of you, and try to bargain, as it were, over a perfectly straightforward course of action? Is it not enough that I feel how much I ask of you? Not only are you asking a great deal, you are asking the impossible. For if my friends have talked about you, they have done so simply out of concern for me. And even if they are mistaken, their intentions were none the less good. And you are proposing that I should acknowledge this mark of friendship on their part by betraying their trust! I have already put myself in the wrong by telling you about it, and now you make me only too aware of this. What with anyone else would have been just candour is madness where you are concerned, and I should be guilty of great wrongdoing if I yielded to your demands. I appeal to you, on your honour, did you believe I was capable of doing that? Should you ever have proposed such a thing? No, of course not. And I am sure when you reflect upon it further you will no longer press me on the matter.

Your request that I write to you is scarcely easier to grant. And, in all fairness, you cannot lay the blame for this on me. I do not wish to offend you, but in view of the reputation you have acquired and which, on your own admission, you at least partly deserve, how could any woman admit to being in correspondence with you? And how could an honest woman be capable of resolving to do what she knows she must keep secret?

And another thing: if I could be certain your letters were such that I would never have reason to complain of them, that I might always be able to justify in my own mind the receiving of them, then perhaps the desire to prove to you that I am guided by reason and not hatred would make me override these powerful considerations, and go much further than I ought in allowing you to write to me occasionally. If indeed you desire this as much as you say you do, you will abide willingly by the single condition which could make me agree to it. And if you are at all grateful for what I am doing at this moment for your sake, you will not put off your departure any longer.

Allow me to observe, while on this subject, that you received a letter this morning but did not take advantage of it to announce your departure to Madame de Rosemonde, as you promised. I hope henceforth that nothing will stop you keeping your word. I trust above all that you will not on that account wait for me to grant the interview you ask for, and which I absolutely do not wish to have with you. And instead of the orders you say you find necessary, you will make do with this plea, which I make to you now once again. Farewell, Monsieur.

From —, 27 August 17**

LETTER 44

The Vicomte de Valmont to the Marquise de Merteuil

Share my joy, my dearest. She loves me. I have triumphed over her unruly heart. In vain she pretends to hide it; happily my cleverness has discovered her secret. Thanks to my painstaking exertions I have found out everything I need to know. Since last night – oh blessed night! – I am once more in my element.

I have come into my own again. I have lifted the veil from a twofold mystery of love and infamy. I shall enjoy the one and be revenged for the other. I shall fly from pleasure to pleasure. The very thought of it transports me into a state in which I have some trouble reminding myself to proceed with caution; and I may have trouble too in putting some order into my account of what occurred. But let me try.

Only yesterday, after writing you a letter, I received one from the celestial being. I am sending it to you. You will see that she gives me, in the least clumsy manner possible, permission to write to her. But she urges me to leave, and I knew I should not be able to postpone it much longer without damaging my cause.

However, I was still uncertain what to do, because I was tormented by the desire to know who could have said things about me. I made an attempt to win over the maid and have her empty her mistress's pockets for me, which she could easily do in the evening and put things back next morning without arousing the least suspicion. I offered her ten *louis* for this small service, but she turned out to be a timid or conscientious prude of a girl who could be won over by neither money nor eloquence. I was still lecturing her when the supper bell went. I had to leave her. I was only too relieved when she said she would keep my secret, though I was none too sure she would.

Never before had I been in such bad humour. I felt compromised. And I blamed myself all evening for my lack of caution.

When I had returned, not without some disquiet, to my room, I spoke to my valet, who ought to have some credit with the girl because of his successful love affair with her. I asked him either to obtain from her what I had asked or at least ensure her discretion. But though usually so confident, he seemed rather dubious about the success of the undertaking, and made an observation on this subject which astonished me by its depth:

'Monsieur surely knows better than I do,' he said, 'that going to bed with a woman simply makes her do what she likes doing. But it is often a far cry between that and making her do what we want her to do.' '*The rascal's good sense appals me at times.*'*

---

* Piron, *Métromanie*.[21]

'I vouch for this girl even less,' he added, 'because I have reason to believe she has another lover and that I only owe my success with her to the fact that there is so little to do in the country. So, were it not for my eagerness to serve Monsieur, I should only have had her once.' (This fellow is a real treasure!) 'As to the secret,' he continued, 'what would be the use of making her promise, since she will risk nothing by telling lies? If we mention it to her again, that would only make her more aware of its importance, and she would be all the more likely to go trying to curry favour with her mistress.'

The more sensibly he reasoned, the greater the difficulty I was in. Luckily the fellow was in a garrulous mood and, as I needed his services, I let him run on. In the course of his telling me about his affair with this girl I learned that, since the room she occupies is only separated from that of her mistress by a partition, through which suspicious noises might be heard, it was in his own room that they met each night. I immediately made my plans. I told him about them and we carried them out successfully.

I waited until two in the morning. And then, as agreed, I went to the room where they met, carrying a light, and pretending that I had rung several times without getting an answer. My confidant, who plays his parts to perfection, executed a little scene of surprise, despair and apology, which I brought to a conclusion by pretending I needed some water and sending him to heat some up for me. And the conscientious chambermaid was even more ashamed, for my man tried to outdo me in ingenuity by making sure she was attired in a manner admissible for, though not excused by, the time of year.

Knowing that the more humiliated the girl was, the more easily I could deal with her, I did not allow her to change either her position or her state of undress. And when I had ordered my valet to wait for me in my rooms I sat down beside her on the bed, which was in extreme disarray, and began to talk to her. I needed to retain the authority that circumstances had given me over her. So I remained composed, in a manner which would have done credit to the restrained Scipio himself;[22] and without taking the smallest liberty with her – which, however, the occasion and her exposure would seem to give her reason to expect – I talked business to her as calmly as if I were talking to the public prosecutor.

My conditions were that I would keep the secret faithfully as long as she would hand over to me at roughly the same time the following day the contents of her mistress's pockets. 'Moreover,' I added, 'I offered you ten *louis* yesterday. I am promising you them again today. I do not wish to abuse your position.' All was granted, as you can guess. So I retired and allowed the happy couple to make up for lost time.

I used mine to get some sleep. And when I woke, needing an excuse to leave my beauty's letter unanswered before going through her papers, something I should not be able to do until the following night, I decided to go out hunting and I spent nearly the whole day in that pursuit.

On my return I was received rather coldly. I incline to believe there was a touch of pique that I was showing so little eagerness to make the most of the time I had left, especially since that kinder letter she had written to me. I suppose this because Madame de Rosemonde chided me a little for my long absence, and my beauty replied, with some asperity: 'Oh, we must not scold Monsieur de Valmont for enjoying the one pleasure he may find here.' I complained of the unfairness of this remark and took the opportunity to assure them that I enjoyed the company of the ladies so much that I would put off writing a very interesting letter that I had to send. I added that, since for several nights I had been unable to get any rest, I wished to see whether being very tired would restore my sleep to me. And my look was enough to make her understand both what my letter was about and the cause of my sleeplessness. Throughout the evening I was careful to retain an air of gentle melancholy, which seemed to have some success, and beneath which I hid my impatience for the hour when the secret being so obstinately hidden from me should be revealed. Finally we separated, and a little while later the faithful chambermaid came to bring me the reward that we had agreed for my discretion.

Once I had my hands on this treasure I proceeded to its examination with my customary prudence. For it was vital to put everything back in its place. First I found two letters from the husband, an indigestible hotchpotch of details about legal proceedings and outpourings of conjugal love, which I was patient enough to read in their entirety, and where I found not a single mention of myself. They made me cross, and I put them back. But my temper was improved by finding in my hand the pieces of my famous letter from Dijon, carefully joined together. Fortunately, upon a whim, I glanced through it again. You can imagine how delighted I was to detect upon it the quite distinct traces of tears of my adorable devotee. I admit I gave in to an adolescent impulse and kissed this letter with a passion I no longer thought myself capable of. I continued my happy research. I rediscovered all my letters together in the order they were written. And an even more agreeable surprise was to find the very first one, the one I thought had been sent back to me by the cruel woman, faithfully copied out in her hand, in writing that was shaky and distorted, proof enough of the sweet agitation of her heart during this activity.

Up to that point I was full of love. Soon this gave way to fury. Who do you suppose it is who wants to ruin me in the eyes of the woman I adore? What Fury do you think is vicious enough to engage in such villainy? You know her. It is your friend, your relative. It is Madame de Volanges. You cannot imagine what unspeakable lies that devilish shrew has spun about me. She is the one, the only one, who has made this angelic woman worried that she is in danger. It is through her advice, because of her pernicious warnings, that I am forced to leave. It is to her that I am being sacrificed. Oh, there is no doubt at all I must seduce her daughter. But that is not enough; I must ruin her. And since the age of this wretched woman protects her from my blows I must attack her through the object of her affections.

So she wants me to come back to Paris! She is obliging me. Very well, then, I shall return. But she will rue the day I came. I am very sorry that Danceny should be the hero of this adventure. He is fundamentally an honest man and that will get in our way. However, he is in love, and I see him frequently. Perhaps there may be some way of profiting from this. But I am forgetting myself in my rage, and that I must tell you all about what happened today. Let us resume.

This morning I saw my sensitive prude again. I had never seen her look so beautiful. It was inevitable. A woman's finest moment and the only one when she can induce that intoxication of the soul, so often talked about but so rarely experienced, is the one when we are certain of her love but not of her favours. And it was exactly that situation I found myself in. Perhaps also the idea that I was going to be deprived of the pleasure of seeing her served to make her more beautiful. Well, when the post arrived, I received your letter of the 27th. And while I was reading it, I was still in two minds about whether to keep my promise. But I caught my beauty's eye and it would have been impossible for me to refuse her anything.

So I announced my departure. One moment later Madame de Rosemonde left us alone together. But I was still four feet away from the timid girl when she got up in a fright saying: 'Leave me, leave me, Monsieur, for pity's sake, leave me.' This fervent prayer, which revealed the extent of her emotion, only excited me more. I was already close to her and had caught hold of her hands, which she had placed together with a most touching gesture, and begun my tender expressions of love when some fiend brought Madame de Rosemonde back again. The timid devotee, who does indeed have good reason to be fearful, saw her opportunity and departed.

But I offered her my hand, which she accepted. And, thinking this unwonted gentleness augured well, I tried to squeeze hers, while at the same time renewing my protestations. At first she tried to pull away. But when I insisted, she gave in with a good enough grace, though without responding either to my gesture or my words. At the door to her room I tried to kiss her hand before leaving. To begin with I met with firm resistance: but my *just remember I am leaving*, uttered in my most tender voice, made her ill at ease and uncertain. Scarcely had the kiss been bestowed when her hand recovered the strength to escape, and my beauty entered her room where her maid was waiting. This is where my story ends.

As I presume you will be at the house of the Maréchale de

— tomorrow, where I shall certainly not come to find you, and as I am sure as well that at our first meeting we will have more than one affair to discuss, and notably that of the little Volanges, which I have not forgotten, I have decided to send this letter on ahead. And, though it is lengthy, I shall close it only just before sending it to the post. For in my present situation everything can depend on a moment's opportunity. I am leaving you, in order to go and lie in wait for it.

P.S. At eight o'clock in the evening.

Nothing new; not a single moment of liberty; even some care taken to prevent it. However, as much regret as decency permits, at least. Another event which is perhaps not without interest: I am the bearer of an invitation from Madame de Rosemonde to Madame de Volanges to come and stay a while with her in the country.

Farewell, my dear. Till tomorrow, or the day after at the latest.

From —, 28 August 17**

LETTER 45
The Présidente de Tourvel to Madame de Volanges

Monsieur de Valmont left today, Madame. I felt that you so much wished for his departure I should inform you of it. Madame de Rosemonde misses her nephew greatly, and it must be said that his company was agreeable. She spent the entire morning talking to me about him, with her usual perceptiveness. She did not stop singing his praises. I thought I should show enough consideration to listen without contradicting her, particularly because she is right, one must admit, on many counts. And I felt that I was to blame for this separation, and am not hopeful of being able to compensate for the pleasure I have deprived her of. As you know my nature is not normally a particularly cheerful one, and the sort of life we lead here is unlikely to alter that.

Had I not conducted myself according to your advice, I should fear I had acted a little impulsively. For I have been truly troubled by my dear friend's unhappiness. She touched me so deeply I should gladly have mingled my tears with hers.

We are living now in hopes that you will accept the invitation that Monsieur de Valmont will give you from Madame de Rosemonde to come and spend some time with her. I need not tell you the pleasure it will give me to see you here. Indeed, it is your duty to make up for our loss. I shall be delighted to have this earlier opportunity to make the acquaintance of Mademoiselle de Volanges and to be in a position to further assure you of my respectful regards, etc.

From —, 29 August 17**

LETTER 46

The Chevalier Danceny to Cécile Volanges

What has happened to you, my darling Cécile? What has brought about such an abrupt and cruel change in you? What has become of your vow that you would never change? Only yesterday you were so glad to say those words again and again! Who has made you forget them today? However closely I look, I cannot find the reason within myself and it is a terrible thing for me to have to look for it in you. You are not fickle or unfaithful, I am certain of that. And even in this moment of despair I shall not insult you with suspicions which would cause my heart to wither. But what twist of fate has made you no longer what you were? No, cruel girl, you are no longer the same! My sweet Cécile, the Cécile I adore, who made her promise to me, she would not have avoided my eyes, would not have objected to the lucky chance which placed me by her side;

or if, for some unfathomable reason, she had been obliged to treat me with such severity, she would at least not have scorned to tell me why.

Oh, you do not know, you will never know, my Cécile, how you have made me suffer today, and how much I suffer now. Do you believe I can live without your love? Yet when I begged you for a word, one word to allay my fears, instead of answering, you pretended you were afraid of being overheard; and then you immediately created that very obstacle, that had not existed before, by the seat you chose among the company. When I was obliged to leave you and asked what time I might see you again tomorrow, you pretended not to know, and Madame de Volanges had to give me the information. And so that moment which brings me close to you and which I have always so very much looked forward to, will tomorrow cause me nothing but anxiety. The pleasure of seeing you, which until now has been my only joy, will be replaced by the fear of being unwelcome.

I already feel inhibited by this fear, and dare not speak of my love. That *je vous aime*, which I so delighted in saying when I could hear it from your lips too, those gentle words, which were enough to make me a happy man, now, if you have changed, will bring me nothing but the image of eternal despair. However, I cannot believe that this talisman of love has lost all its power, and so I still try what it may do.* Yes, my Cécile, *je vous aime*. Say after me those words which make me happy. Remember you have accustomed me to hear them, and depriving me of them means condemning me to a torture which, like my love for you, will end only with my life.

From —, 29 August 17**

---

* Those who have never had the opportunity of feeling the value of a word or expression hallowed by love will find this sentence meaningless.

LETTER 47

The Vicomte de Valmont to the Marquise de Merteuil

I shall still not be able to see you today, my love, and these are
my reasons, which I beg you to accept with indulgence.

Instead of coming straight back, I stopped off at the home of
the Comtesse de —, whose chateau was not far off my route,
and invited myself to dinner. It was almost seven when I got to
Paris, and I went to the Opera, where I hoped you might be.

When the opera was over I went to look up my ladies of the
green room;[23] there I found my old friend Émilie, surrounded
by numerous admirers, as many women as men, to whom she
was giving supper that evening at P—. I had no sooner joined
the company than, by popular assent, I was asked to eat with
them. I was also issued with an invitation by a short, fat little
man who jabbered in double Dutch and who, I realized, was
the real hero of the hour. I accepted.

On the way I learned that the house we were bound for was the
price agreed for Émilie's favours to this grotesque fellow, and
that tonight's supper was to be a real wedding feast. The little
man could not contain his delight in the expectation of the happiness he was going to enjoy; he appeared so self-satisfied he made
me want to throw a spanner in the works. And this indeed I did.

The one problem I had was to convince Émilie, who had a
few qualms because of the burgomaster's wealth. But she
agreed, after protesting a little, to the plan I had of filling up
this little beer belly with wine and putting him hors de combat
for the night.

The high expectations we had of Dutch drinkers induced us
to employ all possible means. We succeeded so well that at dessert
he no longer had strength enough to hold his glass. But the obliging Émilie and I vied with one another to fill it up. Finally he fell
under the table in such a drunken stupor it must last at least a
week. Then we decided to send him back to Paris; and, as he had
not retained his cab, I had him loaded into mine, and I stayed in
his stead. Then I received the congratulations of the assembled

company, who withdrew shortly afterwards and left me in command of the field. These merry japes and perhaps also my long time away made me find Émilie so desirable that I have promised to stay with her until the Dutchman comes back to life.

This indulgence on my part is in exchange for her kindness in serving as a desk on which to write to my beautiful devotee. I thought it would be amusing to send from the bed, from the arms almost, of a girl a letter – interrupted, indeed, for a downright infidelity – and in which I give her an exact account of my situation and conduct! Émilie, who has read the letter, laughed and laughed, and I hope you will too.

As my letter must be postmarked Paris, I am sending it to you. I am leaving it open. Would you please read it, seal it and have it sent to the post? Be particular not to use your own seal, nor any emblem of love. Just a head[24] will do. Farewell, my dear.

P.S. I have opened my letter again. I have persuaded Émilie to go to the Théâtre des Italiens . . . I will take advantage of that time to come and see you. I shall be with you at six at the latest. And if agreeable to you, we will go to Madame de Volanges together at seven. It will be best if I do not put off giving her the invitation I have for her from Madame de Rosemonde. And besides, I shall be very happy to see the little Volanges girl.

Farewell, my darling. I intend to welcome you with such passion, the Chevalier will be jealous.

P —, 30 August 17**

LETTER 48

The Vicomte de Valmont to the Présidente de Tourvel
(Postmarked Paris)

After a tempestuous night during which I have not once closed my eyes; after the constant agitation of an all-consuming love, the total annihilation of all my faculties, I have come to seek in your company, Madame, a calm which I need but as yet do not expect to enjoy. In fact, as I am writing this to you, the situation I am in makes me more conscious than ever of the irresistible power of love. I have difficulty in keeping enough self-control to order my ideas. And already I foresee that I shall not be able to finish this letter without being obliged to break off. Surely I may hope that you will one day share the passion I feel at present? I hope that if you got to know it better you would not remain completely indifferent to it. Believe me, Madame, cold tranquillity and the torpor of the soul, the very image of death, do not make for happiness. Only the active passions can lead you to it. And in spite of the torments you put me through I think I can assure you, without hesitation, that at this moment I am happier than you. Your treating me with such depressing harshness is to no avail. In no wise does it prevent me giving myself up totally to love and forgetting, in my delirious state, the despair into which you cast me. This is how I shall avenge the exile to which you are condemning me. Never did I have so much pleasure in writing to you. Never did I feel as I do now such sweet but such keen emotion. Everything seems to increase my passion. The very air I breathe is burning with sensuality. The very table on which I am writing, dedicated for the first time to this use, has become for me the sacred altar of love.[25] How much more beautiful it will be now in my eyes! I shall have traced upon it my vow to love you for ever! Forgive me, I implore you, the confusion of my senses. Perhaps I should not abandon myself so to these passions which you do not share. I must leave you a moment to assuage a madness which increases every instant, and is stronger than I am.

I come back to you, Madame, and there is no doubt that I return as urgently as before. But the feeling of happiness has fled far from me. It has given way to cruel privation. Of what use is it to me to talk to you of my feelings if I look in vain for the means to convince you? After so many repeated efforts, my confidence and strength are both leaving me. If I recount the pleasures of love again, it is so that I may feel more keenly my sorrow at being deprived of them. The only help I can see is in your indulgence, and I am only too aware at the moment how much will be necessary for me to have any hope of obtaining it. But my love was never more respectful, and never less capable of giving offence. I might say it is such that the strictest virtue would have nothing to fear from it. But I am myself afraid to discourse longer on the pain I am experiencing. Since I am assured that she who has caused it does not share it, I must be sure, at least, not to abuse her goodness. And if I spent any more time painting such a sorry picture to you, I should be doing just that. I shall only take the time to beg you to reply, and never to doubt the truth of my feelings.

Written from —, dated from Paris, 30 August 17**

LETTER 49
Cécile Volanges to the Chevalier Danceny

I am not fickle or deceitful, Monsieur, but it is enough for me to be shown my conduct in its true light to feel I need to change it. I have promised this sacrifice to God until I can offer Him also the sacrifice of my feelings for you, which the religious order to which you belong renders even more wicked. I am very well aware that it will cause me suffering and I shall not even conceal from you that since the day before yesterday I have wept every time I thought of you. But I hope that God will give me the grace and the necessary strength to forget you, as I pray night and morning that He will. I even hope that your honour and friendship will keep you from upsetting the good resolutions I have been induced to make and which I am trying to keep. As a consequence, I am asking you to be good enough not to write to me any more, especially as I am warning you that I shall not answer, and that if you do I should have to inform Mamma of everything. And that would completely deprive me of the pleasure of seeing you.

I shall still remain as attached to you as I possibly can be

without doing anything wrong. And I wish you, with all my
heart and soul, every happiness. I know you are not going to
love me now as much and perhaps you will soon love some
other girl better than me. But it will be one more penance for
the sin I committed in giving you my heart, which I should have
given only to God, and to my husband when I have one. I hope
divine mercy will have pity on my weakness and not inflict
upon me any more suffering than I can bear.

Farewell, Monsieur. I can assure you that if I were allowed
to love anybody, it would never be anyone but you. But that is
all I can say, and it is perhaps more than I should have said.

From —, 31 August 17**

LETTER 50

The Présidente de Tourvel to the Vicomte de Valmont

So is this how you fulfil the conditions on which I agreed to
receive your letters from time to time? And how should I *not
have reason to complain about them* when all you talk about
are feelings which I should still fear to indulge in, even if I could
do so without neglecting all of my duties?

Besides, if I needed any new argument to give weight to this
salutary fear, it seems to me I could find it in your last letter.
For at the very time you think you are extolling the delights of
love, what are you doing except the exact opposite, by proving
how fearful and tempestuous they are? Who could wish for a
happiness bought at the expense of reason, one whose passing
pleasures have for consequence, at the very least, regret if not
remorse?

You yourself, in whom the effects of this dangerous madness
must be rendered less serious through force of habit, do you
nevertheless not have to admit that it is often stronger than you
are, and are you not the first to complain of the helpless distress
it occasions in you? What terrifying ravages would it then cause

in a fresh and sensitive heart, so much more at their mercy by the size of the sacrifice she was obliged to make?

You think, Monsieur, or so you pretend, that love leads to happiness. And I am so persuaded that it would make me unhappy that I should wish never to hear the subject mentioned. It seems to me that just to speak of it disturbs one's peace of mind. And it is as much through preference as through duty that I beg you to keep your silence on this subject.

After all, this request must be very easy for you to grant at present. Being in Paris again, you will find plenty of opportunities to forget a feeling which perhaps only came about in the first place through your habit of occupying yourself with these matters, and owed its strength to the fact that there is so little to do in the country. Are you not in the same place you saw me in before, when you were quite indifferent to me? Can you go anywhere there without coming across instances of your inconstancy? And are you not surrounded there by women, all of whom are more attractive than me and have more claim on your attentions? I have not the vanity that my sex is often blamed for. Even less do I possess that false modesty which is only a refinement of pride. And it is in all good faith that I say to you here and now that I know very few ways of pleasing a man. Were I to possess every one of them I should not think them enough to hold your interest for long. So in asking you not to concern yourself with me I am only asking you to do today what you have already done, and what you would most certainly do before long even if I were to beg you not to.

This truth, which I do not lose sight of, would be on its own a valid reason for not wishing to listen to you. I have a thousand more. But without entering into a long discussion I will confine myself to begging you, as I have already done, not to speak to me of feelings to which I must not listen, and, even less, respond.

From —, 1 September 17**

PART TWO

The Marquise de Merteuil to the Vicomte de Valmont

You really are impossible, Vicomte. You treat me as casually as if I were your mistress. You know very well you will make me angry; just now I am in a terrible mood. What is it you are saying? You have to meet Danceny tomorrow morning; but you know how important it is for me to talk to you before you see him; and you run around like that, keeping me waiting for you the whole day long? You are the reason I arrived *indecently* late at Madame de Volanges's and had all the old ladies thinking I was a *Merveilleuse*.[1] I had to be nice to them the whole evening to pacify them: for one must not upset old ladies. They are the ones who make or break the reputation of young ones.

It is now one in the morning, and instead of going to bed, as I desperately wish, I have to write you a long letter and that will make me twice as sleepy, for I shall be so bored by it. Fortunately for you I do not have the time to scold you further. Don't imagine just because of that that I forgive you. It is simply that I am in a hurry. So listen to me, and I'll be quick.

Tomorrow, if you use your expertise, Danceny should confide in you. The time is ripe for confidences. He is unhappy. Our young friend has been to confession. She has blurted everything out, just like a child. And since then she has been tormented to such a degree by the fear of the devil that now she wants to break it off completely. She confided in me all her little worries, so passionately that it made me realize what a state she is in. She showed me the letter in which she had broken it off; it is full of religious nonsense. She babbled to me for an hour without uttering a word of common sense. But she made it difficult for me all the same. For, as you can see, I could not risk being completely frank with someone of such feeble intelligence.

None the less I could see in the midst of all this chatter that she is no less in love with her Danceny. I even noticed she is, rather amusingly, the victim of one of those little tricks that love invariably plays. Tormented by the desire to think about her lover, and afraid of damning herself by so doing, she has hit upon the idea of praying to God to make her forget him. And, as she repeats this prayer at each and every moment of the day, she finds the means to think of him constantly.

With someone more *experienced* than Danceny this little circumstance would perhaps be more favourable than otherwise. But he is such a Céladon[2] that if we do not help him along he will take an age to surmount the easiest of obstacles, and we shall not have enough time to carry out our plans.

You are quite right. It is a pity and I am as sorry as you are that he should be the hero of this adventure. But there we are. What is done is done. And it is your fault. I asked to see his reply.* It was pitiful. He reasons with her till he is blue in the face to prove to her that an involuntary feeling cannot be a crime. As if it did not stop being involuntary from the moment one ceases to fight it! This is such a simple idea it even occurred to the girl. He complains of his misfortune in quite a touching way, but his suffering is so sweet and seems so strong and sincere that I believe a woman who finds the opportunity to make a man despair to this degree, and with so little danger, would find it impossible not to be tempted to indulge her fancy. He ends up explaining to her that he is not such a monk as she believes. And that is undoubtedly the best part. For if one went so far as to yield to a monk's embraces, one would most certainly not give the preference to Messieurs the Knights of Malta![3]

Whatever the case, instead of wasting my time in argument with her, which would have compromised me, and perhaps not convinced her, I approved of her plan to break it off. But I told her that in such cases it was more honest to tell the person why to their face instead of writing to them. And that it was also customary to give back the letters and other fripperies one might have received. So, while appearing to see eye to eye with the girl, I persuaded her to accord Danceny a rendez-vous. We immediately joined forces, and I took it upon myself to persuade

* This letter has not been found.

the mother to go out without her daughter. Tomorrow afternoon is to be the fateful occasion. Danceny has already been
informed. But for God's sake, if you have a chance, use your
influence to make this lovesick swain less indolent, and teach
him, since you must be quite frank with him, that the real way
to overcome other people's scruples is to ensure that they have
nothing to lose.

As to the rest, I took care to raise a doubt or two in our
young friend's mind about the discretion of the confessors, so
that there should be no repetition of this ridiculous episode.
And I assure you that she is presently paying for the fright she
gave me, since she fears the priest might go and tell her mother
everything. I hope that after I have had another chat or two
with her she will no longer go and prattle to the first person
she sees.*

Adieu, Vicomte. Take hold of Danceny, and steer him along.
It would be shameful if we did not do as we liked with two
children. If we find in the process that we have more trouble
than we expected, let us not forget – and this will give us
strength – that you are dealing with the daughter of Madame
de Volanges and I with the wife-to-be of Gercourt. Farewell.

From —, 2 September 17**

LETTER 52

The Vicomte de Valmont to the Présidente de Tourvel

You forbid me, Madame, to speak of my love. But how can
I find the courage to obey you? Occupied solely as I am with a
feeling which should be so sweet, and which you are rendering
so cruel; languishing in the exile to which you have condemned

* The reader will have guessed a long time ago from Madame de Merteuil's
behaviour in what little respect she held religion. This whole paragraph should
perhaps have been omitted; on the other hand it was thought that while
showing the effects, we should not neglect to make people aware of their
causes.

me; living only on privation and regret, a prey to torment that is all the more painful because it reminds me constantly of your indifference; must I then also lose the one consolation left to me? And how can I have any other but that of laying bare to you from time to time a soul which you fill with trouble and bitterness? Will you turn away your eyes from those tears you caused to flow? Will you refuse even the homage of the sacrifices you have exacted? Would it not be more worthy of you, of your sweet and honourable soul, to take pity on a poor unfortunate who is so only because of you, rather than inflict further sufferings on him by a prohibition which is both unjust and severe?

You pretend to be afraid of love, and are unwilling to see that it is you alone who have caused the ills you blame love for. Oh yes, this feeling is most certainly painful when the person who inspires it does not share it. But where may happiness be found if not in reciprocated love? Tender friendship, mutual trust, the only trust that is unconditional, pain diminished, pleasure increased, sweet hopes, delicious memories, where can they be found but in love? You misrepresent it, you who, in order to enjoy all the good things it has to offer, need only not resist its pleasures. And in defending it I forget my suffering.

You force me to defend myself as well. For while I devote my life to adoring you, you spend your time in finding fault with me. You already assume I am frivolous and deceitful. And you persist in holding against me certain mistakes which I have freely admitted to you; you are pleased to confuse what I was then with what I am now. Not content with having delivered me to the torture of living far from you, you also tease me mercilessly about pleasures to which you know perfectly well you have rendered me totally impervious. You believe neither my promises nor my oaths. Well, there remains one guarantee I can offer you that at least you will not be suspicious of: yourself. All I ask is that you put the question honestly to yourself. If you do not believe in my love, if you doubt for one moment that you alone have dominion over my soul, if you are not assured of the fact that you have captured this heart, which has been too wayward until now, I agree to bear the consequences of this error. I shall bemoan my lot, but not make an appeal. But if, on the other hand, to be fair to both of us, you are forced to admit to yourself that you do not nor ever will have a rival, I entreat you, do not oblige me any longer to fight with this chimera, but allow me at least the consolation of seeing that you no longer doubt my feelings, which will only end, can only end, with my life. Permit me, Madame, to beg a positive response to this item in my letter.

But if I cease talking about that period in my life which appears to be harming me so in your eyes, it is not that I am short of arguments in my defence.

What did I do, after all, but fail to struggle against the whirlwind into which I was thrown? Entering society young and inexperienced; passed around from one to another by a crowd of women who were all in a hurry to anticipate, by the readiness with which they gave themselves, an opinion which they felt would be in any case unfavourable; was it up to me then to set an example by resisting what was being so freely offered? Or was I to punish myself for momentary lapses, which had all too often been provoked, by a constancy which was certainly pointless and which would have been considered quite simply ridiculous? What else, except breaking it off immediately, can excuse a shameful choice!

But I can tell you that this intoxication of the senses, which I might even call a deranged vanity, never touched my heart. Born for love, I might have been amused by these adventures, but they have never been enough to occupy my life. I have been surrounded by seductive but contemptible creatures and not one has touched my soul. Pleasures were offered to me, but I was seeking virtue. And I often believed myself inconstant, being in fact both delicate and sensitive.

It was when I set eyes on you that I saw the light. I realized that the charm of love resides in the qualities of the soul. That they alone can cause its excesses and provide the excuse for them. Then I felt it was equally impossible either not to love you, or to love another.

So here, Madame, is the heart to which you fear to give yourself, and upon whose fate you must pronounce. But whatever destiny you reserve for it, you will change nothing in the feelings by which it is bound to you. They are as unalterable as the virtues which brought them into being.

From —, 3 September 17**

LETTER 53

The Vicomte de Valmont to the Marquise de Merteuil

I have seen Danceny, but he was not entirely open with me. He particularly insisted on not mentioning the name of the little Volanges girl, only speaking of her as a very good and even rather religious young woman. But he did recount the affair truthfully enough, and especially what happened that last time. I led him on as much as I could, and teased him a great deal about his delicate scruples. But he seems to set great store by them, and I cannot answer for him. For the rest, I shall be able to tell you more the day after tomorrow. I am taking him to Versailles today and shall make it my business to interrogate him on the way.

The rendez-vous supposed to have taken place today also gives grounds for hope. It is possible that everything may have worked out to our satisfaction. And perhaps all we have to do now is extract a confession and collect the evidence. This task will be easier for you to do than it will for me. For the girl is more confiding than her discreet lover, or more talkative, it comes to the same thing. However, I shall do what I can.

Farewell, my dearest. I am in a great hurry. I shall not see you tonight, nor tomorrow. If you find out anything on your side write me a note for when I return. I shall certainly be back in Paris for the night.

From —, 3 September 17** in the evening

LETTER 54

The Marquise de Merteuil to the Vicomte de Valmont

Oh yes! There is so much about Danceny it is worth our while
to know! If he told you that, he was flattering himself. I don't
know anyone as stupid as he is in matters of love, and increas-
ingly I regret how good we have been to him. Do you realize
I thought I might be compromised on his account! And to think
that everything would have been to no avail! Oh, I shall get my
revenge, never fear.

When I arrived yesterday to fetch Madame de Volanges she
did not want to go out; she did not feel very well. I had to use
all my powers of persuasion, for I saw how it would be if
Danceny arrived before we left. It would have been particularly
bad planning, since Madame de Volanges had told him the day
before she would not be at home. Her daughter and I were on
tenterhooks. Finally we left, and our young friend shook my
hand with such affection when she bade me farewell that in
spite of her plan to break it off, which she honestly believed
she was still considering, I predicted wonderful things would
happen that evening.

But my worries were not over. We had scarcely been chez
Madame de — half an hour when Madame de Volanges really
did take ill, seriously ill, and, quite rightly, wanted to go home.
I, of course, was most reluctant, because I was afraid that if we
surprised the young folk, as we most certainly should, all would
be lost, and my efforts to persuade the mother to go out might
look suspicious. I resolved to scare her about her health, something that fortunately is not hard to do. And I kept her there
for an hour and a half before I agreed to take her back home,
pretending to be afraid that the motion of the carriage might
be dangerous. In the end we only returned at the time we had
said we would. And the embarrassment I detected when we
arrived gave me some hope, I admit, that all the trouble I had
gone to would at least not have been in vain.

My desire to learn more made me stay with Madame de

Volanges, who went straight to bed. After taking supper at her bedside, we left her very early on the pretext that she needed to rest, and went into her daughter's rooms. She had done, for her part, everything I expected of her; scruples quite gone, renewed vows of eternal love, etc., etc. She finally acquitted herself with very good grace. But that idiot Danceny did not advance one inch beyond his previous position. Oh, I shall fall out with that young man. Mere reconciliations will get us nowhere.

Our little friend assures me that he wanted more, but that she was able to defend herself. I guess she is flattering herself, or that she is making excuses for him. I am even fairly sure of it. In fact, I took it into my head to find out how far I could be satisfied with the defence she was able to put up. And I, a mere woman, by talking worked her up to such a degree that . . . Well, you may take my word for it, nobody was ever more susceptible to having her senses awakened. She really is a charming girl! She deserves another lover. At least she will have a nice woman friend, for I am sincerely attached to her. I have promised to tutor her and I believe I shall keep my word. I have often felt the need to take a woman into my confidence, and I should prefer this one to another. But I cannot do anything with her as long as she is not . . . what she must become. And that is yet another reason to bear Danceny a grudge.

Adieu, Vicomte. Do not come to me tomorrow unless it be in the morning. I have yielded to the demands of the Chevalier for an evening at home.

From —, 4 September 17**

LETTER 55

Cécile Volanges to Sophie Carnay

You were right, my dear Sophie. Your prophecies were more sound than your advice. Danceny, as you predicted, was stronger than the confessor, stronger than you, stronger than myself. And we are back precisely where we started. Oh, I do not regret it. And if you scold me it will be because you do not know how delightful it is to be in love with Danceny. It is easy for you to say what should be done; there is nothing to stop you. But if you had felt how much pain the sorrow of someone we love causes us, how their joy becomes our own, and how hard it is to say no when you want to say yes, you would not be surprised any more. I myself who have felt this, and felt it so keenly, do not yet understand it. For instance, do you believe that I can see Danceny weep without weeping myself? I assure you it is impossible. And when he is happy I am happy too. Whatever you say will not change anything, I am certain of that.

I wish you were in my shoes. No, that is not what I mean, for I certainly should not wish to change places with anyone. But I wish you were in love with someone too. Not just because you would understand me more, and scold me less, but because you would also be happier or, rather, only then would you begin to be happy.

Our fun and laughter, all that, you see, is only child's play. When it is over, it is over. But love, ah, love! . . . a word, a look, just knowing he is there – well, that is happiness. When I see Danceny I want nothing more. When I do not see him he is all I want. I don't know how to explain it, but it is as though everything I like resembles him. When he is not with me I think about him. And when I am able to think about him properly, without being distracted – when I am on my own, for example – I am still happy. I shut my eyes and immediately it seems to me I can see him. I remember what he has said and I believe I am hearing him speak those words. It makes me sigh. And then I feel a flame within me, an excitement . . . I can't keep still. It's like torture, and that torture gives me a pleasure I cannot express.

I even think that once you are in love, it spills over into your friendships; though the friendship I have for you has not changed, it's just the same as it was at the convent. But what I am talking about is the way I feel about Madame de Merteuil. It seems to me that I love her more how I love Danceny than how I love you, and sometimes I wish she were him. Perhaps it is because it is not a childhood love, as ours was, or else it is because I see them so much together, and that makes me confuse the two. But anyway, the truth is that between the pair of them they make me very happy. And, in any case, I do not believe there is any great harm in what I am doing. So all I ask is to stay the way I am. It is only the thought of my marriage which worries me. For if Monsieur de Gercourt is the kind of man they say he is, and I am in no doubt of this, I do not know what will become of me. Farewell, my Sophie. Your affectionate and loving friend.

From —, 4 September 17**

LETTER 56

The Présidente de Tourvel to the Vicomte de Valmont

What good would it do to send you the reply you ask for, Monsieur? If I believed your feelings, would it not be just one more reason to fear them? And without attacking or defending their sincerity, is it not enough for me, and should it not be enough for you as well, to know that I do not wish, nor have any right, to reciprocate them?

Supposing you do truly love me (and it is only so that I need not revert to this matter that I allow this supposition), would the obstacles separating us not be any less insurmountable? Would I have any other option but to wish you might soon conquer that love and, by hastening to banish all hope, help you towards that end with all my might? You yourself acknowledge that *this feeling is painful when the person who inspires it does not share it.* Now you know perfectly well it is impossible for me to share it. And even were this misfortune to befall me, I should be the more to be pitied, and you none the happier. I hope you respect me enough not to be in any doubt of that for one moment. So stop, I implore you, stop wishing to distress a creature to whom peace and quiet is necessary. Do not make me sorry I ever met you.

I am respected and cherished by a husband I love and respect, duty and pleasure combining in the same person. I am happy, that is right and proper. If keener pleasures than these exist, I do not desire them. I do not wish to know them. Can there be a sweeter pleasure than to be at peace with oneself, to enjoy days of unbroken calm, to fall asleep without anxiety and to wake without remorse? What you call happiness is but a tumult of the senses, a tempestuous sea of passions, a fearful spectacle even when it is viewed from the shore. So how can I confront these storms? How dare I embark upon a sea covered in the debris of thousands upon thousands of shipwrecks? And with whom? No, Monsieur, I shall stay on land. I cherish the bonds which tie me to it. Even if I could break them, I should not wish to. If I did not have them I should make haste to acquire them.

Why do you dog my footsteps? Why do you insist upon pursuing me? Your letters were supposed to be occasional, but they follow one another in rapid succession. They were going to be reasonable, but all you talk about is how madly you love me. You besiege me with the idea of your love more than you did with your person. You have distanced yourself in one way, but reproduced yourself in another. Things I ask you not to repeat any more you say again, except with different words. You enjoy confusing me with arguments that are specious; you avoid mine. I do not wish to reply to your letters, I shall not ... Look how you treat the women you have seduced! With what contempt you speak of them! I can believe that some deserve it. But are they all therefore contemptible? Oh, no doubt, in that they have all betrayed their duties to give themselves up to unlawful love. From that moment on they lost everything, including the respect of the man to whom they sacrificed everything. Their suffering is justly deserved, though the very idea of it makes me tremble. But what is it to me, after all? Why should I concern myself with them or you? What right have you to come disturbing my peace and quiet? Leave me, do not see me any more, do not write to me any more. I beg you. I demand it of you. This is the last letter you will receive from me.

From —, 5 September 17**

LETTER 57

The Vicomte de Valmont to the Marquise de Merteuil

I found your letter here yesterday when I got back. Your anger is delightful. You could not be more sensitive to Danceny's bad behaviour had it been intended for you personally! There is no doubt it is revenge that motivates you to make his mistress acquire the habit of these small infidelities; what a bad girl you are! But you are very attractive and I am not a bit surprised she finds you more irresistible than Danceny.

Well, finally I know him inside out, our fine romantic hero! He has no more secrets where I am concerned. I told him so often that true love was the supreme good, that one passionate experience was worth ten affairs, that, as I said it, I was myself quite the shy young lover again. Anyway, he found my way of thinking so exactly reflected his own that he was enchanted by my candour and told me everything, swearing everlasting friendship. But for all that we have scarcely advanced at all with our plans.

First, his reasoning seems to be that a young girl deserves to be treated with far more consideration than a woman, since she has more to lose. He believes, especially, that when that girl is infinitely richer than the man, as in his case, nothing can justify his placing her in a position where she has to marry him or be dishonoured ever after. The mother's wealth, the girl's innocence, he finds it all intimidating and constraining. The difficulty lies not in combating his arguments, however well-founded they may be. With a little skill and passion I could have demolished them soon enough; all the more easily since they invite ridicule and one does have on one's side the authority of what is normally done. But what prevents me from having any influence over him is that he seems quite content with the situation. First love usually seems more true, and more pure, if you like. It may proceed more slowly, but this is not, as one might expect, through delicacy or timidity. It is that the heart, surprised by an unknown feeling, stops, as it were, at each step to enjoy the delight it is experiencing, and this is such a powerful enchantment for an innocent heart that it takes over completely, and makes one forgetful of every other pleasure. So the truth of the matter is that a libertine in love, if indeed a libertine can be in love, becomes from that moment in less of a hurry to enjoy the pleasures of the flesh. And when all is said and done, between the conduct of Danceny with the little Volanges girl and mine with the prudish Madame de Tourvel, there is only a difference in degree.

It would have taken many more obstacles than he has encountered so far to excite this young man. He needs more mystery, for mystery leads to daring. I am not far from thinking that you did us a disservice in looking after him so well. Your conduct would have been excellent with an *experienced* man, who would have had only his desires. But you might have foreseen that for a young, upright man in love, what is most valuable in a woman's favours is that they are proof of love. And that consequently the more sure he is of being loved, the less enterprising he will be. What shall we do now? I do not know. But I do not expect that he will have our young friend before she is married, and we shall be let down. I am annoyed about it, but I don't see any solution.

While I prattle on like this you are doing better with your Chevalier. And that reminds me that you have promised an infidelity in my favour. I have your written promise of it, and I wish to make sure it is honoured. I agree that payment is not yet due. But it would be kind of you not to wait too long. And for my part I shall keep an account of the interest. What have you to say, my love? Are you not weary of your faithfulness? Is this Chevalier so very wonderful? Oh, let me have my way and I shall oblige you to admit that if you have found some merit in him it is because you had forgotten me.

Adieu, my love. I kiss you and desire you. And I defy all the kisses of the Chevalier to be as ardent as mine.

From —, 5 September 17**

LETTER 58

The Vicomte de Valmont to the Présidente de Tourvel

What have I done to deserve, Madame, both rebukes and anger
from you? A most ardent and yet most respectful attachment,
my utter submission to your slightest wish, that is the whole
story of my sentiments and conduct. Overwhelmed by the pain
of an unhappy love, my one consolation was in seeing you. You
commanded me to deprive myself of it. I obeyed without so
much as a word of complaint. As a reward for this sacrifice you
permitted me to write to you, but today you wish to take this,
my only pleasure, away from me. Shall I allow it to be snatched
away without trying to defend it? No, of course not! What!
How should it not be dear to my heart? It is the only pleasure
left to me, and it is you who have granted it.

You say my letters are too frequent! Remember, I beg you,
that for the last ten days of this exile, not one moment has
passed without my thinking of you, and yet you have received
only two letters from me. *All I talk about in them is my love!*
What can I talk about, except what is on my mind? Yet all I
can do is moderate its expression. And you may take it from
me I have only allowed you to see what was impossible to hide.
You threaten that you will reply to my letters no more. So, not
content with cruelty, you now show contempt towards the man
who prefers you above all others and who respects you even
more than he loves you! And why all these threats, this anger?
Why do you need them? Are you not certain of being obeyed,
even when your commands are unjust? Is it possible for me to
deny you any one of your desires; have I not already proved as
much? Will you abuse this power you have over me? After
making me unhappy, after being unjust to me, will you find it
easy to enjoy the peace and quiet that you declare is so necessary
to you? Will you not ever say to yourself: 'He has left me to be
mistress of his destiny and I have caused his unhappiness; he
implored my help and I looked on him without compassion'?
Do you know to what extremes my despair might lead me? No.

To assess the extent of my suffering you would have to know how much I love you, and you are not privy to my heart.

To what are you sacrificing me? To chimerical fears. And who inspires these fears? A man who adores you. A man over whom you will never cease to have absolute power. What do you have to fear, what can you possibly fear, from feelings you will always have the power to direct as you will? Your imagination is creating monsters, and the terror they cause you, you attribute to love. With a little trust these ghosts would disappear.

A wise man once said that to rid oneself of fears it suffices in almost every case to go to the root of the problem.*[4] This truth applies especially to love. Love, and your fears will vanish. In place of the things that frighten you, you will discover feelings of delight and a lover who is tender and ready to do your will. And all your days, devoted to happiness, will leave you with no other regret than that of having wasted so many through indifference. I myself, since I have mended my ways, live only for love, regretting the days I believed I was spending in pleasure. And I feel that it is you alone who can make me happy. But, I beseech you, may the pleasure I have in writing to you be no longer troubled by the fear of displeasing you. I have no wish to disobey you: I am prostrate before you, claiming the happiness you wish to snatch from me, the only one I have left. I cry out to you: listen to my prayers, observe my tears. Oh, Madame, will you tell me no?

From —, 7 September 17**

* Probably Rousseau in *Émile*, but this is not an exact quotation and Valmont's application of it here is quite wrong. Would Madame de Tourvel have read *Émile*?

LETTER 59

The Vicomte de Valmont to the Marquise de Merteuil

Tell me, if you can, what this Danceny nonsense means. What has happened, and what has he lost? Is his little beauty perhaps irritated by his everlasting respect? It is true one would, at the very least, be put out. What shall I tell him tonight at the meeting he has requested and which I casually agreed to? I shall most certainly not waste my time listening to his grievances if it does not advance our cause. Lovers' complaints are only worth listening to when there is a recitative or a grand aria. So instruct me in the matter and tell me what I should do, or I shall abandon him and avoid the boredom I can see coming. Will I be able to talk to you this morning? If you are *occupied*, at least send me word and give me my cue.

By the way, where were you yesterday? I never manage to see you. It really was not worth keeping me in Paris the whole of September. But make up your mind, for I have just received a most pressing invitation from the Comtesse de — to visit her in the country and, as she rather pleasingly puts it, 'her husband has the finest woods in the world, and preserves them carefully for the entertainment of his guests'. Now you know I have a good few rights in those woods, and shall go and visit them if I cannot be of use to you. Goodbye. Remember that Danceny will be with me on the stroke of four.

From —, 8 September 17**

LETTER 60

The Chevalier Danceny to the Vicomte de Valmont
(Enclosed in the previous letter)

Oh Monsieur, I am in despair! All is lost![5] I dare not entrust
the secret of my unhappiness to paper, but I need to unburden
myself to a loyal and trusted friend. At what time may I see you
and seek consolation and advice? I was so happy the day I
opened my heart to you! What a difference now! Everything
has changed. Yet my own suffering is the least of my trials. My
anxiety about a person who is much dearer than myself is much
more unbearable. You are more fortunate than I: you can go
and see her, and I hope you will do me this favour in the
light of our friendship. But I must speak to you, and tell you
everything. You will take pity on me, you will come to my
rescue. You are my only hope. You are a man of feeling, you
know what love is, and you are the only one in whom I can
confide. Do not refuse me your help.

Adieu, Monsieur; the only comfort I have in my misery is to
remember that I still have a friend like you. Let me know, I beg
you, at what time I may meet you. If not this morning, I should
like it to be early this afternoon.

From —, 8 September 17**

LETTER 61

Cécile Volanges to Sophie Carnay

My dear Sophie, pity your Cécile, your poor Cécile, for she is
so unhappy! Mamma knows everything. I cannot imagine how
she could have had the least suspicion, but she has found out
everything. Last night I was fairly sure there was something
wrong, but I did not pay much attention to it. And, even while
I was waiting for her to finish her game, I was chatting very

merrily with Madame de Merteuil, who had supped with us, and we spoke a great deal about Danceny. But I do not think we were overheard. She left and I retired to my rooms.

I was getting undressed when Mamma came in and told my maid to leave. She asked for the key to my *secrétaire*. Her tone of voice made me tremble so much I could scarcely stand. I pretended I had lost the key, but in the end I had to do as she bade me. The first drawer she opened was the very one which contained the Chevalier Danceny's letters. I was so distressed that when she asked me what it was, all I could answer was that it was nothing. But when I saw her begin to read the one on top I only just had time to reach my chair before I felt so ill I fainted. As soon as I regained consciousness my mother, who had recalled my maid, went away, telling me to go to bed. She took all Danceny's letters with her. I shudder every time I think I shall have to face her again. I have done nothing but cry all night long.

I am writing this at dawn in the hope that Joséphine will come. If I am able to speak to her on her own, I shall ask her to deliver a message that I am going to write to Madame de Merteuil. Or else I shall put it in with your letter and ask you to send it as though it were from you. She is the only one who will be able to comfort me. At least we should be able to talk of him, for I do not expect to see him again. I am so unhappy! Perhaps she will be so kind as to take charge of a letter to Danceny for me. I dare not trust Joséphine with it, and still less my chambermaid. For she is perhaps the one who told my mother I had letters in my writing desk.

I shall not write any more, because I want to have time to write to Madame de Merteuil* and to Danceny as well, so that my letter will be all ready in case she can deliver it for me. After that I shall go back to bed, so that if anyone comes in to my room they will find me there. I shall say I am ill in order not to have to go and see Mamma. I shall not be telling such a big lie.

* The letter from Cécile Volanges to the Marquise has been omitted since it contains only the same facts as the above letter but with fewer details. The letter to the Chevalier Danceny has not been found. We shall see the reason for this in Letter 63 from Madame de Merteuil to the Vicomte.

It is certain that I am suffering more than if I had a fever. My eyes are stinging with crying so, and there is a weight on my stomach which is stopping me breathing. When I think I shall never see Danceny again, I wish I were dead. Adieu my dear Sophie. I cannot go on. Tears are choking me.

From —, 7 September 17**

LETTER 62

Madame de Volanges to the Chevalier Danceny

After your abuse of a mother's trust and a child's innocence, I am sure it will come as no surprise to you, Monsieur, that you will no longer be received in a house where you have repaid the proof of a most sincere friendship with a complete disregard for correct behaviour. I prefer to ask you not to come to my house any longer rather than give orders at my door, for we should all be compromised alike by the remarks that the footmen would be certain to make. I have a right to expect that you will not oblige me to have recourse to such measures. I must also warn you that if in the future you make the least attempt to carry on leading my daughter astray in this manner, she will be removed from your sight and placed in strict seclusion for good. It is for you, Monsieur, to decide if you care as little about bringing misfortune as you do dishonour upon her. As for me, I have made up my mind, and informed her of my decision.

I enclose a packet of your letters. I trust you will send me all those of my daughter in exchange, and that you will take steps not to leave any trace of an event which cannot but be remembered with indignation on my part, shame on hers and remorse on yours. I have the honour to be, etc.

From —, 7 September 17**

LETTER 63

The Marquise de Merteuil to the Vicomte de Valmont

Indeed I will explain Danceny's note. The occasion of it is my own doing, and I like to think it is my *chef d'oeuvre*. I have not wasted any time since your last letter, and, like the Athenian architect, I have said: 'What *he* has said, I shall do.'[6]

So our romantic hero is slumbering in felicity and needs a few obstacles placed in his way! Then let him come to me with his problem; I shall give him plenty to do. And if I am not mistaken his sleep will no longer be so peaceful. He needed to be shown that time flies, and I flatter myself that at present he is regretting the time he has wasted. You say too that he needed more mystery. Well, that need will be met from now on. It can be said to my credit that all you have to do is to show me where I have gone wrong and I do not rest until I have made proper amends. Let me tell you, then, what I have been doing.

On returning home the day before yesterday, in the morning, I read your letter. I thought it most enlightening. I was convinced that you indicated very clearly the cause of the problem and my one concern was to find a way of dealing with it. However, the first thing I did was go to bed. For the indefatigable Chevalier had not allowed me a moment's rest and I thought I must be sleepy. But it was not at all the case. Danceny was on my mind the whole time; I was unable to sleep a wink for thinking how much I wished to drag him out of his inertia or punish him for it, and it was only after I had finalized my plan that I was able to get a couple of hours' rest.

That same evening I went to Madame de Volanges's house and, as planned, confided in her that I was sure there existed a dangerous liaison between her daughter and Danceny. This woman, so discerning where you are concerned, was so blinded in this case she immediately replied that I must be mistaken. That her daughter was a child, etc., etc. I could not tell her everything I knew. But I provided some instances of how they looked at one another and what they said, and told her how shocking it was to me *with my standards and bearing in mind our close friendship*. Well, I was almost as eloquent as a devotee! And just to ram the point home I went as far as to say that I thought I had seen a letter being given and received. 'That reminds me,' I added, 'that one day while I was there she opened a drawer in her writing desk, and I could see a great many papers inside, which she was no doubt preserving. Do you know if she is having a frequent correspondence with someone?' Here Madame de Volanges's face changed and I saw her eyes moisten. 'I thank you, my dear friend,' she said, wringing my hand. 'I shall take steps to shed light on the situation.'

After that conversation, which was too short to arouse suspicion, I approached the young lady. Soon afterwards I left her, to ask her mother not to compromise me in the eyes of her daughter; which she agreed to all the more willingly when I made her see how useful it would be if the child trusted me enough to be completely frank with me, for it would put me in a position where I could give her the benefit of my *wise counsel*. What reassures me she will keep her word is that I am positive she wishes her daughter to think her most perceptive. I thought in that way I would be justified in keeping on friendly terms with the girl without appearing to be false in the eyes of Madame de Volanges, which is what I wished to avoid. The consequence being that my position would be even better since I could stay with the young person for as long and as secretly as I wished without the mother ever taking exception to it.

I made use of my advantage that very evening. After my game was over I cornered the girl and got her talking about Danceny, a subject on which she never dries up. I amused myself by exciting her with the prospect of seeing him the next day. I made her say no end of silly things. I had to compensate her in hope for what I was depriving her of in reality. And all that will make the blow even harder, for I am persuaded that the more she suffers, the more anxious she will be to make up for it at the first opportunity. In any case it is good to accustom someone to major calamities if they are destined for life's great adventures.

After all, is it not worth a few tears for her to have the

pleasure of possessing her Danceny? She is besotted with him! Well, I promise she will have him, and even sooner than she would have without this upset. It is a bad dream, from which waking will be delightful. And, when all is said and done, it seems to me she owes me a debt of gratitude. In fact, if I have been rather wicked, well, one has to amuse oneself:

Fools are on earth to keep us all amused.*

So I left, much pleased with myself. Either, I reckoned, Danceny will be spurred into action by these obstacles in his path, and will become more amorous than ever, in which case I shall do my utmost to help him; or, if he is nothing but a fool, as I am sometimes inclined to think, he will be in despair and accept defeat. So in that event at least I shall have had my revenge on him, insofar as I can, and, in so doing, I shall have increased the mother's respect for me, the daughter's friendship and the confidence of both. As for Gercourt, the principal object of my attentions, it would be extremely unfortunate or inept of me if I did not find plenty of ways to guide his future wife's thinking in whatever manner I wish, since she is now, and will be even more in future, under my tutelage. I went to bed with these happy thoughts. And so I slept well and woke late.

On waking I found two notes, one from the mother and one from the daughter. And I could not help chuckling when I found literally the same sentence in both: 'It is from you alone that I may hope for consolation.' It is pleasing, would you not say, to offer consolation for and against, and to be the only agent of two directly contrary interests? I am like the Deity, receiving the opposing wishes of blind mortals, and not changing my immutable decrees one whit. And yet I have abandoned this august role to take on that of comforting angel; and have accordingly been to visit my friends in their affliction.

I started with the mother. I found her in such a pathetic state that this already avenges you partly for what you have had to put up with from her with regard to your beautiful prude.

* Gresset, *Le Méchant*, Comédie.[7]

Everything passed off to perfection. My one anxiety was that Madame de Volanges might profit from that moment to gain the confidence of her daughter. It would have been very easy to do so had she spoken to her as a friend, offering her reasonable advice with a look and tone of indulgent tenderness. As luck would have it, she armed herself with severity. In fact, she conducted herself so badly that I could only applaud her. It is true that she thought she could destroy all our plans by the decision she had taken to put Cécile back in the convent. But I fended this off. And I enjoined her simply to leave the threat of it hanging over her daughter, in the event of Danceny continuing his suit and in order to force them both into a circumspection I believe necessary to success.

Then I went to see the daughter. You would not credit how beautiful she is in her grief! I guarantee that if she were trying to be charming she would often be in tears. This time it was not a ploy ... At first I was very struck by this new allurement which I had not previously encountered and which I was very glad to observe, and I only offered consolation in a clumsy fashion, which made her feel worse rather than better. And thus I brought her to a point where she really did seem to be suffocating. She was no longer weeping, and for a moment I feared she might have convulsions. I advised her to go to bed and she acquiesced. I took on the role of lady's maid. She had not yet begun to dress and soon her fine hair fell down over her shoulders and bosom, which were entirely uncovered. I kissed her. She let herself go into my arms and her tears once more began to flow effortlessly. My God, how beautiful! Ah, if Magdalene was like that, she must have been much more dangerous as penitent than sinner![8]

When my grief-stricken beauty was in her bed I set myself to consoling her in good faith. I reassured her first of all on the subject of the convent. I instilled in her the hope of seeing Danceny secretly. 'If only he were here,' I said, sitting on the bed; then, elaborating on that theme, I led her, by one distraction or another,[9] to forget her suffering entirely. We should have parted totally content with one another if she had not wished me to take charge of a letter for Danceny, which I steadfastly refused to do. These are my reasons, which you will surely approve of.

First, I would be compromising myself with Danceny; and though that was the only reason I could give her, there are many more you and I might have between us. Would it not be risking the fruit of my labours to give our young friends so immediate a means of lessening their suffering? And then, I should not be displeased if I obliged them to implicate servants in this affair. For truly, if this succeeds as I hope, it will have to be made public immediately after the wedding, and there are few means more sure to put it about. Or, if by some miracle the servants did not talk about it, we would have to, you and I, and it would be more convenient for us to have them commit the indiscretions.

So you will have to communicate this idea to Danceny today. And, as I am not sure about the little Volanges's chambermaid, whom she herself appears to distrust, I suggest he try my faithful Victoire. I shall take care that the stratagem succeeds. This idea pleases me all the more because the confidence will serve only our purposes, not theirs: for I have not finished telling my tale.

While I was protesting about taking the girl's letter, I was afraid from one moment to the next that she was going to ask me to put it in the post,[10] and I could not possibly have refused. But as luck would have it, whether it was through worry or ignorance, or perhaps because she was less concerned about the letter than the answer, which she would not have been able to receive by this means, she did not mention it; but so that it should not enter her head or, at least, before she could allude to it, I acted. And when I went back to her mother, I persuaded her to let her daughter go away for a while, to take her to the country . . . And where do you think? Does your heart not beat with joy? To your aunt's, to your old Aunt Rosemonde's. She is to let her know today. So there you are; you have permission to go back to your devotee and she will not be able to object to the scandal of being there alone with you. And, thanks to my care, Madame de Volanges will herself repair the wrong she has done to you.

Listen to me and do not be so occupied with your own affairs that you lose sight of this one. Remember my interest in it. I want you to appoint yourself go-between and adviser to these two young people. Tell Danceny about this visit and offer him your services. Let there be no difficulty in the way except that of getting your credentials into the hands of his beauty, and remove that obstacle immediately by indicating that my maid will convey them. There is no doubt whatsoever he will accept. And, as the reward for your pains, you will have the confidence of an innocent heart, something which is always worth having. Poor little thing! How she will blush when she gives you her first letter! Truly the role of confidant, so frowned upon these days, seems to me a pleasant way of amusing oneself when one is busy with other matters – which you will be.

The dénouement of this intrigue depends on you. You must judge when the moment arrives for the reunion scene; there are always a hundred opportunities in the country, and Danceny, for sure, will be ready to play his part the moment you give the sign. Nightfall, a disguise, a window . . . what else? But anyway, if the girl comes back still in the state in which she went, I shall blame you for it. If you are of the opinion that she needs some encouragement from me, tell me. I believe I have given her a good enough lesson on the dangers of keeping letters that I may dare write to her at present. And I still intend to keep her as my pupil.

I think I forgot to tell you that her suspicions on the subject of her betrayed correspondence fell first of all upon her chambermaid, and I diverted them on to the father confessor, thus killing two birds with one stone.

Adieu, Vicomte. This is a very long letter and because of it I am late for lunch. But my letter was dictated by friendship and self-esteem, and both have made me run on a bit. In any case, it will be with you at three o'clock, and that is all that is necessary.

Now complain about me if you dare. And go back, if you feel so inclined, to the woods of the Comte de B——.[11] You say he keeps them for the entertainment of his friends! So, is the whole world his friend? But farewell, luncheon beckons.

From ——, 9 September 17**

LETTER 64

The Chevalier Danceny to Madame de Volanges
(Document sent with Letter 66 from the Vicomte
to the Marquise)

Without seeking to justify my conduct, Madame, and without
complaining of yours, I can only feel very sorry for an occur-
rence which has caused the unhappiness of three people, all of
whom are worthy of a better fate. More painfully conscious of
being the agent rather than victim of this disaster, I have tried
several times since yesterday to do myself the honour of replying
to you, without being able to find the strength to do so. I have
so much to say to you, however, that I have to make an effort
with myself. And if this letter has little order or coherence, you
must be well enough aware of how truly distressing my situation
is to grant me some indulgence.

Permit me first of all to object to the first sentence in your
letter. I have not abused, I dare affirm, either your trust or the
innocence of Mademoiselle de Volanges. I have respected both
in whatever I have done. They were the sole regulators of my
conduct. And if you hold me responsible for an involuntary
feeling, I do not fear to add that the sentiments which Mademoiselle, your daughter, has inspired in me are such that they
might be displeasing to you but could never give offence. In
this matter, which touches me more than words can say, I only
want you to be the judge and my letters the witness.

You forbid me to present myself at your house in future, and
of course I shall agree to everything you may be pleased to
command. But will my sudden and total absence not give rise
to as many remarks, which you are anxious to avoid, as would
the order that, for the same reason, you did not wish to issue
to your servants at the door? I shall all the more insist on this
point since it is of much greater concern for Mademoiselle de
Volanges than for myself. I beg you therefore to weigh these
matters with all due attention and not allow your strict principles to affect your prudence. Persuaded that the sole interest

of Mademoiselle your daughter will dictate your decision, I shall await new orders from you.

Nevertheless, in the event that you would allow me to come visiting sometimes, I engage, Madame, and you may rely upon my word, not to take advantage of those occasions to try and speak privately to Mademoiselle de Volanges or to pass any letter to her. The fear of anything compromising her reputation causes me to make this sacrifice. And the happiness I shall have in seeing her from time to time will compensate me for it.

This part of my letter is also the only response that I can make to what you have said to me concerning the fate you reserve for Mademoiselle de Volanges, and that you wish to make dependent upon my conduct. If I pretended otherwise, I should be deceiving you. A vile seducer can bend his projects to circumstance, and calculate his actions according to events; but the love inspiring me permits of only two feelings: courage and constancy.

Could I ever possibly consent to be forgotten by Mademoiselle de Volanges, or to forget her myself? No, no, never! I shall be faithful to her; she has received my vow and I renew it again today. Forgive me, Madame, I am forgetting myself. I return to the matter.

There remains one more thing I have to discuss with you. The letters you have asked me for. It truly pains me to add my refusal to the other wrongs that in your opinion I have already been guilty of. But I beg you, listen to my reasons and deign to remember, in order to appreciate them, that my only consolation for the misfortune of having lost your friendship is the hope of preserving your respect.

Mademoiselle de Volanges's letters, always so precious to me, have become even more so at present. They are the only treasures left to me. The only things I have left to recall a feeling which has been the one delight of my life. However, you may depend upon it, I should not hesitate for one instant to make this sacrifice to you, and my regret at being deprived of them would yield to my wish to prove my respectful deference to you. But powerful considerations hold me back, and I am certain that you yourself would not find them unjust.

It is true that you know Mademoiselle de Volanges's secret, but, if you will allow me to say so, I believe it is because you discovered it rather than that she has confided in you. I would not seek to blame what you have done – your maternal anxiety no doubt authorizes this. I respect your rights, but they will not go as far so to dispense me of my duties, the most sacred of which is never to betray the trust accorded to us. I should be failing in this were I to expose to another's eyes the secrets of a heart which wished only to reveal itself to mine. If Mademoiselle, your daughter, consents to entrust them to you, let her say so. Her letters are of no use to you. If she wishes, on the other hand, to lock up her secrets in her heart, you would not, I suppose, expect me to be the one to tell you what is in them.

As for the obscurity in which you desire this event to remain buried, have no fear, Madame; on everything which is in the interest of Mademoiselle de Volanges, I can challenge even a mother's heart. To set your mind entirely at rest, I have thought of everything. This precious deposit, which until now was labelled 'Papers to be burned', bears at present the label 'Papers belonging to Madame de Volanges'. This position I am taking must be proof to you that my refusal does not bear at all on the fear that you would find in them one single sentiment of which you could find reason to complain.

So, Madame, this is a very long letter. But it would not be long enough if it allowed you to remain in the slightest doubt that my sentiments are honourable, or that I most sincerely regret having displeased you. It is with profound respect that I have the honour to be, etc.

From —, 9 September 17**

LETTER 65

The Chevalier Danceny to Cécile Volanges
(Sent unsealed to the Marquise de Merteuil in letter 66
from the Vicomte)

Oh my dear Cécile, what is to become of us? What god will
save us from the ills which threaten us? May love at least grant
us the courage to bear them! How can I describe to you my
shock and despair at the sight of my letters, and on reading
Madame de Volanges's note? Who can have betrayed us?
Whom do you suspect? Could you have done something indis-
creet? What are you doing at this moment? What have they
said? I want to know everything but know nothing. Perhaps
you yourself are no wiser than I.

I am sending you your Mamma's letter and the copy of my
reply. I hope you will approve of what I have said. I really need
your approval too for the actions I have taken since this fateful
event; they have all been to one end, that of receiving news of
you and sending you mine. And who knows? Perhaps I shall be
able to see you again and more freely than before.

Imagine, Cécile darling, what a pleasure it will be to see each
other, to be able to swear anew our eternal love, and to see in
our eyes, feel in our hearts, that this vow will be for ever. Surely
a moment as sweet as that will make us forget all our sorrows.
Well, I have hopes that it may come about, hopes I owe to the
same actions for which I am begging your approval. What am
I saying? I owe them to the consolation of a most loving friend.
And my only request is that you allow this friend to become
your friend as well.

Perhaps I should not have told your secrets without your consent, but my excuse is unhappiness and necessity. It is love which
has brought me to this; it is love which demands your indulgence, which asks you to forgive a necessary confidence without
which we should perhaps have remained separated for ever.*

* Monsieur Danceny is not being totally honest. He had already confided in
Monsieur de Valmont before this happened. See Letter 57.

You know the friend of whom I speak. He is the friend of the woman you love best in the world. It is the Vicomte de Valmont.

My idea in approaching him was first to beg him to engage Madame de Merteuil to take a letter for you. He did not believe this means could succeed. But if not the mistress, he is sure of her maid, since she owes him a good turn. She will be the one who will give you this letter, and you can give her your answer.

This will scarcely help us if, as Monsieur de Valmont believes, you are leaving immediately for the country. But then it will be he himself who will come to our aid. The woman in whose house you are to stay is related to him. He will use this pretext to visit at the same time as you. And he will be the one to pass letters between us. He even assures me that if you do what he says he will procure the means for us to see each other without risk of compromising you in any way.

Meanwhile, my Cécile, if you love me, if you pity my unhappiness, if, as I hope, you share my sorrow, can you refuse to trust a man who will be our guardian angel? Without him I should be reduced to despair, for I should not even be able to alleviate the troubles I have caused you. There will be an end to them, I hope. But, my love, promise me not to give in to them too much, promise me not to be too cast down by them. The idea that you are in pain is unbearable torment for me. I would give my life to make you happy! You know that only too well. May the certain knowledge that you are adored bring some consolation to your heart! My heart needs to know that you forgive love for the suffering it is causing you.

Goodbye, my Cécile; goodbye, my love.

From —, 9 September 17**

LETTER 66

The Vicomte de Valmont to the Marquise de Merteuil

You will see, my love, as you read the two letters enclosed, that I have carried out your plan thoroughly. Although both are dated today they were written yesterday at my house and in front of me. The letter to the girl says everything we wished. One can only feel humble before your insight if we may measure this by the success of your actions. Danceny is ready and willing, and I am certain that as soon as he has the opportunity you will no longer be able to criticize him for anything. If his fair *ingénue* will do as she is told, everything will be over shortly after her arrival in the country. I have a hundred schemes up my sleeve. Thanks to your care I am definitely *Danceny's friend*. And all he has to do is be the *Prince*.*[12]

Our Danceny is still so young! Would you believe that I have never been able to obtain his word that he would promise the mother to renounce his love; as though it were very difficult to promise something when you are decided upon not keeping it! 'It would be lying,' he kept saying to me. Are not such scruples edifying, considering that he wants to seduce the girl? A typical man! We are all equally wicked in our plans, and whatever weakness we show in carrying them out we call probity.

Your job is to prevent Madame de Volanges from taking fright at the little things he could not help saying in his letter. Preserve us from the convent. Try too to make her forget her request for the girl's letters. For one thing, he will not give them up; he is determined not to, and I share his opinion. Here love and reason are in agreement for once. I have read these letters; I have consumed their boredom. But they could be useful. Let me explain.

In spite of our prudence there could still be a scandal and that would mean the wedding would not go ahead, would it? Then all our plans for Gercourt would come to nothing. But if this happens, I, who also have to avenge myself on the mother,

* Reference to a passage in a poem by Monsieur de Voltaire

reserve for myself the right to dishonour the girl. If I choose carefully from this correspondence and only produce part of it, the little Volanges girl will appear to have made all the initial moves and to have absolutely thrown herself at him. Some of the letters might even compromise the mother and at least *taint* her with unpardonable negligence. I feel that the scrupulous Danceny would resist this at first, but as he would be under attack himself, I believe he could be persuaded. It is a thousand to one against things working out like this, but we have to be prepared for every eventuality.

Goodbye, my lovely. It would be nice of you to come and sup with me tomorrow at the Maréchale de —'s; I was not able to refuse. I suppose I do not need to tell you to keep my plan to go to the country secret from Madame de Volanges? She would immediately decide to stay in town. Once in the country, she will not leave next day. If she gives us a week, I can answer for everything.

From —, 9 September 17**

LETTER 67

The Présidente de Tourvel to the Vicomte de Valmont

I did not intend to answer your letter, Monsieur, and perhaps my present trouble is itself proof that I ought not to be doing so. However I do not wish to leave you with any reason whatsoever to complain of my conduct; I hope to persuade you that I have done everything I could for you.

You say I allowed you to write to me. Well, that is true. But when you remind me of this, do you imagine I forget the conditions of that promise? If I had observed those conditions as faithfully as you have ignored them, would you have had one single reply from me? And yet this is the third. And whereas you do all you can to oblige me to stop our correspondence, it is I who take measures to maintain it. There is a way, only one, to achieve this; if you refuse to take it, you will prove, despite what you say, how low a value you place upon it.

So please stop using these words that I cannot and will not hear. Renounce these feelings which both offend and frighten me, and to which, perhaps, you would attach less importance if you realized they are the thing that is keeping us apart. Are these truly the only feelings you can entertain? Must I think even worse of love than I do already in that it excludes the possibility of friendship? And you, will you be guilty of not wanting as a friend the woman in whom you hoped to find more tender sentiments? I do not wish to believe so. I should find such a shameful idea degrading, and it would estrange me from you for ever.

In offering you my friendship, Monsieur, I give you everything which is mine, everything which is mine to give. What more can you desire of me? To surrender to this delightful feeling, to which my heart is open, I await only your consent and your promise, which I insist upon, that friendship with me will be enough to make you happy. I shall forget all that people have said. I shall rely on you to prove my decision justified.

You can see how honest I am being; my frankness must prove my confidence. It will be up to you to strengthen that. But I must warn you that the very first word of love you utter will destroy it for ever, and will revive all my fears. I warn you that for me it will betoken eternal silence as far as you are concerned.

If, as you say, you have *mended your ways*, would you not rather be the object of a respectable woman's friendship than the object of a guilty woman's remorse? Farewell, Monsieur. You will understand that, having spoken thus, I can say nothing further until I have received an answer from you.

From —, 9 September 17**

LETTER 68

The Vicomte de Valmont to the Présidente de Tourvel

How can I reply, Madame, to your last letter? How may I dare
to be frank when sincerity might mean the end of everything?
No matter, I must. I shall be brave. I tell myself time and again
that it is better to be worthy of you than to obtain you. And
even though you were to refuse me forever a happiness that I
shall always desire, I must none the less prove to you that my
heart is worthy.

What a pity I have *mended my ways*, as you put it! With
what transports of delight might I have perused the very letter to
which I fear to answer today! You talk to me with *frankness*, you
profess your *confidence* and finally you offer me your *friendship*.
What treasures, Madame, and what regrets at not being able
to take advantage of them! Why am I not the man I was?

And what if I were? Let us suppose this was only a vulgar
attraction for you, a passing desire born of lust and intrigue,
that today none the less goes by the name of love; I should
hasten to take advantage of anything I could get. Caring little
about the means, as long as it procured me success, I should
encourage your frankness by the need to divine your secrets. I
should try to gain your trust, with the intention of betraying
it. I should accept your friendship in the hope of leading
you astray ... Well, Madame, does this picture frighten you?
... Yet it would be a true likeness of me if I were to tell you
I agreed to be no more than your friend ...

How could I consent to share with anyone else a feeling that
emanated from your soul? If I ever say such a thing, do not
believe it. From that moment on I should be seeking to deceive
you. I might desire you still, but it is certain I should no longer
love you.

It is not that frankness, quiet trust and sympathetic friendship
have no value in my eyes ... But love! True love of the kind
that you inspire, uniting all these sentiments and giving them
more intensity, cannot lend itself as they do to that tranquillity,

that peace of mind, which permits one to make comparisons and have preferences. No, Madame, I shall not be your friend. I shall love you truly and tenderly, even ardently, though always respectfully. You can make me lose hope, but you can never quench my love.

By what right do you claim to command a heart whose homage you refuse? By what refinement of cruelty do you begrudge me even the happiness of loving you? That belongs to me, independently of you. I shall defend it. If it is the source of my misfortune, it is also the remedy.

No, no, and again, no. Persist in your cruel refusals. But leave me my love. You delight in making me unhappy! Well, so be it. Try to wear down my resolve; I shall force you at least to decide my fate. And perhaps one day you will be more just towards me. It is not that I hope to ever make you feel anything for me. But though you may not be persuaded, you will think otherwise. You will say to yourself: I was unfair to him.

Let us put it another way: it is to yourself that you are being unfair. To know you without loving you, to love you without being constant to you, are both equally impossible. And despite your cloak of modesty it must be easier for you to protest than wonder at the feelings you inspire. As for me, my only merit is that I have learned to love you, and I do not wish to lose it. And far from consenting to your insidious suggestions, I renew my vow, at your feet, to love you for ever.

From —, 10 September 17**

LETTER 69

Cécile Volanges to the Chevalier Danceny
(Note written in pencil and copied out by Danceny)

You ask me what I am doing. I am loving you and weeping. My mother refuses to speak to me any more. She has taken away my paper, pens and ink. I am using a pencil which I still have, luckily, and I am writing to you on a piece of your letter. Of course I approve of all you have been doing. I love you too much not to do everything in my power to have news of you and to send you mine. I did not like Monsieur de Valmont, and did not realize he was such a good friend of yours. I shall try to get to know him and like him because of you. I don't know who betrayed us. It can only be my maid or my confessor. I am so unhappy. We leave for the country tomorrow. I do not know for how long. Oh God, how shall I bear not seeing you! I have run out of space. I hope you can read this. These pencilled words will one day perhaps fade, but the feelings engraved on my heart, never.

From —, 10 September 17**

LETTER 70

The Vicomte de Valmont to the Marquise de Merteuil

I have something important to tell you, my love. I was having supper yesterday at the Maréchale de —'s. We were discussing you and I was expressing not all the good opinions I have of you, but all I do not have! Everyone seemed to be of my mind and the conversation was running out, as it always does when all you do is praise your neighbour, when someone contradicted me: Prévan.

'Far be it from me,' said he, getting up, 'to be sceptical of Madame de Merteuil's virtue! But I believe she may owe it more to her fleet-footedness than to her principles. It is perhaps harder to catch her than to please her. And as one inevitably meets other women when one is chasing a woman; as, when all's said and done, others may be as good or better than her, some men will be distracted by meeting someone new, others will give up because they are tired, so she is perhaps the one woman in the whole of Paris who has least often been put to the trouble of defending herself. I for my part,' he added, spurred on by the smirks of a few women, 'shall only believe in Madame de Merteuil's virtue after I have run half a dozen horses into the ground in pursuit of her.'

This bad joke had a great success, like all those which rely on slander. And during the laughter that ensued, Prévan sat down again and people began talking about something else. But the two Comtesses de B—, sitting near our sceptic, engaged him in a conversation of their own and fortunately I was within earshot.

A challenge that he should try to win you was accepted, and the promise was given that he would conceal no detail. And of all the promises made in the course of this affair, I am certain none will be more religiously kept than that one. But now you are forewarned, and you know the old saying.

I have to tell you as well that this Prévan – you don't know him – is a most agreeable fellow, and even more clever than he is agreeable. If you have sometimes heard me say anything else, it is just that I don't like the man; I take pleasure in placing obstacles in his way, and I am not unaware of how much weight my opinion carries with thirty or so of the most fashionable women around.

In fact, I have prevented him for quite some time by this means from appearing on what we call the world stage,[13] and he did extraordinary things without ever acquiring the reputation for doing so. But the glory of his triple affair focused all eyes upon him and gave him the confidence which he did not have until then, and made him into someone truly to be reckoned with. So he is today perhaps the only man whom I should not care to have cross my path; and, setting aside your own interest, you would do me a great service if you had occasion to make him look ridiculous. I leave him in good hands. And I hope when I get back he will have sunk without trace.

I promise you in return to bring your pupil's affair to a successful conclusion and to take as much care with her as with my beautiful prude.

The latter has just sent me an offer of surrender. Her whole letter cries out her longing to be led astray. And she could not have hit upon a more convenient and well-worn method. She wants me to be *her friend*. But I like novel and intricate ways of going about things, and it is not my intention to let her off so lightly. Indeed, I have not taken so much trouble with her in order for it all to end with a run-of-the-mill seduction.

Quite the opposite, in fact; my plan is that she should feel most acutely the value and extent of each of the sacrifices she makes to me; not to lead her along so fast that she does not feel guilt; to let her virtue expire in a long-drawn-out agony; to concentrate her mind incessantly upon this desolating spectacle; and not to allow her the happiness of having me in her arms until I have forced her no longer to hide the fact that she wants it. For I am not worth much if I am not worth the asking, that's for sure. And can I exact a lesser vengeance on a high and mighty woman who seems ashamed to admit she adores me?

I have therefore refused this precious friendship, and have insisted on my claim to be her lover. As I do not deceive myself that this title (which seems at first a mere quibbling with words) is none the less really important to obtain, I took a lot of trouble with my letter, and tried to reproduce the impression of disorder, the only thing that can depict feeling. Anyway, I reasoned as badly as I knew how; for without talking nonsense, one cannot express one's love. And that is why, in my view, women are better than men at writing love letters.

I ended mine by flattering her, and that too is a consequence of my profound observations. After a woman's heart has been exercised for some time it needs rest. And I have observed that a little flattery is for all of them the softest pillow one may offer.

Farewell, my love. I leave tomorrow. If you have any orders to give me for the Comtesse de —, I shall stop at her place, for dinner at least. I am sorry to leave without seeing you. Send me your excellent instructions and give me the benefit of your sage counsel at this critical time.

And especially defend yourself against Prévan; I hope I may one day make it up to you for this sacrifice! Farewell.

From —, 11 September 17**

LETTER 71

The Vicomte de Valmont to the Marquise de Merteuil

My pea-brained valet has gone and left my letter-case in Paris! My beauty's letters, Danceny's to the little Volanges girl, everything is still there, and I need it all. He is going to go back and make up for his stupidity. And while he is saddling his horse I'll tell you what happened last night. For I beg you to believe I am not wasting my time.

The affair in itself was nothing special. Just the reigniting of an old flame with the Vicomtesse de —. But the details were of interest to me.[14] I am very pleased in any case to show you that, though I have a talent for ruining women, I have just as fine a talent, when I like, for saving them. I always opt for the most difficult or the most amusing course of action; and I do not regret a good action as long as it is entertaining or challenging.

So I found the Vicomtesse here, and as she added her pressing invitation to the others I received to spend the night in the chateau, I said: 'All right, I agree, on condition I may spend it with you.' 'That is impossible,' she said, 'Vressac is here.' Up to that point my one concern had been to be polite. But as usual that word 'impossible' made me defiant. I felt humiliated to be sacrificed to Vressac, and determined I would not put up with it. So I insisted.

The circumstances were not favourable. Vressac has been silly enough to get on the wrong side of the Vicomte, so the Vicomtesse cannot receive him any longer. And this trip to the good Comtesse had been planned between the pair of them to try to steal a few nights together. At first the Vicomte was rather put out by finding Vressac there; but, as his interest in hunting is stronger than his jealousy, he stayed. And the Comtesse, in her usual fashion, after having settled the wife in a room off the long corridor, put the husband on one side of her and the lover on the other, and let them sort it out between them. Unfortunately for them both, I had the bedroom opposite.

That very same day, that is to say, yesterday, Vressac who,

as you may imagine, likes to keep the Vicomte sweet, was hunting with him, in spite of not caring very much for it, and was looking forward to making up for the boredom of being with the husband all day by lying in the arms of his wife at night. But I decided he should have some rest after his exertions and set to thinking up ways of persuading his mistress to allow him time for that.

I succeeded, and managed to obtain her consent that she would pick a quarrel with him about that same hunting expedition which, of course, he had only agreed to because of her. You could not have hit upon a worse pretext. But there is no one more talented than the Vicomtesse at substituting a bad mood for reasoned argument – though all women do it – and at never being so hard to appease as when she is in the wrong. Anyway, it was not the time for arguments. And only wanting one night I consented to them making it up the next day.

So she was in a sulk with Vressac when he came back. He wanted to know why, and she picked a quarrel with him. He attempted to stand up for himself, but the husband was present, which served her as an excuse to bring the conversation to a halt. So he tried to take advantage of a moment when the husband was not there to ask her if she would see him in the evening. It was then that the Vicomtesse surpassed herself. She railed at the audacity of men who, because they have won a woman's favours, believe they always have a right to them, even when she has reason to complain about their behaviour. And, skilfully changing the subject, she talked so eloquently on the subject of delicacy and sensibility that Vressac remained confused and tongue-tied. Even I was inclined to believe she was right. For as you know I am a friend of both and was party to their conversation.

Finally she roundly declared that she would not add the fatigues of love to those of hunting, and that she would feel guilty if she were to spoil such agreeable pleasures. The husband came in. Vressac was desolated, being no longer at liberty to reply, and addressed himself to me. And after he had at length expounded his arguments, which I knew as well as he did, he begged me to talk to the Vicomtesse, and I promised I would. I did indeed speak to her. But only to thank her, and fix the time and place for our rendez-vous.

She told me that since her room was in between her husband's and Vressac's she had thought it was more prudent to go to Vressac's room than to receive him in hers. And since I was in the room opposite, she thought it was safer to come to my room. She would come as soon as her chambermaid left her; I only had to leave my door ajar and wait.

Everything happened as we had agreed. And she arrived in my room at about one in the morning,

> . . . wearing no more
> Than beauty snatched from sleep would wear.*[15]

As I am not a vain man I shall not linger over the night's details. But you know me, and I was satisfied with my performance.

At dawn we had to separate. And this is where it begins to get interesting. The silly woman thought she had left her door ajar, but we found it shut with the key inside. You cannot imagine the first desperate words of the Vicomtesse: 'Oh no! I am ruined.' It must be said it would have been rather amusing to leave her in this situation. But could I allow a woman to be ruined on my account, and I not do the ruining? And should I, like most men, allow myself to be overcome by circumstance? I had to find a stratagem. What would you have done, my love? This is what I did, and it succeeded.

I soon realized that the door in question could be broken open, as long as it did not matter if we made a noise. I therefore persuaded the Vicomtesse, not without some difficulty, that she should utter fearful piercing cries such as *Stop thief! Murder!* etc., etc. And we agreed that at the first shout I would break down the door, and she would leap into bed. You would not believe how long it was before she could bring herself to do it even after she had agreed. But in the end there was no other possibility, and the door gave way at the first kick.

The Vicomtesse did well not to waste any time. For at the

---

* Racine, the tragedy of *Britannicus*.

same instant the Vicomte and Vressac were in the corridor; and the chambermaid came running without delay to her mistress's bedroom.

I was the only one to preserve my composure, and I took advantage of it to go and extinguish a nightlight which was still burning and knock it over. For you can see how ridiculous it would have looked to simulate panic and terror with the light still on. I then scolded the husband and the lover for their lethargy, assuring them that I had come running as soon as I heard the shouting and my efforts to kick the door down had lasted a full five minutes.

The Vicomtesse who, back in bed, had recovered her courage, once more ably backed me up, and swore to God there had been a thief in her room. She protested, with greater sincerity, that she had never been so frightened in her whole life. We hunted everywhere but found nothing. Then I called the over-turned nightlight to everyone's attention and concluded that a rat must have caused the damage and the alarm. My opinion was echoed by everyone, and after the usual old chestnuts about rats,[16] the Vicomte was the first to return his room and his bed, begging his wife in future to keep rats of a more peaceable temperament.

Vressac remained, and approached the Vicomtesse to tell her tenderly that it was Love's revenge; to which she answered, with a glance in my direction: 'He must have been very angry then, because he took his revenge many times over. But,' she added, 'I am exhausted and I wish to sleep.'

I was feeling well-disposed towards everyone. Consequently before we separated I pleaded Vressac's cause and brought about a reconciliation. The two lovers kissed and I was kissed by them both in turn. I was no longer interested in the Vicomtesse's kisses, but I admit that I took pleasure in Vressac's. We left together. And once I had received his lengthy expressions of gratitude we each went back to our beds.

If you find this story amusing, I shall not insist you keep it secret. Now I have had my laugh it is only fair that the public should have its turn. For the moment I am only talking about the plot; perhaps soon we shall say the same of its heroine?

Farewell, my valet has been waiting for an hour. I shall only take one moment to kiss you and urge you above all to beware of Prévan.

From the Chateau de —, 13 September 17**

LETTER 72

The Chevalier Danceny to Cécile Volanges
(Not delivered until the 14th)

Oh Cécile! How I envy Valmont! He will be seeing you tomorrow. It is he who will give you this letter, whereas I, languishing far away, shall drag out my cruel existence in sorrow and misery. My love, my darling, pity my misfortunes, but especially pity me for yours. It is in the face of those that my courage deserts me.

How terrible it is for me to have brought about your unhappiness! Without me you would be happy and at peace. Can you forgive me? Tell me, oh tell me you forgive me. Tell me as well that you love me and that you always will. I need to be told again and again. It is not that I do not believe you. But it seems to me that the more certain one is, the sweeter those words are. You do love me, don't you? Yes, you love me with all your heart and soul. I have not forgotten that those were the last words I heard you utter. How I took them to my heart! How deeply they are engraved there! And with what rapture my heart responded!

Alas! At that happy moment, I was far from seeing what dreadful fate awaited us. My Cécile, let us try to find ways of making it more bearable. All that is needed to achieve this, if I am to believe my friend, is that you place in him the trust which he deserves.

I must admit I was pained that you appeared to think so badly of him. I detected your Mamma's prejudices there. It was in order to bow to your mother's opinion that I neglected this truly kind man who has done so much for me for so long; he is working to bring us together, whereas your Mamma has torn us apart. I beseech you, my darling, try to look upon him more favourably. Remember he is my friend, he wants to be yours, and it is in his power to give me back the happiness of seeing you again. If these reasons do not persuade you, Cécile my love, you do not love me as much as I love you, you do not love me as much as you did love me. Oh, if ever you were to love me less . . . But no, my Cécile's heart belongs to me until I die. And if I have to fear the pain of an unhappy love, her constancy will save me at least from the torments of a love betrayed.

Farewell, my dearest. Do not forget that I am suffering, and that it is you, and you alone, who can make me happy, perfectly happy. Hear the avowal of my heart and accept the most tender kisses love can bestow.

Paris, this 11 September 17**

LETTER 73

The Vicomte de Valmont to Cécile Volanges
(Included in the preceding letter)

The friend who is at your service has learned you have no writing materials, and has already made provision for you. You will find in the large cupboard on the left, in the antechamber of the room you are occupying, a stock of paper, pens and ink; he will replenish them whenever you wish, and believes it would be best to leave them in that same place if you do not find a safer one.

He asks you not to take offence if he appears to pay you scant attention in company, and to treat you as a mere child. This behaviour appears to him necessary. It will give him the security he needs to work more safely and effectively for his friend's happiness and yours. He will try to engineer opportunities to speak to you when he has something to tell or give you, and if you put all your efforts into supporting him he has every hope of success.

He also advises you to give him back the letters you receive as they arrive, so that you will run less risk of being compromised.

He concludes by assuring you that if you place your trust in him, he will do everything in his power to alleviate the over-harsh persecution inflicted by a mother upon two people, one of whom is already his dearest friend, and the other who would seem to merit the most affectionate interest.

In the Chateau de —, 14 September 17**

LETTER 74

The Marquise de Merteuil to the Vicomte de Valmont

Since when have you been so easily frightened off, my friend? Is this Prévan really so very terrifying? You see how simple and unassuming I am, for I have come across this Casanova many times and yet I have scarcely given him a glance! It took your letter to bring him to my notice. I put this right yesterday. He was at the Opera, almost opposite me, and I paid him careful attention. He is certainly good-looking, very good-looking. Such fine, delicate features! He must surely be seen to advantage at close quarters. And you say he is pursuing me! He would surely be doing me an honour and a pleasure. Seriously I dream of it, and I may as well tell you now that I have made the first move. I don't know whether it will succeed, but this is what happened.

He was standing right next to me on our way out of the Opera when in a very loud voice I told the Marquise de — I would meet her for supper on the Friday at the Maréchale's. I believe it is the only house where I am likely to meet him. I am certain he heard me . . . Supposing the rogue were not to turn up? Tell me, do you think he will come? If he does not, I can tell you I shall be in a bad mood all evening. You will see he will not find it so very hard to *catch me*. And what will surprise you more is that he will find it even less hard *to please me*. So he says he wants to ride six horses into the ground running after me! Oh, I shall spare their lives, those horses. I shall never be patient enough to wait that long. As you know, on principle I do not make anyone wait once my mind is made up, and I have made up mine about him.

So admit there is some pleasure to be had in talking seriously with me! Your *important advice* is a great success, is it not? But what do you expect? I have been here twiddling my thumbs for so long! I have not allowed myself any fun for six weeks! Then this comes along. Can I say no? Is he not worth it? Is there any more agreeable fun, in whatever sense you take the word?

You yourself are obliged to give him his due. You do more than praise him; you are jealous of him. Well, I shall be the judge of you both. But first I need to acquaint myself with the facts, and that is what I intend to do. I shall be your impartial judge, and you shall both be weighed in the same balance. As far as you are concerned the case is already well-documented and perfectly prepared. Is it not fair that at present I busy myself with your adversary? Come now, do not be difficult. To start with, tell me about this 'triple adventure' and its hero. You talk as though I was perfectly *au courant* when I do not know the first thing about it. Apparently it all happened during my journey to Geneva, and your jealousy prevented you from writing to me about it. Repair this omission as soon as possible. Remember that *nothing that concerns him is strange to me*.[17] I seem to recall they were still talking about it when I got back. But I was busy doing something else, and I rarely listen to news of this sort when it is more than two days old.

If what I am asking you annoys you a little, is it not a very small price to pay for the trouble I have taken on your behalf? Was it not I who reconciled you to your Présidente when your stupid behaviour had wrenched you apart? And was it not I who placed within your grasp the means to avenge yourself for the zealous harshness of Madame de Volanges? You have often complained about the time you waste looking for adventures! At present you have them to hand. Love, hate, you have only to choose, everything under the same roof. And you can live two lives: stroke softly with one hand, strike hard with the other.

You even owe your affair with the Vicomtesse to me. That pleases me well enough, but, as you say, it should be talked about. For if in the circumstances you incline, as I suppose, to keep quiet rather than boast about it, yet you must agree this woman does not deserve to be treated so considerately.

Moreover, I have reason to complain about her. The Chevalier de Belleroche thinks her prettier than I could wish. And there are many reasons why I should be very happy to have an excuse to break off relations with her. Now there is no more convenient excuse than to have to say: one cannot possibly see that woman any longer.

Farewell, Vicomte; remember that in your position time is precious. I am going to devote mine to making Prévan happy.

Paris, 15 September 17**

LETTER 75

Cécile Volanges to Sophie Carnay
(In this letter Cécile Volanges goes into great detail about everything concerning her in the events the reader has encountered in Letter 59 and those following. We felt it better to avoid repetition. At the end of the letter she talks about the Vicomte de Valmont thus:)

I do assure you he is a most remarkable man. Mamma does not have a good word to say about him, but the Chevalier Danceny sings his praises and I believe he is the one who is right. I have never seen such a clever man. When he gave me back Danceny's letter it was in full view of everyone, and nobody noticed anything. I was really scared because I did not know what to expect. But from now on I shall. I have already understood exactly what he wants me to do when I give him my reply. He is very easy to understand because his eyes speak volumes. I don't know how he does it. In the note I was telling you about he said he would appear not to be taking any notice of me in front of Mamma, and you would think, in fact, that it never crossed his mind. Yet every time I look at him I am certain of meeting his eyes straight away.

There is a good friend of Mamma's here, whom I did not know before, who also seems as if she does not care greatly for Monsieur de Valmont, although he is most attentive to her. I am afraid he may very soon become bored with the life we lead here and return to Paris. That would be most disappointing. He must be exceedingly good-hearted to come on purpose to render a service to his friend and me! I should like to show him how grateful I am, but I don't know how to find a way of speaking to him. And even if I found the opportunity, I should be so embarrassed I probably would not know what to say.

When I speak of my love I can really only talk freely with Madame de Merteuil. Perhaps I should be embarrassed about talking of it even with you, to whom I tell everything. With Danceny himself I have often felt, in spite of myself, a certain timidity which prevented me saying all I wished. I regret that now, and would give anything in the world to find the opportunity to tell him once, just once, how much I love him. Monsieur de Valmont has promised him that if I do as he asks he will procure the chance for us to see each other again. I shall do whatever he says; but I cannot imagine it will be possible.

Farewell, my friend, I have run out of space.*

From the Chateau de —, 14 September 17**

---

* Mademoiselle de Volanges having shortly afterwards changed confidante, as we shall see by the ensuing letters, none of those which she continued to write to her friend in the convent will be found here. They would provide no further information for the reader.

LETTER 76

The Vicomte de Valmont to the Marquise de Merteuil

Either you are teasing me in your letter and I have misunderstood; or else you were seriously deranged when you wrote it.
If I did not know you as well as I do, my dear, I should be very
frightened indeed. And whatever you may say, I am not one to
be so easily frightened.

Though I have read and re-read it, I can make no headway.
For your letter cannot possibly be taken at face value. So what
did you mean?

Is it simply that you felt you need not trouble to guard
yourself against such a feeble adversary? If you believe that,
then you are wrong. Prévan is actually a very likeable man,
more likeable than you might suppose. In particular he has a
knack, which is very useful to him, of involving everyone else
in his love life by the skilful weaving of the subject into the
conversation, in everyone's hearing, at any opportunity. Only
very few women do not fall into the trap of responding, for
they all wish to be thought very discerning, and not one of them
is inclined to lose the chance of showing it. Now, as you very
well know, a woman who consents to discuss matters of the
heart soon ends up falling in love, or at least behaving as though
she were. And more often than not with this tactic, which he
really has perfected, he is able to call upon the women themselves to witness their own defeat. And I know what I am
talking about because I have seen it happen.

I only heard about it at second hand. For I have never been
intimate with Prévan. But anyway, there were six of us. And
the Comtesse de P—, thinking she was being very witty, and
seeming, except to those in the know, to be making general
conversation, related in the greatest detail how she had surrendered to Prévan, and all that had passed between them. All this
was recounted with such composure that she was not in the
least disconcerted by all six of us simultaneously screaming
with laughter; and I shall always remember that when someone,

by way of excuse, pretended not to believe what she was saying, or rather appeared to be saying, she answered with some gravity that for certain none of us knew as much as she did about the matter. And she did not hesitate to appeal to Prévan himself and ask him whether she had told the least little fib.

And so I believe this man is a danger to everybody. But for you, Marquise, is it not enough that he is *good-looking, very good-looking,* as you say yourself? Or that he may launch *one of those attacks that you are sometimes pleased to reward, for no other reason than that you find them executed with style?*[18] Or that you find it amusing to give yourself to him for whatever reason? Or ... what else? How can I guess at the thousands upon thousands of fancies that reign in the minds of women, by virtue of which alone you remain typical of your sex? Now that you are warned of the danger I am sure you will easily escape. But it was my duty to warn you. So I come back to my theme. What was it you meant in your letter?

If it was only a joke about Prévan, apart from it being a rather laborious one, it was wasted on me. It is in public that he needs to be well and truly held up to ridicule, and I renew my plea to you in this regard.

Oh, I believe I have the clue to the mystery! Your letter is a prophecy, not of what you will do, but of what he thinks you will be ready to do at the moment of his downfall. I don't disapprove of your plan; yet it will be necessary to organize it with great care. You know as well as I that, as far as society is concerned, being a man's mistress and receiving his attentions amounts to exactly the same thing, unless that man happens to be a fool. And Prévan is by no means a fool. If he can only make it look as if he has won you, he will brag about it, and that will be that. Fools will believe him, and malicious people will pretend to believe him. What will you do then? I do not like to think. It is not that I do not believe in your competence. But it is always the good swimmers who drown.

I like to think I am no more stupid than the next man. I have found hundreds, no thousands of ways of dishonouring a woman. But when I try to think of ways she might save herself, I can never see how it might be done. Even you, my darling, who conduct yourself so masterfully, I have seen you triumph a hundred times, I believe, more through luck than judgement.

But when all's said and done, I am perhaps looking for a reason where none exists. I wonder at my taking seriously for the past hour something that must be meant as a joke on your part. You will have fun at my expense. Well then, so be it. But hurry up and let us talk of something else. Something else! No, it is always about the same thing: possessing or ruining women, often both of these.

Here, as you have so well observed, I have plenty of opportunity for practising both, though not in equal measure. I foresee that revenge will prosper more quickly than love. The little Volanges girl has given in, I guarantee; she is only waiting for an opportunity, and I shall be responsible for providing that. But it is not the same with Madame de Tourvel. This woman depresses me; I do not understand her at all. I have a hundred proofs of her love, but a thousand of her strength to resist, and the truth is I fear she may yet escape me.

Her initial reaction when I got back raised my hopes. As you may imagine, I wanted to judge for myself. Therefore I had not announced my arrival so that I might better observe her first reaction, and I had timed my journey to arrive when everyone was at supper. In fact, I fell out of the sky like a *deus ex machina* at the Opera arriving in the last act.

Since I made enough noise upon entering for all eyes to be turned upon me, I was able to observe simultaneously the joy of my old aunt, the vexation of Madame de Volanges and the confusion and pleasure of her daughter. My beauty had her back to the door. She was busy cutting something at that moment and did not even turn her head. But I spoke to Madame de Rosemonde. And at the first word I uttered the sensitive devotee recognized my voice and let out a cry in which I thought I could detect more love than surprise or alarm. I had by then moved forward into the room sufficiently to be able to see her face. The turmoil in her soul, the struggle between ideas and feelings, was manifest there in a score of different ways. I sat down beside her. She did not know what she was doing or saying. She tried to carry on eating, but there was no posssibility of that. Finally, less than a quarter of an hour later, her embarrassment and agitation got the better of her and she had to resort to asking permission to leave the table; whereupon she escaped into the park, on the pretext of needing some fresh air. Madame de Volanges offered to go with her, but the gentle prude would not allow it, only too happy no doubt to have an excuse to be on her own and give herself up wholeheartedly to her sweet emotions!

I cut dinner as short as possible. Dessert had scarcely been served when that infernal Volanges woman, apparently with a pressing need to be malicious towards me, rose from her seat and went to look for our suffering beauty. But I had seen this little trick coming and I countered it. I pretended to think this move on her part was a signal that everyone was leaving and I got up at the same time as she did, her daughter and the local curate also allowing themselves to be influenced by our example. So Madame de Rosemonde found herself alone at table with the old Commandeur de T— and they both also decided to leave. We all went in search of my beauty and found her in the little grove beside the chateau. And as it was solitude and not a walk that she needed it made no difference to her whether she came back with us or had us remain with her.

When I was certain Madame de Volanges would not have an opportunity to speak to her on her own, I turned my attention to carrying out your commands and busied myself furthering the interests of your pupil. Immediately coffee was over I went upstairs to my rooms and through the other rooms as well to see how the land lay. I made sure that all was in order for the little Volanges girl to write her letters. And after that preliminary good deed I wrote her a note to tell her, and ask her to trust me. I put my letter in with Danceny's. I went down to the salon again. And there I found my beauty reclining on a chaise longue in an attitude of delightful abandon.

My face lit up at this sight and my desire was aroused. I sensed that my face must have assumed an expression of tender longing, and placed myself in a position where I could take advantage of that. The immediate effect of this was that the heavenly prude lowered her big, modest eyes. I considered this angelic face for some time; then, my eyes travelling over her whole body, I amused myself imagining her curves and shapes underneath her flimsy, yet all too inhibiting garment. After descending from her head to her feet my gaze lifted once more from feet to head ... My love, her sweet eyes were upon me; in a trice they were lowered again: but I averted my own, with the intention of making her look at me again. And so this tacit convention established itself between us, the first treaty ratified by shy lovers, which, in order to satisfy the need to look at each other, allows glances only in succession, until they can meet.

Persuaded that my beauty was entirely occupied with this new pleasure, I took it upon myself to check on our safety. But, after assuring myself that the conversation was animated enough to prevent us being noticed by the company, I tried to make her eyes express her feelings more plainly. To this end I first surprised a few glances, but with so much reserve that her modesty could not be alarmed. And to put the shy woman more at ease I myself pretended to be as embarrassed as she was. Gradually our eyes got accustomed to meeting and fixed each other at greater and greater length. Finally they no longer looked away, and I perceived in hers that sweet languor, the happy sign of love and desire. But it was short-lived. Soon she regained her composure and, with some embarrassment, her attitude and expression altered.

Not wishing to leave her in any doubt that I had observed her various emotions, I got up quickly and asked, with a look of alarm, whether she was unwell. Immediately everyone clustered round. I allowed them all to pass in front of me. And as the little Volanges girl, who was at her tapestry by a window, needed a moment to set aside her work I seized the moment to slip her Danceny's letter.

I was a little way off. I threw the epistle on to her lap. She really did not know what to do. You would have laughed heartily at her air of surprise and embarrassment. I, however, was not laughing, for I was afraid that we should be betrayed by so much clumsiness. But a wink and an emphatic nod finally made her understand she was to put the letter in her pocket.

The rest of the day passed uneventfully. Subsequent events

will perhaps develop to your satisfaction, at least as far as your pupil is concerned. But it is better to use one's time in executing these projects than in relating them. Anyway, I am on to my eighth page and weary of writing. So farewell.

I don't need to tell you, of course, that the girl has replied to Danceny.* I have also had a reply to the letter I wrote my beauty the day after my arrival. I am sending you both letters. Read them or not as you wish. For going over and over the same old thing is already becoming rather less than amusing, and must be exceedingly dull for anyone not personally involved.

Again, farewell. I love you still very much. But if you speak of Prévan again, then please do it so that I may understand what you are saying.

From the Chateau of —, 17 September 17**

LETTER 77

The Vicomte de Valmont to the Présidente de Tourvel

Madame, how can you be so cruel as to keep running away from me like this? How can it be that the most loving attentions on my part are answered on yours by conduct that a man who had given you most cause for complaint would scarcely merit? How can this be? Love brings me to your side; and although by good fortune I am placed next to you, you feign illness and cause your friends alarm rather than consent to remain beside me! How many times yesterday did you turn your eyes away and deny me the favour of a glance? And though for one brief moment I thought I could detect in you a little less severity, it was so short-lived that I believe you were not so concerned that I should enjoy it as that you might make me aware of what I was losing when you deprived me of it.

Might I suggest that this is not the sort of treatment love deserves nor friendship should tolerate? Yet, as you are well

* This letter has not been found.

aware, it is one of these two sentiments that I live by, and I had been led to believe that you would not refuse the other. What have I done since, then, to forfeit this precious friendship, of which you certainly once thought me worthy, because you were willing to offer it? Am I to suffer because of my trusting nature? Will you punish me for being frank with you? Are you not afraid, at least, of abusing one or the other? Is it not indeed in the bosom of my friend that I have laid the secrets of my heart? It is surely for her sake, and hers alone, that I felt obliged to refuse conditions which, had I accepted, would have been easy not to adhere to, and which I could have turned to my own advantage. Finally, would you have me believe, by reason of this unmerited severity, that all I would have had to do in order to obtain greater indulgence from you is deceive you?

I do not regret my conduct, which I owed to you as well as to myself. But what is this fate which decrees that every praiseworthy deed must become a source of fresh unhappiness for me?

It was after receiving the only compliment for my conduct you have so far condescended to utter that I had reason for the first time to bemoan my misfortune in having displeased you. It was after I had proved my total subservience to you and deprived myself of the happiness of seeing you, solely out of regard for your finer feelings, that you desired to break off all correspondence with me and deny me this paltry compensation for the sacrifice you demanded, taking everything from me, even the love which could alone give you that right. And now it is after speaking to you with a sincerity that even my love's self-interest could not diminish that you flee from me today, as though I were a dangerous seducer whose perfidy you have recognized.

Will you never tire of such injustice? Tell me at least what new wrongs have provoked you to such unkindness; do not refuse to dictate the orders you wish me to obey. As I undertake to carry them out, is it too much to ask that you tell me what they are?

From —, 15 September 17**

LETTER 78

The Présidente de Tourvel to the Vicomte de Valmont

You seem, Monsieur, surprised by my conduct and almost to be asking me to justify it, as if you had a right to blame me. I confess I should have thought I had more grounds for surprise and grievance than you. But ever since the refusal contained in your last reply I have taken the decision to envelop myself in an indifference which no longer leaves room for any criticism or reproach. However, since you ask for explanations and, thanks be to God, I feel nothing within me that should prevent me giving them, I will once more try to explain my reasoning to you.

Anyone reading your letters would think I was unjust or very strange. I do not think I deserve anyone to have this opinion of me. I had thought that you were less likely than others to entertain it. I am sure you felt that in obliging me to justify myself you were forcing me to remember everything that has passed between us. Apparently you thought only to gain from this scrutiny. Since for my part I do not believe I have anything to lose, at least in your eyes, I do not fear to expose myself to it. Perhaps this is, in fact, the only way of ascertaining which of us has the right to complain of the other.

You will, I believe, acknowledge that from your first day in this chateau, Monsieur, your reputation gave me, at the very least, the right to treat you with some reserve. And I might, without being accused of excessive prudery, have confined myself simply to expressions of the coolest politeness. You yourself would have treated me with indulgence, and would have found it quite natural that a woman of so little experience had not the necessary qualities to appreciate yours. That would certainly have been the more prudent course. And had I pursued it, it would have cost me much less; for I shall not hide from you the fact that when Madame de Rosemonde came to tell me about your arrival I had to remind myself of my friendship for her and hers for you, so that she might not perceive how displeased I was by this news.

I am willing to agree that at first you appeared in a more favourable light than I imagined. But you will in your turn concede that it did not last long, and that all too soon you tired of a constraint for which you believed you were not sufficiently compensated by the positive impression it made upon me.

It was then that you abused my innocence and compromised my safety by daring to speak to me of feelings you must surely have realized I should find offensive. And while you yourself were only making matters worse by increasing your misdemeanours, I was attempting to find a way of forgetting them by offering you the opportunity to make amends, at least in part. My demands were so fair that even you did not feel able to refuse them. But you asked my indulgence as of right and took advantage of it to ask a favour, which I certainly ought not to have granted, and yet which you obtained from me. You observed none of the conditions that were attached to it. And your letters have been such that each of them imposed upon me a duty not to reply to them. It was at the very moment when your obstinacy obliged me to put a distance between us that I tried – and perhaps I should not have gone to those lengths – the only means that might allow me to effect a reconciliation between us. But what currency does an honourable feeling have in your eyes? You hold friendship in contempt and, in your blind folly, set at nought both shame and unhappiness, seeking nothing but your own pleasure and victims to sacrifice to it.

As frivolous in your actions as you are inconsequential in your rebukes, you forget about your promises, or rather you make a game of breaking them. Having consented to stay away from me, you come back here without being asked, without any regard for my pleading or for my reasoning, and without even taking the trouble to let me know in advance. You did not fear to expose me to a shock, the effect of which was quite natural, yet which could have been interpreted unfavourably by people around us. And, far from seeking to distract attention or dispel this embarrassing moment which you had caused, you seemed to be doing everything you could to make it worse. At table you deliberately chose your place next to mine. A slight indisposition forced me to leave before the others, and instead of respecting my wish to be alone you engaged everyone to come and disturb me. Back in the drawing room, if I move an inch I find you there next to me. If I utter one word you are always the one who answers. The most casual remark serves as a pretext to revert to a conversation that I do not wish to hear, and which might well compromise me. For, Monsieur, however clever you are, what I can understand I believe others can understand too.

So, though I am forced by you into immobility and silence, you still continue to pursue me. I cannot raise my eyes without encountering yours. I am constantly obliged to avert my gaze. And with an incomprehensible disregard for the consequences you make all eyes focus upon me at the moment when I should have wished to hide away even from my own.

And you complain about my behaviour! You are surprised at my haste to flee from you! Oh, blame me rather for being too kind, and be surprised that I did not leave the instant you arrived. Perhaps I should have done, and you will force me into this rather desperate but necessary course of action if you do not cease your offensive pursuit of me. No, I do not forget, I shall never forget, what I owe myself, or what I owe to the bonds I have formed, which I respect and cherish. And I beg you to believe that if I ever found myself reduced to the unhappy choice of having to sacrifice them or myself, I should not hesitate. Farewell, Monsieur.

From —, 16 September 17**

LETTER 79

The Vicomte de Valmont to the Marquise de Merteuil

I was hoping to go out hunting this morning, but the weather is foul. All I have to read is a modern novel which would be tedious even for a convent girl. Luncheon will be another two hours at the earliest, so despite my long letter of yesterday I am going to chatter to you again. I am positive I shan't bore you, for I am going to speak of *the very handsome Prévan*. I am surprised you do not know about his famous affair, the one which separated the Inseparables.[19] I'll wager you will remember as soon as I start. But here it is, since you ask.

You remember that the whole of Paris was astonished that three women, all very pretty and all three equally talented and able to have similar aspirations, should remain very close from the moment they entered society. At first people thought it was because of their extreme shyness. But soon, surrounded as they were by innumerable suitors whose homage they shared, and made aware of their worth by being the object of so much interest and attention, they none the less became closer. And it always seemed that the success of any one of them was a success for the two others also. We all hoped at least that the advent of love would bring with it some rivalry. Our eligible young men were quarrelling over the privilege of being the apple of discord, and I myself would have joined the ranks if the Comtesse de — had not risen so high in favour at that time that I could not permit myself to be unfaithful to her before I had obtained the pleasure I was seeking.

However, our three beauty queens made their choices at the same ball, as it were in concert. And far from it causing the storm everyone had promised themselves it only rendered their friendship more interesting by the way they confided so charmingly in one another.

The throngs of unhappy suitors then joined the hordes of jealous women, and this scandalous display of loyalty was subjected to public censure. Certain people claimed that in this society of the Inseparables (that was what they called them) the basic law was that all possessions should be held in common, and even love was subject to that law. Others asserted that the three gallants, though safe from male rivals, had women rivals to contend with.[20] People even went so far as to say men had only been admitted for the sake of decency and had only obtained their title without their function.

These rumours, true or false, failed to produce the intended effect. Quite the opposite: the three couples felt that if they did not stick together at this juncture they would be lost. They decided to ride out the storm. Society, which gets bored with everything, soon got bored with its ineffectual satire and, carried along by its natural frivolity, occupied itself with other matters; then, in its usual inconsequential manner, reverted to this subject and, instead of criticizing, praised them. As everything here goes by what is fashionable, enthusiasm won the day. It was becoming a real craze when Prévan took it upon himself to investigate these prodigies, and settle his own and the public's opinion about them.

So he sought out these models of perfection. He was admitted readily into their society, and believed this augured well. He was perfectly aware that happy people are not so easy to approach. But he soon saw in fact that this much vaunted happiness was like that of kings, more envied than desirable. He noticed that among these so-called Inseparables some were starting to seek their pleasures outside the circle and that they were even eager for other entertainment. And he concluded that the bonds of love or friendship were already loosened or broken, and that any strength that remained was only preserved through vanity or habit.

The women, drawn together out of mutual need, kept the appearance of the old intimacy between them. But the men, who were more at liberty with regard to their behaviour, found things they had to do or business they had to attend to. They still complained about it, but no longer neglected it, and evenings were rarely spent all together.

This conduct on their part afforded the assiduous Prévan an advantage; since he was naturally placed next to the woman who was on her own that day, he was able to pay court in turn to all three friends, according to the circumstances. He quickly realized that if he made a choice between them he would be the loser. That the false shame of finding herself the first to be unfaithful would frighten off the one who had been singled out; that wounded vanity would make the other two into enemies, who would be sure to bring strict and lofty principles to bear against him. And lastly he realized that jealousy would most certainly bring back the attention of a rival, who might still be someone to be feared. There would be so many problems; but by proceeding in triplicate, everything became easy: each woman was in favour of it because she had an interest; each man because he thought he did not.

Prévan, who at the time had only one woman to sacrifice, was lucky in that she had become something of a celebrity. The fact that she was a foreigner and had adroitly turned down the homage of a great prince had focused the attention of both court and town upon her. Prévan shared the glory and went up in the estimation of his new mistresses. The only problem was to keep all three intrigues going at the same time, and they all necessarily had to be conducted at the pace of the slowest. As it happens, I have it from one of his confidants that the greatest difficulty was in stopping one of them from reaching maturity nearly a fortnight before the others.

Finally the great day arrived. Prévan, who had obtained the avowals of all three, was already in charge and organized the proceedings, as you will see. Of the three husbands, one was away, another was leaving at dawn the next day and the third was in town. The inseparable friends were supposed to have supper at the future grass-widow's house. But the new lord did not allow them to invite their former suitors. That very morning he divided the letters from his mistress into three packets: in the first he put the portrait she had sent him; in the second a cameo sketch that she had done herself; and in the third, one of her locks of hair. Each took this third part of the sacrifice as complete surrender, and consented in exchange to send a decisive letter breaking off the relationship with her disgraced lover.

This was a great deal, but it was not enough. The one whose husband was in town was only free in the daytime. It was agreed that a feigned indisposition would excuse her from supping at her friend's house, and that the evening would be devoted to Prévan. The night was accorded by the one whose husband was away. And dawn, the lovers' hour, the time the third husband was to leave, was set aside by the last.

Prévan, who thinks of everything, rushed to his beautiful foreign mistress, threw the fit of temper he needed and was repaid in kind, and only left after picking a quarrel which guaranteed him twenty-four hours of freedom. Having made his arrangements, he went back home in the hope of getting some rest. But other business was waiting for him.

The letters of dismissal had been an eye-opener for the disgraced lovers. Each was certain he had been sacrificed to Prévan. And all three, piqued at having had a trick played on them, and in the bad humour that almost always results from the minor humiliation of being abandoned, without telling each other but as if with one mind, resolved to demand satisfaction from their fortunate rival.

So when he got home the latter found their three challenges, which he duly accepted. But, not wishing to lose either the pleasures or the glory of the adventure, he fixed the rendez-vous for the following morning, assigning all three to the same place and time, at one of the gates of the Bois de Boulogne.

When evening came he accomplished his triple task with equal success. At least, he has boasted ever since that each of his new mistresses received in triplicate the vows and proof of his love. Here, as you may guess, the authentication of his story is lacking. All the impartial historian can do is to point out to his incredulous reader that vanity embellished by imagination can bring forth miracles; and moreover that the morning after such a brilliant night appeared to dispense with the need for any care for the future. Whatever the truth of the matter, the following facts are more certain.

Prévan was punctual for the meeting he had arranged. He found his three rivals a little surprised at meeting each other there, and perhaps each already partly consoled by the sight of his companions in misfortune. He approached them in an affable and casual manner and made this speech to them, which has been faithfully reported to me.

'Gentlemen,' he said, 'you must have guessed when you found yourselves all together here that you had the same grounds for complaint about me. I am ready to give you satisfaction. All three of you have an equal right to revenge, so let it be decided by lot who will be the first to try his luck. I have brought neither witness nor second with me. I did not need any when I committed the offence and I do not ask for any now for the reparation.' Then, true gambler that he was, he added: 'I know one rarely wins with *le sept et le va*;[21] but whatever fate awaits me, one has always lived long enough when one has had time to acquire the love of women and the esteem of men.'

While his astonished adversaries looked at each other in silence and were beginning to think, like the gentlemen they were, that perhaps this combat of three against one was not quite fair, Prévan started to speak again: 'I cannot hide from you,' he went on, 'that the night I have just spent has worn me out. It would be generous of you to permit me to mend my strength. I have given orders for breakfast to be served here. Do me the honour of joining me. Let us eat together and, above all, let us eat with gaiety. We may fight over such trifles, but it is my opinion that we should not allow them to spoil our temper.'

The invitation was accepted. They say that Prévan was never more amiable. He was clever enough not to humiliate any of his rivals; he persuaded them that they would all easily have had the same success as he did, and, above all, he made them admit that they would not have let slip such an opportunity either. Once these facts were admitted everything went as smoothly as could be. Before breakfast was finished it had already been said a dozen times that such women did not deserve to be fought over by men of honour. This idea inspired an air of conviviality. Wine reinforced it. And so only a few moments later, no longer just content with not bearing a grudge, they were swearing eternal friendship to one another.

Prévan, no doubt as pleased as anyone by this turn of events, did not wish to forfeit any of the glory. In consequence, adapting his plans to the circumstances with some skill, he said to the three men who had been offended: 'It is not upon me but upon your faithless mistresses you must take revenge. I shall offer you the opportunity to do this. I already feel for you this injury that soon I shall be sharing. For if none of you has managed to keep one single one of them for himself, how could I expect to hold on to all three? Your quarrel has become mine. Please accept supper in my *petite maison* this evening, and I hope I shall not have to defer your revenge any longer.' They asked him to explain. But, with the tone of superiority that he was entitled to take in the circumstances, he replied: 'Gentlemen, I believe I have proved to you that I am skilled in these matters. Count on me.' They all agreed and, after embracing their new friend, they separated until the evening, to await the fulfilment of his promises.

Prévan, without delay, returned to Paris and, as is customary, visited his new conquests. He obtained a promise from all three that they would come that very evening and partake of supper alone with him in his *petite maison*. Two of them certainly raised a few objections. But after the night before, what was there left to refuse? He told them to come at intervals of an hour, which was the time he needed to carry out his plans. After these preparations he retired, warned his three partners in crime, and all four went off with a light heart to await their victims.

They heard the first one arrive. Prévan appeared on his own, receiving her with tender solicitude, conducting her into the sanctuary whose presiding goddess she believed herself to be. Then, disappearing suddenly on some slight pretext, he was himself immediately replaced by the outraged lover.

As you may guess, at that moment the consternation of a woman not yet accustomed to having affairs made his victory very easy. Every reproach he did not make was accounted a favour, and the fugitive slave, once more delivered up to her former master, was only too happy to hope for forgiveness by resuming her former chains. The peace treaty was ratified in a more secluded place. And the stage, now empty, was filled by the other actors, each in their turn in more or less the same manner, and of course with the same dénouement.

Each of the women, however, believed herself to be the only one to have the trick played on her. Their astonishment and embarrassment increased when at suppertime the three couples all met up. But the confusion reached its climax when Prévan, reappearing in their midst, was cruel enough to make his excuses to the three unfaithful women and, thus revealing their secrets, made it perfectly obvious to them to what extent they had been tricked.

Meanwhile they sat down to eat and soon began to feel more comfortable. The men gave themselves up to it and the women submitted. There was some hatred in all their hearts, but the conversation went smoothly just the same. Gaiety led to desire, which lent in its turn a new charm to the proceedings. This astonishing orgy lasted till morning. And when everyone left the ladies must have thought they were forgiven. But the men, who still harboured resentment, broke it off the next day once and for all. And not content with leaving their fickle mistresses, they completed their revenge by publicizing the whole affair. Since that time one of the women is in a convent; the two others are languishing in exile on their estates.

So that is the story of Prévan. It is up to you if you want to add to his glory, and yoke yourself to his triumphal chariot. Your letter really has given me cause for anxiety and I await with impatience a more sensible and intelligible reply to the last one I wrote.

Farewell, my love. Beware of the pleasing or fanciful ideas which so easily lead you astray. Remember that in the kind of life you lead it is not enough to be clever; one single unwise step may mean irremediable disaster. Permit a prudent friend to be sometimes your guide in your pleasures.

Farewell. I still love you just as if you were a reasonable being.

From —, 18 September 17**

LETTER 80

The Chevalier Danceny to Cécile Volanges

Cécile, my darling, when shall we see each other again? How shall I ever learn to live without you? Who will give me the strength and the courage? Never, no, never will I be able to bear this dreadful absence. Each day adds to my sorrow. I see no end to it! Valmont promised me his help and comfort. But

Valmont neglects me and has perhaps forgotten me. He is near his beloved. He no longer knows what one suffers when one is apart from her. When he passed your last letter to me he did not add anything. And yet it is he who is supposed to tell me when I can see you and how. So has he nothing to tell me? You yourself do not speak of him. Is that because you no longer share my longing? Oh Cécile, Cécile, I am so unhappy. I love you more than ever. But this love, which is the delight of my life, is becoming a torment to me.

No, I can no longer live like this. I must see you, I have to, if only for a moment. When I get up, I say: 'I shall not see her today.' I go to bed saying: 'I have not seen her today.' The days so long and not a moment of happiness in them! All is privation, regret, despair. And all these ills spring from the place where I used to obtain all my pleasure! Add to these mortal sufferings my worries about your own pain and you will have some idea of how I feel. I think of you continually and never without anxiety. If I see you afflicted or unhappy, I suffer all your grief. And if I see you are calm and consoled, then my own worries are redoubled. So there is unhappiness wherever I turn.

Oh, it was not like that when you dwelt where I did! Everything then was pleasure. The certainty of seeing you even made the moments of absence more delicious. The time I had to spend away from you brought me nearer to you as it passed. The use I made of it was never strange to you. If I went about my duties, they made me more worthy of you. If I cultivated my talents, I hoped you would be more pleased with me. Even when the distractions of society carried me far away from you I was not separated from you. At the theatre I tried to guess what might have pleased you. A concert made me think about your talents and our sweet occupations together. In company and when I went walking I seized upon the slightest likeness to you. I compared you with everything and always you had the advantage. Each moment of the day was marked by some new homage and every evening I brought the tribute to your feet.

What is there left for me now? Painful regret, eternal privation and a slight hope that Valmont will break his silence and that yours will change to concern. Only ten leagues[22] separate us

– such a short distance to cross, but for me an insurmountable obstacle! And when I implore my friend and my mistress to help me surmount it, they both remain cold and indifferent! Far from coming to my aid, they do not even reply.

So what has happened to Valmont's commitment and friendship? And especially what has become of your tender sentiments, which made you so ingenious at finding a way for us to see each other every day? Sometimes I remember that my desire to see you had to be sacrificed to other considerations or things I had to do, though I did not cease to want to see you. And then, what did you not find to say to me? With how many pretexts did you not combat my arguments? And if you remember, my Cécile, my reasons always gave way to your wishes. I take no credit for that. I did not even feel it was a sacrifice. What you wanted I was only too eager to grant. But now it is my turn to ask you something. And what is my demand? To see you for a moment, to renew and receive the vows of eternal love. Is that no longer the thing that would make you as happy as it would me? I reject this desperate thought, which would crown my misery. You do love me, you will always love me. I believe it, I am certain of it, I never wish to doubt it. But my situation is terrible, and I cannot put up with it much longer. Adieu, Cécile.

Paris, 18 September 17**

LETTER 81

The Marquise de Merteuil to the Vicomte de Valmont

How pitiful your fears are, and how thoroughly they prove my superiority over you! And you want to teach me, to guide me? Oh my poor Valmont, what a distance there still is between us! No, all the vanity of your sex would not suffice to close the gap separating us. Because you yourself would not be able to carry out my plans, you say they are impossible! You are a weak and vain man; how ill it becomes you to try to assess my methods or weigh up my resources! Truly, Vicomte, your advice has put me in a bad humour, I can tell you.

That, in order to disguise the quite extraordinary ineptitude of your dealings with your Présidente, you boast about momentarily disconcerting this timid woman who is in love with you as though you have won some kind of victory, I can accept; that you have managed to obtain a look, one single look, I can smile at and allow; that, in spite of yourself, you feel how little your conduct is worth, and hoped to divert my attention by telling me about your superhuman efforts to bring together two children who are both longing to see one another, and who, it should be said in passing, owe the ardour of their desire to me alone, I even grant you as well; and, finally, that these remarkable achievements authorize you to lecture to me that *it is better to use one's time in executing these projects than in relating them* – this vanity does me no harm either, and so I forgive you. But that you can believe I need your wisdom, or that I shall go astray if I do not defer to your advice, or that I must sacrifice to it my pleasures or my fancies – really, Vicomte, you are becoming too conceited about the confidence I am willing to place in you!

What have you ever done that I have not outdone a thousand times? You have seduced, even ruined, numerous women. But what problems did you have to conquer? What obstacles did you have to overcome?[23] So where is the real merit in that? A handsome face, the result of pure chance. Nice manners, which can almost always be acquired with a little practice. Wit, certainly, but prattle will do instead at a pinch. A certain admirable boldness that one might attribute solely to the ease of your first conquests. And, if I am not greatly mistaken, that is all. For as far as celebrity goes, you will not ask me, I suppose, to believe that your talent for creating and seizing the opportunity for scandal counts for very much.

As for wisdom, sensibility, name me one woman, not counting myself, who does not possess more of that than you? Huh! Your Présidente is leading you like a child.

Believe me, Vicomte, one rarely acquires the qualities one

can do without. As you fight without any risk, you do not have to take precautions. For you men defeat is only one victory less. In this unequal contest we are lucky not to lose, and you are unlucky not to win. If I were to grant you as many talents as we have, we should still surpass you by far through our continual need to make use of them!

Supposing I grant that you put as much skill into victory as we do into defence or surrender, you must at least agree that that skill becomes useless after you have achieved success. Occupied solely with your new pleasure, you deliver yourselves up to it unreservedly, without hesitation. Whether it lasts or not is of small consequence to you.

In fact, to talk the jargon of love, those reciprocal promises given and received can be made or broken at will by you alone. We are fortunate if you, contenting yourselves with our total, humiliating submission, decide in your unpredictable way upon secrecy rather than scandal, and do not turn yesterday's idol into tomorrow's victim!

But if the unfortunate woman is the first to feel the weight of her chains, what risks she has to run in her attempts to escape or simply lighten them! It is only in fear and trembling that she tries to rid herself of the man her heart struggles to reject. If he insists on remaining, what she once granted to love becomes a tribute to fear.

> Her arms still open though her heart is closed.

Caution obliges her to skilfully untie these same bonds that you would simply have torn apart. She is at the mercy of her enemy, and if he is ungenerous she is without resources. And how may men be expected to show generosity when they, although sometimes praised for this quality, are never thought any the less of if they show none?

I am sure you will not deny these truths that are so obvious they have become banal. Since, then, you have seen me controlling events and opinions; making these formidable men the playthings of my caprices or fantasies; depriving some of the will, others of the power to harm me; since, then, according to the impulse of the moment, I have been able to attach or reject as suitors

These unthroned tyrants now become my slaves*

and, in the midst of these frequent vicissitudes, kept my reputation pure; have you not perforce come to the conclusion that, born to avenge my sex and conquer yours, I have succeeded in inventing strategies for doing so that before me were quite unheard of?

So keep your advice and your fears for those silly women who say they are women 'of feeling'; who fondly believe that Nature has placed their senses in their heads; who, without ever thinking about it, invariably confuse love with the lover; who foolishly imagine that the only source of pleasure is the man with whom they have sought it, and, like all truly superstitious people, accord to the priest the respect and the faith which is due to the Deity alone.

Keep your fears too for those women, more vain than prudent, who cannot bear the thought of being abandoned when needs be.

Tremble, above all, for those women whose minds are active while their bodies are idle; you call them 'sensitive' women – who fall in love so easily and overpoweringly. They feel they have to, even when they take no pleasure in it. And, abandoning themselves unreservedly to their seething imagination, they give birth to letters full of tenderness, but fraught with danger, and are not afraid to confide these proofs of their weakness to the object of their love. They are imprudent creatures, for in their present lover they fail to perceive their future enemy.

But I, what have I in common with these empty-headed women? When have you ever seen me break the rules I have

---

* It is not known whether this line, like the one above, 'Her arms still open though her heart is closed', are quotations from little-known works, or whether they form a part of Madame de Merteuil's prose. What inclines us to the latter view is the multitude of errors of this nature which may be found in the whole of this correspondence. Those of the Chevalier Danceny are the only exception to this. Perhaps as he sometimes read poetry his ear was more attuned and he was able to avoid the error more easily.

laid down for myself or betray my principles? I say my principles, and I use that word advisedly. For they are not, like those of other women, discovered by chance, accepted uncritically or followed out of habit. They are the fruit of my deepest reflections. I have created them, and I can say that I am what I have created.[24]

When I entered society I was still a young girl, condemned by my status to silence and inaction, and I took advantage of this opportunity to observe and reflect. They were under the impression that I was scatterbrained and woolly-headed; I was indeed paying scant attention to what they were so anxious to tell me, but I thought long and hard about what they were trying to hide from me.

This useful curiosity, while it increased my knowledge, also taught me to dissemble. I was often forced to hide the objects of my attention from the eyes of the people around me, but I tried to direct my own wherever I wished. From that time on I managed to put on at will that air of detachment you have so often admired. Encouraged by this first success, I learned then to control the various expressions on my face. If I was feeling unhappy, I practised adopting a look of serenity or even joy. I even went so far as to deliberately cause myself pain in order to make an attempt at the simultaneous expression of pleasure. I laboured, with as much care and even more difficulty, to suppress the symptoms of an unexpected joy. And that is how I have been able to exercise over my physiognomy the power that you have on occasions found so astonishing.

I was still very young and almost completely lacking seriousness, but I had only my thoughts to call my own and was indignant if anyone tried to wrest them from me or surprise me against my will. Armed with these first weapons, I practised using them. No longer content with remaining enigmatic, I amused myself taking on different personas, and once I was sure of my bodily gestures I set myself to study my speech. I determined both according to circumstance, or even just according to my fancy. From that moment on my thoughts were for my benefit and mine alone, and I only revealed to others what I found it useful to reveal.

This work on my self focused my interest on facial expressions and the nature of their physiognomy. And through this my eye has become sharper, though experience has taught me not to trust it totally. But all in all it has rarely let me down.

At not quite fifteen I already possessed the talents to which a great many of our political figures owe their reputation, and yet I was still only learning the first elements of the science I intended to master.

As you may guess, in common with all young girls I was trying to find out about love and its pleasures. But never having been in the convent, not having a best friend, and watched over continually by a vigilant mother, my notions about it were of the vaguest and I was unable to clarify them. My own nature, on which I have since then most certainly had reason only to congratulate myself, offered me no clue at that time. You might almost have thought it was silently working towards perfecting what it had begun. Only my head was in a whirl. I did not desire to *enjoy* these pleasures, I just wished to know. This desire for knowledge suggested to me the means of acquiring it.

I felt that the only man I could talk to about this matter without compromise was my confessor. So I took my decision. I got over my slight feeling of shame. And, laying claim to a sin I had not committed, I accused myself of having done *all that women do*. That was what I said. But even as I said it I truthfully had no idea what I was talking about. My hopes were not completely dashed nor entirely fulfilled; the fear of betraying myself prevented me from further explanation. But the priest made it out to be such a big sin that I came to the conclusion the pleasure must be exquisite. And after the desire for knowledge came the desire for gratification.

Who knows where this desire might have led me? With my total lack of experience at that time, perhaps one single occasion would have been my ruin. Luckily for me, my mother announced only a few days later that I was to be married. Straight away my curiosity was quelled by the certainty that I should soon know everything; I was a virgin when I landed in the arms of Monsieur de Merteuil.

I waited confidently for the moment of enlightenment, and

I had to remind myself to show embarrassment and fear. That first night, generally considered 'cruel' or 'sweet', offered me only an opportunity for experience. Pain or pleasure, I observed it all precisely and viewed these different sensations simply as facts to be collected and meditated upon.

I soon acquired a taste for this sort of study. But, sticking to my principles, and with a perhaps instinctive feeling that the one person I should not confide in was my husband, I resolved to appear to him to be indifferent to things I felt quite keenly. This apparent frigidity was subsequently the unshakeable foundation of his blind trust in me. On further reflection I then also indulged in the sort of harebrained behaviour to be expected at my age. And he never thought me more like a child than when I was most flagrantly deceiving him.

However, I confess I allowed myself at first to be drawn into the social whirl, and I gave myself up utterly to futile distractions. But after a few months, Monsieur de Merteuil having carried me off to his gloomy country house, the fear of boredom revived my interest in study. And, finding myself surrounded only by people so remote from me as to put me above all suspicion, I took advantage of it to widen my experience. It was then that, more than at any other time, I was convinced that love, which people pretend is the cause of our pleasures, is at most only an excuse for them.

Monsieur de Merteuil's illness came to interrupt these agreeable occupations. I had to accompany him to Town where he went to seek treatment. He died, as you know, a short time afterwards. And although, all in all, I had no reason to complain about him, I appreciated just as keenly the value of the freedom my widowhood was about to afford me, and I promised myself I would make the most of it.

My mother thought I would enter the convent, or come back and live with her. I refused to do either. And the only concession I made to decency was to go back to the same house in the country, where I still had some observations to make.

I backed them up with some reading. But do not imagine it was all the sort of reading that you have in mind. In novels I studied manners; in the philosophers, opinions; I even tried to find out from the strictest moralists what they demanded of us, to be certain of what it was possible to do, what it was best to think and how one must appear to be. Once focused upon these three, only the last presented a few difficulties in practice; these I hoped to overcome, and I pondered how this might be done.

I began to tire of my country pleasures, which were not varied enough for my active mind. I felt the need for a flirtation that would reconcile me to love. Not that I might truly feel it, but that I might inspire it and feign it. Although I had been told and had read that one could not feign this feeling, I saw that to achieve it all I need do was combine the talents of an actor with the wit of a writer. I practised these two genres, perhaps with some success. But instead of striving for vain applause in the theatre I resolved to use for my own happiness what so many others have sacrificed to vanity.

A year went by in these different occupations. My period of mourning over, I emerged and returned to town full of great projects. The first obstacle I encountered took me by surprise.

The long period of austere retreat had given me a veneer of prudishness which frightened away our most eligible men. They kept their distance, abandoning me to a host of bores who all were asking my hand in marriage. My problem was not how to refuse them. But several of these refusals displeased my family, and I was wasting time in domestic squabbles, a time I had promised myself I was going to pass in far more pleasant occupations. So, in order to attract some and repel others, I was obliged to flag up a few misdemeanours, and take as many pains to harm my reputation as I had thought I would need to preserve it. I easily succeeded, as you can guess. But, not being carried away by passion, I did only what I thought necessary, and measured out my doses of flightiness with great care.

As soon as I had achieved my goal I retraced my steps and laid the honour of my reformed character at the feet of some of those women who, being devoid of charm, have to rely on merits and virtue alone. This was a move which was worth a great deal more to me than I had hoped for. The grateful duennas appointed themselves my apologists. And their blind enthusiasm for what they called their 'handiwork' was carried to the point where, at the least suggestion of any remark made about me, the whole battalion of prudes would cry 'scandal' and 'slander'. The same means also earned me the support of those women who did have pretensions, for they, being persuaded that I was renouncing my pursuit of the same career as themselves, singled me out as an object for praise every time they wanted to prove they did not speak ill of everyone.

In the meantime my aforementioned conduct had brought me lovers. And, in order to operate between them and my loyal protectors, I showed myself to be a sensitive but fastidious woman, whose excessive delicacy was her defence against passion.

And so I began to display on the stage of life the talents I had acquired. My first objective was to acquire the reputation of being invincible. To achieve this, I pretended to receive only the homage of men I did not like. I made use of them to gain credit for resisting, while I abandoned myself fearlessly to the lover of my choice. But the shyness I affected never permitted him to accompany me in society, and so everyone's attention was always fixed upon the suitors who were unhappy.

You know how quickly I take decisions: that is because I have observed that it is nearly always preliminary planning that betrays a woman's secret. Whatever one does, one's manner is never the same after as it is before success. This difference never escapes the close observer, and I have found it is less dangerous to make a wrong choice than to have my reasons for making it exposed. I further gain by this in that I remove the likely assumptions by which alone we may be judged.

These precautions, along with that of never writing things down and never providing any proof of my defeat, might seem excessive, but to me they have never seemed enough. In exploring deep in my own heart I have studied the hearts of others. And I have perceived that there is no one without a secret which it is in his interest never to reveal: a truth which they seem to have understood better in ancient times than they do now, and of which the story of Samson is perhaps just a clever allegory. A latter-day Delilah, I have always used my powers, as she did, to discover this important secret.[25] Ha! How many modern Samsons have had their hair held to my scissors! They are the ones I have stopped being afraid of. They are the only ones I have sometimes allowed myself to humiliate. More subtle tactics with the rest have guaranteed their discretion: artfully causing them to be unfaithful to me, so as not to appear fickle myself, a pretence of friendship, an apparent trust, a few generous gestures, the notion they all flatter themselves with that they have been my one and only lover. Finally, when these means have failed, I have been able to foresee the break-up of the affair and quash in advance by means of smears and ridicule any credence these dangerous men may have obtained.

What I am telling you now you have seen me constantly putting into practice; and yet you question my prudence! Well, just remember the time when you started paying court to me. Never had anyone's attentions flattered me so much. I desired you before I set eyes upon you. Seduced by your reputation, it seemed to me that I needed to have you before I could account myself a success. I was longing to cross swords with you. It is the only one of my desires which has ever momentarily had power over me. Yet had you wished to ruin me, what means would you have found? Empty words that left no trace and which your own reputation would have helped to render suspect, and a series of unlikely facts which, had you recounted them, would have seemed like a badly structured novel. I have since, it is true, told you all my secrets. But you know what our common interests are, and whether, of the two of us, I am the one who should be taxed with lack of prudence.*

Since I am giving an account of myself, I wish to be precise. I can hear you saying that I am at least at the mercy of my chambermaid. It is true that even though she is not party to my innermost feelings, she is to my actions. When you spoke to me about this matter before, my only answer was that I was sure of her. And the proof that this reply was enough for your peace of mind is that since then you have confided some fairly dangerous secrets to her on your own account. But now that you are resentful towards Prévan and getting agitated about all

---

* We shall learn later in Letter 152 not Monsieur de Valmont's secret, but its nature, more or less. And the reader will understand why we have not been able to clarify it further.

this, I am sure that you will not take my word for it, so I shall explain further.

First, this girl and I were nursed at the same breast, and this bond, which you and I may not regard as a bond, carries a considerable weight with people of that class. Moreover, I know her guilty secret, and better than that: she was the victim of a disastrous love affair and would have been lost but for me.[26] Her parents positively bristled with honour, and all they wanted to do was have her locked up. They approached me. I saw at a glance how useful to me their anger might be. I gave my support, applied for and obtained the order for arrest. Then, suddenly shifting to the side of clemency, and managing to convince her parents of it as well, I turned my credit with the old minister to advantage, and made them all agree to leave this order in my hands, with the power to prevent or demand its execution according to my judgement of the girl's future conduct. So she knows that I hold her fate in my hands. And if this were not enough to prevent her, is it not evident that, as soon as her behaviour and her just punishment became public knowledge, that would very soon deprive what she says of all credibility?

To these precautions, which I should call basic, I might add, as necessary, and according to circumstance and opportunity, a thousand more which are suggested to me by reflection or habit. It would be tedious to go into too much detail, but nevertheless they are important, and you must take the trouble to review them in the light of my whole conduct if you wish to arrive at a proper understanding of them all.

But to expect that, after I have gone to such lengths, I should not reap the rewards, or that, having raised myself so much above other women by my painstaking efforts, I should now consent to creep along as they do, in between recklessness and timidity; or, above all, that I should so fear a man that I saw no safety anywhere except in fleeing him? No, Vicomte, never. One must conquer or die. As for Prévan, I want him, and I shall have him. He wants to be able to say so, and he shall not say so. And there, in brief, is our story. Adieu.

From —, 20 September 17**

LETTER 82

Cécile Volanges to the Chevalier Danceny

Dear God, how your letter distressed me! And to think how
impatient I was to receive it! I hoped to find consolation, but
now I am sadder than before. I wept so much when I read it,
but that is not what I blame you for. I have wept many times
already on your account, without it greatly troubling me. But
this time it is not at all the same.

What do you mean, your love has become a torment to you,
you cannot live like this any more, and you cannot put up with
this situation any longer? Are you going to stop loving me
because it is not so pleasurable as it was before? It seems to me
that I am no happier than you, quite the opposite, and yet I
love you all the more. If Monsieur de Valmont has not written,
it is not my fault. I have not been able to ask him to because
I have not been on my own with him, and we have agreed never
to speak to each other when everyone is there. And that is for
your sake as well, so that he can do what you wish all the
sooner. I am not saying that I do not wish it too; you cannot
be in any doubt of that. But what do you expect me to do? If
you believe it is so easy, why don't you find a way? Nothing
would please me more.

Do you think it is nice for me being scolded every day by
Mamma when at one time she never said anything? Quite the
contrary. At the moment it is worse than when I was in the
convent. I have been consoling myself, thinking it was for your
sake, and there have even been moments when I found I was
quite happy about it. But now I see that you are angry as well,
without me being in any way to blame, it makes me more
unhappy than anything that has ever happened to me before.

Even receiving your letters is difficult, and, if Monsieur de
Valmont were not as agreeable and clever as he is, I should not
know what to do. Writing to you is even more difficult. In the
mornings I do not dare because Mamma's room is right next
to mine and she comes into my room the whole time. Sometimes

I can in the afternoons, on the pretext of singing or playing the harp. But I still have to break off at each line so that I can be heard practising. Luckily my chambermaid sometimes falls asleep in the evenings and I tell her I can make ready for bed on my own, so that she will go away and leave me the light. And then I have to hide behind the curtain so that my light cannot be seen, and listen for the tiniest sound so that I can hide everything under the bedclothes if anybody comes. I wish you were there to see! You would realize that you have to be really in love to do things like that. Anyway, I truly am doing all I can and I wish I could do more.

Of course I do not refuse to tell you that I love you and always will. I have never meant it more. And yet you are angry! Before I said it, you assured me that that was all you needed to make you happy. You cannot deny it. It is in your letters. Though I do not have them any more, I remember them as if I read them every day. But because we are not together you no longer feel the same way! But presumably this absence will not last for ever! Oh God, how unhappy I am! And you are the reason for it!

About your letters, I hope you have kept the ones that Mamma took away from me, that she sent back to you; surely there will come a time when things won't be so difficult as they are at present and you can give them all back to me. How happy I shall be when I can keep them for ever and ever without anybody interfering! At present I shall give mine to Monsieur de Valmont because otherwise it will be too risky. All the same, I never give them back without feeling greatly troubled.

Goodbye, my dearest. I love you with all my heart. I shall love you all my life. I hope you are not annoyed any more now. If I were certain of that, I should not be anxious any more either. Write to me as soon as you can, for I feel that I shall not be happy until then.

From the Chateau of —, 21 September 17**

LETTER 83

The Vicomte de Valmont to the Présidente de Tourvel

Let us, I earnestly beg you, Madame, resume the conversation
that was so unfortunately interrupted! Then I may finally prove
to you how different I am from the odious portrait people have
painted of me and, most of all, continue to enjoy that delightful
confidence you were beginning to show in me! What charms
you bestow upon virtue! How much more lovely and beautiful you render all honest feelings! Indeed, that is your special
magic, the most potent; and the only one both powerful and
honourable.

Merely to see you is to desire to please you. Simply hearing
your voice in company suffices to increase this desire. But he
who has the good fortune to know you better, he who at times
is privileged to look into your heart, soon gives in to a more
noble passion: he loves and worships you utterly, and adores
in you the image of all goodness. I am perhaps more inclined
than another to love and seek this out, after being led astray by
one or two errors that made me a stranger to these virtues; you
are the one who has drawn me back to them, you who have
made me feel once again how perfectly delightful they are. Will
you call this new love a crime? Will you find fault with your
handiwork? Will you even blame yourself for participating in
this? What harm can come from such a pure feeling, and what
sweet delight would you not find in tasting it?

My love frightens you; you find it violent, unbridled! Temper
it with a gentler love. Do not refuse the power over me that I
am offering you, from which I vow never to seek to escape; a
power which, I venture to believe, might indeed further the
cause of virtue. What sacrifice would I find too painful to make
if I were sure that your heart would know what it had cost
me? Is there a man so unfortunate that he may not enjoy the
privations he imposes on himself? Which man would not prefer
one word, one gracious look bestowed, to all the pleasures he
might take or seize by force! And you believed I was such a

man! And you were afraid of me! Ah, why does your happiness not depend upon me! What sweet revenge would there be for me in making you happy! But barren friendship cannot create this gentle power. Only love can.

This word intimidates you! Why? It means a more tender attachment, a closer intimacy, a meeting of minds, the same happiness, the same unhappiness, and what is so strange to your nature in that? That is what love is! The love that you inspire and I feel! And especially it is unselfishness, the ability to appreciate an action on its merit and not on its value. An inexhaustible treasure-house for sensitive souls, everything becomes precious when done in its name.

These truths are so easy to grasp, so sweet to practise! What is so frightening about them? What fear can a sensitive man cause you, a man whose love does not allow him any happiness but your own? That is now my only wish. I shall sacrifice every-thing to fulfil it, apart from the feeling which has inspired it. Consent to share this feeling, and you shall order it as you choose. But no longer let it divide us when it ought to unite us. If the friendship you have offered me is not an empty word; if, as you told me yesterday, it is the sweetest feeling known to your heart, let your heart decide. I shall not question its decision. But if it is to be a judge of love, let it give love a hearing. To refuse would be unjust, and friendship is never unjust.

A second meeting would have no more disadvantages than our first. Chance will perhaps yet provide the occasion. You may yourself be able to indicate when. I am willing to believe I have done wrong. Would it not be preferable for you to bring me back to the fold rather than struggle against me, and do you doubt that I shall do what you say? If we had not been interrup-ted by that importunate third party, perhaps I should already have quite come round to your way of thinking. Who knows how far your power may reach?

Shall I say it? At times I am afraid of this invincible power, to which I yield, not daring to count the cost; afraid of this irresistible fascination, which makes you sovereign over my thoughts as well as my actions. Perhaps, alas, it is I who am in the greater danger from this tête-à-tête I am asking for!

Afterwards, a prisoner of my vows, I shall find myself reduced to burning with a love which I know will never die, but without even daring to implore your help! Oh Madame, do not, I beg you, abuse the dominion you have over me! But if you should be happier because of it, if because of it I may seem worthier of you, how greatly my pain will be assuaged by that consolation! Yes, I know. To speak to you again would be to provide you with more powerful weapons against me. I should be utterly subject to your will. I find it easier to defend myself against your letters. They are your words still, but you are not there in person to add strength to them. But the pleasure of hearing your voice makes me face these dangers. At least I shall have the happiness of doing everything for you, even to the detriment of myself. And my sacrifices too will become a homage. It will make me so happy to prove to you in a thousand ways, to prove what I feel a thousand times over, that, not even excepting myself, you are and always will be the object dearest to my heart.

From the Chateau de —, 23 September 17**

LETTER 84

The Vicomte de Valmont to Cécile Volanges

You saw how everything was against us yesterday. All day long I was unable to pass on the letter I had for you. I do not know if I shall find it any easier today. I'm afraid of compromising you by being more zealous than adroit. Such carelessness would be fatal to you, and I should never forgive myself. It would make my friend despair and cause you to be unhappy for the rest of your life. But I know how impatient love is; I feel how painful it must be to experience a delay in what must, in your present circumstances, be your only consolation. By dint of continually mulling over how to remove these obstacles in our path, I have come up with one plan which would be easy to put into operation if you were careful.

I believe I have noticed that the key to the door of your room, which gives on to the corridor, is always on your mother's mantelpiece. Everything would be easy if we had this key, you must see that. But if you cannot get hold of it, I will obtain a similar one instead. All I should need is to have the other one at my disposal for an hour or two. You will easily find an opportunity to take it. And, so that they don't notice it is missing, I am sending you one of mine which looks quite similar, so that no one will know the difference unless they try it. Which they will not. All you have to do is be careful to tie a ribbon on it, a faded blue ribbon like the one on yours.

You should attempt to get this key for tomorrow or the day after, at breakfast-time. It will be easier for you to give it to me then and it can be put back in its place by evening, when your Mamma might notice it more. I can give it back to you at dinner, if we can agree how to do this.

You know that when you go from the salon to the dining room it is always Madame de Rosemonde who brings up the rear. I shall give her my arm. All you must do is put your tapestry away slowly or else drop something on the floor so that you lag behind. Then you will easily be able to take the key that I shall be sure to hold behind my back. As soon as you have taken it, you must make sure you go over to my old aunt again and be attentive to her. If by any chance you were to drop the key, do not allow yourself to look embarrassed. I shall pretend that it was I who did so, and you can totally rely on me.

The fact that your mother trusts you so little and treats you so harshly justifies this small deceit. But, chiefly, this is the only way you can carry on receiving Danceny's letters and pass yours to him. Every other means is really too dangerous and could leave you both with nothing, so as a cautious friend I would feel I were to blame if I were to choose another method.

Once masters of the key we shall have to take a few precautions against the noise of the door and the lock. But that is not a problem. Under the same cupboard where I put your paper you will find some oil and a quill. Sometimes you go to your room and are alone. You must make the most of that time to oil the lock and the hinges. The one thing you must avoid is making any spots which would incriminate you. And it would be best to do it after dark because if you are clever enough to do it properly, it will not show the next day.

If anyone notices, do not hesitate to say that it was the chateau's *frotteur*[27] who did it. In that case you will have to specify the time, and even say what he said to you. As, for instance, that to prevent them rusting he was seeing to all the locks that were not in general use. For you realize it would not have been likely that you witnessed this disturbance without asking the reason for it. It is these little details which make it more realistic, and thus render lies unimportant, because they take away any wish people might have to query them.

After you have read this letter, please read it again and think it over. First, because to do a thing properly you must have a good idea of what it is you are aiming at. But also to make sure I have not forgotten anything. I am so unaccustomed to employing such strategies on my own account that I am not practised in them, and nothing but my close friendship for Danceny and my liking for you would induce me to make use of these means, innocent as they are. I hate everything which seems deceitful. That is the sort of man I am. But your unhappiness has touched me so deeply that I shall do everything possible to alleviate it.

As you can imagine, once we have established this communication between ourselves it will be much easier to secure the meeting Danceny wishes. However, do not speak to him yet about all this. You would only make him more impatient, and the time for satisfaction has not yet quite arrived. You owe it to him, in my view, to calm him down rather than increase his anxiety. I rely on your tact. Goodbye, my dear pupil; for you are indeed my pupil. Try to like your tutor a little, and, most of all, be guided by him. You will reap the benefit. Your happiness is my concern, and you may be sure I shall, in that, find my own.

From —, 24 September 17**

LETTER 85

The Marquise de Merteuil to the Vicomte de Valmont

Now set your mind at rest and, above all, admit I was right. Listen to me, and do not confuse me with other women. I have put a stop to my affair with Prévan. A *stop*! Do you realize exactly what that means? You may now decide which of us may boast about it, him or me. The telling will not be as amusing as the doing; but in any case it would go against the grain, when all you have done is reason and pontificate about the whole affair, that you should get as much pleasure as I, who have put so much time and trouble into it.

However, if you are planning some *coup*, or wish to attempt some enterprise in which he is to figure as the dangerous rival, then now is the moment. He has left the field to you, at least for the time being. And it is possible he will never get over what I have done to him.

How lucky you are to have me for a friend! I am a fairy godmother to you![28] You languish far away from the beautiful woman who obsesses you; one word from me and you find yourself at her side again. You wish to take revenge upon a woman who is harming you; I indicate the place you need to strike and leave her to your tender mercies. Finally, in order to remove a redoubtable rival from the lists, yet again you summon me, and I grant you your wish. And may I say that if you do not spend your life thanking me, you are an ungrateful wretch. So, let us go right back to the beginning of my affair.

The rendez-vous that I fixed so loudly on my way out of the Opera* was overheard, as I had hoped it would be. Prévan was there. And when the Maréchale obliged him by saying how gratified she was to see him twice running at her evenings, he was particular to say that since Tuesday evening he had undone a thousand arrangements in order to have this evening free. *A nod is as good as a wink!* But, as I wished to reassure myself that I was the real object of this flattering enthusiasm, I decided

* See Letter 74.

to force my new suitor to choose between me and his favourite pastime. I declared I would not play cards. He found, therefore, a thousand pretexts not to play. And so it was over the game of *lansquenet*[29] that I scored my first triumph.

I engaged the Bishop of — in conversation. I chose him because of his relationship with the hero of the day, wanting to give him every opportunity of approaching me. I was also very happy to have a respectable witness who could, if necessary, provide evidence of my conduct and conversation. This plan succeeded.

After the usual generalities, Prévan soon dominated the conversation and tried various lines in turn to see which one I would find most pleasing. I refused to speak of sentiment, since I do not believe in it; I put a halt to his frivolous remarks with my serious tone, since they seemed to me too flippant for a beginning. He was reduced to a tone of courteous friendship. And it was under this flag of banality that we joined battle.

The Bishop did not come down for supper.[30] So Prévan gave me his arm and naturally found himself placed next to me at table. One must be fair. He kept up our private exchanges with a great deal of skill while still apparently making general conversation, of which he appeared to be bearing the entire burden. At dessert there was talk of a new play that was supposed to be put on the following Monday at the Comédie Française. I expressed a few regrets that I did not have my box that night; he offered me his and I refused first of all, as one does. To which he responded rather amusingly that I did not understand him; that of course he would not give up his box to someone he did not know, but he meant simply to inform me that it would be at Madame la Maréchale's disposal. She went along with this little joke, and I accepted.

Once back in the salon, as you can guess, he asked for a seat in this box. And as the Maréchale, who is very kindly disposed towards him, promised he could have it *if he behaved himself*, he took the opportunity to conduct one of these conversations with a double meaning, of the kind you have said he is so talented at. Going down on his knees to her like an obedient child, as he put it, while ostensibly asking what she meant and begging her to explain, he passed many flattering, affectionate remarks which quite plainly were intended for me. Several people did not return to cards after supper and the conversation became more general and less interesting. But our eyes spoke volumes. I say our eyes. I should say his, for mine registered only surprise. He must have thought I was startled and that my mind was extremely preoccupied with the prodigious effect he was having upon me. I think I left him very satisfied with himself, and I was no less pleased.

The following Monday I was at the theatre as agreed. Despite your interest in literary matters, I have nothing to say about the spectacle except that Prévan has a prodigious talent for flattery and the play was a flop. That is all I gathered. But I was sorry when the evening was over, for in fact I enjoyed it enormously. And to make it last longer I asked the Maréchale to come and sup with me, which gave me a pretext to invite my amiable flatterer, who asked only time to hurry to the Comtesses de P—* and make his excuses. Their name filled me with rage again as I saw quite clearly that he was going to start sharing confidences with them. I remembered your wise advice and determined to pursue the affair, sure that I would be able to cure him of such dangerous indiscretions in future.

As a newcomer among my friends, of whom there were not very many that evening, he was obliged to pay me the usual attentions. So when we went in to supper he offered me his hand. As I accepted it, I was wicked enough to make my own tremble just a little in his. I lowered my eyes and my breath quickened as I walked, as if I could foresee my defeat and was in awe of my conqueror. He fell for it straight away. The traitor! In a split second his tone and attitude changed. He had been gallant, he became tender. Not that the remarks themselves were very different. Circumstances saw to that. But the expression in his eyes grew softer, more caressing. There was a gentler inflection in his voice. His smile was no longer calculated but more contented. And when he spoke his salvos became fewer and kinder, and cleverness gave way to compliments. I ask you, would you have done better?

* See Letter 70.

I, for my part, became so pensive that people could not but notice. And when they chided me for it, I was adroit enough to make a clumsy defence of myself, and to flash a quick but timid and disconcerted glance at Prévan, one that was designed to make him think I was afraid he might guess the reason for my agitation.

After supper, when the good Maréchale was telling one of the stories she is always telling, I availed myself of the opportunity to arrange myself in an attitude of dreamy abandon and sweet reverie upon my ottoman. I was quite content that Prévan should see me like this. In fact, he honoured me with a quite particular attention. You can guess that my shy glances did not dare meet those of my conqueror. But as I aimed them in a more modest manner in his direction I quickly realized that I was obtaining the effect I hoped to produce.[31] I still had to persuade him that I shared his feelings. So when the Maréchale announced she was about to leave I cried in a soft and tender voice: 'Oh, I was so comfortable here!' But I got up. Before leaving her I asked what her plans were, so that I could have a pretext to say what mine were and let it be known that two days hence I would be at home. Upon which everyone went their way.

Then I began to think it over. I did not doubt that Prévan would take advantage of the kind of rendez-vous I had just given him; that he would come early enough to find me alone, and that he would launch a strong attack. But I was also very sure that, given my reputation, he would not treat me in the casual fashion in which men, if they ever do, treat only loose or inexperienced women. And I could foresee certain success for me if he uttered the word *love*, and especially if he attempted to make me say it.

How easy it is to deal with you *men of principle*! Sometimes a mawkish lover will disconcert you by his shyness, or embarrass you with his transports of passion. He may be in a fever that, like any other, has moments when one shivers and sweats; sometimes the symptoms vary. But a well-regulated advance is so predictable! The arrival, the comportment, the tone, the speech – I knew it all from the day before. So I will not give you an account of our conversation, which you will have no trouble supplying for yourself. Only observe that I gave him every possible help in my feigned defence. Embarrassment, to allow him time to speak; faulty arguments, to allow him to counter them; fear and mistrust, to make him return to his protestations; and I met his perpetual refrain, 'I ask only one word from you', with a silence which seemed to keep him waiting only in order to increase his desire. And in addition to all that, a hand taken a hundred times, always withdrawn but never refused. You could spend the whole day doing that. We spent one mortal hour, and should perhaps still be at it if we had not heard a carriage enter the courtyard. This happy contretemps made his demands all the more insistent, as you might expect, and, seeing I would now be safe from a surprise attack, I prepared myself with a long-drawn-out sigh and allowed myself to utter the blessed word. Someone was announced and a short time later quite a few had arrived.

Prévan asked if he might call the next morning, and I agreed. But, taking care to defend myself, I ordered my chambermaid to stay in my bedroom the whole time, from which, as you know, one can see everything that goes on in my dressing room, and it was there that I received him. We talked freely and, as we were both wanting the same thing, we were soon in agreement. But we had to get rid of our unwelcome spectator. And that was my moment to strike.

Painting a fictitious picture of my domestic arrangements, I easily managed to persuade him that we should not be free, not for one moment, and that we should regard the time we had enjoyed together the day before as a sort of miracle, but that all the same it had exposed me to too great a danger, since anyone could have entered my drawing room at any moment. I did not fail to add that all these habits had become established because until now they had never got in my way. And I insisted at the same time on how impossible it was to change them without compromising myself in the eyes of my servants. He feigned sadness, became moody, told me I did not love him. And you can guess how touching I found that! But, wishing to strike the final blow, I sought help in tears. It was exactly like 'Zaïre, you are weeping.'[32] The power he supposed he had over me, and the hopes he entertained of ruining me as he chose, did duty with him for all Orosmane's love.

This *coup de théâtre* accomplished, we got back to our arrangements. Since there was no possibility in the day we wondered about night time. But my porter proved to be an insurmountable obstacle, and I did not allow him to be bribed. He suggested the small garden gate. But I had foreseen this and I invented a dog, who was calm and quiet by day but a real demon at night. The ease with which I went into all this detail was just what was necessary to make him more determined. So then he suggested the most ridiculous expedient of all, and that was the one I agreed to.

First, his manservant was as trustworthy as he was. In that he was not wrong, one was as bad as the other. I was to give a big supper party at my house; he would be there; he would choose his moment and leave alone. The servant, in on the plan, would quickly call his cab and open the door, and he, Prévan, instead of getting in, would adroitly slip away. His coachman would not notice a thing. And thus having left, as everyone else thought, he would still be in the house, and it was simply a question of knowing if he would be able to reach my room. At first, I admit, my problem was to find objections to this plan that were weak enough for him to appear to be demolishing them. He countered with examples of its previous use. To hear him you would think there was nothing more banal than this tactic; he had often used it himself. It was indeed the one he used most frequently, being the least dangerous.

Crushed by this irrefutable expertise, I candidly admitted that I did have a secret stairway leading very near to my boudoir. I could leave the key to it, and it would be possible for him to lock himself in and wait there without too much danger until my women retired. And then, to make my consent seem more believable, a moment later I pretended I no longer wanted that, and was only persuaded again on condition of his perfect submission, of his discretion . . . Ah, what discretion! Anyway, I was very happy to give proofs of my love, but not to satisfy his.

His departure, which I was forgetting to tell you about, was supposed to be by the little garden gate. He would only have to wait until dawn and Cerberus would not make a sound. Not a soul passes that way at that hour and people are fast asleep. If you are surprised by this string of feeble arguments, it is because you are forgetting the nature of the situation between us. Why bother to invent better ones? He was quite happy for all of this to be known, and I was very sure that it should not be known. The day was fixed for the next but one.

You will observe that the affair is all arranged and no one has seen Prévan with me as yet. I meet him for supper at a friend's house, he offers her his box for a new play and I accept a seat in it. During the performance and in front of Prévan I invite this woman to supper. I can scarcely not invite him as well. He accepts and comes to see me two days later, as custom demands. In fact, he comes to see me the following morning. But apart from the fact that morning visits are no longer thought anything out of the ordinary, I am the only one who should judge whether it is too improper. And I place him in the category of people who are not such close friends by a written invitation to a formal dinner. I may well remark, like Annette, 'That's all there is to it in fact.'[33]

The fateful day arrived, the day I was to lose my virtue and my reputation. I gave my orders to the faithful Victoire, and she carried them out, as you shall soon see.

Evening came. I already had a great many people at my house when Prévan was announced. I received him with studied politeness, a mark of how little I knew him. And I put him at the Maréchale's table for cards, since she was the person through whom we had met. The evening only produced a very short note, which my discreet suitor managed to pass to me, and which I burned, according to my custom. In it he declared that I could count on him, and these important words were buried under the usual parasitical words like love, friendship, etc., which are invariably used on such occasions.

At midnight when the card games were over, I proposed a short *macédoine*.* I had the twofold plan of making Prévan's

* Some readers may not know that a *macédoine* is a medley of several games of chance, among which each player has the right to choose when it is his turn to deal. It is one of the novelties of our day.

escape easier and at the same time making sure it was noticed, which was certain to happen, given his reputation as a card player. I was also very happy for people to remember, if the need arose, that I had not been in a hurry to be left alone.

The card game lasted longer than expected. The devil was tempting me, and I succumbed to the desire to go and console the impatient prisoner. I was just en route to my downfall when I reflected that once I had given myself to him completely I should no longer have the authority over him to keep him in the decent costume which was necessary to my plans. I had the strength to resist. I went back and took my place again, not without a little annoyance at this everlasting card game. But finally it was over and everyone left. As for me, I rang for my women, undressed with all speed and sent them away.

Can't you just see me, Vicomte, scantily clad, walking timidly and looking around me as I did so, and, with an uncertain hand, opening the door to my conqueror? He saw me, quick as a flash. What can I say? I was overcome, completely overcome, before being able to say a word to stop him or protect myself! Then he wanted us to adopt a more convenient position, more suited to the circumstances. He cursed his fine clothes which, he said, meant he could not get near me. He wanted to enter into equal and close combat with me. But my extreme timidity baulked at this project, and my tender kisses did not allow him time. He was busy with other things.

His rights being increased twofold, he again became demanding. But then I said: 'Listen to me, until now you will have a pretty tale to tell to the two Comtesses de P— and to a thousand others: but I am curious to know how you will recount the end of the affair.' With these words I pulled on the bell with all my strength. Instantly I had the advantage, and my action spoke louder than his words. He had done no more than stammer out a word or two when I heard Victoire come running and call the servants she had kept with her, just as I had ordered. Then, adopting my regal tone and raising my voice, I continued: 'Go, Monsieur, and never darken my door again.' Upon which a crowd of my domestics came in.

Poor Prévan lost his wits and, believing it was a trap, when basically it was just a joke, tried to draw his sword. This was most unfortunate, for my intrepid and muscular valet seized hold of him and threw him to the floor. I feared for his life, I must admit. I shouted to them to stop and ordered them to let him go, and just make sure he left my house. My servants obeyed. But rumour was rife among them. They were indignant that someone had insulted *their virtuous mistress*. They all accompanied the unfortunate cavalier out, with a great deal of noise and cries of scandal, as I was hoping. Only Victoire remained, and we busied ourselves during this time with putting my bed to rights.

My servants came upstairs again, still in an uproar, and I, *still greatly distressed*, asked how it was that they had by good fortune been up at that hour. And Victoire recounted that she had given supper to two of her friends, that they had spent the evening with her – in short, all that we had agreed together. I thanked them all and told them to retire, but ordered one of them to go and fetch my doctor immediately. It seemed to me I was right to fear the effects of *my terrible shock*, and it was a sure method of giving currency and fame to this piece of news.

So the doctor came and sympathized a great deal, but only ordered me to rest. As for me, I ordered Victoire to do more than that, and sent her out early to gossip to all the neighbours.

Everything worked out so well that before midday, in fact as soon as my curtains were opened, my devoted neighbour was already at my bedside to know the truth and all the details of this ghastly affair. I was forced to spend a whole hour with her deploring the corruption of our age. A moment later and I received from the Maréchale this note I enclose with mine. Lastly at five o'clock, to my great astonishment, I saw Monsieur —* arrive. He came, he said, to present his apologies that an officer of his corps could have so insulted me. He had only learned of it at dinner with the Maréchale, and had immediately sent an order that Prévan should go to prison. I asked pardon

* Commanding officer of the regiment in which Monsieur de Prévan was serving.

for him, but he refused. So I thought that as his accomplice
I should do likewise and at least stay strictly within walls. So I
had my doors closed to the outside world and gave out that
I was indisposed.

You owe this long letter to my solitude. I shall now write one
to Madame de Volanges, which she will be certain to read
aloud, and where you will hear this story again as it should be
told to the world.

I was forgetting to tell you that Belleroche is beside himself
with anger, and is determined to fight Prévan. The poor boy!
Luckily I shall have time to calm him down ... Meanwhile
I am going to rest, as I am tired of writing. Adieu, Vicomte.

Chateau de —, 25 September 17**, evening

LETTER 86

The Maréchale de — to the Marquise de Merteuil
(Note included in the preceding letter)

Heavens above! What is this I hear, my dear? Can it be that
Prévan has behaved so abominably? And to you! What dangers
one is exposed to! Shall we no longer be safe in our own
homes? Truly these events console one for being old. But what
I shall never be able to console myself for is having been to
some extent the cause of your receiving such a monster in your
house. I promise you that if what they have told me is true, he
will never set foot in my house again. And that is how all
respectable people will behave towards him, if they do their
duty.

I have been told you are very ill, and I am worried about
your health. Let me know how you are, my dear. Or let me
know through one of your women if you cannot yourself. I
only ask one word to set my mind at rest. I should have come
straight round to see you this morning had it not been for my
baths, which my doctor does not allow me to interrupt;[34] and

this afternoon I have to go to Versailles, still on my nephew's business.

Adieu, my dear. Count on my sincere friendship always.

Paris, 25 September 17**

LETTER 87

The Marquise de Merteuil to Madame de Volanges

I am writing to you from my bed, my dear friend. The most disagreeable and unexpected event has made me ill with shock and worry. Of course, it is not that I blame myself at all. But it is always so upsetting for a respectable woman who maintains the modesty becoming to her sex to focus public attention upon herself, when I would have given anything to have avoided this unfortunate affair. And I do not know yet whether I might not decide to go to the country and wait for it all to blow over. This is what it is all about.

At the Maréchale de —'s I met a certain Monsieur de Prévan – you very likely know him by name – with whom I was not acquainted before. But since I met him at her house, I thought I could legitimately think him fit company. He is quite presentable, and seemed not to be lacking in intelligence. Since I was tired of playing cards, I remained the only woman, as it happened, with him and the Bishop of — while everyone else was busy playing *lansquenet*. We all chatted until suppertime. At table a new play that was being discussed provided him with the opportunity to offer his box to the Maréchale, who accepted. And it was agreed that I should have one of the seats. It was for last Monday at the Comédie Française. As the Maréchale was coming to have supper with me after the performance, I suggested to this gentleman that he should accompany her – which he did. Two days later he paid me a visit, which passed in polite conversation, and without there being anything especially remarkable about it. The following day he came to see me in the morning, which did seem a little *unusual*, but instead of making him aware of this by the manner in which I received him, I thought it would be best to warn him politely that we were not yet so intimate as he seemed to believe. And so I sent him a very cool, formal invitation to a supper party I was giving the day before yesterday. I spoke to him no more than three or four times in the course of the evening. And he, for his part, withdrew as soon as his game was over. You will agree that up to this point nothing looked less likely to lead to an affair. After the games we had a *macédoine*, which did not finish until almost two o'clock. And finally I went to bed.

At least half an hour had elapsed after my women had retired when I heard a noise in my room. I opened my curtains in a fright and saw a man come in by the door that leads to my boudoir. I uttered a piercing scream. And with my nightlight I recognized this Monsieur de Prévan, who with inconceivable effrontery told me not to be alarmed, that he would explain his mysterious behaviour, and begged me not to make any noise. As he spoke, he lit a candle. I was so paralysed I was unable to speak. I think it was his easy, unruffled appearance that petrified me still more. But he had not said two words when I saw what this so-called mystery was. And my only reply, as you may guess, was to pull hard on my bell.

By an incredible stroke of luck all the servants on duty had stayed up late in one of my women's rooms and had not yet retired to bed. My chambermaid, who, on entering my room, heard me talking very angrily, was alarmed and summoned everyone. You may imagine the scandal! My servants were furious. For one moment I thought my valet might have killed Prévan. I admit that at the time I was very happy to see them all rally round me. Thinking it over now, I should have preferred only my chambermaid to have come. She would have been enough, and I would have perhaps avoided this public scandal which is causing me such distress.

Instead of that the tumult woke the neighbours, my servants talked, and ever since yesterday it has been all over Paris. Monsieur de Prévan is in prison by order of the commandant of his corps, who was civil enough to call and present his apologies, as he said. This imprisonment is going to make tongues wag even more. But I did not succeed in persuading him of any other course. The Town and Court have been leaving their names at my door, which I have closed to everyone. The few people I have seen since then have told me that justice has been done, and that public indignation against Monsieur de Prévan is at its height. Of course he deserves it, but that does not make the whole affair any less disagreeable.

Moreover, this man must have friends, and ones who are capable of making mischief. Who knows, who can know, what they will think up to harm me? Heavens, how unfortunate a young woman is! She achieves nothing simply by avoiding conduct that might excite gossip; she must defend herself against calumny as well.

Tell me please what you would have done, what you would do in my position; tell me what you think. It is always from you that I have received the sweetest consolation and the wisest advice. It is from you as well that I prefer to receive this.

Goodbye, my dear, good friend. You know what feelings unite us for ever. My love to your dear daughter.

Paris, 26 September 17**

PART THREE

PART THREE

LETTER 88

Cécile Volanges to the Vicomte de Valmont

Despite the real pleasure it gives me, Monsieur, to receive Monsieur le Chevalier Danceny's letters, and though I desire no less than he does that we might be able to see each other again without hindrance, I have still not dared do what you suggest. In the first place, it is too dangerous. This key which you want me to put in the other one's place indeed does look quite a lot like it. Yet there is still some difference, and Mamma looks at everything, and notices everything. Moreover, although it has not been used since our arrival here, it would only take one stroke of ill luck. And if it were noticed I should be ruined for ever. It does seem to me that it is definitely not a good idea, and is going rather far, to make a duplicate key like that! It is true that it is you who would be the one responsible; but, in spite of that, if people were to find out about it, the fault and blame would still be mine, since it would be for me that you would be doing it. I have tried to remove the key twice, and I am sure it would be quite easy if it were for anything else. But, I don't know why, I keep starting to tremble, and I have not been able to summon up the courage to do it. So I think it would be best if we leave things as they are.

If you would kindly continue to be as helpful as you have been until now, I am sure you will always be able to find a way to pass a letter to me. Even the last one, without the unfortunate circumstance that meant you had to turn round suddenly at a certain moment, would have been quite easy. I realize of course that, unlike me, you have other things to do apart from thinking about all this. But I prefer to contain my impatience and not risk so much. I am sure that Monsieur Danceny would be of my opinion. For each time he wanted something which was going to cause me too much distress he always agreed not to do it.

I will return Monsieur Danceny's letter at the same time as this letter, your own and your key. I am none the less most grateful for your kindness and I beg you to continue in it. It is true that I am very unhappy, and were it not for you I should be more so. But it is my mother, when all is said and done. One has to be patient. And as long as Monsieur Danceny still loves me, and you do not abandon me, perhaps there will be happier times.

I have the honour to be, Monsieur, with deepest gratitude, your humble and very obedient servant.

From —, 26 September 17**

LETTER 89
The Vicomte de Valmont to the Chevalier Danceny

If your affair is not proceeding as quickly as you would wish, my dear fellow, I am not entirely to blame. I have here more than one obstacle to overcome. The vigilance and severity of Madame de Volanges are not the only ones. Your young friend is also putting a few obstacles in my way. Either through indifference or timidity she does not always follow my advice. And yet I believe I know better than she does what has to be done.

I had found a simple means that was convenient and safe for giving her your letters, and so facilitate the meetings you desire. But I have not been able to persuade her to make use of it. I am all the more sorry since I see no other way of bringing you together and since, even with regard to your correspondence, I am in constant fear that we shall all three be compromised. Now obviously I do not wish to run that risk, nor expose the pair of you.

I should be sorry, however, if the lack of trust displayed by your little friend should prevent me from being useful to you. Perhaps it would be a good idea if you were to write to her about it. See what you wish to do; it is entirely up to you. For it is not enough to help one's friends, one has to help them after their own fashion. This could also be a further opportunity to make certain of her feelings for you. For the woman who has a will of her own is not as much in love as she professes.

It is not that I suspect your mistress of inconstancy. But she is very young. She is terrified of her Mamma who, as you are well aware, is only out to harm you. And perhaps it would be dangerous if you let too much time go by without her dwelling on you. Do not, however, imagine you need to worry overly about what I am telling you. At bottom there is no reason for misgiving. It is just the concern of a friend.

I shall not write any more, because I also have a few things of my own to attend to. I have not made as much progress as you. But I am as much in love, and that is some consolation. And even if I do not succeed on my own account, if I can be of any use to you I shall think I have used my time wisely. Adieu, my friend.

From the Chateau de —, 26 September 17**

LETTER 90

The Présidente de Tourvel to the Vicomte de Valmont

I very much hope, Monsieur, that this letter will not cause you pain. Or if it does, then at least let it be assuaged by the pain I feel in writing to you. You must know me well enough by now to be assured it is not my intention to distress you. But I am sure you, for your part, do not wish to plunge me into ever-lasting despair. I beg you therefore, in the name of the loving friendship which I have promised you, and indeed in the name of the feelings you have for me, which may be more keen, but are in no wise more sincere, let us see each other no more. Go. And, until then, let us above all avoid these intimate, dangerous conversations in which some inconceivable force compels me to spend my time listening to things I should not be hearing, while I am never able to speak of what I wish.

Only yesterday, when you came to join me in the park my

one intention was to tell you what I am putting in this letter today. But instead, what did I do? Only concern myself with your love ... With your love, which I must never reciprocate! Leave me, leave me, I entreat you.

Do not fear that absence could ever change my feelings for you. How could I manage to conquer them, when I no longer have the strength even to fight them? As you can see, I tell you everything, but I am less fearful of admitting my weakness than of succumbing to it. Yet the control that I have lost over my feelings I shall maintain over my actions. Yes, I am resolved to maintain this, though it cost me my life.

Alas, it was not so very long ago that I thought I should be certain never to have such battles to fight. I was congratulating myself that I was safe from such things. Perhaps I was too triumphant. God has punished me, cruelly punished me, for my pride. But at the very moment He strikes, He still, in His compassion, gives me warning before my fall. And I should be more than ever to blame if I continued to be anything less than prudent, given that my strength is failing.

You have told me a hundred times that you would not wish for a happiness bought by my tears. Oh, let us no longer talk of happiness, but allow me some peace and quiet again.

In granting my request, what new rights will you not acquire over my heart? And I shall not have to struggle against them since they are founded in virtue. How I shall enjoy my gratitude to you! To you I shall owe the pleasures of delightful feelings, free from remorse, whereas now I am frightened by my feelings and thoughts, and am afraid to think about either you or me. The very idea of you fills me with terror. When I cannot escape from it, I fight it. I cannot banish it, but I push it away from me.

Would it not be better for both of us to put a stop to this distressing and troubled situation? With your sensitive nature, which has inclined you to love virtue even in the midst of your wrongdoing, you will respect my anguished state, you will not reject my prayer! A gentler but no less tender relationship will take the place of these violent emotions. And then, because of your generosity, I shall be able to breathe freely again, to hold life dear and say with joy in my heart: 'This peace that I feel, I owe to my friend.'

If I subject you to some small privations, which I am not imposing upon you but which I ask of you, do you think that will be too high a price to pay for the end of my torments? Ah, if all I had to do to obtain your happiness was to consent to be unhappy, you can believe me, I should not for a moment hesitate ... But to become a sinner! ... No, my friend, I had rather die a thousand deaths.

Already beset by shame, and near to remorse, I am afraid of other people, and of myself. I blush when in company and tremble when alone. My life is nothing but pain. I shall have peace only if you consent. My most admirable resolutions are not sufficient to reassure me. I only made this one yesterday and yet I spent last night in tears.

So you see before you your friend, the one you love, mortified, pleading, asking you for peace and innocence. Oh God! Without you, would she ever have been reduced to this humiliating demand? I do not blame you for anything. I feel only too keenly how difficult it is to resist an overpowering feeling. An appeal is not a complaint. Do out of generosity what I am doing out of duty. And to all the feelings you have inspired in me I shall add that of eternal gratitude.

Adieu, adieu, Monsieur.

From —, 27 September 17**

LETTER 91

The Vicomte de Valmont to the Présidente de Tourvel

I am dismayed by your letter, Madame, and do not, as yet, know how to respond. Undoubtedly, if it is a question of choosing between your unhappiness and mine, I must be the one to sacrifice myself, and I should not hesitate. But I believe these important matters deserve to be first discussed and clarified.

And how can we achieve that if we are not to see or speak to each other?

What! When the sweetest of feelings unites us, is a senseless fear all that it takes to separate us, perhaps for ever? In vain shall loving friendship and ardent love demand their rights! Their voices will not be heard; but why? What is this imminent danger hanging over you? Ah, believe me, such fears, so lightly conceived, are already, I should say, powerful enough reasons to guarantee your safety.

Allow me to suggest that I see in all this evidence of the unfavourable impressions that you have received about me. A woman does not fear a man she respects. And especially she does not seek to banish from her side the man she has judged to be worthy of her friendship. It is the dangerous man she fears and flies from.

Yet who was ever more respectful and submissive than I am? Already, as you perceive, I am studying my language. I no longer allow myself to use those sweet names so dear to my heart, which I still call you in secret. No longer am I the faithful, unhappy lover receiving counsel and consolation from a loving and sympathetic friend. I am the accused before the judge, the slave in front of his master. These new roles no doubt impose new duties. I declare I shall fulfil them all. Listen to me, and if you condemn me I shall subscribe to it and leave. I promise you even more. Do you prefer to act like a despot and arrive at a judgement without a hearing? Do you have the courage to be unjust? Command and I shall yet obey.

But this judgement, this command, let me hear it from your own lips. Why, you will ask in your turn. Ah, if you put this question to me, how little you know of love and my heart! Is it then nothing for me to see you just one more time? If you bring despair to my soul, perhaps one consoling glance will save me from giving in to it. And if in the end I have to renounce love and friendship, for which alone I exist, at least you will see what you have done, and your compassion will remain with me. Though I might not deserve this poor recompense, I am, I believe, paying a high price in the hope of obtaining it.

What! Are you going to send me away? Is it your will that

we should become strangers to each other? What am I saying? It is your will. And while you assure me that my absence will not change how you feel about me, you are only hastening my departure in order to destroy those feelings the sooner.

Already you speak of substituting gratitude for love. So, what any stranger could, for the slightest service, expect from you, and what even your enemy, in ceasing to harm you, might obtain, that is what you are offering me! And you think I should be content with that! Ask yourself this question: If your lover, your friend, came to talk to you one day of his *gratitude*, would you not say to him in indignation: 'Begone, ungrateful wretch'?

I shall stop and beg your indulgence. Pardon me for giving vent to a grief that you have brought into being. It will make no difference to my total submissiveness. But I beseech you in my turn, in the name of these sweet feelings which you yourself have so often mentioned, do not refuse to hear me. And, out of pity for the mortal agony into which you have plunged me, do not put off the hour. Adieu, Madame.

From —, 27 September, 17**, in the evening

LETTER 92

The Chevalier Danceny to the Vicomte de Valmont

Oh my dear friend! Your letter terrifies me, and has turned my heart to ice. Cécile – oh God, is it possible? – Cécile does not love me any more. Yes, I perceive this terrible truth through the veil your friendship has thrown over it. You wished to prepare me for this mortal blow. I thank you for your care, but can love ever be deceived? It runs ahead of its interests. It does not learn its fate, but divines it. I am no longer in any doubt about my own. Speak to me frankly. You can, and I beg you to. Let me know everything. What has given rise to your suspicions, what has confirmed them. The tiniest detail is precious. Especially try to remember what she said. One word instead of another can change the whole sense of a sentence. The same word sometimes has two meanings. Perhaps you have misunderstood? Alas, I am trying to make myself feel better. What did she say? Does she blame me in some way? Does she not, at least, make excuses for herself? I should have foreseen this alteration, given the difficulties she has been finding for so long in everything. Love would not place all these obstacles in its way.

What ought I to do? What do you advise? Supposing I tried to see her? Is that impossible? Absence is so cruel, so distressing . . . and she refused a means of seeing me! You do not say what that was. If there was indeed too much danger, she knows very well that I would not want her to take too many risks. But I know how cautious you are as well, and I, unfortunately, cannot doubt it for a minute.

What am I going to do now? What shall I say to her in my letter? If I let her see my suspicions, she will perhaps be distressed. And if they are unjust, how could I forgive myself for hurting her? If I hide them from her, it would be deceiving her, and I cannot dissemble with her.

Oh, if she knew what I am going through, she would be touched by my sufferings. I know how sensitive she is. She has a heart of gold and I have a thousand proofs of her love. She is so timid, so inexperienced, so young! And her mother treats her with such severity! I shall write to her. I shall be restrained. I shall ask her only to put herself entirely in your hands. Even if she refuses, still she will not be able to be angry with me for asking; and she may perhaps consent.

My friend, I offer you a thousand apologies, both on my behalf and on hers. I do assure you that she appreciates your kindness and is grateful. It is not mistrust, but fearfulness. Be indulgent. That is the best part of friendship. Yours is very precious to me, and I do not know how to repay you for all you are doing for me. Adieu, I shall write to her without delay.

I feel all my fears returning. Who would have thought how much it would cost me to write to her! Alas, only yesterday it was my sweetest pleasure.

Goodbye, my friend. I ask you to continue in all you are doing for me and to pity my plight.

Paris, 27 September 17**

LETTER 93

The Chevalier Danceny to Cécile Volanges
(Included in the preceding letter)

I cannot pretend I am not extremely pained to learn from Valmont how little trust you still place in him. You are aware that he is my friend, and that he is the only person who can bring us together. I had thought these considerations would be enough for you, but I now see to my distress that I am wrong. May I hope that at least you will explain your reasons? Or will you still find some obstacle that will prevent you doing so? Whatever the case, without you I cannot solve the mystery of this conduct. I do not dare to doubt your love, and I am sure you would not betray mine. Oh Cécile!

So is it really true that you refused a way of seeing me? A way that was *simple, convenient and safe*?* So that is how you love me! Such a short absence has certainly changed your feelings. But why deceive me? Why tell me you still love me, that you love me more than ever? Has your mother, in destroying your love, also destroyed your frankness? If, at least, she has left you with some mercy, you will not hear without sorrow of the terrible torments you are causing me! Oh, if I were dying, I should suffer less.

So tell me, is your heart closed to me for ever? Have you forgotten me utterly? Your refusal means I know neither when you will hear my appeals nor when you will answer them. Valmont's friendship made our correspondence safe. But you did not want this. You found it painful; you preferred our

* Danceny does not know what this is. He is simply repeating Valmont's words.

correspondence to be only occasional. No, I can no longer believe in love, in honesty. Alas, whom can I trust if my Cécile has deceived me?

So answer me. Is it true you no longer love me? No, it is not possible. You are deceiving yourself. You are insulting your feelings. A passing fear, a moment of discouragement, that will soon be banished by love. Is that what it is, my darling? Oh yes, it must be that, and I am wrong to accuse you. How happy I should be if I were wrong! How I should like to make my loving apologies to you, to atone for this moment of injustice with an eternity of love!

Cécile, Cécile, have pity on me! Consent to see me. Take every opportunity you can! See what absence does! Fears, suspicions, perhaps even indifference! One single look, one single word, and we shall be happy. But how can I still speak of happiness? Perhaps it is gone from me, gone for ever. Tormented by my fears, and cruelly oppressed by unjust suspicions and a truth more cruel still, I can no longer take comfort in any thought. I continue my existence only to suffer, and to love you. Ah Cécile! You alone have the power to make my life dear to me. And the first word you utter will signal the return of happiness or the certainty of eternal despair.

Paris, 27 September 17**

LETTER 94

Cécile Volanges to the Chevalier Danceny

I do not understand any of your letter apart from the fact that it hurts me. What was it, then, that Monsieur de Valmont told you, and what makes you think I no longer love you? If that were the case, it would be a good thing for me, for I should surely be less tormented. But, loving you as I do, it is very hard for me to see you still think I am in the wrong, and that, instead of consoling me, you are yourself the cause of all the things which distress me most. You think I am deceiving you and telling you untruths. You must have a strange idea of what I am really like! But if I were telling lies, as you say, what would be my motive? For surely, if I did not love you any more, all I should have to do is say so, and everyone would approve. But unfortunately it is stronger than me. To think it has to be for someone who is not in the least grateful for it!

So what have I done to make you so angry? I did not dare take a key because I was afraid Mamma would notice, and that would make me even more unhappy, and you too because of me. But it was also because I think it is wrong. And it was only Monsieur de Valmont who talked of it, and I could not know whether you wanted that or not, because you did not know anything about it. But now I know you wish it, how could I refuse? I shall take it tomorrow. And then we shall see what you have to say.

Monsieur de Valmont may well be your friend, but I believe I love you at the very least as much as he does. And yet it is always he who is in the right, and I in the wrong. I am very angry, I can tell you. That does not make any difference to you because you know I get over it immediately. And if I have the key now I shall be able to see you whenever I want to. But I can assure you that I shall not want to if you behave like this. I prefer the distress I feel to be caused by me rather than you. Consider what you will do.

Oh, if you wished, we would love each other so much! And at least we should only have to put up with the troubles inflicted upon us by other people! I assure you that if it were in my control you would never have cause for complaint. But if you do not believe me, we shall always be really unhappy, through no fault of mine. I hope we shall soon be able to meet and no longer have occasion to upset each other as we do at present.

If I had been able to foresee this, I should have taken the key straight away. But I truly believed I was doing the right thing. So do not hold it against me, I beg you. Do not be sad any more, love me still as much as I do you. Then I shall be perfectly happy. Adieu, my dear friend.

From the Chateau de —, 28 September 17**

LETTER 95

Cécile Volanges to the Vicomte de Valmont

I beg you, Monsieur, to be so kind as to give me back the key that you gave me to put in place of the other. Because everyone wishes it, I must consent to it as well.

I do not know why you told Monsieur Danceny I did not love him any more. I do not think I ever gave you cause to think so. And it made him very unhappy, as it did me. I know you are his friend. But that is no reason to distress him, or me. You would do me a great service if you told him the opposite the very next time you write to him, and say that you are certain of it. For it is you he trusts most implicitly. And when I have said something and people do not believe me, I do not know what else to do.

As to the key, you can rest assured. I have remembered everything you told me in your letter. However, if you still have the letter and wish to give it back to me with the key, I promise you I shall give it my utmost attention. If it could be tomorrow when we go in to dinner, I would give you the other key the day after tomorrow at luncheon, and you could give it back in the same way as the first. I should prefer not to leave it any later because there would be more danger of Mamma noticing then.

And once you have that key would you still also be kind enough to make use of it to take my letters? In that way Monsieur Danceny will be able to have news of me more often. It is true that it will be much more convenient than at present. But at first I was too scared. I beg you to forgive me, and hope you will still continue to be as helpful as you have been up until now. I shall always be very grateful.

I have the honour, Monsieur, to be your humble and most obedient servant.

From —, 28 September 17**

LETTER 96

The Vicomte de Valmont to the Marquise de Merteuil

I shall wager you have been waiting every day since your affair for compliments and praise from me. I am even certain you have become a little piqued by my long silence. But what do you expect? I have always thought that when all there was left to offer a woman was praise one might as well leave it to her and attend to other matters. However, I thank you on my own account and congratulate you on yours. I even concede, to make you totally happy, that for once you have surpassed my expectations. After that you will see whether I have fulfilled yours, at least in part.

It is not about Madame de Tourvel that I wish to speak. That affair displeases you because it is proceeding at such a slow pace. You only like things that are over and done with. Long-drawn-out scenes annoy you. But I have never tasted pleasure such as I am experiencing at present in these so-called *lenteurs*.[1]

Yes, I love to watch and contemplate this cautious woman engaged without realizing it along a path from which there is no return, which, in spite of herself, drags her rapidly and perilously down after me. Terrified of the danger she is in, she wants to stop, but cannot hold herself back. Her caution and adroitness do of course mean that she may take smaller steps; but taken they must be, one after the other. Sometimes, not daring to face the danger, she shuts her eyes and lets herself go, abandoning herself to my tender care. More often a fresh fear revives her efforts. In mortal terror she tries once more to take a step back. She expends her strength on climbing up again briefly, with great difficulty; but soon a magic power draws her down closer to the danger which she has been vainly attempting to flee. So, having no one but me as her guide and support, without blaming me further for her inevitable downfall she implores me to delay it. The fervent prayers and humble supplications all God-fearing mortals offer up to the divinity, she offers them to me. And you wish me to be deaf to her wishes and destroy the cult she is devoting to me; and the power she invokes to sustain her, you want me to make use of only in order to hurry the affair along! Oh, let me at least have time to observe these touching struggles between love and virtue.

Can you suppose that the same spectacle which makes you rush to the theatre and applaud with such enthusiasm is less spell-binding in real life? These feelings of a pure and loving soul who dreads the happiness she desires and never stops defending herself, even when she ceases to resist, you listen to them enthusiastically; are they not then priceless for the man who has brought them into being? And yet these are the treasures that this heavenly woman offers me every day; and you blame me for tasting their delights! Ah, the time will come only too soon when, degraded by her fall, she will be for me nothing but an ordinary woman.

But while I speak of her I am forgetting that I did not mean to speak of her. I do not know what spell binds me to her, continually taking me back to her, even if it is only to insult her. Let us put this dangerous topic to one side. Let me become myself once more, and reflect upon a lighter matter. I mean your pupil, who has now become mine, and I hope when I tell you this you will recognize me for the man you know.

For some days I have been treated in a more loving fashion by my dear devotee, and consequently have been less obsessed by her. I noticed that the little Volanges girl is in fact very pretty. And that even if it were foolish to be in love with her, as Danceny is, perhaps it would be no less foolish on my part not to be seeking some distraction with her, rendered necessary by my solitude. It also seemed fair that I should be recompensed for my efforts on her behalf. I remembered, quite apart from that, that you had offered her to me before Danceny had any rights over her. And I felt I was justified in claiming a few of those rights over a property that he only possessed because of my refusal and neglect. The girl's pretty little face, the freshness of her lips, her childlike air, even her gaucheness reinforced these sensible ideas of mine. So I resolved to act upon them, and success crowned my enterprise.

Already you are wondering what method I used to supplant

the beloved lover so speedily; what kind of seduction technique is appropriate for this age and inexperience. Spare yourself the trouble; I employed none. While you, handling the weapons of your sex so adeptly, were victorious by your subtlety, I restored to man his inalienable rights and subjugated her with my authority. Sure of seizing my prey if I were able to reach her, I only needed a stratagem in order to approach her, and even the one I used was scarcely worthy of the name.

I took advantage of the next letter I received from Danceny for his mistress and, after warning her by using the agreed signal, I exercised my ingenuity, not in giving it to her, but in finding a way of not giving it to her. I pretended to share her impatience at this, and after causing the harm I pointed out the remedy.

The girl occupies a bedroom, one of whose doors gives on to the corridor. But, as you might expect, the mother has taken the key. All I needed to do was to get hold of it. Nothing easier than to achieve this. I asked only to have it at my disposal for two hours, after which I could guarantee I would be in possession of a similar one. So then correspondence, conversation, nocturnal rendez-vous, everything would have become convenient and safe. However, would you believe it, the timid child took fright and refused. Anyone else would have been crushed by this, but I saw only the opportunity for a more piquant pleasure. I wrote to Danceny to complain of this refusal, and succeeded so well that our stupid fellow did not stop until he had obtained, demanded even from his fearful mistress that she should grant what I asked, and deliver herself up totally to my discretion.

I was very relieved, I admit, to have exchanged roles in this way, and that the young man should be doing for me what he thought I would be doing for him. This idea doubled the value of the adventure in my eyes. So, as soon as I had the precious key, I hastened to make use of it. That was last night.

Having made sure everything in the chateau was quiet, I armed myself with my shaded lantern and, in the state of undress normal for that hour and demanded by the circumstances, I paid my first visit to your pupil. I had everything arranged – by

her, in fact – for me to enter without any noise. She was in that
first deep sleep, so characteristic of the young, and I arrived at
her bedside without waking her. At first I thought I would
venture further and pretend to be a dream,[2] but, fearing the
effect of surprise and the accompanying noise, I decided instead
to wake my sleeping beauty carefully, and actually managed to
prevent the cry I was dreading.

As I had not come there for a chat, after calming her initial
fears, I took a few liberties. Probably they did not teach her in
the convent what different dangers timid innocence may be
exposed to, or all she must protect so as not to be taken by
surprise. For, bringing all her attention and strength to bear
upon defending herself from my kiss, which was just a false
attack, everything else was left undefended. How could I not
take advantage! So I changed tactics, and immediately took up
my position. At that point I thought we were both lost. The
girl, terrified, tried to cry out, but luckily her voice was stifled
by tears. She had also thrown herself upon her bell-pull, but I had
the presence of mind to grab her by the arm in the nick of time.

'What do you want to do?' I said then. 'Ruin yourself for
good? If someone comes, what difference would it make to me?
Who would you be able to persuade that I am not here with
your permission? Who else could have provided me with the
means to get in? And this key I have from you, that I have only
been able to obtain through you, will you take responsibility
for explaining what it was for?' This short harangue did nothing
to calm her pain or her anger. But she submitted. I don't know
whether it was my eloquent tone of voice or what; it certainly
could not have been my gestures. One hand busy restraining,
the other caressing, what orator could aspire to be graceful in
such a situation? If you can imagine what she looked like, you
will agree at least that she laid herself open to attack. But there,
I don't understand a thing about it, and, as you say, the simplest
woman, a little schoolgirl, can lead me like a child.

Although in despair, she realized she had to decide one way
or another and come to terms with the situation. Finding me
adamant to all entreaties, she was reduced to saying what she
would and would not allow. You may be thinking I sold my

important position for a high price; but I promised everything for a kiss. It is true that, once the kiss was over, I did not keep my promise, but I had good reason. Had we agreed it should be taken or given? Through bargaining, we agreed upon a second. And that one, it was promised, would be received. So, guiding her timid arms around my body, I clasped her more amorously with the one that was free, and that sweet kiss was indeed received. But well and truly received. So well, in fact, that love itself could not have done better.

All this trust merited some reward, so I immediately granted the request. Her hand withdrew. But by some extraordinary chance I found myself taking its place. You will suppose I was in a great hurry, very urgent, will you not? Not at all. I have acquired a taste for *lenteurs*, I tell you. Once you are sure of arriving, why hasten the journey?

Seriously, I was very glad for once to observe the power that opportunity brings, deprived here of any external help. Yet she had to contend with love, a love sustained by embarrassment or shame and, above all, fortified by the angry mood I had provoked, which was considerable. Opportunity was alone. But it was there, still offered, still present, and yet love itself absent.

In order to make certain of my observations, I was mischievous enough to use no more strength than could be easily resisted. It was only when my charming enemy took advantage of my lenience and seemed about to escape that I restrained her with the same threats whose happy effects I had already enjoyed. Well, without further ado, this *amoureuse* forgot her vows, first yielding, then consenting. Which is not to say that after that first moment there were no more tears and reproaches. I do not know whether they were real or faked. But, as always happens, they ceased just as soon as I busied myself with giving her the opportunity for more. Anyway, between surrender and accusation, and accusation and surrender, we only separated when quite satisfied with one another and both of us in agreement that we should meet again that evening.

I did not go back to my room until dawn, worn out and dying of sleep. Yet I sacrificed both of these to my desire to appear at breakfast this morning. I passionately love the expressions on

their faces the morning after! You cannot imagine what hers
was like. So self-conscious in her gestures! The awkward way
she walked! Eyes permanently cast down, and so large and
pale! Her little round face so drawn! Nothing was so amusing.
And her mother, alarmed for the first time at this dramatic
change, showed quite an affectionate interest in her! And so
did the Présidente, who showered attentions on her! Oh, as far
as those attentions go, they are but lent awhile! The day will
come, and it is not very far off, when she will need them back.
Farewell, my friend.

From the Chateau de —, 1 October 17**

LETTER 97

Cécile Volanges to the Marquise de Merteuil

Oh Madame, Heaven knows what a sorry plight I am in! How
unhappy I am! Who will console me in my misery? Who will
advise me in my predicament? Monsieur de Valmont . . . And
Danceny! No, the very thought of Danceny fills me with despair
. . . How can I tell you? What can I say? I don't know what to
do. But my heart is full . . . I have to tell someone, and you are
the only one in whom I can and dare confide. You are always
so good to me! But do not be good to me on this occasion; I
am not worthy of it. What am I to say? I do not wish to say
anything. Everyone here has offered me sympathy today . . .
They have all made my misery greater. I so much felt I did not
deserve it! Scold me instead. Give me a good scolding for I am
very guilty. But afterwards, come to my aid. If you do not have
the goodness to advise me, I shall die of chagrin.

So let me tell you . . . My hand is trembling, as you see, I can
scarcely write, my face is burning . . . It must be red with shame.
Well, I shall bear it. It will be the first punishment for my sins.
Yes, I shall acquaint you with everything.

You will know that Monsieur de Valmont, who has until

now been giving me Monsieur de Danceny's letters, suddenly decided it was too difficult. He wanted the key to my room. I can assure you I did not wish to give him one. But he went so far as to write to Danceny about it and Danceny wanted me to as well. And it made me so unhappy to refuse him anything, especially since my absence, which had made him so unhappy, that in the end I agreed. I could not foresee the ills that would befall me as a result.

Yesterday Monsieur de Valmont used this key to come into my bedroom while I was asleep. I was not expecting it at all, so when I woke I was really scared. But as he spoke to me straight away I recognized who it was and did not cry out. And my first thought was that he was perhaps bringing a letter from Danceny. But it was not that at all. A short time after that he tried to embrace me, and as I was defending myself, as was natural, he succeeded in doing what I would not have done for all the world . . . But he wanted a kiss first. I had to, what else could I have done? Especially since I had tried to call someone, but apart from the fact that I could not, he also told me that if someone came he would be able to put all the blame on to me, and of course that would have been easy because of the key. And then he did not move an inch. He wanted another kiss. And I don't exactly know why, but that one troubled me a very great deal. And afterwards, it was worse than before. Oh, it was terrible. Then after that . . . You will forgive me if I don't tell you the rest, but I am as unhappy as can be.

What I blame myself for most, and yet this is what I must talk to you about, is that I am afraid I did not look after myself as well as I might have done. I don't know how it happened. I certainly am not in love with Monsieur de Valmont – quite the opposite. But there were moments when it seemed as though I did love him . . . As you may imagine, that did not prevent me saying no to him all the time. But I could feel that my actions did not reflect my words. And it was as if I could not help it. And then I was very agitated as well. If it is always so difficult to defend oneself, one must need a lot of practice! It is true that Monsieur de Valmont is so persuasive that it is hard to know how to answer him. Well, anyway, would you believe that when he left I was almost sorry, and I was weak enough to agree to him coming back this evening. And that is what makes me feel the worst of all.

Oh, in spite of that, I promise you I shall stop him coming back. He had scarcely left the room when I realized I had been very wrong to make him any promises. So I cried the rest of the night. It was especially the thought of Danceny that upset me so. Every time I thought of him I cried twice as much, so that my tears choked me, and I kept on thinking about him . . . And still am, and you can see what has happened. My paper is soaked through. No, I shall never get over it, if only because of him. Well, I was exhausted and yet I could not sleep a wink. And this morning, when I got up and looked at myself in the mirror, it frightened me because I looked so different.

Mamma noticed as soon as she saw me, and asked what the matter was. I started weeping straight away. I thought she was about to scold me, and perhaps that would have caused me less pain. But quite the contrary. She spoke to me quite gently! I did not deserve it at all. She told me not to take on so. She did not know why I was so upset that I should make myself ill! There are times when I wish I were dead. I could not bear it. I threw myself into her arms, sobbing: 'Oh Mamma, your daughter is so unhappy!' Mamma could not help weeping a little herself; and all that only increased my sorrow. Fortunately she did not enquire why I was so unhappy, for I should not have known what to say to her.

I beg you, Madame, write to me as soon as you can, and tell me what to do. For I have no strength to think about anything, and all I do is make myself feel worse. Please send me your letter via Monsieur de Valmont; but I beg you, if you are writing to him at the same time, do not tell him I have said anything to you.

I have the honour to be, Madame, with the most sincere friendship, your most humble and obedient servant.

I dare not put my name to this letter.

From the Chateau de —, 1 October, 17**

LETTER 98

Madame de Volanges to the Marquise de Merteuil

Only a very few days ago, my dearest friend, you were the one writing to me to ask for consolation and advice. Today it is my turn. And I am making to you the same request you made to me. I am really very distressed, and fear I have not gone about things in the best way to avoid the worries I am experiencing.

It is my daughter who is causing this anxiety. Since leaving, she has been constantly depressed and miserable. But that I was expecting, and I had prepared myself to be as strict with her as I might deem necessary. I was hoping that absence and distractions would soon put an end to a love that I regarded more as a childish crush than a veritable passion. However, far from gaining anything by our stay here, I perceive the child is falling more and more into a dangerous melancholy. And I am afraid, truly afraid, that her health may be impaired. Particularly in the last few days she is visibly changed. It struck me especially yesterday, and everyone here was really alarmed.

The further proof of how keenly she is affected is that she is evidently prepared to overcome the reserve she has always felt towards me. Yesterday morning, when I asked her straight out if she was unwell, she flung herself into my arms saying she was dreadfully unhappy. And she wept and sobbed. I cannot describe how upset I was. Tears rushed to my eyes. And I just had time to turn away so that she could not see. Fortunately I was prudent enough not to question her at all, and she did not dare confide in me further. But all the same it is evident that it is this unfortunate passion that is tormenting her.

But what is to be done, if this goes on? Shall I be the cause of my daughter's ills ? Shall I turn her most precious qualities, sensibility and constancy, to her disadvantage? Is it for this that I am her mother? And if I stifle this natural feeling, which makes us wish for our children's happiness, if I view as weakness what I believe on the contrary to be the first and most sacred of our duties, if I force her choice, shall I not have to answer for the possibly dire consequences? What misuse of my maternal authority it would be to place my own daughter between crime and misery!

I shall not emulate what I have so often criticized. I have undoubtedly tried to make a choice for my daughter. By doing that I was simply giving her the benefit of my experience. It was not a right exercised, but a duty fulfilled. But on the other hand I should be failing in my duty were I to disregard an inclination which I was unable to prevent and of which neither she nor I can know the extent or duration. No, I shall not allow her to marry one man and fall in love with another. I prefer to compromise my authority rather than her virtue.

So I think I shall take the wiser course and withdraw the promise I made to Monsieur de Gercourt. You have just heard my reasons. They seem to me to be stronger than my promises. I will say more. With the state of things at present, to fulfil my engagement would be, in fact, to breach it. For if I owe it to my daughter not to divulge her secret to Monsieur de Gercourt, I at least owe it to him not to abuse the ignorance in which I leave him, and to do on his behalf whatever he would, in my view, do himself if he were apprised of everything. Shall I let him down in this unworthy fashion, when he trusts me and honours me in choosing me as his second mother; am I to deceive him in the choice he wishes to make for the mother for his children? These thoughts, both honourable and inescapable, alarm me more than I can say.

I compare all these fearful and possible ills with the happiness of my daughter, choosing the husband of her heart and knowing her duty only through the delights she finds in its fulfilment; my son-in-law equally satisfied, and congratulating himself every day upon his choice; each only finding their happiness in that of the other; and the happiness of both uniting to increase my own. Must the hopes of such a sweet future be sacrificed to such vain considerations? And what are they, after all? Only financial ones. And what advantage will it be for my daughter to be born rich if she must none the less be a slave to fortune?

I concede that Monsieur de Gercourt is a better party than I might have hoped for my daughter. I even admit that I was extremely flattered that his choice fell upon her. But, after all, Danceny is from as good a family as his. And he has nothing to learn from him as far as personal qualities go. He has the advantage over Monsieur de Gercourt in loving and being loved. He is not, it is true, a man of means. But is my daughter not rich enough for two? Why snatch away from her the sweet satisfaction of enriching the man she loves!

These arranged marriages, which are not real matches but what are called *mariages de convenance*, where everything is mutually agreeable apart from the tastes and character of the parties involved, are they not the most fertile ground for these scandals which are becoming more and more common every day? I prefer to delay the whole thing. At least I shall have time to get to know my daughter, who is a stranger to me. I feel I have the strength to cause her some passing disappointment if she can receive a more solid happiness as a result. But to risk delivering her up to eternal despair, I cannot find in my heart.

These are the ideas tormenting me, my dear friend, and for which I ask your advice. These serious matters contrast greatly with your liveliness and gaiety, and are scarcely suitable for someone of your tender years. But your judgement is so far ahead of your years! Your friendship, moreover, will come to the aid of your wisdom. I am not afraid that you will on either count disregard my maternal solicitude in requesting your help.

Goodbye, my charming friend. Never doubt the sincerity of my feelings for you.

From the Chateau de —, 2 October 17**

LETTER 99

The Vicomte de Valmont to the Marquise de Merteuil

More news, my darling, but it is all dialogue and no action, so contain your soul in patience. You will need a great deal of it. For whereas my Présidente moves forward very gingerly, your pupil is withdrawing, and that is even worse. Oh well, my nature is such that I rather enjoy these little contretemps. I am actually accustoming myself very well to my time here. And I must say that in the gloomy chateau of my aged aunt I have not been bored for one second. In fact, do I not have here pleasures, privation, hope and uncertainty? What more does one have in a larger theatre? Spectators? Ha! Just wait, I shall have plenty of them. Though they may not see me at work, I shall show them the finished product. All that will remain for them to do is admire and applaud. Yes, they will applaud. For I can finally predict with certainty the instant of my austere devotee's downfall. I have been present this evening at the death-throes of virtue. A sweet helplessness will reign in its place. I fix the time no later than at our next rendez-vous. But already I hear you cry: 'The arrogant man, proclaiming victory, boasting about it before it has happened!' Oh, calm yourself, my dear! To prove to you how modest I am, I shall begin by telling you the story of my defeat.

Your little pupil is indeed a ridiculous young person! She really is nothing but a child who should be treated as such, and it would be doing her a favour to punish her. Would you believe that after what took place the night before last between her and me, after the friendly way we left each other yesterday morning, when I tried to return in the evening as agreed, I found her door locked from the inside? Now what do you think of that? Sometimes one encounters such childish things the day before – but the day after! Is that not ridiculous?

At first, however, I did not think it so very funny. I had never before felt the force of my own character so keenly. It is certain that I attended this rendez-vous only as a matter of course, and without taking any pleasure in it. My own bed, which I certainly felt the need of, seemed to me at that moment far preferable to any other, and it was only with some regret that I left it. However, no sooner had I encountered an obstacle than I passionately desired to remove it. And it was especially humiliating that a mere child had played a trick on me. So I retired in a very bad mood. And, thinking I would no longer have anything to do with the silly girl and her affairs, I immediately penned a note that I hoped to give her today, in which I told her just how little she was worth. But, as they say, it is best to sleep on it. This morning I bethought myself that since I do not have much choice of entertainment here I should do better to stick to what I do have. So I destroyed the stern note. After reflecting upon it I cannot get over the fact that I had in mind to bring the affair to a conclusion before I had obtained a means of ruining its heroine. But see what happens when one gives in to impulse! Happy are those who, like you, my dear, have acquired the habit of never giving in to it! I have, then, put off my revenge awhile. I have made this sacrifice in view of your designs on Gercourt.

Now I am no longer angry, I can only perceive how ridiculous your pupil's conduct is. I must say I should love to know what she can hope to gain from it! It's a mystery to me. If it is only to protect herself, you have to agree it is a little late in the day. She will have to give me a clue to the conundrum one day! I am dying to know the answer. Perhaps it was just that she was tired? Frankly that is possible. For undoubtedly she is still unaware that the arrows of love, like Achilles' sword, carry with them the remedy for the wounds they cause.[3] But no, to judge from the little expression on her face all day long I wager that repentance comes into it somewhere ... something of the sort ... something to do with virtue ... Virtue! She's a fine one to be feeling virtuous! Oh, let her leave such things to the woman who is truly born for virtue, the only one who knows how to enhance it, who would make virtue worthy of love! ... I am sorry, my dear, but it was this very evening that there took place between Madame de Tourvel and myself the scene I have to describe to you – and I am still in an emotional state about it. I need to shake off the effect it had on me. It is actually for that reason that I began a letter to you. You must forgive me that first impulse.

Madame de Tourvel and myself have for some days been in agreement about our feelings for each other. We only disagree about what to call it. It has always been *her friendship* and *my love*. But these conventions of language did not change anything fundamental. And had things remained thus, my progress might

possibly have been slower, yet it would have been no less
certain. For already, in fact, it was no longer a matter of me
keeping my distance as she wished at first. And as for our daily
conversations, if I took care to offer her the opportunity, she
took care to seize it.

Since it is usually during walks that our little rendez-vous
take place, the dreadful weather we have had all day left me
nothing to hope for. In fact, I was badly put out. I could not
foresee how much I was to gain from this inconvenience.

We could not go for a walk, so we began playing cards as
soon as we left the table. And, as I do not play very much and
am no longer necessary to the game, I took the opportunity to
go up to my rooms with no thought but to wait there, more or
less, for the game to finish.

I was returning to join the company when I met the charming
creature outside her room, and, whether it was lack of prudence
or through weakness, she said in her dulcet tones: 'Where are
you going? There is no one in the drawing room.' That was
enough for me, as you may imagine, to try to enter her room.
There I encountered less resistance than I was expecting. It is
true I had taken the precaution of beginning the conversation
at the door, and to begin it on quite a neutral topic. But scarcely
had we settled down when I brought it round again to the real
issue, and spoke about *my love for my friend*. Her first reply,
though simple, seemed to me to speak volumes. 'Oh,' said she,
'please do not talk of that here,' and she was trembling. Poor
woman! She foresees her imminent defeat.

Yet she was wrong to be afraid. For some time now, since
I was assured of success sooner or later, and seeing her waste
so much effort in this useless struggle, I had resolved to moderate my own efforts and, without my doing anything, wait for
her to give herself up out of weariness. As you know, one seeks
total victory in these cases, and I did not wish to put anything
down to circumstance. It was precisely for this reason, and so
that I could be more insistent without engaging myself too
much, that I reiterated the word love, which she so obstinately
refused to utter ... Sure that my passion was not in doubt, I
tried a gentler tone. Her refusal no longer angered but distressed

me. Surely, as a sympathetic friend, she owed me some consolation?

By way of consolation, one hand was laid upon mine. Her
lovely body was leaning against my arm and we were very very
close to each other. I am sure you will have noticed how, in
such situations, as defences gradually melt away, demands
and refusals are exchanged in closer and closer proximity?
Heads are averted, eyes are lowered and words, pronounced in
a feeble voice, grow few and disjointed. These precious signs
proclaim, without the shadow of a doubt, the heart's consent.
But rarely until this point does it pass into the realm of the
senses. I even take the view that it is always risky to attempt
too obvious a move at times like these, because this state of
abandon is never accompanied by anything other than very
sweet pleasure, and one can never force a person out of it
without causing a change of mood which invariably turns to
the advantage of the defence.

But in the present case prudence was all the more vital since
I had to fear over and above everything the alarm that this
heedlessness would be bound to cause in my beautiful dreamer.
So I did not even ask her to utter the longed-for word. One
look would be enough. One single look would make me a
happy man.

My dear, her beautiful eyes were indeed raised to mine. The
heavenly lips even uttered: 'Well yes, I . . .' But suddenly her
eyes misted over, words failed, and this adorable woman fell
into my arms. Hardly had I time to catch her when with a
convulsive effort she pulled herself away from me and cried out
distractedly: 'God . . . oh my God, save me', with her hands
held out to Heaven. And immediately, in a trice, she was on
her knees ten steps away from me. I could hear her almost
choking. I went forward to help. But, taking hold of my hands,
which she drenched with her tears, and sometimes even embracing my knees, 'Yes,' she cried, 'it is you, you who will save me!
You do not wish me to die: leave me, save me, leave me, in the
name of God, leave me!' And her sobs redoubled as these
disjointed words came painfully out. However, she held on to
me so tightly that I could not free myself; so, gathering up my

strength again, I lifted her into my arms. At the same moment the tears stopped; she spoke no more; her limbs stiffened and violent convulsions followed this storm.

I admit I was deeply moved, and I believe I should have consented to her request even if circumstances had not compelled me to do so. The fact is that after coming to her aid I left her as she begged me to, and I congratulate myself on that. I have already almost obtained my reward.

I was expecting that, as on the day of my first declaration, she would not appear in the evening. But towards eight she came down into the drawing room and announced quite simply to the assembled company that she had been very unwell. Her face was drawn, her voice weak, but her bearing composed. Her eyes were soft and often rested upon me. Her reluctance to play cards having obliged me to take her place, she even sat down at my side. During supper she remained alone in the drawing room. When we returned there I thought I could discern that she had been weeping. To be certain of it, I told her I thought she was still a little unwell, to which she obligingly replied: 'This malady will not go away as quickly as it came.' At last, when people left, I gave her my hand and, at the door to her room, she pressed mine hard. It is true this gesture seemed to me a little involuntary, but so much the better. It is another proof of my power over her.

I wager that now she is delighted to be at this stage. All sacrifices have been made and only pleasure awaits. Perhaps, as I am writing to you right now, she is occupying herself with this sweet thought! And even if not, and she were thinking up a new strategy of defence, we both know very well what becomes of all such projects, do we not? I ask you, it cannot happen later than at our next meeting, can it? So I am definitely expecting that she will still raise some difficulties. But so be it. Can these strict devotees stop themselves once they have taken the first step? Their love is a veritable explosion. Resistance makes it even more violent. If I were to stop chasing her, my timid devotee would be running after me.

And then, my love, I shall arrive post haste at your house to make you keep your promise to me. You have surely not forgotten what you promised me after my success – that little infidelity to your Chevalier? Are you ready? As for me, I desire it as much as though we had never known one another. Besides, knowing you is perhaps a reason to desire it more:

I speak with justice not with gallantry.*[4]

So this will be the first time I am unfaithful to my all-important conquest. And I promise you I shall take advantage of the first pretext to leave her for twenty-four hours. That will be her punishment for having kept me away from you so long. Do you realize that this affair has been taking up more than two months of my time? Yes, two months and three days. It is true I am counting tomorrow, since it will only finally be consummated then. Which reminds me that Madame de B— resisted for three whole months. I am delighted to perceive that frank coquetterie can defend itself better than strict virtue.

Farewell, my love. I must go, for it is very late. This letter has made me run on more than I expected. But as I am sending tomorrow morning to Paris, I wanted to take advantage of it so that you could share in your friend's joy one day earlier.

From the Chateau de —, 2 October 17**, in the evening

LETTER 100

The Vicomte de Valmont to the Marquise de Merteuil

My dear, I am tricked, betrayed, lost! I am in despair.[5] Madame de Tourvel has left! She has gone without my knowledge! And I was not there to forestall her departure, to deplore this unworthy betrayal! Oh, you may be sure I should not have let her go. She would have stayed. Yes, she would have stayed even had I had to use violence towards her. But what could I have done? There I was, fast asleep, not knowing a thing. I was

* Voltaire, *Comédie de Nanine.*

sleeping when the thunderbolt fell. No, I do not understand the first thing about this departure. I give up trying to understand females.

When I think about what happened yesterday! What can I say? The very same evening! That gentle look, that tender voice! And the way she squeezed my hand! And all that time she was planning her escape! Oh women, women! Can you complain if we deceive you? Every act of treachery we commit we have learned from you.

What pleasure I shall take in avenging myself! I shall track this perfidious woman down and recover my power over her. If love on its own was enough to achieve this, what may it not do with vengeance at its side? I shall see her yet at my feet, trembling and bathed in tears, crying for mercy in that deceitful voice. And I shall be pitiless.

What is she doing at present? What is she thinking? Perhaps she is congratulating herself on playing me false? And, true to her sex, finds this pleasure the sweetest of them all? What her much-vaunted virtue has not achieved, her natural cunning has done effortlessly. Fool that I was! I was afraid of her righteousness, but it was her dishonesty I should have feared.

And to be obliged to swallow my resentment and dare to show nothing but regretful concern when my heart is filled with rage! To see myself reduced to pleading again with a rebellious woman who has escaped my dominion over her! Did I have to be humiliated so? And by whom? By a timid woman who has never in her life fought before. What good has it done me to establish myself in her heart, to have set her on fire with flames of love, to have carried her troubled senses to the point of delirium, if, secure in her refuge, she can today take more pride in her escape than I can in my victories? Shall I endure this? My friend, you cannot believe so. You cannot entertain such a humiliating idea of me!

What strange power draws me to this woman? Are there not a hundred others clamouring for my attention? Will they not rush to respond? Even if none can hold a candle to this one, the attraction of variety, the charm of new conquests, the glory in numbers, do they not offer sweet enough pleasures? Why chase after the one who flees from us and neglect those who offer themselves? Ah why? I do not know, but I feel it most grievously.

There is no more peace, no more happiness for me unless I possess this woman whom I hate and love with equal passion. I shall be able to bear my fate only when I have become master of hers. Calm and contented then, I shall see her in her turn buffeted by the storms which blow on me now, and I shall stir up a thousand more. I want all the hopes and fears, the trust and suspicion, all the ills invented by hatred, all the blessings accorded by love to fill up her heart, to succeed one another at my will. That time will come ... But what a lot of work is still to be done! How close I came yesterday, and how far I am from that today! How may I draw closer to her again? I do not dare to try any manoeuvre. I feel that in order to come to a decision I must remain calm, and yet the blood is boiling in my veins.

What is making my torment so much worse is the cool manner in which everyone here replies to my questions about this incident, about the reason for it, about everything that is remarkable about it ... No one knows anything, no one cares; they would scarcely have broached the subject if I had allowed them to talk about anything else. Madame de Rosemonde, to whom I flew this morning when I learned the news, replied to me with the indifference typical of her age that it was the natural consequence of Madame de Tourvel's state of health yesterday. That she had feared she might fall ill and preferred to be at home. She sees nothing untoward in that. She would have done the same, she told me. As if those two could have anything in common! Between the one, who has nothing but death awaiting her, and the other, who is the delight and the torment of my life!

Madame de Volanges, whom I had at first suspected of being an accomplice, seems to have been affected simply by the fact that she was not consulted about this move. I admit I am glad she has not had the pleasure of doing harm to me. I also see this as proof that she is not so much in this woman's confidence as I first feared. That is one enemy less. How she would congratulate herself if she knew I am the one she is running away from! How puffed up with pride she would be, had it been on her advice! How her self-importance would have increased! My God! How I detest her! Oh, I shall resume my relations with her daughter; I intend to do with her as I please. And so I think I shall remain here for some while. At least the few reflections I have made incline me to this course.

Do you not think, in fact, that given such unambiguous behaviour, the ungrateful woman must be afraid I shall reappear? So if she gets hold of the idea that I might follow her, her doors will be closed to me, for sure. And I do not wish her either to make a habit of that, nor do I wish to suffer the humiliation of it. I much prefer to let her know that I am remaining here. I shall even implore her to return. And when she is completely persuaded of my absence, I shall arrive on her doorstep. We shall see how she takes that meeting. But it must be put off awhile in order to increase its effect, although I do not yet know if I have the patience. Twenty times today I have opened my mouth to summon my horses. However, I shall contain myself. I promise to receive your reply here. I only ask, my love, that you do not keep me waiting for it.

What would annoy me most would be not to know what is going on. But my valet, who is in Paris, has some rights of access to the chambermaid; he could be useful to me. I am sending him my instructions and some money. I hope you will not object to me including both with this letter, and also that you will take care to send them to him by one of your servants with orders to hand them over to him in person. I am taking this precaution because the fellow has a habit of never receiving the letters I write to him when I ask him to do something he does not wish to. And for the moment he does not seem to me so taken with his conquest as I hoped he might be.

Farewell, my love. If you have a good idea, some way of hastening my affairs, let me know. More than once I have acknowledged how useful your friendship is to me. I feel it again at this moment. For I am calmer than when I began this letter. At least I am talking to someone who will listen and not to the stuffed dummies in whose company I have been vegetating ever since this morning. Truly the more I live the more tempted I am to think that you and I are the only people in the world who are worth a jot.

From the Chateau de —, 3 October 17**

LETTER 101

The Vicomte de Valmont to Azolan, his valet
(Enclosed in the previous one)

You must be a real fool, leaving here this morning not knowing that Madame de Tourvel was leaving too. Or if you did know, not coming to warn me. What is the point of you wasting my money getting drunk with the valets and spending time which you should be spending in my service, flirting with the chamber-maids, if I am not to be better informed about what is going on? So much for your negligence! But I am warning you that if you make just one mistake in this present affair it will be the last one you make in my service.

You must keep me informed about everything that goes on with regard to Madame de Tourvel. Her health; whether she sleeps; if she is sad or happy; whether she often goes out and to whose house; whether she receives at home; and who goes to see her. How she spends her time. If she is out of sorts with her women servants, particularly with the one she brought here. What she does when she is on her own. Whether, when she reads, she does so uninterruptedly or breaks off to daydream. And the same when she is writing. Take care as well to make friends with the person who takes her letters to the post. Offer frequently to run this errand for him. And whenever he accepts, only post the ones which seem unimportant and send the rest to me. Especially the ones to Madame de Volanges, if you should come across any.

Make arrangements to carry on as Julie's fond lover yet awhile. If she has someone else, as you suspect, make her agree to share her favours. And do not be so foolish as to be over-scrupulous about this. You will be in the same predicament as many others who are worth far more than you. If, however, the second makes a nuisance of himself and you notice, for example, that he is too often with Julie during the day and that she is not so often with her mistress as a result, find some means to get rid of him or pick a quarrel with him. Do not worry about the consequences; I shall stand by you. Above all, do not leave the house. By paying constant attention you will be able to observe everything and observe accurately. And if by chance any of the servants were to be dismissed, propose yourself as a replacement as though you were no longer in my service. In that case just say you have left me to look for a quieter and more well-regulated household. Anyway, try to get taken on. I shall still keep you in my service during this period. It will be as it was with the Duchesse de—, and eventually Madame de Tourvel will reward you equally well.

Were you endowed with enough adroitness and enthusiasm, these instructions should suffice. But in order to make sure you are not lacking in either, I am sending you money. The attached note, as you will see, authorizes you to draw twenty-five *louis* from my agent. For I am sure you don't have a sou. You will use whatever is necessary from this amount to persuade Julie to enter into correspondence with me. The rest you may use to buy drinks for the servants. Take care, as far as possible, to let that happen in the janitor's quarters so that he is glad to see you arrive. But do not forget that it is not your pleasures but your services that I wish to fund.

Make Julie acquire the habit of observing everything and telling you everything, even what might seem to her the most minute detail. It is better for her to write ten useless sentences than to omit an interesting one. Often what seems to be of no importance, is. As it is necessary for me to be informed immediately if something happens which seems to merit atten-tion, as soon as you receive this letter you will send Philippe on the messenger's horse to establish himself in —.* He will remain

---

* A village halfway between Paris and Madame de Rosemonde's chateau.

there and await further orders, as a staging post if I need him. For ordinary correspondence the post will do.

Take care you do not lose this letter. Read it again every day, as much to assure yourself you have forgotten nothing as to be sure you still have it. Do everything expected of someone honoured by my confidence. You know that if I am satisfied with you, you will be satisfied with me.

From the Chateau de —, 3 October 17**

LETTER 102

The Présidente de Tourvel to Madame de Rosemonde

You will be very surprised, Madame, at this sudden departure of mine. This move will seem most extraordinary to you. But you will be doubly surprised when you learn the reasons for it! You may think I have not paid enough attention to the peace and quiet necessary to someone of your years; even that I am ignoring those feelings of respect and admiration due to you on so many counts. Forgive me, Madame. My heart is heavy and I must slake my grief in the bosom of a friend who is both gentle and wise. And whom should I choose but you? Look upon me as your child. Show me the kindness of a mother. I do perhaps have a right to this through my feelings for you.

The time is past, alas, when, entirely given over to these praiseworthy sentiments, I was unacquainted with those which affect the soul with mortal anguish and take away one's strength to fight, while at the same time necessitating the duty to do so. Oh, this fateful journey has been my downfall . . .

What can I say? I am in love, hopelessly in love. Alas, that word, which I have written here for the very first time, that word so often asked for in vain, I should give my life for the sweet delight of uttering it just once to the person who has inspired it. Yet I must forever deny myself that pleasure! He will still be in doubt about my feelings for him. He will believe he has reason to grieve. How unhappy I am! Why is it not as easy for him to read my heart as to reign supreme in it? Yes, I should suffer less if he were aware of all my suffering. But you yourself, to whom I am saying this, will still have only the faintest notion of it.

In a few moments I shall leave him and cause him pain. While he imagines he is still near me I shall already be far away. At the time when I was in the habit of seeing him every day I shall be in places he has never been, where I must never allow him to come. Already I have made all my preparations. Everything is here before my eyes. I can rest them upon nothing that does not announce this cruel departure. Everything is ready, except my self! And the more my heart denies it, the more it proves to me the need to submit to it.

For submit I surely shall. It is better to die than to live a guilty life. I feel I am already more than guilty. All I have rescued is my good conduct – my virtue has vanished. And I must admit that what is left still I owe to his generosity. Intoxicated with the pleasure of seeing him, of listening to his words, of the sweet delight of feeling him near, of the greater happiness of being able to make him happy, I have lost all power and strength. I had almost none left to be able to fight back, no more strength to resist. I trembled at the danger, unable as I was to escape. Well, he saw my plight and took pity on me. How should I not cherish him? I certainly owe him more than my life.

Oh, if by staying near him it was only my life I had to fear for, do not suppose I should ever have brought myself to leave. What is my life without him? Should I not be more than glad to lose it? Condemned to his and my own eternal misery; unable to complain or console him; defending myself every day against him, against my own self; putting my energies into causing him pain when I wish to devote them entirely to his happiness; living like that, is it not like dying a thousand times over? Yet that is to be my fate. But I shall bear it, I shall be brave. I herewith make this vow to you, whom I have elected to be my mother.

I also vow not to hide any of my actions from you. I beg you will receive this vow. I am asking you this as in my hour of need. Thus obliged to tell you everything, I shall acquire the habit of believing myself to be always in your presence. Your virtue will take the place of mine, for I shall certainly never allow myself to blush in your sight. And under this powerful constraint, while I shall cherish in you the indulgent friend, confidante of my weakness, I shall still honour in you the guardian angel who will save me from my shame.

It is shame enough simply to make such a request, the inevitable effect of a presumptuous trust! Why did I not fear sooner this desire that I have felt growing inside me? Why did I flatter myself I could master it or conquer it at will? Fool! I knew so little of love! Ah, if I had fought it more diligently, perhaps it would not have seized hold of me in this way! Perhaps then this departure would not have been necessary; or even if I had submitted to this painful decision, I might have been able to avoid destroying a liaison which it would have perhaps sufficed to render only less frequent! But to lose everything all at once! And for ever! Oh my friend! But alas! Even as I write, my thoughts stray and become wicked desires. Ah, let me leave, let me leave, and at least let these involuntary sins be expiated by my sacrifices.

Farewell, my honourable friend. Love me as a daughter, adopt me as your own and be assured that, in spite of this weakness of mine, I should die rather than render myself unworthy of your choice.

From —, 3 October 17** at one o'clock in the morning

LETTER 103

Madame de Rosemonde to the Présidente de Tourvel

My dearest friend, I am more affected by your departure than surprised by the reason for it. Long experience and my concern for you were enough for me to realize the condition of your heart. And, to be perfectly honest, you have told me in your

letter almost nothing I did not know already. If I had only
your letter to go by, I should still be in ignorance of whom it is
that you love. For while you speak of *him* all the time, you have
not once written his name. I did not need it. I know very well
who it is. But I make that observation because I remember that
love was always so. I see it has not changed.

I never thought I should be in the position of recalling old
memories which are so distant from me and so strange to one
of my years. Yet since yesterday I have beeen dwelling on them
a great deal in the hope of discovering in them something which
could prove useful to you. But what can I do except admire you
and sympathize? I approve of the sensible decision you have
taken, but it alarms me because I conclude from this that you
have judged it necessary. When one has reached that stage it is
very difficult to keep oneself remote from the man to whom
one's heart is constantly drawn.

Do not, however, be discouraged. Nothing is impossible to
your beautiful soul. If you were to have the misfortune to give
in to it one day (God grant it may not be so!), believe me, my
dear, you must reserve for yourself at least the consolation of
having fought with all your might. What human wisdom cannot
achieve, divine grace may bring about when it pleases. Perhaps
you are on the verge of receiving that help, and your virtue,
sorely tried in these painful struggles, will emerge more pure
and more resplendent than ever. The fortitude that you do not
possess today, pray that you will receive tomorrow. Do not,
however, count upon it to support you, but rather to encourage
you to use every ounce of your own strength.

Leaving it to Providence to protect you from a danger against
which I can do nothing, I confine myself to sustaining and
consoling you as best I can. I shall not assuage your pain, but I
shall share it. It is in that capacity that I willingly accept your
confidences. I feel that your heart must needs pour out its pain.
I open my heart to you. Age has not yet cooled it to the point
of being insensitive to friendship. You will always find it ready
to receive you. It will be a feeble comfort to your pain but at
least you shall not weep alone. And when your unhappy love,
gaining too much power over you, forces you into speaking

about it, it is better that it should be with me than with *him*. Now I am talking like you. I believe that we two will never come to the point of naming him: in any case we understand each other.

I do not know if I should tell you that he seemed to me greatly affected by your departure. Perhaps it would be wiser not to tell you about this. But I do not care for the sort of wisdom that hurts one's friends. I am obliged, however, not to speak of it any longer. My failing sight and my shaking hand do not allow me to write lengthy letters, when I have to write them myself.

So farewell, my dear. Farewell, sweet child. Yes, I shall willingly take you for my daughter, and you certainly have everything necessary to make a mother proud and delighted.

From the Chateau de —, 3 October 17**

LETTER 104

The Marquise de Merteuil to Madame de Volanges

I must admit, my dear, good friend, that I could not help feeling a rush of pride when I read your letter. Can it be that you really are honouring me by taking me entirely into your confidence and even going so far as to ask my advice? If I truly deserve your favourable opinion and do not simply owe it to your predisposition as my friend, it makes me very happy. Well, whatever prompted it, it is most precious to me, and, in my view, obtaining it is but one more reason why I should strive harder to deserve it. I shall therefore tell you frankly (but without presuming to give you advice) my own opinion. I am rather mistrustful of it, as it differs from yours. But after I have expounded my reasons to you, you may be the judge. And if you think ill of them, I bow to your judgement in advance. I shall at least be wise enough not to imagine that I am wiser than you.

If, this once, however, my view were to be preferred, we should seek the reasons in the illusions of maternal love. Since this is such a praiseworthy sentiment, it must dwell in your heart. And how evident it is in the decision you are inclined to take! If occasionally you chance to make a mistake, it is only ever when you have to choose between two virtues.

Prudence is the course which should be adopted, or so it seems to me, when the fate of others is in one's own hands, and especially when an indissoluble, holy bond like that of matrimony is in question. It is then that a wise and tender mother must *give her daughter the benefit of her own experience*, as you put it so well. I ask you, what does she have to do to give her that – other than distinguish for herself between what she may wish to do and what is right and proper?

So would it not debase and reduce a mother's authority to nothing, if she were to subordinate it to some idle fancy, whose illusory power only makes itself felt to those who are fearful of it and vanishes as soon as scorn is poured upon it? I must say that, as far as I am concerned, I never set great store by these passionate, irresistible love affairs which it is apparently quite acceptable now to use as a general excuse for flouting the conventions. I do not comprehend how an inclination, here one moment and gone the next, can have more force than the immutable principles of decency, modesty and respectability. And I do not understand either that a woman who betrays those qualities can feel her so-called passion justified, any more than a thief would be by his passion for money or an assassin by his thirst for revenge.

For who can in all honesty say they have never had to struggle? I have always sought to convince myself that to resist it was enough simply to want to resist. And my experience, so far at least, has confirmed me in that opinion. What would virtue be without the duties she imposes? Devotion to her demands sacrifices; she rewards us in our hearts. These truths cannot be denied except by those in whose interest it is to misconceive them. Already depraved, they hope to create a moment's illusion by trying to justify their bad conduct with bad reasons.

But could one fear such a thing from an innocent, timid child? And from a child of yours, whose pure, modest education has only served to reinforce a naturally happy temperament? Yet it is to this apprehension, which I would venture to call humiliating, that you wish to sacrifice the advantageous marriage you have so carefully arranged for your daughter! I like Danceny a great deal and I have not seen much of Monsieur de Gercourt for some time now, as you know; but my friendship for the one and my indifference to the other do not prevent me from appreciating the enormous difference which exists between these two.

They are equal in birth, I admit. But one is without fortune, and the other's wealth is such that even without his high birth it would have taken him anywhere. I allow that money does not equal happiness. Still, one has to admit that it is a great help. Mademoiselle de Volanges is, as you rightly say, rich enough for two. However, the sixty thousand *livres* of income that she will enjoy are not so very much when one bears the name of Danceny, or when one has to furnish and keep up an establishment that befits that name. We are no longer in the days of Madame de Sévigné.[6] Luxury has overtaken everything. One may criticize it, but one must nevertheless do as others do. And in the end superfluities deprive one of necessities.

As far as personal qualities go, and you so rightly hold them in high regard, Monsieur de Gercourt's are certainly beyond reproach, and he has given us proof of them. I like to think, and do truly believe, that Danceny is no less a man than he is. But can we be so sure? It is true that so far he has seemed exempt from the faults of youth, and despite the manners of our age he exhibits a taste for good society which augurs well for him. Yet who can tell if he does not owe this apparent wisdom to the mediocrity of his fortune? However afraid a man may be of becoming corrupt or dissolute, he needs money to be a gambler or a libertine, and it is still possible to love vice and yet fear its excesses. When all's said and done he would not be the first to have frequented good society only for lack of anything better to do.

I am not saying – God forbid – that I do believe all of this about him. But it would be a risk, and you would have only yourself to blame if things did not work out well! How would you answer your daughter if she said: 'Mother, I was young and inexperienced. I was even the victim of a mistake pardonable at my age. But God, who foresaw my weakness, granted me a mother wise enough to remedy this and preserve me from it. So why, forgetting your wisdom, did you consent to my misfortune? Was it up to me to choose a husband when I knew nothing of the estate of marriage? If this was my desire, was it not up to you to oppose it? But I never was so foolish. Determined to obey you, I awaited your decision with respectful resignation. Never did I depart from the obedience I owed you, and yet today I bear the pain which only rebellious children should have to suffer. Oh, your weakness has been my downfall . . .'? Perhaps she would suppress these complaints out of respect for you. But your maternal love would divine her feelings. And your daughter's tears, though they may be hidden from you, would still flow into your heart. So where will you then seek consolation? Will it be in this foolish love against which you should have armed her, but by which instead you have allowed yourself to be persuaded?

My dear friend, I do not know whether I have too strong a mistrust of such a passion. But even within marriage I think it something to be feared. It is not that I disapprove of a true feeling of tenderness coming to enhance the marriage bed and in some wise sweeten the duties it requires. But it is not its place to create this. It is not for the illusion of a moment to regulate our choices of a lifetime. In fact, in order to make a right choice we need to be able to make comparisons. And how can we do so when our attention is entirely taken up by one single being? When we are in a state of blind infatuation and cannot even understand that one person properly?

As you may imagine, I have met several women suffering from this dangerous complaint. I have received the confidences of some. To hear them speak, there is not one whose lover is not perfection itself. But these perfections are chimerical and exist only in their imagination. Their heads are in the clouds. Dreaming of nothing but charming qualities and virtues, they freely adorn the man of their choice with them, which all too often is like dressing some contemptible dummy in the vestment of a god. But whoever it is, hardly have they clothed him thus, than, duped by their own creation, they go down on their knees and adore him.

Either your daughter does not love Danceny or she is under the same illusion. If they love one another, both of them share it. So your reason for uniting them for ever boils down to this, to the certainty that they do not and cannot know one another. 'But,' you will object, 'do my daughter and Monsieur de Gercourt know each other any better?' No, I am sure they do not. But at least they are not deceiving each other; they are simply unaware of each other. What happens in such cases between two married people, assuming they behave correctly? Each studies the other; they observe how they behave to one another, seek and soon recognize what compromises they must make in their tastes and desires for mutual happiness. These small sacrifices are made painlessly because they are reciprocal and have been anticipated. Soon this gives rise to mutual benevolence. And habit, which strengthens all the inclinations that it does not destroy, brings about, little by little, that loving friendship, that tender trust which, together with respect, form, or so it seems to me, the true and solid basis of a happy marriage.

The illusions of love may be sweeter. But everyone knows that they are also less durable. And what danger the instant they are destroyed! It is then that the slightest faults seem shocking and unbearable by contrast with the ideal of perfection which had seduced us. Yet each party believes that it is the other who alone has changed, and that they themselves should still be appreciated for what a momentary illusion once rendered attractive. They are astonished that they no longer inspire the charm they no longer feel. They are humiliated by this. Hurt pride embitters their spirits, increases wrongs, produces bad feelings, gives birth to hatred. And in the end frivolous pleasures are paid for by long periods of misery.

So that, my dear friend, is my view of the matter under discussion. I do not defend it, I merely state it. It is up to you.

But if you continue to hold to your opinion I ask you to acquaint me with your arguments, which are opposed to mine. I shall be very happy to know your views, and especially to be reassured upon the fate of your lovely daughter, whose happiness I most ardently desire both because of my friendship for her and because of our own, which unites us as long as we live.

Paris, 4 October 17**

LETTER 105

The Marquise de Merteuil to Cécile Volanges

Well, my dear, so you are very ashamed and angry! And Monsieur de Valmont is a wicked man, isn't he? What! Does he dare treat you like the woman he loves best in the world? Has he taught you those things that you were simply dying to know? What unforgivable behaviour! And you for your part wish to keep your virtue for your lover (who has not abused it). You attend only to the pain of love, not to its pleasures! What could be better? You would make a marvellous character in a novel. Passion, misfortune and, most of all, virtue. What a wonderful array! One is sometimes bored, it is true, with all this glittering display, but one cuts a fine figure.

So the poor dear child is to be pitied, is she! And did she have shadows under her eyes next day! What will you say when your lover has shadows beneath his as well? Come come, darling, you will not always look like that. All men are not Valmonts. And then not daring to raise those little eyes! Oh my goodness, you were quite right not to! Everyone would have seen the whole adventure written in them. But, believe me, if that were the case, then the eyes of all our women and even our young girls would be more downcast.

In spite of the compliments I am obliged to pay you, as you see, you must admit that you have failed to deliver your master stroke; that is, telling your Mamma everything. And it all started so well! You had already thrown yourself into her arms; you were sobbing, she was weeping as well. What a pathetic scene! And what a pity you did not finish it! Your loving mother, in rapturous satisfaction, and by way of assisting your virtue, would have immured you in a cloister for good. And there you could have loved Danceny as much as you wanted without fear of rivalry or sin. You could have despaired as much as you wished, and Valmont for certain would not have been able to disturb your grief with his annoying pleasures.

Seriously, how can you be so childish when you are past fifteen years of age? You are right to say you do not deserve my kindness. Yet I wished to be your friend. And I should say you need that, with the mother you have, and the husband she wishes to give you! But if you do not take steps to improve your education, what do you expect people to do with you? What hope is there if what makes girls come to their senses seems on the contrary to have deprived you of yours?

If you would make up your mind to be sensible for a moment, you would soon realize that you need to congratulate yourself rather than complain. But you are ashamed, and that is a worry to you! Well, calm down. The shame caused by love is like the pain, you only experience it once. You can pretend later, but you do not feel it any more. Yet the pleasure remains, and that is something. Do I understand through all your babbling that you could even set great store by it? Come now, be honest. This *trouble* which prevented you from *doing what you said*, which made you find it *so difficult to defend yourself*, which made you *almost sorry* when Valmont departed, was it really shame that caused it or was it pleasure? And his *way of talking*, so that *it is hard to know how to answer him*, would that not be because of his way of behaving? Ah my girl, you are telling lies and lying to your friend! That is not good enough. But let us say no more about it.

What might be a pleasure and no more than a pleasure for the rest of us has been a real stroke of fortune as far as you are concerned. For caught as you are in between a mother whose love you need and a lover whose love you want for ever, do you not see that the only way of obtaining these contrary outcomes is to occupy yourself with a third party? You will be distracted by this new affair, and while vis-à-vis your Mamma you will appear to be making a sacrifice and submitting to her wishes, you will acquire in the eyes of your lover the honour of putting up a good defence. Assuring him constantly of your love, you will not grant him the final proof of it. And in the circumstances he will be sure to attribute these refusals, which will not cause you any pain at all, to your virtuous character. He might complain about them, but he will love you all the more. And while you appear to be doubly deserving – to the one in the sacrifice of your love, and to the other in your resisting – all it will cost you is the enjoyment of its pleasures. Oh, how many women whose reputations have been ruined would have kept them intact had they seen their way to sustaining them in this manner!

Does the course I am suggesting not seem the most reasonable as well as the most attractive? Do you realize what you have achieved from the decision you have taken? Your Mamma has attributed your excessive grief to an excess of love; she is outraged by this and, to punish you for it, all she is waiting for is to be quite certain. She has just written to me about it. She is going to try every means to make you admit it and, to make you talk, she will even go so far as to suggest you marry Danceny. But if you allow yourself to be taken in by this false display of affection, and reply according to the dictates of your heart, you will soon be locked away for a very long time, perhaps for ever, and will repent your blind credulity at leisure.

You have to counteract the trick she is trying to play on you by playing one on her. So start by not making such a display of your melancholy, so as to make her believe your mind is not continually on Danceny. She will be persuaded of it so much more easily as this is the usual result of absence. And she will be all the more pleased with you, for she will find she has occasion to congratulate herself on her prudence, which has suggested to her this course of action. But if she still has her doubts and, persists in putting you to the test, and comes to discuss marriage with you, like the well-born girl you are, just contain your feelings and give in completely. For what risk do you run? As far as husbands go, one is just as good as another. And even the most unaccommodating is much less of a trial than a mother.

Once she is more content with you, your Mamma will finally arrange your marriage. And then you will have more freedom of action and be able to, if you wish, leave Valmont and take Danceny, or even keep them both. For, mark my words, your Danceny is a nice young man. But he is one of those men you can have whenever you want and as often as you want, so you may feel easy about him. Valmont is quite another matter. He is a difficult man to keep and a dangerous one to leave. You need to exercise a great deal of skill with him, and if you do not have skill, then a great deal of docility. On the other hand, if you were able to form a friendship with him, it would be a real piece of good fortune! He would immediately place you in the first rank of our women of fashion. That is the way one acquires a certain substance in society, not by blushing and weeping as you did in the days when your nuns made you kneel at supper.

So if you are sensible you will try to make it up with Valmont, who must be very angry with you. And as you must learn to repair these foolish mistakes, do not be afraid to make advances to him. You will soon learn that though men are the ones who make the first move, we are almost always obliged to make the second. You have a pretext for this, for you must not keep this letter: I insist that as soon as you have read it you give it to Valmont. But do not forget to seal it again before you do. First, because you must be allowed to take the credit for your actions towards him, and not seem to be acting simply upon advice. And then because I am the only friend that you have in the whole world close enough to speak to you as I do.

Farewell, my angel. Follow my advice and tell me if you feel better for it.

P.S. By the way, I was forgetting ... One word more. Take more care with your style. You still write like a child. I can see why. It is because you say everything you think and never what you do not think. That is all right between you and me, since we have nothing to hide from each other. But with everyone else! And especially with your lover! You will always be thought of as a silly little girl. When you write to someone, you see, you are writing for them, not for yourself. You should attempt to talk less about what you think and more about what the person you are writing to will wish to hear.

Farewell, dear heart. I shall kiss you instead of scolding you, hoping that you will be more reasonable in future.

Paris, 4 October 17**

LETTER 106

The Marquise de Merteuil to the Vicomte de Valmont

Bravo, Vicomte, this time I love you madly! In any case, after the first of your two letters I was expecting the second, so I did not find it very surprising. And while you were already boasting about your future successes and claiming your reward, and asking if I were ready, I could see that I had no need to hurry. Yes, on my honour. As I was reading your touching account of this love scene which *deeply moved you*; as I observed your restraint, worthy of the best tradition of chivalry, I said to myself a dozen times: 'He has bungled it!'

But how could it be otherwise? What do you expect a poor woman to do if she gives herself to you and you do not take her? In such cases, for Heaven's sake, one must at least save face. And that is what your Présidente has done. My impression is that this march she has stolen upon you is not without its effect, and I intend to make use of it myself on the first important occasion that arises. But, I promise you, if the person for whom I pay that price does not take advantage of it any better than you have done, he can forget about me for ever, and that's for sure.

So now you are reduced to absolutely nothing! And by two women, one already the affair of the *morning after*, and the other longing to be one! My goodness! You will think I am showing off and that it is easy to be wise after the event, but I swear to you I was expecting it. You do not really have a genius for your role in life; you know nothing except what you have learned, and you invent nothing. So, as soon as circumstances no longer lend themselves to your usual formulas and you have to depart from the normal routes, you are brought up short like a schoolboy. On the one hand childish behaviour and on the other a return of prudery are enough to disconcert you totally because you do not come across them every day. And you can neither prevent nor remedy them. Ah Vicomte! Vicomte! You teach me not to judge men by their successes. But soon we shall have to say about you: 'He was a fine fellow once.' And when you have committed one foolishness after another you come running back to me! It would seem I have nothing else to do except make good your mistakes. It is true I should have more than enough to keep me busy.

Whatever the rights and wrongs of these two affairs, the one is undertaken against my wishes and I do not want to become involved. As to the other, as you have been to some extent helpful to me, I will concern myself with it. The letter that I append here, which you must read first and then deliver to the little Volanges girl, is more than enough to bring her back. But I beg you to take pains with the child, and let us unite in causing her to be the despair of her mother and of Gercourt. Do not be afraid to increase the dose. It is plain that she will not be the least bit frightened if you do. And once our designs are fulfilled she will have to cope as best she can.

I shall pull out of the whole affair completely. I had a vague notion of making her a subsidiary in the plot and have her play a supporting role, but I see she is not the right material. She has a silly ingenuousness which has not been cured even by your medicine, which scarcely ever fails. And that is in my opinion the most dangerous illness a woman can have. It denotes, above all, a weakness of character which is almost always incurable and resistant to everything. So while we were busy schooling the child for intrigue, all we should make of her would be a woman of easy virtue. Now I know nothing so dull as that faculty for stupidity that gives itself without knowing how or why, but only because it is being attacked and cannot resist. That kind of woman is nothing but a pleasure machine.

You will say that we may as well do that, and that that is enough for our purposes. Well, all right! But let us not forget that everyone soon becomes familiar with the springs and motors of that sort of machine. So in order to make use of this one without danger you have to be quick, and stop in good time, and then destroy it. In truth we shall have plenty of ways of getting rid of her, and Gercourt will have her safely put away as soon as we like. In fact, when he no longer has any doubts about his discomfiture and the whole thing is very public and notorious, what difference does it make if he takes his revenge, as long as he does not console himself? What I say about the husband, you no doubt are thinking about the mother. So it is as good as done.

This decision I have reached seems to me the best and has convinced me we should lead the child along rather rapidly, as you will see from my letter. That makes it also very important not to leave anything in her hands that could compromise us, and I beg you to pay attention to this. Once we have taken this precaution I will look after the moral side and the rest is up to you. If, however, we see that the ingenuousness corrects itself afterwards, we shall still have time to alter the plan. We should in any case one day have had to consider what we are going to do. But our attention to detail will in no circumstances be wasted.

Did you know that mine very nearly was, and that Gercourt's lucky star almost triumphed over my prudence? That Madame de Volanges had a momentary maternal weakness? That she wanted to give her daughter to Danceny? That was the meaning of the more tender interest manifested *the morning after*. And again you are the one who would have been the cause of this fine state of affairs! Fortunately her loving mother wrote me a letter about it, and I hope my reply will turn her against that idea. In it I go on such a lot about virtue and flatter her so much, she must be persuaded I am right.

I am annoyed I did not have time to take a copy of my letter, so that I could edify you about the strictness of my morality. You would see how I pour scorn on women depraved enough to take lovers! It is so easy to be moralistic when one is writing! It never hurts anyone but other people, and troubles oneself not at all ... And I am very well aware that the good lady had, like everyone, her own little *faiblesses* in her younger days, so I was pleased to humiliate her, if only to prick her conscience. It would console me a little for the praise I lavished on her against my own conscience. And so it was that in the same letter the idea of hurting Gercourt gave me the strength to speak well of him.

Farewell, Vicomte. I am greatly in favour of your decision to remain for a time in your present situation. I can think of no way to hasten your progress, but I invite you to relieve your boredom with the pupil we have in common. As for me, in spite of your polite quotation you must see that we still have to wait a while. And you will no doubt agree that it is not my fault.

Paris, 4 October 17**

LETTER 107

Azolan to the Vicomte de Valmont

Monsieur,
In accordance with your instructions I went to Monsieur Bertrand's house as soon as I received your letter and he gave me twenty-five *louis*, as you had told him to. I asked him for two more for Philippe, whom I had told to leave straight away as Monsieur ordered, and who had no money. But your agent refused, saying he had not received any such order from you. So I was obliged to give him them myself, and perhaps Monsieur will be so good as to bear that in mind.

Philippe left last night. I instructed him carefully to stay in the inn so that we could be sure of getting hold of him if necessary.

I went to Madame la Présidente's house immediately afterwards to see Mademoiselle Julie. But she had gone out and I
was only able to speak to La Fleur, who could tell me nothing,
because since her arrival he has only been in the house at
meal-times. It was his assistant on duty and, as Monsieur
knows, I am not acquainted with him. But I made a start on
my work today.

I went back to Mademoiselle Julie's this morning and she
seemed most happy to see me. I questioned her as to the reason
for her mistress's return, but she told me she did not know and
I believe she was telling the truth. I scolded her for not warning
me of her departure and she assured me she did not know about
it until the same evening when she went to help Madame to
bed. The poor girl spent the whole night packing and did not
have more than a couple of hours' sleep. She did not emerge
from her mistress's bedroom until past one o'clock in the morning, leaving her on her own and about to write a letter.

In the morning, as she was leaving, Madame de Tourvel gave
a letter to the housekeeper in the chateau. Mademoiselle Julie
does not know who it was for. She said it was perhaps for
Monsieur. But Monsieur has not said anything about it.

During the whole journey Madame had a large hood covering
her face, and therefore could not be seen, but Mademoiselle
Julie is sure she wept frequently. She did not say a word on the
way, and she did not wish to stop at —,* as she had done on
the way down. That was not very pleasant for Julie, who had
not breakfasted. But, as I told her, a mistress is a mistress.

On arrival Madame retired to bed, but she only remained
there for two hours. When she rose she summoned her porter
and gave him orders not to allow anyone in. She did not wash
or dress. She went down to dinner, but she only ate a little soup
and then left immediately. They took her coffee up to her and
Mademoiselle Julie went in at the same time. She found her
mistress tidying papers in her desk and saw they were letters.
I'll wager they were letters from Monsieur. And of the three
that arrived for her in the afternoon there was one she still had

* Still the same village, halfway to Paris.

in front of her in the evening! I am sure it was another one from Monsieur. But why did she run away like that? I am most astonished! Anyway, Monsieur must know why, and it is none of my business.

Madame la Présidente went into the library in the afternoon and took two books which she carried off to her boudoir. Mademoiselle Julie assures me she did not read them for more than a quarter of an hour the whole day, and all she did was read that letter, dream and hold her head in her hands. As I expect Monsieur would dearly like to know what those books were, and Mademoiselle Julie had no idea, I got someone to take me to the library today on the pretext of visiting it. There was only an empty space for two books: one was for the second volume of *Christian Thoughts* and the other the first volume of a book entitled *Clarissa*.[7] I am writing it down exactly as it is. Monsieur will perhaps know the book.

Yesterday evening Madame did not have supper. She only drank tea.

She rang early this morning. She called for her horses immediately and she was at the Feuillants[8] before nine o'clock, where she observed Mass. She wished to go to confession, but her confessor was away and will not be back for eight or ten days. I thought it was best to inform Monsieur of that.

She came back afterwards and started to write, and was writing for nearly an hour. I took an early opportunity to do what Monsieur most wished me to do. I was the one to take the letters to the post. There were none for Madame de Volanges, but I am sending one to Monsieur which was for the Président. I thought that one would be the most interesting. There was one for Madame de Rosemonde too, but I thought Monsieur would be able to see that whenever he wished and I let it go. Moreover, Monsieur will soon know everything because Madame la Présidente has written to him as well. From now on I shall have all the ones he wants. For it is almost always Mademoiselle Julie who gives them to the servants, and she has assured me that out of friendship for me and also for Monsieur she is happy to do what I want.

She did not even wish to take the money I offered. But I am

sure Monsieur would like to make her a little present and, if he does and he wishes me to do so on his behalf, I can easily find out what she would like.

I hope Monsieur will not find I have neglected my duties. I believe it is important to give him reasons why I did what he has accused me of. If I was not aware of the departure of Madame la Présidente, it was because of my zeal to serve Monsieur, since he was the one who made me leave at three in the morning, which meant that I did not see Mademoiselle Julie the evening before, as I usually do, since I slept at Tournebride,[9] so that I would not wake anyone in the chateau.

As to Monsieur scolding me for being so often penniless, first it is because I like to keep up a good appearance, as Monsieur can see; and I have to uphold the honour of the coat I wear. I know I should perhaps save a little for the future, but I put my entire trust in the generosity of Monsieur, who is such a good master.

As for entering the service of Madame de Tourvel while remaining in Monsieur's service, I hope Monsieur will not require this of me. It was very different at Madame la Duchesse's. But I certainly shall not wear the livery and especially not that of the Law after having had the privilege of being Monsieur's valet.[10] As to the rest, Monsieur may do what he likes with the man who has the honour of being his most respectful, affectionate and humble servant.

Roux Azolan, valet

Paris, 5 October 17**, at eleven o'clock at night

LETTER 108

The Présidente de Tourvel to Madame de Rosemonde

My dear, kind mother, how grateful I am to you and how I needed that letter of yours! I read and re-read it, over and over. I could not tear myself away. The only moments I have found bearable since my departure I owe to that letter. How kind you are! Wisdom and virtue have compassion for my *faiblesse*! You pity my misfortune! Oh, if you only knew! . . . It is terrible. I believed I had felt the pangs of love. But the inexpressible torment, and you must feel it yourself to have any idea what it is like, is to be separated from your beloved, to be separated from him for ever! . . . Yes, the overwhelming pain I feel today will be there again tomorrow, and the day after, and through my whole life! My God, I am still so young, what a deal of time is left for suffering!

To be the architect of my own misfortune; to tear my heart out with my own hands; and, while I am suffering this unbearable pain, to know that I could end it with a single word, except that the word is a crime! Oh, my friend! . . .

When I took that painful decision to leave him, I hoped that absence would increase my courage and strength. How wrong I was! Quite the opposite seems to be the case; it has destroyed them utterly. I know I had more to fight against. But even when I was resisting him I was not totally deprived of him. At least I saw him sometimes. Often, even, without daring to raise my eyes and look at him, I could feel his eyes fixed upon me. Yes, my dear, I could feel them. They seemed to be giving warmth to my soul. And though his gaze did not meet mine, it nevertheless entered my heart. But now, in my painful solitude and isolated from everything which is dear to me, cloistered with my misfortune, all moments of my sad existence are bathed in tears and nothing sweetens the bitterness. My sacrifices have brought me no consolation. And those I have made so far have served only to render more painful still the sacrifices I have yet to make.

Only yesterday this was brought home to me. In the letters they delivered there was one from him. From two yards away I recognized it from among the others. I rose involuntarily. I was shaking; I could scarcely hide my emotion. But this state was not unpleasurable. One moment later, as soon as I was alone, this deceptively sweet feeling vanished and left me with but one more sacrifice to make. For how could I open this letter that I was nevertheless longing to read? Because of the fate that pursues me, the consolations which seem to offer themselves

only impose new privations. And these become still more cruel
when I reflect that Monsieur de Valmont is experiencing them
as well.

So there it is finally, the name that is obsessing me, the one I
had so much trouble writing. When you almost rebuked me for
this it truly alarmed me. I beg you to believe that a false modesty
has not lessened my trust in you. Why should I be fearful of
naming him? Oh, I blush for my feelings and not for the person
who causes them. Who is worthier than he to inspire them! Yet
I do not know why this name does not come naturally to my
pen. And this time I still needed to reflect before I wrote it. But
let us return to the subject again.

You tell me he seemed *greatly affected by my departure.* So
what did he do? What did he say? Did he speak of returning to
Paris? I beg you to persuade him not to, if it lies in your power.
If he has judged me well, he should not bear me a grudge if I
act in this way. But he must also realize that it is a decision
I cannot go back on. One of my greatest torments is not knowing what he thinks. I have his letter still here . . . But you will
probably agree that I must not open it.

It is only through you, my understanding friend, that I am
not entirely separated from him. I do not wish to abuse your
kindness. I know perfectly well that you cannot write long
letters. But you will not refuse your child two words, one to
sustain her courage and the other to console her. Farewell, my
honourable friend.

Paris, 5 October 17**

LETTER 109

Cécile Volanges to the Marquise de Merteuil

It is only today, Madame, that I gave Monsieur de Valmont the
letter you did me the honour of writing to me. I kept it for four
days in spite of my frequent fears that it would be discovered,

but I did hide it very carefully. And when I was overcome by despair again I shut myself away and read it once more.

I quite see now that what I thought was such a great misfortune is scarcely one at all. And I must admit there is a great deal in it that is pleasurable. So that I am hardly sad at all any more. It is only the thought of Danceny that still torments me sometimes. But now for much of the time I don't think about him at all! Monsieur de Valmont is so amiable!

I made it up with him two days ago. It was very easy for me. For I had only just opened my mouth to speak when he said that if I had something to say to him he would come to my room that evening, and all I had to do was say yes. And then, as soon as he got there, he did not seem any more put out than if I had never done anything to upset him. He only scolded me afterwards and then it was very gently, and it was like ... Just like you did. And that proved to me that he was also my good friend.

I can't tell you how many funny things he recounted to me. I would never have believed them, especially about Mamma. I should love to know from you if they are true. What is certain is that I could not stop laughing. Once I laughed right out loud and we were both scared, for Mamma might have heard us, and if she had come to see what was going on, what would have become of me? She would certainly have sent me back to the convent!

As I must be careful and as Monsieur de Valmont said himself he would not want to risk compromising me, we agreed that in future he would just come and open the door, and that we would go into his bedroom. There is no danger there. I was there yesterday already and at the time of writing I am expecting him to come again. So I hope, Madame, you will not scold me any more.

But there was one thing that really surprised me about your letter. It's what you said about when I am married, concerning Danceny and Monsieur de Valmont. It seems to me that one day at the Opera you were telling me something quite different, that once married I would only be able to love my husband and have to forget all about Danceny. But perhaps I did not quite understand you and I would much prefer it to be different, because now I shall no longer be afraid to be married. I even desire it, for then I shall have more freedom. And I hope I shall be able to manage in such a way that I need think of no one but Danceny. I feel that I shall only be truly happy with him. For at the moment the thought of him keeps tormenting me, and I am only content when I can stop thinking about him, which is very difficult. As soon as I do, I immediately become very depressed again.

What consoles me a little is that you assure me that Danceny will love me more. But are you absolutely certain? Oh yes, you would not wish to tell me falsehoods. Yet it is funny that it should be Danceny I love and that Monsieur de Valmont ... But, as you say, perhaps it is fortunate! Well, we shall see.

I do not quite understand what you say about my style. I think Danceny likes my letters just how they are. Yet I know I must not say anything to him about what is going on with Monsieur de Valmont. So you need not worry.

Mamma has not spoken to me yet about my marriage. But let us wait. When she mentions it, since it is to trick me, I promise I shall be able to conceal the truth.

Farewell, my dear friend. I am so grateful to you and I promise I shall never forget all your kindness to me. I must stop, for it is almost one and Monsieur de Valmont will be here before long.

From the Chateau de —, 10 October 17**

LETTER 110

The Vicomte de Valmont to the Marquise de Merteuil

*Heavenly powers, my soul was fit for sorrow; give me a soul fit for happiness!**[11] It is, I believe, the tender Saint-Preux who expresses himself thus. I am better endowed than he was; I

* Rousseau, *La Nouvelle Héloïse*.

possess both at one and the same time! Yes my friend, I am both very happy and very unhappy. And since you have my absolute trust I owe you the twofold account of my pain and of my pleasure.

Do you know that my ungrateful devotee is still being cruel to me? She has now sent my fourth letter back. Perhaps I am wrong to say fourth, for I guessed after the first it would be followed by many others, and not wishing to waste my time like that I decided to couch my complaints in platitudes and not put any dates on them. And ever since the second it is always the same letter going back and forth. All I do is change the envelope. If my beauty ends up doing what they all do as a rule and one day takes pity, if only out of weariness, she will finally keep the letter and it will be time then to find out how things are going. As you can see, with this new kind of correspondence I cannot be in command of all the facts.

But I have found out that the fickle creature has changed her confidante. At least I am sure that since her departure from the chateau no letter has arrived from her for Madame de Volanges, whereas two have come for old Rosemonde. And as the latter has not said anything, and as she does not open her mouth any more about her 'dear girl', of whom she used to talk endlessly, I conclude that she is the one who is the confidante. I presume that it is on the one hand her need to discuss me, and on the other the slight shame with regard to Madame de Volanges of reverting to feelings for so long denied, which have produced this momentous change in tactics. I am still afraid I may have lost out; for the older women get, the harsher and stricter they become. The former would certainly have spoken more ill of me, but the latter will speak more ill of love; and the sensitive prude is much more afraid of the feeling than the person who inspires it.

The only way I can learn the facts is, as you see, to intercept the clandestine correspondence. I have already sent my orders about this to my valet and I am expecting him to carry them out day by day. Until then I can do nothing systematic. So for the last week I have been vainly going over every stratagem known to man, those taken from novels and from my own secret diaries. I find none suitable, either to the circumstances of the affair or to the character of the heroine. The difficulty would not be getting into her room, even at night, or yet again to make her go to sleep and create a new Clarissa.[12] But after two months of toiling away and putting myself out for her, to have recourse to means that are not my own! Dragging myself along in that servile way in the wake of others and winning a victory without any glory! . . . No, she shall not have *the pleasures of vice and the honours of virtue.*[*][13] It is not enough for me to possess her, I want her to surrender. Now in order for that to happen, not only must I get into her room, I must arrive there at her invitation, find her alone and ready to listen, and especially to close her eyes to the danger, for if she sees it she must rise above it or die. But the more I know what I have to do, the harder I find it to carry it out. And if you were again to make fun of me, I can tell you that my embarrassment increases the more I think about it.

I should be driven mad, I do believe, were it not for the happy distraction afforded me by our communal pupil. I owe it to her that I still have better things to do than write elegies.

Would you believe that the girl was so terrified that three long days went by before your letter produced its full effect? See how one single false notion can spoil the happiest of natures!

It was not until Saturday that she approached me and stammered out a few words. And they were mumbled so quietly and so shame-facedly that it was impossible to hear them, but the blush they provoked made me guess at their meaning. Until then I had retained my pride. However, yielding to such a pleasing repentance, I was happy to promise that I would go and see the pretty penitent that very evening. And this forgiveness on my part was received with all the gratitude due to such a kindness.

As I never lose sight of your projects or of mine, I have resolved to take advantage of this opportunity to find out the child's potential, and also to accelerate her education. But to pursue this work with greater freedom I needed to change our

---

* Rousseau, *La Nouvelle Héloïse.*

meeting place. For a mere closet, which is all that separates your pupil's room from her mother's, would not afford her enough security to allow her to show herself at her ease. So I had promised myself to make some noise *innocently*, that would cause her enough alarm to make her take a safer refuge in future. She spared me this trouble.

The little lady laughs a lot. And to encourage her gaiety I took it into my head, during the intervals, to tell her all the scandalous adventures that came into my head. And to spice them up and focus her attention more sharply I said they all concerned her mother, whom I very much enjoyed slandering with vice and follies.

My idea was not without an ulterior motive. More than anything else it encouraged my shy little schoolgirl and inspired in her at the same time the deepest contempt for her mother. I have long ago noticed that, if it is not always necessary to use this means to seduce a young girl, it is an indispensable and often the most effective course when one wishes to corrupt her. For the girl who does not respect her mother will not respect herself. A moral truth that I believe to be so useful that I am very glad to provide another example of its application.

However, your pupil, with never a thought for morals, was in fits of laughter all the time. And once she nearly burst. It was easy to make her believe she had made *a terrible noise*. I pretended to be extremely scared, a feeling she was easily persuaded to share. And so that she would not forget it, I did not allow pleasure to rear its head again, but left her three hours earlier than usual. So as we parted we agreed that we should meet in my room from the following day onwards.

I have already received her twice there. And in this short time the schoolgirl has become almost as skilled as her teacher. Yes, I have taught her everything, including the variations! Everything except the precautions.

So being occupied all night I make up for it by sleeping a good part of the day. And as the current society in the chateau holds no attraction for me, I spend scarcely an hour in the salon in the course of the day. I have even, from today, decided to eat in my room and I hope to leave it only for a little walk now and then. This odd behaviour is put down to my health. I declared that I was *overcome by the vapours*.[14] I also told them I had a touch of the fever. All I have to do is speak in a slow, muffled voice. As to the change in my expression, rely on your pupil. *Love will provide the reason.**[15]

I occupy my leisure hours with thinking up how to make good the advantage I have lost over the ungrateful woman and also with composing a sort of catechism of debauchery[16] for my schoolgirl to use. I take pleasure in using only the technical word for everything, and I laugh in anticipation at the interesting conversation that that will doubtless provide for her and Gercourt on their wedding night. Nothing is more amusing than the naivety with which she already uses the little she knows of this language! She has no idea there is any other way of expressing herself! This child is truly seductive! This contrast between her naive candour and the boldness of her language never fails to have its effect on me. I don't know why it is only odd things that please me.

Perhaps I am too occupied with the girl, for I am compromising my time and my health. But I hope that my pretended illness, apart from sparing me from the boredom of the salon, will still be of some use where the austere devotee is concerned, who marries the virtues of a tigress with such sweet sensitivity! I do not doubt that she has already been informed about my grave indisposition, and I am longing to know her opinion of it. All the more so because I wager she will not fail to take the credit for it herself. In future I shall regulate the state of my health by the impression it makes upon her.

So now, my dear, you are as up-to-date as I am about my affairs. I hope soon to have more interesting news to tell; and beg you to believe that, among the pleasures I am looking forward to, I greatly prize the reward I am expecting from you.

From the Chateau de —, 11 October 17**

---

* Regnard, *Folies amoureuses.*

LETTER 111

The Comte de Gercourt to Madame de Volanges

All seems quiet in this country, Madame, and we daily expect permission to return to France. I hope you will not doubt that I am still as anxious as ever to return and tie the knot that will unite me to you and to Mademoiselle de Volanges. However, Monsieur le Duc de —, my cousin, to whom you know I have a great many obligations, has just told me of his recall to Naples. He writes that he hopes to go via Rome and see the parts of Italy he is not acquainted with on the way. He has invited me to accompany him on this journey, which will take about six weeks or two months. I cannot deny that it would be pleasant for me to take advantage of this opportunity, knowing that once I am married I shall find it hard to take the time to absent myself except when military service requires. So perhaps it would be best to wait until winter to get married, since that is the only possible time when all my relatives are together in Paris, and in particular Monsieur le Marquis de —, to whom I owe my hopes of belonging to your family. In spite of these considerations my plans in this respect will be completely subordinated to your own and, should you favour the arrangement we first made, then I am ready to cancel mine. I beg you only to let me know your intentions as soon as possible. I shall await your reply here and that alone will decide my actions.

I am respectfully, Madame, and with all the sentiments that behove a son, your very humble, etc.

Comte de Gercourt

Bastia, 10 October 17**

LETTER 112

Madame de Rosemonde to the Présidente de Tourvel (Dictated)

I have only just received, my dear, your letter of the eleventh* and the gentle reproach it contains. You must admit you would have liked to make many more, and that, had you not remembered you were my *daughter*, you would have really scolded me. That would have been most unjust of you! It was because of my wish and my hope of being able to reply to you myself that I put it off each day. But as you see, even now I am obliged to borrow the writing hand of my maid. My unfortunate rheumatism has taken hold again.[17] It has lodged in my right arm this time, rendering it quite useless. That is what it is like to have such an aged friend, when you are so young and fresh! You suffer from her infirmities.

As soon as my pain lets up a little I promise we will have a long talk. In the meantime, this is to let you know that I have received your two letters, and that they have redoubled, if such a thing is possible, my tender affection for you, and that I shall never cease taking the keenest interest in all your doings.

My nephew is also a little indisposed, but not in any danger, and there is nothing to worry about. It is a minor ailment which in my opinion is affecting his mood rather than his health. We scarcely see him nowadays.

His retirement and your departure have made our little circle less gay. The little Volanges girl especially regrets your absence and yawns so much the whole day long she looks as if she might swallow her fists. For the last few days in particular she has been doing us the honour of falling fast asleep every day after dinner.

Farewell, my dear. I am your very good friend, your Mamma, your sister even, if my great age allowed me to call myself that. Anyway, I am bound to you by all the most tender sentiments.

Signed: Adélaïde on behalf of Madame de Rosemonde

From the Chateau de —, 14 October 17**

* This letter has not been found.

LETTER 113

The Marquise de Merteuil to the Vicomte de Valmont

I feel I must warn you, Vicomte, that people are beginning to talk about you in Paris. Your absence has been noted and already people are guessing the reason for it. Yesterday I was at a supper where there were a great many guests. It was said there authoritatively that a romantic and unhappy love affair had kept you in the country. Immediately the faces of all those jealous of your success lit up with joy, as did those of all the women you have neglected. If you take my advice, you will not allow these dangerous rumours to gain ground, but will come back directly and put an end to them by your presence.

Just remember that if you once allow the idea that you are irresistible to lose credence, you will soon see that in fact people will resist you more easily; that your rivals will also lose respect for you and dare to stand up to you. For which of them does not think himself a match for virtue? Above all, remember that from among the multitudes of women you have flaunted in public, all those you have not possessed will be trying to disabuse people, while the others will be doing all they can to deceive them. But, anyway, you must expect that now you will be rated perhaps as much below your worth as up till now you have been rated above it.

Come back then, Vicomte, and do not sacrifice your reputation to a childish whim. You have made all we wanted of the little Volanges girl. And as to your Présidente, I should imagine it is not by staying ten leagues away from her that you will rid yourself of your fantasies. Do you think she is going to come looking for you? Perhaps she is already no longer thinking about you, or only inasmuch as she is congratulating herself for having humiliated you. At least here you would be able to find some opportunity to reappear with a flourish, which is what you need to do. And if you insist on carrying on with your ridiculous affair, I do not see that your coming back would do any harm ... Quite the contrary.

In fact, if your Présidente *adores you* as you have so often asserted, but seldom proved, her only consolation, her only pleasure, these days must be to talk about you, and to know what you are doing, what you are saying, what you are thinking, and every last detail about you. These paltry things assume some value because of the privations one endures. They are like crumbs falling from a rich man's table. He may scorn them, but the poor man eagerly gathers them up and derives nourishment from them. Now at present the poor Présidente is getting all those crumbs. And the more she has, the less anxious she will be to indulge her appetite for the rest.

Besides, since you know her confidante, you must know that each letter from her contains at least one little sermon and everything she thinks likely to *strengthen her goodness and fortify her virtue.**[18] Why then, leave the one with resources to defend herself and the other with resources to harm you?

Not that I agree with you at all about the loss you believe you have sustained in the change of confidante. In the first place Madame de Volanges loathes you, and hatred is always more clear-sighted and ingenious than friendship. And for all your old aunt's virtues, she will not for a single instant say anything bad about her darling nephew. For virtue also has its failings. Besides, your fears are based on a totally false observation.

It is not true that the *older women get, the harsher and stricter they become.* It is between forty and fifty that the despair of seeing their beauty fade, the rage of feeling that they have to abandon the pretensions and pleasures they still cling to, make almost all women sour and prudish. They need this long interval in order to make such an enormous sacrifice. But as soon as it is accomplished they all divide into two types.

The most numerous, those women who have had only beauty and youth to recommend them, fall into feeble-minded apathy, and only emerge from it to play cards and perform a few acts of devotion. They are always boring, often irritable, sometimes a little aggravating but rarely malicious. But one cannot say these women are, or are not, strict. There is not a thought in

---

* *On ne s'avise jamais de tout!* Comédie.

their heads; they are scarcely alive; they repeat everything other people say indifferently and uncomprehendingly, and remain complete nullities themselves.

The other type, much rarer but precious, are those women who, having once had some personality and not having neglected to look after their intellect, know how to create a life for themselves when nature lets them down. They decide to put into their brains the attributes they previously used to enhance their beauty. These women usually have very sane judgement and considerable intelligence of a gay and gracious kind. They replace their seductive charms with an appealing kindness and also with a cheerfulness whose attraction only increases with age. In making themselves loved by the young, they manage in some sense to recapture their youth. And then, far from being, as you say, *harsh and strict*, their habit of tolerance and their long experience of human frailty, and especially the memories of their youth by which they alone remain reconciled to life, incline them, perhaps sometimes rather too much, to indulgence.

What I can tell you, though, is that, having always sought the society of older women, because I realized at a very early stage that they were very useful to have on my side, I came across several who not only served my interests but whom I also found sympathetic. I shall not labour the point. For since you are getting so easily and so *morally* inflamed these days, I am afraid you might suddenly fall in love with your old aunt, and bury yourself with her in the tomb where you have been living for such a long time. So to go back to what I was saying.

However enchanted you apparently are with your little schoolgirl, I cannot believe she is essential to your plans. You found her at your disposal, you took her. Good for you! But it cannot be a real choice. It is not even, if we are honest, an undivided pleasure. All you possess is her body! I won't even mention her heart, for I am sure you do not care a jot for that. But you are not even in her head. I do not know if you have noticed, but I have the proof of it in the last letter she wrote,* I am sending it so that you can see for yourself. You can see

---

* See Letter 109.

that when she writes about you it is always *Monsieur de Valmont*. All her thoughts, even the ones that you have put into her head, end only in Danceny. And she does not call him 'Monsieur', but always only *Danceny*. In this way she distinguishes him from everyone else. And though she gives herself to you, it is with him that she is intimate. If such a conquest strikes you as *fascinating*, if the pleasure she gives you *makes you grow more fond of her*, then you are surely undemanding and easy to please! I allow you to keep her. That is even part of my plans. But it seems to me that it is not worth inconveniencing yourself another quarter of an hour more. It seems to me that you should also exercise some power over her, and only allow her to get near to Danceny, for instance, after you have made her forget him a little more.

Before I stop talking about your affairs and tell you about mine, I wish to advise you that the strategy of illness you tell me you intend to adopt is very well-known and well-tried. Really, Vicomte, you are not very imaginative! I do repeat myself as well sometimes, as you will see. But my saving grace is in the detail, and the outcome especially does justice to me. I am going to try another one, a new adventure. I agree that it will not have the merit of being challenging, but I am bored to tears.

I do not know why, but ever since the Prévan affair I have found Belleroche unbearable. He has become much more attentive, loving, adoring, and I cannot stand it. At first I found his anger amusing. But then I had to calm him down, for it would have been compromising to allow him to continue. And there was no way I could make him listen to reason. So I decided to be more loving towards him, in order to quieten him down more easily. But he took it seriously. And ever since then he has been getting on my nerves with his everlasting infatuation. I have noticed in particular the insulting confidence he has in me, and his complacency in regarding me as his for ever. I am truly humiliated by this. Does he place such little value upon me that he thinks himself man enough to capture me! Did he not say recently that I could never have loved anyone but him? Oh, at that moment I needed all my prudence not to disabuse him then and there, by enlightening him about the true situation. What an amusing fellow he is, to be sure, thinking he has exclusive rights! I grant you he cuts a fine figure and is quite handsome. But when all is said and done he is in fact only an *unskilled worker* in the matter of love. Well, anyway, the time has come for us to go our separate ways.

For the last two weeks I have been trying to do just that. I have been cool, capricious, moody and quarrelsome by turns; but he is clinging and does not let go that easily. So I have to take more drastic measures. Consequently I am taking him to my country house. We leave the day after tomorrow. There will be with us only a few unattached people, who are not very astute, and we shall have almost as much freedom as if we were by ourselves. Then I shall so overwhelm him with love and caresses, and we shall live so entirely for each other that I wager he, even more than I, will long for the end of this trip, which he now thinks will be so delightful. And if he does not come back more bored with me than I with him, you may declare that I know no more than you about such matters.

The pretext for this kind of retreat is to think seriously about my important court case, which in fact is finally to be decided at the beginning of winter. I am pleased about that. For it is truly disagreeable to have one's whole fortune placed in the balance like this. It is not that I am worried about the outcome. In the first place I am in the right. All my lawyers tell me so. And even if I were not, then I should be extremely incompetent if I couldn't win a case where my adversaries are still only very young minors along with their old tutor! But, as one must not neglect anything in such an important affair, I shall actually have two lawyers with me. Does this trip not seem to you a jolly affair? Yet if it means that I win my case and get rid of Belleroche, I shall not have wasted my time.

So now, Vicomte, guess who his successor is. I'll give you a hundred guesses. But then, do I not know that you never guess anything? Well, it's Danceny. That surprises you, does it not? For surely I am not yet reduced to teaching children! But this one deserves to be made an exception of. He has the grace of youth, but not the frivolity. His considerable reserve among our group of friends means that he is most likely to distance himself from suspicion, and because of that people find him all the more amiable when he does engage in conversation. It is not that I have had a great deal to do with him so far on my own account; I am just his confidante at present. But beneath the veil of friendship I believe I can discern a strong liking for me, and I feel myself taking a strong liking to him. It would be a real shame if so much wit and delicacy should be sacrificed and squandered on that stupid little Volanges girl! I hope he is mistaken in thinking he is in love with her. She is so far from being worthy of him. Not that I am jealous of her. But it would be sheer murder, and I wish to save Danceny from it. So I beg you, Vicomte, take care not to let him get anywhere near *his* *Cécile* (as he is still ill-mannered enough to call her). One's first inclinations are always stronger than one thinks, and I could not be sure of anything were he to see her again at the moment. Especially during my absence. On my return I take responsibility for everything and I shall answer for it.

I did consider bringing the young man along with me. But I have given up the idea in favour of my customary prudence. I should have been worried that he would notice something between Belleroche and me, and I should be desperate if he had an inkling of what was going on. I wish to offer myself pure and spotless, at least to his imagination. How one should be, in fact, to be truly worthy of him.

Paris, 15 October 17**

LETTER 114

The Présidente de Tourvel to Madame de Rosemonde

My dear friend,
I am giving in to my deep anxiety and, although I do not know whether you will be in a position to answer this, I cannot prevent myself questioning you. The health of Monsieur de

Valmont, who you say is not *in any danger*, does not inspire
me with as much confidence as you seem to possess. It is not
unusual that melancholy and disgust for the world are early
signs of some grave illness. The sufferings of the body, like
those of the mind, make one long for solitude. And often people
are blamed for their ill-humour when they should rather be
pitied for their ills.

It seems to me that he should at least consult someone. Surely
you have a doctor nearby since you yourself are not well? Mine,
whom I saw this morning, and whom I confess I consulted
indirectly, is of the opinion that in naturally active people this
sort of sudden apathy should never be neglected. And, as he
also said to me, illnesses do not respond to treatment if they
are not caught in time. So why make someone so dear to you
run this risk?

What increases my concern is that I have had no news of him
for four days. Oh Heavens! You are not telling me falsehoods
about his condition, are you? Why would he have stopped
writing to me so suddenly? If it were only because of my obstinacy in sending back his letters, I think he would have done it
sooner. Well, whatever the case, though I do not believe in
presentiments, I have been dreadfully depressed for some days.
Oh, perhaps I am on the verge of some calamitous misfortune!

You would not believe, and I am ashamed to confess it, how
troubled I am by not receiving these same letters, which I should
none the less refuse to read. But at least then I was sure he still
thought of me! And I could see something which came from
him. I did not open these letters, but the very sight of them
made me weep. My tears afforded me some relief and they
alone alleviated just a little the constant oppression I have
suffered ever since my return. I beg you, my dear, kind friend,
write to me yourself as soon as may be and in the meantime
send me news every day of yourself and of him.

I see I have scarcely mentioned any of your concerns. But
you are aware of my feelings, my unreserved affection, my
sincere gratitude for your sympathetic friendship. You will forgive me the state I am in, my mortal pain, the frightful torment
of having to fear ills of which I am myself perhaps the cause.

Oh God, this desperate thought obsesses me and tears me apart. This was a misfortune I had not yet experienced. But it seems as if I was born to suffer them all.

Farewell, my dear friend. Love me; pity me. Will there be a letter from you today?

Paris, 16 October 17**

LETTER 115

The Vicomte de Valmont to the Marquise de Merteuil

It is inconceivable, my love, how quickly we misunderstand one another as soon as we are apart. All the time I was with you we always shared the same feelings and point of view, but since we have not seen each other for nearly three months we are no longer of the same opinion about anything. Which of us is in the wrong? Surely you would be able to give me an answer to that straight away. But, being wiser or more polite, I shall not pronounce upon it. I shall simply answer your letter and continue to give an account of my conduct to you.

First, I must thank you for your warning that there are rumours going round about me. But I have no anxieties on that score yet. I am sure that I shall soon be in a position to put a stop to them. Do not worry. When I reappear in society I shall be more famous than before and ever more worthy of you.

I hope my affair with the little Volanges girl, which you seem to think so negligible, will count for something. As though it were nothing in the space of one evening to carry off a young girl from the lover she adores; to use her as much as ever I like, with no problems, and absolutely as though she were my property; to obtain from her what one does not even dare to demand from any lady whose *métier* it is;[19] and to do it without upsetting her tender love in the slightest, without making her inconstant or even unfaithful. For you are quite right, her head is not full of me! And when my whim has passed I shall put her back, so to speak, in the arms of her lover without her noticing anything. Is that such a common feat? And, believe me, once she is out of my hands, the ideas I have given her will go on developing. I predict that the shy little schoolgirl will soon spread her wings in a manner that will do honour to her master.

However, if people prefer something in the heroic mode, I shall exhibit the Présidente, that paragon of virtue, respected by even the most libertine among us! And so virtuous, indeed, that everyone has given up all notion of attacking her! I shall exhibit her, I repeat, as a woman who has forgotten duty and virtue, sacrificing her reputation and two years of prudent behaviour in order to pursue the happiness of pleasing me, to become intoxicated with the pleasure of falling in love with me. She will think herself sufficiently compensated for so many sacrifices by a word or a look, which, it must be said, she will not always obtain. I shall do more than this; I shall leave her. And I shall not have a successor, or I do not know this woman. She will resist the need for consolation, the habit of pleasure, even the desire for revenge. Indeed, she will have existed only for me and, however long her career, I alone will have opened and closed the barrier. Once having achieved this triumph, I shall say to my rivals: 'Look at my handiwork and see if you can find another example of it in our time!'

You will ask me where this sudden excess of confidence comes from. It is that for the last week I have known what my beauty is thinking. She does not tell me her secrets, but I find them out. Two letters from her to Madame de Rosemonde have given me enough information, and I shall read the others only out of curiosity. Absolutely all I have to do in order to succeed is to see her again and I have found the means. I shall put this in train straight away.

I suppose you are curious? . . . But no, in order to punish you for believing me uninventive, I shall not tell you. Seriously, you deserve to have me keep things from you at least inasmuch as this affair is concerned. In fact, without the delicious reward you have promised me at the successful outcome of this adventure, I should not speak of it any longer. You see how cross I am. However, in the hope that you will mend your ways, I will content myself with inflicting this slight punishment. And reverting to indulgent mode, I shall put aside my grand projects for the time being in order to discuss yours with you.

So you are out there in the country, which must be as dreary as sentiment and depressing as fidelity itself! And poor old Belleroche! Not content with forcing him to drink the waters of Lethe, you are putting him on the rack. How is he taking it? Is he able to bear the surfeit of love? I would so much enjoy it if that made him become even more attached to you. I am curious to see what more effective remedy you might find to administer. I am truly sorry for you that you have had to resort to this one. I have only made love in cold blood once in my life. And then it was surely for a very good reason, since it was to the Comtesse de —; and a score of times when she was in my arms I was tempted to say: 'Madam, I renounce the position I solicited; kindly allow me to leave the one I am now occupying.' So among all the women I have had she is the only one of whom I take pleasure in speaking ill.

As to your own motives, I find them, if I am honest, extraordinarily absurd. You were right in thinking I should not have guessed who Belleroche's successor was. What! Can it be for Danceny that you are going to all that trouble? Dearest, for goodness' sake, leave him to adore *his virtuous Cécile* and do not compromise yourself with these childish games. Allow schoolboys to receive their education from housemaids or play at *innocent little games* with convent girls. Why burden yourself with a novice who will not know how to take you or leave you, and with whom you will have to make all the running? I tell you frankly, I disapprove of your choice, and however secret it remains it will humiliate you at least in my eyes and in your own conscience.

You say you are developing a strong liking for him. Come now, you must be mistaken and I think I have even worked out the reason. This fine distaste for Belleroche has come upon you in a time of famine, and with Paris not there to offer you a choice, as usual, your too lively imagination has lit upon the first object it has encountered. But just think, on your return you will be able to make your choice from among thousands. And if you are

afraid that by putting things off you will risk being too inactive,
I offer myself for your amusement in your leisure hours.

Between now and your arrival my important business will
be finished, one way or another. And surely neither the little
Volanges girl nor the Présidente herself will by that time be
occupying me so much that I could not be at your disposal as
often as you wish. It may even be that between now and then I
shall already have placed the girl back into the arms of her
discreet lover. Though, despite what you say, I cannot agree with
you that it is not a pleasure which makes one grow more fond; I
intend her to view me throughout her whole life as someone who
is superior to all other men, but my behaviour with her has been
such that I should not manage to keep this up for very long without damaging my health. And from this moment on I no longer
care for her except in as far as family obligations require . . .

Do you understand what I am saying? I am waiting for a
second cycle to confirm my hopes[20] and make me certain I have
entirely succeeded in my plans. Yes, my love, I already have the
first indication that my pupil's husband will not run the risk of
dying without descendants. And that the head of the future
house of Gercourt will be just a younger son of the house of
Valmont. But allow me to finish this affair in my own way, for
I only took her on because you begged me to. Remember that
if you cause Danceny to be inconstant you will deprive the story
of all interest. Consider, finally, that by offering myself as his
representative I am owed, in my opinion, preferential treatment.

So confident am I that this will be forthcoming, I shall not
hesitate to obstruct your plans and am working instead towards
increasing the tender passion of the discreet lover for the first
and most worthy person of his choice. So, having yesterday
discovered your pupil busy writing to him, and having interrupted this sweet occupation to replace it with a sweeter one still,
I asked her afterwards if I might see her letter. And finding it
cold and constrained, I made her realize that that was no way to
console her lover, and persuaded her to write another one at my
dictation, in which, imitating her nonsense as best I could, I
attempted to encourage the young man's love with a more certain
hope. The girl was absolutely delighted, she said, to find she could

write so well. So henceforth the correspondence will be my responsibility. What shall I not have done for this man Danceny? I
shall have been at one and the same time his confidant, rival and
mistress! And what is more, at this moment I am doing him the
service of keeping him out of your dangerous clutches. Yes, I
mean dangerous. For to possess you and then lose you is to
purchase a moment's happiness with an eternity of regrets.

Farewell, my love. Have the courage to dispatch Belleroche
as soon as you can. Leave Danceny alone, and prepare to
rediscover and renew the delicious pleasures of our first liaison.

P.S. My compliments on the impending decision in the important court case. I should be very pleased for this happy event to
take place under my regime.

From the Chateau de —, 19 October 17**

LETTER 116

The Chevalier Danceny to Cécile Volanges

Madame de Merteuil has left for the country this morning and
so, my charming Cécile, I am deprived of the only pleasure
remaining to me in your absence, that of talking about you to
your friend and mine. For some time now she has allowed me
to call her friend. And I was all the more eager to do that
because it seemed that by this means I could draw closer to
you. Heavens, what a lovely woman! And with what flattering
charm she cloaks her friendship! It seems that this sweet sentiment becomes stronger and more beautiful the more she refuses
her love. If you knew how much she loves you, and how she
loves to hear me talk about you! . . . That is undoubtedly what
binds me to her so closely. What joy to be able to live only for
you two, to pass continually from the delights of love to the
sweetness of friendship, to consecrate my whole life to it, to be
in some way the point of contact of your mutual attachment;

and to feel always that in concerning myself with the happiness of the one I should be labouring equally for the happiness of the other! I hope you will love her, my dear; I hope you will love her very much. She is an adorable woman. The attachment I have for her will be given still more value by your sharing in it. Since experiencing the charms of friendship I wish you to experience them too. The pleasures that I do not share with you I feel I only half enjoy. Yes, my Cécile, I should like to fill your heart with all the sweetest feelings; I should like each emotion to make you experience a new sensation of happiness; but I should nevertheless believe I could only ever give you back a fraction of the happiness I have received from you.

Why should these delightful projects be nothing but a dream, and reality offer me the very opposite, only painful and endless privation? I can see I must abandon the hopes you have given me of seeing you in the country. The only consolation I have left is to persuade myself that in fact it is impossible for you. But you neglect to tell me of it, to share my suffering! My reproaches have twice already remained unanswered. Oh Cécile! Cécile, I believe you love me with all your heart and soul, but your soul does not burn like mine! If only it were my task to remove the obstacles! Why is it not my interests that are in need of managing rather than yours? I should then soon be able to prove to you that nothing is impossible in love.

You do not say either when this cruel separation is to be at an end. At least here perhaps I might see you. Your charming eyes would revive my vanquished soul. Their tender look would comfort a heart which is at times in need of reassurance. Forgive me, Cécile. This fear is not a suspicion. I believe in your love, in your constancy. Oh, I should be so unhappy if I was unsure of that. But there are so many obstacles! More and more! My love, I am sad, so sad. It seems that this departure of Madame de Merteuil has reawakened in me all my feelings of unhappiness.

Farewell, my Cécile. Farewell, my beloved. Remember that your lover is suffering, and that you alone can give him back his happiness.

Paris, 17 October 17**

LETTER 117

Cécile Volanges to the Chevalier Danceny
(Dictated by Valmont)

Do you really believe, my dear, that I need scolding for being sad when I know how upset you are? And do you doubt that I am suffering as much as you are, with all your woes? I share even the ones I cause you knowingly. And I have more to put up with than you because you are not being fair to me. Oh, that is not kind of you. I can see what makes you cross. It is that the last two times you asked to come here I did not answer your request. But is that answer such an easy one to give? Do you think I do not know that what you want is very wrong? And yet if I already have so much pain in refusing you when you are at a distance, what would it be like if you were there? In wishing to afford you momentary consolation I should suffer for the rest of my life.

Let me tell you that I have nothing to hide from you. Here are my reasons; be the judge of them yourself. I would perhaps have done what you want, were it not, as I have told you, that Monsieur de Gercourt, the cause of all our worries, will not be arriving as soon as expected. And, as Mamma has been much nicer to me lately and I for my part am doing what I can to please her, who knows what I may not be able to obtain from her? And if we could be happy without me having anything to reproach myself for, would that not be a great deal better? If I am to believe what everyone tells me all the time, men love their wives less when the wives have loved them too much before marriage. This fear holds me back even more than all the rest. My dear, are you not sure of my heart, and will there not always be time?

Listen, I promise you that if I cannot avoid the ill fortune of marrying Monsieur de Gercourt, whom I heartily detest before I even make his acquaintance, nothing will keep me from being entirely yours, first and foremost. As my only concern is that you will love me, and that you see that if I do anything wrong it will not be my fault, then I don't mind at all about anything else as long as you promise me you will always love me as much as you do now. But until then, my friend, let me continue as I am. And do not ask me any more for something I have good reason not to do, especially when it makes me sorry to have to refuse.

I could also wish that Monsieur de Valmont were not so pressing on your behalf. That only adds to my difficulties. Oh, you have there a very good friend, I assure you! He does everything just as you would yourself.[21] But farewell, my dear friend. I have started writing to you very late and have spent half the night doing it. I'm going to bed to make up for lost time. I send you my love, but do not scold me any more.

From the Chateau de —, 18 October 17**

LETTER 118

The Chevalier Danceny to the Marquise de Merteuil

If I am to believe my diary, my beloved friend, you have only been away for two days. But if I believe my heart, it is two centuries. Now I have it from yourself, it is always the heart that one must go by. So it is high time you returned, for all your business must be more than complete. How can you expect me to take an interest in your lawsuit if, win or lose, I must pay the costs in boredom at your absence? Oh, I am minded to pick a quarrel with you! How sad it is, when I have such good reason to be cross, that I have no right to show it!

But is it not indeed a true infidelity, a base treachery, to leave your friend behind after rendering him incapable of doing without you? You may consult your lawyers in vain, for they will find no justification for this wicked procedure. And then, those people only deal in arguments, and arguments will not do to answer feelings.

As for me, you have so frequently said that you were making this trip for a reason that you have made me absolutely fall out with reason. I will not listen to reason. Not even when it tells me to forget you. And yet that reason is very reasonable. In fact, it would not be so hard as you might think. I should only need to get out of the habit of thinking about you the whole time. And there is nothing here, I can assure you, to remind me of you.

Our prettiest women, the ones people say are the most attractive, are still so far beneath you that they can only give the very faintest notion of the being you are. I even believe that, with a practised eye, the more one might have thought they were like you, the more one would find afterwards they were different. Whatever they do, whatever arts they may employ, they still fail to be you, and that is positively your charm. Unfortunately when the days are so long, and one has not much to do, one dreams, one builds castles in Spain, one creates one's fantasies. Gradually the imagination takes over. One wishes to embellish one's work and, gathering up everything that would give pleasure, one finally arrives at perfection. And as soon as that happens the portrait recalls the model, and one is surprised to see that one has done nothing but think of you.

At this very moment I am the victim of a more or less similar mistake. Perhaps you believe that it was in order to think about you that I began this letter? Not at all. It was to stop myself thinking about you. I had a hundred things to tell you, which did not have to do with you, but which, as you know, are of the greatest concern to me. Those are what I have been distracted from. And since when have the delights of friendship distracted one from the delights of love? Oh, if I looked into that more closely, perhaps I would have reason to blame myself a little! But hush! Let us forget this trifling fault for fear of committing it again. Let my lady remain unaware of it.

So why are you not there to answer me, to bring me back when I go astray, to talk about my Cécile, to increase, if that were possible, the happiness that I find in loving her by the sweet idea that it is your friend I love? Yes, I admit it, the love she inspires in me has become even more precious to me since you have been so good as to let me talk to you about it. I so much love to open my heart to you, to tell you my feelings, to pour them out to you! It seems to me that the more you deign to listen, the more I treasure them. And then I look at you and I think: 'It is in her that my entire happiness is contained.'

I have nothing new to tell you about my situation. The last letter I received from *her* increased and confirmed my hopes, but puts off their fulfilment. However, her motives are so kind and honourable that I cannot blame her for them or complain. Perhaps you do not quite understand what I am saying? Oh, why are you not here? Although one can say anything to one's friend, one dares not write everything down. The secrets of love especially are so delicate that one cannot let them out just like that. If sometimes one allows them to appear, one must not at least allow them to be lost sight of. One must, in a sense, see them safely to their new home. Oh, come back, my adorable friend. You see how necessary your return is. So forget the *thousand reasons* which keep you where you are, or teach me how to live wherever you are not.

Respectfully yours, etc.

Paris, 19 October 17**

LETTER 119

Madame de Rosemonde to the Présidente de Tourvel

Although I am still in a great deal of pain, my dear, I shall try to write to you myself so that I can speak about your concerns. My nephew is still in misanthropic mood. He sends to hear news of me most regularly each day; but he has not come to enquire himself, although I have sent a message begging him to do so. So I do not see any more of him than if he were in Paris. However, I chanced upon him this morning in a place I hardly expected to see him. It was in my chapel, which I visited for the first time since my sad affliction. I learned today that he has been going there regularly for four days to hear Mass. God grant that it lasts!

When I entered he came up to me and congratulated me most warmly on my improved state of health. As Mass was starting I cut short our conversation, very much hoping to resume it later.

But he disappeared before I could speak to him again. I shall not hide from you my impression that he had altered a little. My dear, do not make me sorry I trusted in your good sense by giving way to excessive anxiety. But let me above all assure you that I should prefer to cause you distress rather than tell you untruths.

If my nephew continues to be so distant with me, as soon as I am better I shall go and see him in his rooms and try to get to the bottom of this extraordinary eccentricity, which I am certain must have something to do with you. I will tell you what I learn. I must leave you, as I am unable to move my fingers any more. If Adélaïde knew I have been writing, she would scold me all evening. Farewell, my dear.

From the Chateau de —, 20 October 17**

LETTER 120

The Vicomte de Valmont to Father Anselme (Cistercian monk in the convent of the rue Saint-Honoré)

I do not have the honour of your acquaintance, Monsieur, but I am aware of the complete trust that Madame la Présidente de Tourvel has in you, and I also know how eminently worthy you are of it. I believe I may therefore address myself to you in all discretion to obtain a most essential service, one that is truly worthy of your holy ministry and in which Madame de Tourvel's interests are at one with my own.

I have in my hands important documents concerning her which may be entrusted to no one, but which it is my desire and duty to put into her hands alone. I have no means of telling her, since reasons, of which perhaps she has made you aware – but about which I do not believe I am permitted to inform you – have made her decide to refuse all correspondence with me. That decision I today willingly admit I cannot blame her for, since she could not foresee events which I was myself very far from expecting, and which were only able to be brought about, as

I am compelled to acknowledge, through supernatural powers.

So I beg you, Monsieur, to inform her of my new resolutions and ask her on my behalf for a private interview where I can at least partly make amends for my wrongdoing by offering my apologies, and, by way of a final sacrifice, wipe out the only remaining traces of a mistake or fault of which I have been guilty in relation to her.

It will be only after this preliminary expiation that I should dare lay at your feet my humiliating confession of many past misdemeanours, and implore your intercession for a much more important and unfortunately more difficult reconciliation. May I hope, Monsieur, that you will not refuse me the care that is so necessary and precious to me, and that you will condescend to sustain me in my weakness and guide my feet into the path I so ardently desire to follow, but admit, to my shame, that I do not yet know?

I await your response with the impatience of a penitent who wishes to make amends. Please accept my gratitude and reverence in equal measure.

Your very humble, etc.

P.S. I authorize you, Monsieur, if you were to think it proper, to communicate this letter in its entirety to Madame de Tourvel, whom I shall make it my duty to respect for the rest of my life, and in whom I shall never cease to honour the person who, by her own inspiring example, has been used by God to bring my soul back to the paths of righteousness.

From the Chateau de —, 22 October 17**

LETTER 121

The Marquise de Merteuil to the Chevalier Danceny

I have received your letter, my young – my too young – friend. But before I thank you I must scold you and warn you that if you do not mend your ways there will be no more replies from me. So take my advice and leave off this tone of flattery, for, when it is not the expression of love, it becomes nothing but cant. Does friendship speak in that vein? No, my friend. Every sentiment has its own language. And if you use any other you disguise the idea you wish to express. I am very well aware that young women of today do not understand anything one says to them if it is not translated somehow into this common jargon. But I admit that I think I deserve to be treated differently from them. I am truly sorry – perhaps more than I ought to be – that you have so ill judged me.

You will only find therefore in my letter what is lacking in your own: frankness and forthrightness. I might tell you, for example, that I should take great pleasure in seeing you and that I am annoyed to have around me only people who bore me, instead of people who amuse me. But you would translate this same phrase as 'Teach me to live where you are not', so I suppose that when you are with your mistress you would not be able to live unless I too were present. Shame on you! And these women, *who fail to be me*, will you perhaps find that your Cécile is lacking in that regard too! Yet that is where it leads, this language which, through the way it is abused today, means even less than those inane compliments. It has come to be simply a formula in which one cannot believe, any more than one believes in 'your very humble servant'.

My friend, when you write to me, let it be to tell me what you think and feel, and not to send me what I can read, without your help, more or less well expressed in the latest fashionable novel. I hope you will not be cross with me when I say this, even though you might think I am being rather critical. For I do not deny I am. But, to avoid the slightest suspicion of being guilty of the fault I am ascribing to you, I shall not mention that my mood is possibly made rather worse by the fact that I am so far away from you. It seems to me that all in all you are worth more than a court case and two lawyers, and perhaps even more than the *attentive* Belleroche.

So you see that instead of being saddened by my absence you should congratulate yourself. For I never before paid you such a fine compliment. I think I must be following your example and

wishing in my turn to write flattering things to you. But I prefer
to stand by my honesty, and so it is that alone which assures you
of my loving friendship and the interest it inspires. It is very sweet
to have a young friend whose heart is engaged elsewhere. Not
every woman would think like this. But I do. It seems to me that
one can more fully enjoy sentiment when one has nothing to fear.
So I have taken on the role of your confidante, perhaps rather
early in the day. But you choose to have such young mistresses
that you have made me perceive, for the first time, that I am growing old! You do well to prepare yourself in this way for a long life
of constancy; I hope with all my heart it is reciprocal.

You are right to give way before the *kind and honourable
motives* which, according to what you tell me, *are putting off
the fulfilment of your happiness*. A long defence is the only
merit remaining to those who do not always resist. And what I
should find unpardonable in anyone but a child like the little
Volanges girl would be not being able to flee a danger of which
her own confession of love had given her ample warning. You
men have no idea what virtue is, and what it costs to sacrifice
it! If a woman reasons at all, she must realize that, independently of the wrong she is doing, weakness is for her the worst
of misfortunes, though I cannot understand how anyone could
succumb to it if she took a moment to reflect.

Do not dispute this idea, for it is chiefly because of it that I
am attached to you. You will save me from the dangers of love.
And though I have been able to defend myself from them quite
well until now without you, I am grateful and shall love you
more and better for it.

On which note, my dear Chevalier, I pray God to keep you
under His holy and worthy protection.

From the Chateau de —, 22 October 17**

LETTER 122

Madame de Rosemonde to the Présidente de Tourvel

I had hoped, my dear girl, to allay your anxieties at last, and I
see with dismay that it is quite the reverse and I shall only
increase them. But do not be distressed. My nephew is not in
danger. It cannot be said that he is really ill. Nevertheless, there
is certainly something extraordinary going on in him. I do not
understand it at all. I came out of his room feeling unhappy –
you might even say alarmed – and I am loath to share this with
you, and yet I cannot refrain from discussing it. Here is an
account of what happened. You may rely upon its accuracy. If
I were to live another eighty years, I should not forget the
impression this sorry scene made upon me.

Well, I went to my nephew's room this morning. I found him
writing, surrounded by various piles of paper, which seemed to
be the object of his labours. He was so busy that I was already
in the middle of the room before he turned his head to see who
it was. As soon as he saw me he rose, and I could tell quite
plainly that he was trying to compose his face, and perhaps that
was what made me examine him more closely. He was indeed
not fully dressed and his wig was unpowdered.[22] I found him
pale and in disarray, and in particular his face had changed.
His normally gay and lively air was gloomy and disconsolate.
Anyway, between you and me, I should not have wanted you
to see him like that, for he had a most touching air, and one
very likely, in my opinion, to inspire the tender sympathy which
is one of the most dangerous snares of love.

Although greatly struck by my observations, I yet began the
conversation as though I had not noticed anything. First, I
spoke to him about his health and, though he did not say it was
good, he in no way implied that it was bad. Then I complained
that his keeping out of everyone's way seemed more than a little
eccentric, and I tried to introduce a touch of lightness into my
little reprimand. But all he said in reply and with his voice full
of meaning was: 'That is another of my crimes, I admit. But it

shall be paid for, along with the rest.' It was his manner more than what he actually said that dampened my jocular tone, and I hastened to tell him that he was treating what was simply the rebuke of a friend with too great a seriousness.

We then calmly resumed our conversation. A short while afterwards he told me that business, *perhaps the most important business of his life,* would soon recall him to Paris. But as I was afraid to guess what that might be, my dear, and as this beginning might lead to a disclosure I did not wish to hear, I did not question him about it, but contented myself with answering that a little more amusement would benefit his health. I added that this time I would not persuade him to stay, since I loved my friends for their own sake. It was at this simple remark that, seizing hold of my hands, and speaking with a vehemence I cannot describe, he said: 'Yes, Aunt, love me; love your nephew who respects and esteems you a very great deal. As you say, love him for his own sake. Do not distress yourself about his happiness and do not trouble with any regrets the eternal peace he very soon hopes to enjoy. Tell me again that you love me, that you forgive me. Yes, you will forgive me; I know you are kind. But how can I expect the same indulgence from those to whom I have given such offence?' Then he leaned over me in order to hide, I think, the signs of grief that, despite himself, the sound of his voice revealed to me.

More moved than I can say, I got up abruptly. And he must have noticed my alarm for immediately he recovered his composure and went on: 'Forgive me, forgive me, Madame. I was beside myself. I beg you to forget what I said and only remember my profound regard for you. I shall not neglect,' he added, 'to come and renew my respects to you before I go.' It seemed to me that this last sentence obliged me to terminate my visit and so I left.

But the more I think about it, the less I can puzzle out what he meant. What is this business, *the most important business of his life?* What is he asking me to forgive him for? Where did that involuntary emotion as he spoke come from? I have already asked myself these questions a thousand times without finding the answer. I do not even see anything in all of this which relates to you. But as the eyes of a lover see more clearly than those of a friend, I did not wish to leave you in any ignorance of what passed between my nephew and myself.

I have tried four times to write this long letter, and it would be still longer but for the tiredness I feel. Farewell, dear girl.

From the Chateau de —, 25 October 17**

LETTER 123

Father Anselme to the Vicomte de Valmont

I have received, Monsieur le Vicomte, your honoured letter, and yesterday I called on the person in question directly, in accordance with your wishes. I explained to her the object and motives of the meeting you propose. Although I found her determined to abide by the prudent decision she had first made, upon my indicating that a refusal perhaps risked putting an obstacle in the way of your blessed return to the fold, and thus in some way opposing the merciful designs of Providence, she consented to receive your visit on condition that it should at any event be the last, and charged me to tell you that she would be at home next Thursday, the 28th. If that day is not convenient, would you kindly inform her and suggest another. Your letter will be received.

However, Monsieur le Vicomte, allow me to request you not to postpone this without a very good reason, so that you may yield more swiftly and thoroughly to the praiseworthy dispositions of which you have given me some indication. Remember that he who delays seizing the moment of grace is exposed to the possibility of its being taken away from him altogether. Though divine goodness is infinite, its dispensation is still regulated by justice. And there may come a moment when the God of mercy is transformed into the God of vengeance.

If you continue to honour me with your trust, I beg you to believe that I shall give you my whole attention, whenever you desire. However busy I am, my most urgent business will always be to fulfil the duties of the holy ministry to which I have so particularly devoted myself. And the happiest moments of my life are when I see my efforts prosper by the blessing of the Almighty. Feeble sinners that we are, we can do nothing of our own volition! But the God who is calling you is all-powerful. And it is to His goodness that we owe, in your case, the constant desire you have to reach out to Him and in mine the means to lead you to Him. It is with His help that I hope soon to persuade you that it is the holiness of religion alone that can give you in this world the solid and lasting happiness that one seeks vainly in the blindness of human passions.

I have the honour to be with respectful regard, etc.

Paris, this 25 October 17**

LETTER 124

The Présidente de Tourvel to Madame de Rosemonde

In the midst of the astonishment occasioned me by the news I learned yesterday, Madame, I am not unmindful of the satisfaction it will cause you, and I hasten to tell you about it. Monsieur de Valmont is no longer concerned with me or with his love, and only wishes to make amends, by leading a more edifying life, for the wrongdoing or rather the errors of his youth. I have been informed of this wonderful news by Father Anselme, to whom he has turned for guidance in the future and also to arrange an interview with me, the principal object of which I assume must be to give me back the letters he has kept till now, in spite of my request to the contrary.

Naturally I can only applaud this happy change of heart and congratulate myself if, as he claims, I have played some part in it. But why was I chosen to be the instrument, so that it cost me all my peace of mind? Could Monsieur de Valmont's happiness never come about except through my misfortune? Oh, my dear,

understanding friend, forgive my complaining like this. I know
that it is not up to me to question the judgement of God. But
whereas I am always asking Him – and always in vain – for the
strength to conquer my unhappy love, He lavishes it on someone who was not asking for it, and leaves me helpless and
entirely prey to my weakness.

But let us suppress these guilty murmurings. Do I not know
that the Prodigal Son on his return obtained from his father
more grace than the son who had never been away from home?
What account may we ask of One who owes us nothing? And
if it were possible that we had some rights where He is concerned, what could mine be? Could I boast of a virtue I already
owe to Valmont alone? He has saved me; should I dare complain of suffering for his sake? No, I shall cherish my suffering
if his happiness is the price. Undoubtedly it had to be that he
should return to the Father of us all. The God who made
him must treasure what He has made. He did not create this
charming being only to make a reprobate of him. It is for me
to bear the pain of my foolhardiness. Should I not have known
that because I was forbidden to love him I ought not to have
allowed myself to see him?

My mistake or my misfortune is to have refused for too long
to acknowledge this truth. You are witness, my dear and worthy
friend, that I subjected myself to this sacrifice as soon as I
recognized the need for it. But what was lacking to make it
complete was that Monsieur de Valmont did not share in it.
Shall I admit that now it is that thought that torments me most?
Insufferable pride that softens the pain we bear with the pain
we cause to others! Oh, I shall subdue this rebellious heart; I
shall accustom it to humility.

It is with this especially in my heart that I have consented to
receive the painful visit of Monsieur de Valmont on Thursday
next. Then I shall hear from his own lips that I mean nothing
to him any more and that the feeble and ephemeral impression
I made upon him has been completely effaced! I shall see his
dispassionate eyes upon me while the fear of revealing my
emotion will make me lower mine. He will return with indifference to me these same letters that he refused for so long to give

me at my repeated request. He will put them into my hands like so many useless objects which are no longer of interest to him. And my hands, trembling as they receive this shameful bundle, will feel them placed there by hands that are steady and calm! Then finally I shall see him go ... go for ever, and my eyes will follow him, but will not see him look back!

And I must suffer all this humiliation! Oh, let me at least use it to pierce my soul with an awareness of my utter frailty ... Yes, I shall treasure these letters he does not care to keep any longer. I shall impose upon myself the shame of reading them each day until my tears have blotted out the least trace. And I shall burn his, as if infected with that dangerous poison which has eaten into my soul. Oh, what then is love if it makes us regretful even of the dangers to which it has exposed us? And especially if we still have to fear we may feel it even when we no longer inspire it! Let us flee from this baleful passion, which leaves us no choice except shame or misfortune and often entails both of these. And let prudence at least prevail instead of virtue.

How long it is till Thursday! Why can I not bring this painful sacrifice to a conclusion now this minute and forget both cause and object at the same time! This visit is an intrusion. I am sorry I gave my promise. Why oh why should he need to see me again? What are we now to one another? If he has offended me, I forgive him. I even congratulate him for wanting to make amends for his wrongdoing. I commend him for it. I shall do more; I shall imitate him. I have been led into the same errors but shall follow his example and resume my former state. But if his plan is to flee from me, why does he start by seeking me out? Is not the most pressing thing for both of us to forget one another? Oh, surely it is, and that shall henceforth be my sole aim.

With your permission, my dear friend, and in your company, I shall set about this difficult task. If I need help and perhaps consolation, I wish to receive it from no one but you. You alone understand me and speak to my heart. Your precious friendship shall fill my whole life. Nothing will seem difficult if it is to justify your kind help and support. I shall owe to you my peace of mind, my happiness and my virtue. And the reward of your goodness for me will be to have made myself worthy of it at last.

I believe I have been very incoherent in this letter. I presume so at least, judging from the agitation I have constantly felt as I have been writing. If I have expressed any sentiments in it which I ought to have been ashamed of, draw the veil of your indulgent friendship over them. I have complete trust in that. From you I cannot wish to conceal the slightest impulse of my heart.

Farewell, my honourable friend. I hope in a few days to tell you when I shall arrive.

Paris, 25 October 17**

PART FOUR

PART FOUR

The Vicomte de Valmont to the Marquise de Merteuil

So I have defeated her, this arrogant woman who dared to think she could resist me! Yes, my love, she is mine, all mine! And ever since yesterday there is nothing left for her to give.

I am still too full of happiness to be able to appreciate it, but I am surprised by the unfamiliar delight it gave me. Can it then be true that virtue increases the value of a woman even in the very moment of her weakness? But let us dismiss this childish idea as an old wives' tale. Do we not nearly always come across some resistance, more or less well-feigned, at the first surrender? Have I not found the delights I am speaking of with any other women? And yet this is not love. For I have to say that though with this astonishing woman I have sometimes experienced moments of weakness which resemble that unmanly passion, I have always managed to subdue them and adhere to my principles. Even if yesterday's scene had carried me rather further than I expected in that direction and for a moment I had shared the passion and the delirium I created in her, that passing illusion would be dispelled today. And yet the fascination persists. I should take, I don't mind admitting, a certain sweet pleasure in indulging it if it did not worry me a little. Am I at my age to be mastered, like some schoolboy, by an involuntary and unknown feeling? No. Above all, I must get to the bottom of it, and fight it.

And perhaps I have already perceived the cause! At least I am pleased with this idea and like to think it is correct.

Among the crowds of women with whom I have until now fulfilled the role and function of lover, until that point I had not met a single one who was not at least as eager to give herself to me as I was to persuade her to do it. I had even grown accustomed to calling the ones who did not meet me halfway *prudes*, by contrast with so many others whose provocative defences only ever imperfectly concealed the first advances they made.

In her case, on the other hand, there was an unfavourable prejudice from the very beginning, corroborated afterwards by the advice and tale-telling of an odious but perspicacious woman; a natural and extreme shyness fortified by a refined modesty; an attachment to virtue, guided by religion, which already had two years of triumph to its credit; and some brilliant tactics, inspired by these various feelings, whose sole aim was to escape my pursuit.

This is not, therefore, as it was in my other affairs, a simple capitulation, more or less advantageous to me, easier to profit from than to boast about. It was total victory bought by a difficult campaign and decided by clever manoeuvres. So it is hardly surprising if this success, which has been entirely my own doing, should become all the more precious to me. And the excess of pleasure that I experienced in my triumph, and which I am still enjoying, is but the sweet sensation of glory. I cherish this belief since it saves me from the humiliation of thinking that I am in some way dependent upon the very slave whom I have subjected to my will; that I might not possess the capacity for total happiness within myself alone; or that the ability for making me enjoy it in all its intensity should rest with one woman, to the exclusion of all others.

These judicious reflections will govern my conduct at this important stage. And you may be sure I shall not allow myself to become so involved that I am not capable of breaking, with the utmost ease, these new bonds whenever I feel like it. But I am already speaking of breaking up when you are still ignorant of how I acquired the right to it. So read this and see to what dangers wisdom is exposed when it comes to the help of folly. I took such careful note of what I said and what replies I obtained that I hope I can set out both with an accuracy that will gladden your heart.

You will see from the two copies of the attached letters* which mediator I chose to help me to get near to my lady, and with what zeal the holy man set about uniting us. What I have to tell you still and what I learned by letter – intercepted as usual – is that the fear and the small humiliation of being jilted rather upset the prudence of our austere devotee, filling her

---

* Letters 120 and 123.

heart and mind with feelings and ideas that had no foundation in common sense, but were none the less interesting. It was after these preliminaries, which you need to be aware of, that yesterday, Thursday the 28th, the day duly appointed by the ungrateful creature, I presented myself at her house, a timid and repentant slave, only to emerge as crowned conqueror.

It was six in the evening when I arrived at the house of the fair recluse, for since her return her door has been closed to one and all. She tried to rise when I was announced, but her trembling knees did not permit her to remain in this position. She sat down again immediately. The servant who had let me in had some duty to attend to in the apartments, which seemed to cause her some impatience. We filled the interval with the usual courtesies. But in order not to waste a moment of this precious time I cast a careful eye over my surroundings, and instantly marked out the territory for my conquest. I might have chosen a more appropriate one, for in the same room there was an ottoman and I noticed that immediately opposite it was her husband's portrait. I must admit I was afraid that with such an odd woman a stray glance in this direction might destroy all my painstaking work in a trice. But, anyway, there we were on our own at last, and I began talking.

After venturing a few words about how Father Anselme must have informed her of the reasons for my visit, I complained of the harsh treatment I had received. And I particularly dwelt upon the *contempt* shown to me. This was denied, as I expected. And, as you no doubt expected, I based my proof upon the mistrust and fear I had inspired; on the scandalous way she had fled as a result; her refusal to answer my letters, or even receive them, etc., etc. As she was beginning a justification of her actions, which would have been very easy to make, I thought I had better interrupt. And to ensure I was forgiven for this rudeness I immediately covered it up with flattery. 'If all your charms,' I continued, 'have made such a profound impression upon my heart, all your virtue has made just as deep an impression upon my soul. Carried away, no doubt, by my desire to draw near to such virtue, I dared believe I was worthy of it. I do not hold it against you that you judged otherwise. But I am punished for my error.' As she maintained an embarrassed silence I went on: 'I wished, Madame, either to justify myself in your eyes or to obtain pardon for the wrongs you believe I have done you, in order at least to end my life in some peace and quiet, a life I no longer hold dear, since you have refused to lend it any beauty.'

At this she none the less attempted a reply: 'My duty did not permit me . . .' But the difficulty of finishing the lie that duty demanded did not permit her to finish the sentence. I therefore continued in the tenderest tones:

'So is it true that it was me you were escaping from?'

'This departure was necessary.'

'And you are putting a distance between us?'

'It is necessary.'

'For ever?'

'I must.'

I need not tell you that during this short dialogue the voice of the tender-hearted prude was forlorn and her downcast eyes would not meet mine. I decided I should liven up this languorous scene a little; so, rising with an air of annoyance, I declared: 'Your firm resolve gives me back all my own. Well then, Madame, we shall be separated, separated even more than you imagine. And you will congratulate yourself at leisure on what you have done.' Rather surprised by this tone of rebuke, she made an effort to reply. 'The decision you have come to—' she said. 'Is simply the result of my despair,' I rejoined emphatically. 'It was your wish that I should be unhappy. I shall prove to you that you have succeeded far beyond what you might have hoped.' 'I desire your happiness,' she replied, and her voice began to betray quite deep emotion. So, throwing myself at her feet and in my habitual dramatic style, I cried: 'Ah, cruel woman, can there be any happiness for me if you do not share it? How can I find it if not with you? Ah! Never! Never!' I admit that in having recourse to this expedient I had very much relied upon the assistance of tears: but whether it was due to my being in the wrong mood or whether it was just the effect of the constant and exacting attention that I was putting into the whole thing, the tears would not come.

Happily I remembered that all means are equally good for conquering a woman, and that a grand and unexpected gesture would be all that was required to leave a deep and favourable impression. So I used fear to make up for my lack of sensibility. I changed only my tone of voice and, retaining the same posture, I continued: 'I humbly swear before you, I shall possess you or die.' As I uttered these last words, our eyes met. I do not know what the timid creature could see, or thought she could see in mine, but she rose in alarm and escaped from my embrace. It is true I did nothing to restrain her; for I have several times observed that scenes of despair enacted too enthusiastically become absurd when long-drawn-out, or else leave one with only the tragic option, which was very far from my intention. However, while she made her escape, I added in a low and sinister voice, but loud enough to be heard: 'Well then, death it is!'

Then I rose and, remaining silent for a moment, I threw wild glances in her direction; I appeared distraught but was none the less shrewdly observant. Her hesitant demeanour, her loud breathing, the contraction of every muscle, her trembling half-raised arms, all were sufficient proof of the effect I wished to produce. But as in love nothing is achieved unless one is at close quarters, and since we were at that point rather distant from one another, the first priority was to get closer. It was to this end that as soon as I could I assumed a composure calculated to calm the effects of this violence without taking anything away from the impression I had given.

By way of transition I said: 'I am so unhappy. I wanted to live for your happiness and I have destroyed it. All I desired was your peace of mind and I am destroying that too.' Then, composed but constrained: 'Forgive me, Madame. Unaccustomed as I am to the storms of passion, I have not learned how to repress my emotions. If I was wrong to give way to them, at least remember that it was for the last time. Oh! Calm yourself, calm yourself, I entreat you.' And during this long speech I was getting closer, without her realizing.

'If you wish me to calm myself,' replied the terrified beauty, 'you must calm yourself too.'

'Well then,' I told her, 'I promise.' I added more softly: 'If the effort is great, at least it will not be long. But,' I continued immediately with a distracted air, 'is it not the case that I came to give you back your letters? Take them back, I beg you. This painful sacrifice has still to be made. Do not leave me anything which might weaken my resolve.' And pulling from my pocket the precious package: 'There it is,' I declared, 'this deceitful store of friendship! That was what bound me to life. Take it back. Give me the sign that must separate us for ever.'

Here my fearful beloved yielded utterly to her tender solicitude. 'But Monsieur de Valmont, what is the matter? What do you mean? Is what you are doing today not done of your own accord? Is it not the result of your own reflections? And did this not lead you to approve of the course of action I took because it was my duty?'

'Well,' I returned, 'your action has determined my own.'

'And what is that?'

'The only one which can, by separating us, put an end to my pain.'

'But answer me, what is it?'

At this point I took her in my arms without her making any attempt whatsoever to defend herself. And, judging from this disregard for the proprieties, how strong and powerful her emotions must be: 'You adorable woman,' I said to her, risking a little fervour, 'you have no idea how much I love you. You will never know to what extent you have been adored, and how much dearer to me this sentiment is than my life! May all your days be happy and peaceful. May they be blessed with all the happiness you have deprived me of! At least repay this sincere wish with one regret, with one tear; and believe me when I say that my ultimate sacrifice will not have been the most painful one. Farewell.'

As I spoke I felt her heart beating violently. I observed her face change. To be precise I saw her choked with tears, but unable to shed them except slowly and with great difficulty. It was only then that I decided to pretend to leave. But immediately, holding me back by force, she insisted:

'No, listen to me!'

'Let me go,' I replied.

'You will listen to me, I insist.'

'I must fly from you, I must!'

'No!' she cried ... At this last word she threw herself or rather fell into my arms in a faint. As I was still doubtful of such a happy outcome, I pretended to be dreadfully alarmed. But at the same time I was leading her or carrying her towards the place I had designated before as the field of victory. And, in fact, she only regained consciousness having already submitted and surrendered to her happy conqueror.

Up to this point, my love, you will be pleased, I think, by the purity of my method. And you will see that I have not diverged at all from the true principles of this art, which we have often noticed is so very similar to the art of warfare. Judge me then as you would a Turenne or a Friedrich.[1] I forced into battle an enemy who only wished to use delaying tactics. Thanks to clever manoeuvring I obtained for myself the choice of terrain and dispositions. I was able to inspire a sense of security in the enemy in order to attack her more easily in her refuge. After that I was able to cause terror before joining battle. There was no risk, since there would be a huge advantage if I were successful and I was certain of my other resources in case of defeat. Finally I only went into action when I was assured of a safe retreat by which I could protect and preserve everything I had previously won. I think no one could have done more. But at present I fear I have become soft as Hannibal among the fleshpots of Capua.[2] Here is what later ensued.

I was expecting that such a momentous event would not take place without the usual tears and despair. And if I remarked at first rather more embarrassment and a sort of withdrawal, I attributed them both to her prudish disposition. So, without bothering about these slight differences which I thought purely local, I went down the well-trodden road of consolation, fully persuaded that, as normally happens, sensation would come to the help of sentiment and that one single action would speak louder than any words – which I did not in any case neglect. But I found a truly terrifying resistance, not so much by its excess as by the form it took.

Just imagine a woman seated, stiff and motionless, with a fixed expression on her face, apparently not thinking, nor listening, nor comprehending; from her eyes tears flowing more or less continuously, and effortlessly. Such was Madame de Tourvel while I was speaking. But if I tried to bring her attention back to me by a caress, or by even the most innocent of gestures, her seeming apathy gave way immediately to terror, suffocation, convulsions, sobs and a few cries now and then, but not one single articulate word.

These crises were repeated several times over, each one more violent than the one before. The last was so violent that I was completely discouraged by it and feared for a moment that I had carried off a useless victory. I fell back on the usual commonplaces, and among them was this one: 'And you are in despair because you have made me a happy man?' At this, the adorable woman turned to me and her face, although still a little distraught, had nevertheless already recovered its beatific expression. 'Happy?' she said. You can guess what I said to her. 'Are you . . . happy, then?' I redoubled my protestations. 'And happy because of me!' I added tender words and compliments. While I was speaking all her limbs relaxed; she fell back limply, leaning on her armchair. And, allowing her hand, which I had had the temerity to take, to rest in mine: 'That thought,' she said, 'is a solace and a comfort to me.'

As you may guess, once I had been put back on track I did not deviate from it. It was the right and perhaps the only course. So, when I wished to try for another success at first I encountered some resistance and what had taken place before made me circumspect. But, having summoned to my help that same thought of bringing about my happiness, I soon felt its favourable effects. 'You are right,' said the tender-hearted creature, 'I can no longer bear my existence except inasmuch as it will serve to make you happy. To that I devote myself utterly. From this moment on I give myself to you, and you will have from me neither refusal nor regret.' It was with such naive or sublime candour that she gave herself and her charms to me, and increased my happiness by sharing in it. The delight was complete and reciprocal; and for the first time my happiness lasted longer than the pleasure. I left her arms only in order to fall at her feet, and swear eternal love. And, to be absolutely truthful, I believed what I was saying. For even after we had parted, the thought of her would not leave me, and only by an effort of the will could I think of anything else.

Oh, why are you not here to balance out the delights of action with those of reward? But I shall lose nothing by waiting, shall I? And I hope to be able to take for granted the happy arrangement I suggested in my last letter. As you see, I am keeping my word and, as promised, my affairs will be advanced enough for me to be able to allow you part of my time. So make haste and get rid of your tedious Belleroche, and leave the mawkish Danceny to his own devices so that you can concentrate on me. What can be occupying you so much in that country house that you don't even reply to my letters? Do you know I have a mind to scold you? But happiness makes one indulgent. And then I do not forget that by placing myself back in the ranks of your lovers I must submit again to your little whims. However, just remember that this new lover does not wish to lose any of his former rights as a friend.

Farewell, as in the old days. *Yes, farewell, my angel! I send you all my love and kisses.*

P.S. Did you know that Prévan, at the end of his month in gaol, was obliged to leave the Corps? It is the talk of Paris at the moment. Truly he is punished cruelly for a crime he did not commit, and your success is complete!

Paris, 29 October 17**

LETTER 126

Madame de Rosemonde to the Présidente de Tourvel

I should have replied sooner, my dear child, if the fatigue from
writing last time had not brought on my pain, which again
deprived me of the use of my arm. I was most anxious to thank
you for the good news you gave me of my nephew, and I was
just as eager to offer you my sincere congratulations on your
own account. One is obliged to acknowledge this as a true
stroke of Providence which, by having its effect upon the one,
has saved the other. Yes, my dear, God, who wished only to
put you to the test, has come to your aid at the moment when
your powers were failing. And in spite of your little grievances
I believe you have quite a lot to thank Him for. Not that I do
not feel very keenly that it would have been more agreeable,
from your point of view, for this to have been resolved in the
first place by you, and that Valmont's decision should only have
come later. It even seems to me, humanly speaking, that the
rights of our sex would have been better safeguarded – and we
do not wish to lose any of them! But what are these trifling
considerations next to the great Purpose that is being worked
out? Does a drowning man complain of a lack of choice as to
how he should be saved?

You will soon find, my dear daughter, that the pain you fear
will lessen of its own accord. And even if it were to continue
indefinitely and at full strength, you would still feel it was easier
to bear than remorse for wrongdoing and self-contempt. It
would have been useless to discuss this earlier with you with
such apparent severity; love is an independent feeling which
prudence can help us to avoid, but which it cannot conquer,
and, once created, it will only die a natural death or from an
absolute lack of hope. It is your lack of hope that gives me the
strength and the right to express my opinion freely. It is cruel
to frighten a desperately ill person who only benefits from
comfort and palliatives. But it is wise to enlighten a convalescent
about the risks they have run, in order to inspire in them the

necessary wisdom and submission to advice which may still be necessary.

Since you have chosen me to be your doctor, it is in that capacity I am speaking to you, and I tell you that the little indispositions you feel at present, and which perhaps require some remedy, are nothing in comparison with the terrible sickness of which you are now surely cured. Then as your friend, as the friend of a sensible and virtuous woman, I shall allow myself to add that the passion you fell victim to, unfortunate enough in itself, became yet more so by reason of its object. If I am to believe what people say, my nephew, for whom, I admit, I perhaps do have a weakness, and who certainly has many admirable qualities in addition to a great deal of charm, is not without danger, nor free of wrongdoing, where women are concerned, and sets an almost equal value upon seducing them as on ruining them. I do believe you may have converted him. No doubt there is none worthier than you to do so. But so many others have flattered themselves in the same way only to see their hopes dashed that I would very much rather you did not have to resort to this course of action.

Consider at present, my dear, that instead of all those risks you would have had to run, you will have, apart from a clear conscience and your own peace of mind, the satisfaction of being the main cause of Valmont's return to the fold. As for me, I am positive that this is in large part due to your courageous resistance, and that one moment of weakness from you might perhaps have condemned my nephew to the ways of the unrighteous for ever. I like to think so, and should like you to think so too. You will find your prime comfort in these reflections, and I shall find new reasons to love you more

I expect you here in a very few days, my dear child, as you have told me. Come and rediscover your tranquillity and happiness in the place where you lost them. Especially, come and rejoice with your loving mother that you have by such good fortune kept the promise you gave not to do anything that was unworthy of her or of you!

From the Chateau de —, 30 October 17**

LETTER 127

The Marquise de Merteuil to the Vicomte de Valmont

If I did not reply to your letter of the nineteenth, Vicomte, it is not that I have not had time. It is quite simply that I found its lack of common sense irksome. So I thought the best thing would be to forget it. But since you refer to it, seem to insist upon the proposals it contains and take my silence for consent, I must speak my mind plainly.

Sometimes I may have claimed to replace a whole harem of women in my person,[3] but I have never agreed to *belong* to one, as I thought you knew. At least now that you can no longer be unaware of this, you will be able to see how ridiculous your proposition must seem to me. Yes, me! Shall I sacrifice my inclination, and a new one at that, to devote my time to you? And in what manner? Waiting for my turn, like a submissive slave, for the sublime favours of *His Highness*. When, for example, you wish to distract yourself a moment from *this strange fascination* that *the adorable, heavenly* Madame de Tourvel has alone made you feel, or when you are afraid of compromising, with *the charming Cécile*, the superior idea you are so happy for her to have of you: then, descending to my level, you will come and seek out pleasures which are less exciting, of course, but of less consequence. And your precious favours, though passing rare, will be more than adequate to bring about my happiness!

You are certainly well-endowed with a fine opinion of yourself, but I, apparently, do not possess anything like the same amount of modesty. For, however hard I look at myself, I cannot see that I have sunk that low. Perhaps this is a fault in me. But let me assure you I have many more.

In particular, I have that of believing that *the schoolboy, the mawkish* Danceny, who is utterly devoted to me and has sacrificed, without taking any credit for it, his first passion to me before it has even been satisfied, and who indeed loves me as only at that age one can love, could, despite his twenty years, serve my happiness and pleasure more effectively than you. I shall even allow myself to add that if I took it into my head to provide him with an assistant, it would not be you I chose, at least not at present.

And what are my reasons, you will ask? Well, in the first place, it is perfectly possible I have none. For the fancy that might make you the favourite might equally well cast you aside. However, for the sake of politeness, I will tell you what my motives are. It seems to me you would have too many sacrifices to make. And I, instead of being grateful, as you would certainly expect of me, should be capable of believing that you owed me even more! So you see that, being so far removed from each other in our thinking as we are, there is no way we can reach an understanding. And I fear I should need a long time, a very long time, before my feelings changed. When I do see the error of my ways, I promise to let you know. Until then, believe me; make other arrangements and keep all your kisses; you will surely find better places to bestow them!

Farewell, as in the old days, you say? But in the old days it seems to me you valued me more highly; you had not relegated me totally to a minor role. And above all you were willing to wait for me to say yes before you made sure of my consent. So, instead of my bidding you farewell as I did in the old days, you will have to be satisfied with my bidding you farewell as I do now.

Your servant, Monsieur le Vicomte.

From the Chateau de —, 31 October 17**

LETTER 128

The Présidente de Tourvel to Madame de Rosemonde

It was not until yesterday that I received your tardy reply, Madame. It would have been the instant death of me were there any life left that I could call my own. But my life belongs to

Another. And that Other is Monsieur de Valmont. As you see, I am hiding nothing from you. If you were to find me no longer worthy of your friendship, I am still less afraid of losing it than betraying it. All I can tell you is that, given the choice between the death of Monsieur de Valmont and his happiness, I decided to take the latter course. I do not boast of it, nor blame myself. I am simply stating a fact.

After that, you will readily understand the effect your letter, and the stern truths contained in it, must have had on me. Do not, however, believe that it caused me any regrets nor that it could ever make me change my feelings or my conduct. It is not that I do not suffer cruelly, but when my heart is at breaking point, and when I fear I shall no longer be able to bear its torments, I say to myself: 'Valmont is happy.' And with this thought all of that disappears or rather becomes transformed into pleasure.

So it is to your nephew that I have devoted my life; it is for him that I am ruined. He has become the sole centre of my thoughts, feelings and actions. As long as my life is necessary to his happiness, it will be precious to me, and I shall find it blessed. If one day he should think differently . . . he will hear neither complaints nor reproaches from me. I have already dared contemplate that fateful moment, and my mind is made up.

You can see now how unaffected I am by your apparent fears that one day Monsieur de Valmont will ruin me. For before he could wish for such a thing he would therefore have ceased to love me; and of what use would vain recriminations that I could not hear be to me then? He alone shall be my judge. As I shall live only for him, it will be in him that my memory resides. And if he is forced to acknowledge that I have loved him, that will be sufficient justification for me.

You have just looked into my heart, Madame. By my honesty I have preferred the misfortune of losing your respect to that of rendering me unworthy of it by stooping to lies. I believe I owe you this complete confidence in return for your former kindness towards me. To say any more might be to make you suspect that I am arrogant enough to count on it still, when on the contrary I judge myself to have forfeited those claims.

I am respectfully, Madame, your most humble and obedient servant.

Paris, 1 November 17**

LETTER 129

The Vicomte de Valmont to the Marquise de Merteuil

Tell me then, my love, why this tone of bitterness and mockery that pervades your last letter? So what is this crime I have committed, apparently without realizing, which displeases you so? I seemed, you say, to be counting on your consent without first having obtained it; but I supposed that what might seem presumptuous for anyone else could never be construed as anything but trust between you and me. And since when is this sentiment harmful to friendship or love? In uniting hope with desire I only yielded to the natural impulse which makes us draw as near as possible to the happiness we seek. What you have construed as arrogance was simply the effect of my eagerness. I know very well that it is customary in these situations to display a respectful hesitation. But you also know that it is only a formality, a simple matter of protocol. I was, I think, allowed to believe that these footling preliminaries were no longer necessary between you and me.

It seems to me also that this frank and free intercourse, when based upon a long-standing relationship, is far preferable to the insipid flattery which frequently makes of love such a bland thing. Perhaps the reason I attach importance to this is because of the past happiness it reminds me of. And that is precisely why I should be all the more sorry if you were of a different opinion.

This, however, is my only crime, as far as I know. For I do not imagine that you can seriously believe there exists a woman anywhere in the world whom I could find preferable to you. And still less that I could have such a bad opinion of you as you pretend to think. You have looked at yourself, you say, and you do not find you have sunk so low. Well of course, that simply proves that your looking-glass does not lie. But could you not have more easily and correctly concluded that I had passed no such judgement upon you?

I search in vain for the explanation for this strange idea. Yet it seems to me it has something or other to do with the admiration I have allowed myself to express for other women. At any rate this is what I infer from your deliberate picking out of the epithets *adorable, heavenly, charming* that I used when speaking of Madame de Tourvel or the little Volanges girl. But do you not realize that those words, plucked out of the air more often than considered in any depth, express not what one thinks of the woman so much as the mood one is in when one speaks of her? And since, at the very same moment when my feelings for either was so strong, I did not desire you any the less; and seeing that I could not in any case renew our liaison except to the detriment of the other two, and gave you preference over both, I do not believe you have real grounds for complaint.

It will not be any more difficult for me either to defend myself against the *strange fascination* that also seems to have shocked you a little. For, in the first place, just because it is strange it does not follow that it is more powerful. Who could surpass, my dear, the delicious pleasures that you alone render always new and always more intense? I was only trying to say that this one was of a kind that I had not previously experienced, without claiming to assign a value to it; and I did add, and say again now, that whatever it was I shall be able to fight it and conquer it. And I shall put much more effort into that if I discern in this trifling task a way of offering homage to you.

As far as little Cécile is concerned, I think it is superfluous to speak of her to you. You have not forgotten that it is at your request that I took charge of the child, and I await only your leave to get rid of her. I remarked on her freshness and naivety. I might even briefly have thought her *charming* because one always takes pleasure to some degree in one's own handiwork. But she certainly does not have enough substance in any respect to retain one's interest for very long.

Now, my love, I appeal to your sense of justice and your old kindness to me, to our long and perfect friendship, to the absolute trust which has since made our ties even closer. Have I deserved this harsh tone you are adopting with me? How easy it will be for you to make amends whenever you like! Just say the word and you shall see if all the charms and attractions will keep me here one minute, let alone one day. I shall fly to your side and into your arms, and I shall prove to you a thousand times and in a thousand ways that you are and will evermore be the true queen of my heart.

Farewell, my love. I most anxiously await your response.

Paris, 3 November 17**

LETTER 130

Madame de Rosemonde to the Présidente de Tourvel

And why, my dear girl, should you no longer wish to be my daughter? Why do you seem to be saying that all correspondence between us will cease? Is it to punish me for not having guessed something that was against all the odds? Or do you suspect me of having deliberately hurt you? No, I know your heart too well to believe you think this of me. So the pain your letter caused I feel much less on my own account than on yours.

Oh my young friend! It grieves me to say it, but you are much too worthy of being loved for love ever to make you happy. For where is the truly refined and sensitive woman who has not been made unhappy by this very sentiment which promises so much happiness! Do men ever appreciate the women they possess?

It is not that many of them are not honourable in their conduct, and constant in their affections. But even among those, how few can really understand us in our hearts! Do not suppose, my darling child, that their love is similar to ours. Certainly they experience the same delight, and they may often invest it with more passion. But they are ignorant of that anxious eagerness, that delicate solicitude, which produces in us the loving and constant care whose sole object is always the man we love. A man enjoys the happiness he feels and a woman the happiness she gives. This difference, which is so essential and so infrequently observed, nevertheless influences the conduct of each in a very remarkable fashion. The pleasure of one is to satisfy his desires and that of the other above all to arouse them. To please is for him only one means to an end, while for her it is an end in itself. And the coquetry that women are so often blamed for is nothing but the abuse of this way of feeling and is itself proof of that feeling. Finally, the exclusive attachment which particularly characterizes love is in men only a preference, serving at most to increase the pleasure which, with another woman, would perhaps be diminished but not destroyed. Whereas in women it is a deep feeling which not only nullifies all other desires but, stronger than nature and outside its domination, may cause them to experience only repugnance and disgust in what should, so it seems, be the very source of pleasure.

And do not imagine that the more or less numerous exceptions one could cite can disprove these general truths in any way! They have as their guarantee public opinion, which for men alone has differentiated between inconstancy and infidelity. A distinction they glory in, rather than being humiliated by it, as they should be; and one which has never been adopted by our sex except by those depraved women who are a disgrace to it and to whom all means seem good, if they will save them from the painful consciousness of their own degradation.

I thought, my dear girl, that it might be useful to you to have these thoughts to place beside the fantastical ideas of perfect happiness with which love never fails to abuse our imagination; false hopes to which one clings even when one sees one must abandon them and whose loss aggravates and multiplies the pain that is already only too real, because inseparable from deep passion! This task of alleviating your sorrows or of diminishing their number is the only one I can, or wish to, fulfil at the moment. When the malady is incurable, advice can be only on the subject of the regimen. All I ask is that you remember that to pity a sick person is not the same as to blame her. Ah, who are we to blame one another? Let us leave the right of judgement to Him who alone reads our hearts. I even dare believe that in His paternal sight a host of virtues may redeem one weakness.

But I beg you, my dear friend, defend yourself above all against these violent resolutions which do not indicate your strength so much as a total loss of courage. Do not forget that, as you make another person the possessor of your life – to use your own expression – you have not deprived your friends of the part that belonged to them and that they will continue to demand of you.

Farewell, dear daughter. Think of your loving mother sometimes, and be assured that you will always be above all else the object of her tender thoughts.

From the Chateau de —, 4 November 17**

LETTER 131

The Marquise de Merteuil to the Vicomte de Valmont

Good for you, Vicomte. I am bettter pleased with you this time than last. But now let us talk as good friends, and I hope to persuade you that for you as well as me the arrangement you seem to be wanting would be absolute folly.

Have you not yet noticed that pleasure, which is indeed the one and only reason why the two sexes come together, is nevertheless insufficient to forge a relationship between them? And that if it is preceded by desire which attracts, it is succeeded by disgust which repels? This is a law of nature that love alone can change. But can one have love whenever one wants? Yet it must always be present. And that necessity would be truly embarrassing if one had not perceived that fortunately it is enough for it to exist on one side only. The difficulty therefore becomes halved without much being lost thereby. In fact, one party enjoys the happiness of loving and the other that of pleasing, the latter rather less intense, it is true, but to it is added the pleasure of being unfaithful, which evens things out. And so it is satisfactory all round.

But tell me, Vicomte, which of us two will take responsibility for deceiving the other? You know the story about those two gamblers who realized as they played that they were both card-sharpers: 'We shall not win anything,' they told each other. 'Let us divide the stakes between us.' And they abandoned the game. Believe me, we must follow their wise example and not waste time that we can so usefully employ elsewhere.

To prove to you that it is your interests that are influencing my decision as much as my own, and that I am not acting out of pique or on an impulse, I am not going back on the reward we agreed. I feel perfectly sure that we shall be enough for each other for one night, and I am even certain that it will be so good that we shall be sorry to see it end. But do not let us forget that this regret is necessary to our happiness. And, however sweet the illusion, let us not suppose that it can last.

As you see, I am fulfilling my part of the bargain without you having done what you said you would do. For, after all, I was supposed to have the first letter from the celestial prude. Either you intend to keep your part of the bargain or you are forgetting the terms, which concern you perhaps less than you would have me believe, but I have received nothing, absolutely nothing. However, unless I am much mistaken, the loving devotee must write a lot of letters. What else does she do when she is on her own? Surely she has not enough wit to amuse herself? So I might make a few little complaints about you, if I wished. But I shall let them go, to make up for the slightly bad mood you may have detected in my last letter.

Now, Vicomte, all that remains is to ask you a favour. And I ask it as much for your benefit as mine. It is to delay for the moment what I desire perhaps as much as you, but I think will have to be put off until I get back to Town.[4] For one reason, we should not have the necessary freedom here. And for another, I should be running rather a risk. For it requires but a little jealousy to attach this gloomy Belleroche even more firmly to me, although he is at present only hanging by a thread. He already has to whip himself into loving me. It has got to the point where I am now putting as much malice as prudence into the caresses I lavish upon him. But at the same time you quite see that this is not the sacrifice to make for you! A reciprocal infidelity will make the pleasure much more intense.

Do you know I sometimes regret we are reduced to doing these things! In the time when we were lovers, for I believe it *was* love, I was happy. Were you too, Vicomte? . . . But why must we think about a happiness which can never return? No, whatever you say, it is impossible to go back. In the first place I should demand sacrifices that you would surely not want or be able to give, and which quite possibly I should not deserve. And then again, how to be sure of you? Oh no, no, I definitely do not wish to entertain the idea. And in spite of my pleasure at this moment in writing to you I prefer to leave you at once.

Farewell, Vicomte.

From the Chateau de —, 6 November 17**

LETTER 132

The Présidente de Tourvel to Madame de Rosemonde

I am so deeply grateful for your goodness towards me, Madame, that I should open up my heart entirely to you were I not held back in some way by the fear of defiling what I accept. Why, when I see how precious your kindness is, must I feel at the same time that I am no longer worthy of it? I may at least express my gratitude. I admire above all your indulgent virtue, which views weakness as something only to be sympathized with, whose irresistible charm holds such gentle yet powerful sway over my heart, along with the charms of love itself.

But do I still deserve a friendship which is no longer sufficient for my happiness? I say the same about your advice. I feel how valuable it is yet cannot follow it. And how should I not believe in perfect happiness when I am experiencing it at this moment? Yes, if men are like you say, we should flee from them, for they are detestable. But how unlike Valmont they are! They may have in common these violent feelings, which you call passions, but how far these feelings are exceeded in him by his extreme delicacy! O my friend, you speak to me of sharing my pain. Then enjoy my happiness; it is love I owe it to, and the object of my love makes its value so much greater! You love your nephew, you say, and perhaps have a weak spot for him? Ah, if only you knew him as I do! I idolize him, and that is still a great deal less than he deserves. No doubt he has been led into making some mistakes, he admits it himself. But who ever knew true love like he does? What more can I say? His feelings are equal to the feelings he inspires.

You are going to think that this is *one of those fantastical ideas with which love never fails to abuse our imagination*: but in that case why should he have become more loving and eager now that he has nothing more to obtain from me? I admit that previously I found in him a deliberation, a detachment, which rarely left him and which, in spite of myself, often put me in mind of the false and cruel impression that people had given me of him. But ever since he has been able to give himself up without constraint to the impulses of his heart, he seems to divine all the desires of my own. Who knows, we may have been born for one another! My happiness was perhaps destined to be necessary for his! Ah, if this is an illusion, may I die before it is over.[5] But no, I want to live to cherish him, to adore him. Why should he stop loving me? What other woman would he make as happy as me? I know in my own heart the happiness one gives is the strongest bond; that alone is truly binding. Yes, it is this delightful feeling that ennobles love, that in a sense purifies it and renders it truly worthy of a loving and generous spirit such as Valmont's.

Farewell, my dear, kind and honourable friend. I should like to write more, but it is not possible. This is the time he promised to come and I can think of nothing else. Forgive me! But you desire my happiness, and it is so great at this moment, I am scarcely able to bear it.

Paris, 7 November 17**

LETTER 133

The Vicomte de Valmont to the Marquise de Merteuil

So what are these sacrifices you believe I would not make, my love, and yet whose reward would be to please you? Let me know what they are, and if I hesitate to offer them to you, you may refuse my homage. What opinion have you formed of me lately if you doubt my feelings or my capacities even when you are being kind to me? Sacrifices which I would not or could not make! So do you believe I am in love, enslaved? And the value I have placed upon victory, do you suspect me of now attaching it to the vanquished? Ah, thank God, I am not yet reduced to that state, and I offer proof of that. Yes, I shall prove it even if it were to be at Madame de Tourvel's expense. Surely after that you will not still be in any doubt.

I have, I believe, without compromising myself spent some time on a woman who has at least the merit of belonging to a type one rarely sees. Perhaps, too, this affair having taken place in the off-season, I have devoted more attention to it. And even now when the social whirl has scarcely begun again, it is not surprising that I am almost entirely occupied with it. But remember that I have had not quite one week to enjoy the fruit of three months of labour. So often I have spent longer on what was worth much less and did not cost me so much! ... And you have never because of that drawn such conclusions about me.

But do you want to know what the real cause of my enthusiasm for her is besides? Here it is. This woman is naturally shy. At the beginning she had doubts about her happiness, and those doubts were enough to destroy it. So much so that I have scarcely begun to see how far my powers in this direction will stretch. It is, however, something that I have been curious to find out. And the opportunity does not come along as often as one might think.

In the first place, for many women pleasure is always pleasure and never anything else. And with those women, whatever title they bestow on us, we are only ever servants, mere functionaries, whose whole merit resides in activity; the man who does best is always the one who does most.

Another class of women, and perhaps they are the most numerous today, are occupied almost totally with the prestige of the lover, the pleasure of having taken him away from a rival, the fear of seeing him carried off in turn by someone else. Of course we play some part, more or less, in the happiness they enjoy, but it is more dependent upon circumstance than on the person. It comes to them through, but not from, us.

So for my observations I needed to find a delicate and sensitive woman who made love her unique business and who, in love itself, saw no further than her lover; whose emotions, far from following the ordinary routes, always reached her senses through her heart; whom I saw, for example (and I don't mean from the very first day), emerge from pleasure dissolved in tears and a moment later rediscover her voluptuousness thanks to words which touched her soul. Added to this she had to have a natural candour which, because of her habit of indulging it, was indestructible and did not allow her to hide any of her true feelings. Now you will agree such women are rare. And I can quite believe that, had it not been for her, I might never have met one.

So it would be hardly surprising if she has retained my interest longer than anyone else. And if my experiments with her demand that I should make her happy, perfectly happy, why should I deny her that, especially when it serves, not contradicts, my purposes? But though the mind is occupied, does it necessarily follow that the heart is enslaved? No, of course not. So the value I allow myself to attach to this affair will not prevent me from pursuing others or even sacrificing it to more agreeable ones.

I am so free that I have not even neglected the little Volanges girl, and yet I am scarcely attached to her at all. Her mother is taking her back to Town in three days' time. And yesterday I established my communications: a little tip to the porter and a few compliments to his wife have seen to it. Can you imagine why Danceny did not hit upon such a simple method? And yet they say love makes one ingenious! On the contrary it makes those whom it dominates stupid. And you think I am not able to resist! Oh, do not fret. In a few days I shall already have diminished, by sharing it, the perhaps too vivid impression I have experienced. And if sharing it once is not enough, I shall do so again and again.

I shall be none the less ready to give the young convent girl back to her discreet lover as soon as you decide it is proper to do so. It seems to me you have no longer any reason to prevent it. And, as for me, I agree to make this gesture to poor Danceny. Truly it is the least I owe him for everything he has done for me. At the moment he is gravely worried about whether he will be received at Madame de Volanges's house. I calm his worries as well as I can, reassuring him that one way or another I shall make him happy at the first opportunity. And in the meantime I continue looking after the correspondence, which he wishes to resume as soon as *his Cécile* arrives. I already have six letters from him and I shall certainly have one or two more before the happy day. This young man really must have time on his hands!

But let us leave this childish pair and come back to us, that I may occupy myself solely with the sweet hopes that your letter has given me. Yes, of course you will see me and I should not forgive you for doubting it. Have I ever ceased being constant to you? Our bonds have been loosened but not broken. Our so-called rupture was nothing but an error of our imagination. Our feelings, interests, have none the less remained united. Like the traveller who returns disappointed, I shall recognize, as he did, that I left happiness to chase after false hopes; and I shall say like d'Harcourt:

The more I saw of foreign lands the more I longed for home.[*][6]

---

[*] De Belloy, *Tragedy of the Siege de Calais.*

So do not resist the idea or rather the feeling that brings you back to me. And, having tried all the pleasures in our different pursuits, let us enjoy the happiness of feeling that none of them compares with what we once experienced; when we rediscover it, it will be even more delightful than before!

Farewell, my charming love. I agree to await your return. But make haste, and do not forget how much I desire it.

Paris, 8 November 17**

LETTER 134

The Marquise de Merteuil to the Vicomte de Valmont

In truth, Vicomte, you are just like a child; one cannot say anything in front of them; and one cannot show them anything without them wanting to snatch at it straight away! A simple thought occurs to me, one I warned you I did not wish to consider seriously, and, just because I mentioned it, you harp on it for ever more, forcing me to hold to it when I wish to forget it, and thus make me share your crazy ideas in spite of myself! Is it kind of you to let me assume the entire burden of prudence on my own? I tell you again, and I tell myself again even more often, that the arrangement you are suggesting is absolutely impossible. Even were you to invest it with all the generosity you are showing me at present, do you not understand that I also have my tact, which would not allow me to let you make sacrifices that are injurious to your happiness?

Now is it not true, Vicomte, that you are deluding yourself about your feelings for Madame de Tourvel? It is love, or love has never existed. You deny it in a hundred ways, but you prove it in a thousand. What, for example, is this subterfuge you are using with regard to yourself (for I believe you are sincere with me) which makes you attribute to an interest in experiment your desire, that you cannot conceal or conquer, to keep this woman? One would think you had never made another woman

happy, perfectly happy! Oh, if you doubt that, you certainly
have a very bad memory! But no, it is not that. Quite simply
your heart is interfering with your reason and is deceiving itself
with false arguments. But I, having a keen interest in not being
deceived, am not so easily satisfied.

So while observing that, for the sake of politeness, you were
careful to suppress all the words you imagined had offended
me, I could see that, perhaps without realizing, you still clung
to the same ideas. So it was no longer the 'adorable, heavenly'
Madame de Tourvel, but *she is an astonishing woman, delicate
and sensitive* and to the exclusion of all others. *An exceptional
woman* and one *whose like one will not meet again.* And the
same goes for that strange fascination which is not *of the
strongest kind.* Well, so be it. But as you have not found it until
now, one may suppose you will not find it again, and the loss
you sustain would be no less irreparable. If these are not the
certain symptoms of love, Vicomte, one should give up looking
for them.

Rest assured that this time I am speaking without any ran-
cour. I have promised myself I shall not become annoyed any
more. I have realized only too clearly that it might turn out to
be a dangerous pitfall. Please let us remain friends, and leave it
at that. Be grateful to me only for my courage in resisting you.
Yes, my courage. For it is sometimes necessary, even in avoiding
a decision one feels to be bad.

So it is only to persuade you to my way of thinking that I am
going to answer the question you asked me about the sacrifices
I should demand and that you would not be able to make. I use
this word 'demand' deliberately because I am sure that in a
moment you are going in fact to find that I am too demanding.
But so much the better! Far from taking any offence at your
refusal, I shall thank you for it. Listen, I do not want to pretend
with you, though perhaps I need to.

I should demand, then – and here is the cruel part – that this
rare and astonishing Madame de Tourvel should become for
you nothing but the ordinary woman that she is. For we must
not deceive ourselves. The charm that we believe we find in
other people exists only within ourselves. And it is love alone

that enhances the object of our affections. I know you would probably make an effort and promise, or swear to do even, what I am asking of you here, impossible though it may seem; but I have to say that I should not believe any empty words. I could only be persuaded by your conduct as a whole.

That is still not all, for I should be capricious. This sacrifice of little Cécile that you offer me so readily, I should not care about in the least. On the contrary, I should ask you to continue with this painful duty until further notice. Perhaps because I like to abuse my power in this way or perhaps out of indulgence or fairness towards you, I should be quite satisfied with dictating your feelings without wishing to spoil your pleasures. Whatever the case, I should wish to be obeyed. And my orders would be very strict!

It is true that then I should feel obliged to thank you. And who knows? Perhaps even to reward you. For example, I should certainly cut short an absence that I found intolerable. I should see you again at last, Vicomte, and I should see you . . . how? . . . But remember that this is only a conversation, a simple account of an impossible scheme, and I don't wish to be the only one to forget about it.

Do you know I am a little anxious about my lawsuit? Well anyway, I finally tried to find out what my resources were. My lawyers, of course, cite different laws, and a great many authorities, as they call them. But I do not see much reason or justice in them. I am almost at the point of being sorry I refused the settlement out of court. However, I find it reassuring that the prosecutor is clever, the lawyer eloquent and the plaintiff pretty. If these three qualifications were no longer worth anything, the whole legal procedure would have to be changed, and then, what would become of respect for the old traditions?

This lawsuit is at the moment the only thing that keeps me here. The Belleroche business is over. Case dismissed, costs divided. At the moment he is regretting tonight's ball, truly the regret of someone with time on his hands! I shall give him back his complete liberty when I get back to town. I shall make this painful sacrifice and take comfort in the knowledge that he will think it generous.

Farewell, Vicomte, write to me often. The detailing of your pleasures will make up, at least in part, for the boredom I have to suffer.

From the Chateau de —, 11 November 17**

LETTER 135

The Présidente de Tourvel to Madame de Rosemonde

I am trying to write to you, but do not yet know if I shall be able. Ah God, when I think that in my last letter it was my excess of happiness that prevented me from continuing! Now it is an excess of despair that is crushing me. It leaves me with enough strength to feel my sorrows, but takes away my power to express them.

Valmont . . . Valmont no longer loves me, he has never loved me. Love does not vanish just like that. He has deceived me, betrayed me, insulted me. I am suffering all the misfortunes and humiliations in the world, and he is the cause of them.

Do not suppose it is mere suspicion. I was so far from suspecting anything! I am not so fortunate as to be in any doubt about it. I saw him with my own eyes. What can he possibly say by way of excuse? . . . But he does not care! He will not even try . . . Ah, you unhappy creature! What difference will your reproaches and tears make? He does not care about you! . . .

So it is true that he has sacrificed me, delivered me up, even . . . And to whom? . . . A vile creature. But what am I saying? Oh, I have lost even the right to despise her. She has betrayed fewer duties, she is less to blame than I. Oh, how painful suffering is when it is caused by remorse! I feel my torments multiply. Farewell, my dear friend; however unworthy I have made myself of your compassion, you will still feel some for me if you can imagine what I am going through.

I have just reread my letter, and perceive I have told you nothing. So I shall try to find the courage to tell you this terrible story. It was yesterday. For the first time since my return I was to have gone out to supper. Valmont came to see me at five; never had he seemed so amorous. He gave me to understand that he would prefer me not to go out and, as you can guess, I quickly decided to stay at home instead. However, two hours later all of a sudden his attitude and voice changed noticeably. I don't know if I let fall something that displeased him but, whatever the case, a short time later he pretended to remember some business which obliged him to leave me, and off he went. But not before expressing very strong regrets which seemed tender and that I believed at the time to be sincere.

Left to myself, I judged it more seemly not to neglect my previous engagement, since I was free to fulfil it. I finished my *toilette* and got into my carriage. Unfortunately my coachman took me by way of the Opera and I found I was caught up in the crowds at the exit. Four paces in front of me and in the queue next to mine I saw Valmont's carriage. Immediately my heart started to beat fast, but not with fear; the only desire in my head was that my carriage should move forward. Instead of that it was his that was obliged to draw back next to mine. I immediately leaned forward. How astonished I was to find there was a girl at his side, and a notorious one at that! I withdrew, as you may imagine. This was quite enough to break my heart. But what you will scarcely believe is that this same girl, who had apparently an odious knowledge of who I am, did not leave the carriage window, nor stop staring at me, and was attracting everyone's attention by laughing quite openly.

Though totally devastated by this, I none the less allowed myself to be driven to the house where I was to sup. But I found it impossible to stay. I was ready to swoon at any moment, and worst of all I could not prevent myself weeping.

When I got home I wrote to Monsieur de Valmont, and sent the letter without delay. He was not at home. Wishing at whatever price to escape from this living death, or have it confirmed once and for all, I sent the letter back with orders to await his return. But before midnight my servant returned telling me that the coachman had come back and said that his master was not coming home that night. I thought this morning the only thing to do was ask him for my letters back and beg him not to see me any more. In fact, I gave my orders accordingly, but no doubt they were futile. It is almost midday. He has not reappeared and I have not received one word from him.

Now, my dear friend, I have nothing more to add. You know everything and you know my heart. My only hope is that I shall not have to be a burden upon your kind friendship much longer.

Paris, 15 November 17**

LETTER 136

The Présidente de Tourvel to the Vicomte de Valmont

No doubt after what took place yesterday, Monsieur, you will no longer expect to be received in my house, and no doubt you do not at all desire it! The purpose of this note therefore is not so much to beg you not to come here any more as to ask you to return letters which should never have been written; letters which, though they may have been of interest to you for a short while as proof of the infatuation you occasioned, can only be a matter of indifference to you now that this has vanished, and express only feelings which you have destroyed.

I recognize and admit that I was wrong to place in you a trust of which so many others before me have been victims. I blame only myself. But I did not think, all the same, that I deserved to be delivered up by you to scorn and insult. I believed that in sacrificing everything to you, and giving up for your sake the right to others' esteem as well as to my own, I need not, however, expect to be judged by you more severely than by the public, in whose opinion there still exists a huge distinction between a weak woman and a depraved. These wrongs, which anyone would complain of, are the only ones I shall mention. I shall say nothing about the wrongs of love; you would not understand. Farewell, Monsieur.

Paris, 15 November 17**

LETTER 137

The Vicomte de Valmont to the Présidente de Tourvel

I have only just received your letter, Madame. I trembled when I read it and I scarcely have the strength to reply. What a dreadful opinion you must have of me! Ah! No doubt I have done wrong, and my wrongs are such that I shall never forgive myself even though you draw a veil over them with your kindness. But how far I am from committing those you blame me for! Who, me? Humiliate you! Debase you! When I respect you as much as I cherish you. When I have known no pride save what I felt from the moment when you judged me worthy of you. Appearances are deceptive, and I confess they must have been against me. But did you not then have the necessary strength in your heart to combat them? Did your heart not revolt at the very idea that you might have been treated badly by me? And yet you did think that! So not only did you think I was capable of this terrible folly, but you even feared you had exposed yourself to it through your kindness to me. Ah, if you feel yourself to be degraded to that extent by your love, what a base creature I must myself be in your eyes!

Oppressed by the painful feelings this thought is causing me, I am wasting time refuting it that I should spend destroying it. I shall confess everything. Another consideration still is holding me back. Must I then recall an incident I wish to erase from my memory, must I fix your attention and my own on a moment's transgression which I wish to redeem with the rest of my life, of which I still have to ascertain the reason, and whose memory must bring about my everlasting humiliation and despair? Ah! If in blaming myself I am provoking your anger, you will not have to go very far in seeking your revenge. You have only to leave me to my remorse.

But who would believe it? This event has as its prime cause the all-powerful charm you exert over me. It was this that made me forget for so long the important business which could not be postponed. I left you too late and the person I was looking for was no longer there. I hoped to meet this person at the Opera, but that was an equally fruitless quest; and there I found Émilie, whom I had met at a time when I was very far from knowing you or your love. Émilie did not have her carriage and asked me to drop her at her house a short distance away. I saw no reason not to do so and consented. But it was then that I met you. And I realized straight away that you would be bound to believe I was guilty.

The fear of displeasing you or causing you pain is so strong in me that it had to be, and soon was, in fact, noticed. I even admit it made me try to make the girl promise not to show herself. This delicate precaution, however, worked to the disadvantage of my love. Accustomed, like all women of her class, to being uncertain about the power she has usurped unless she can somehow abuse it, Émilie was careful not to allow such a golden opportunity to pass her by. The more she saw my embarrassment grow, the more delight she took in flaunting herself; and her stupid laughter, which I blush to think you could have supposed was aimed at you, was only caused by my extreme discomfiture, itself the consequence of my respect and my love for you.

Until then, no doubt, I was more unfortunate than blameworthy. And these wrongdoings *which anyone would complain of, the only ones you mention,* since they do not exist, cannot be held against me. But it is useless for you to keep silent about injuries to your love for me. There I shall not keep the same silence, for too great an interest will oblige me to break it.

It is not that in the embarrassment I feel about this inconceivable aberration I can, without extreme pain, bring myself to recall what happened. Overwhelmed by my wrongdoing, I should be willing to bear the pain, or hope, with the passage of time, by my undying love and repentance, to bring about my forgiveness. But how can I be silent when what remains to be said is of so much concern to your delicacy?

Do not imagine I am searching for excuses or trying to extenuate my faults. I admit I am to blame. But I do not and never shall admit that this humiliating mistake could be regarded as a crime against love. What can there be in common between one moment of self-forgetfulness, followed by shame and regret, and a pure sentiment which can only take root in a delicate soul, which is nourished by respect and of which happiness is the ultimate reward? Ah, do not debase love in this way. And especially, beware of debasing yourself by speaking of what can never be compared in the same breath. Leave vile and degraded women to fear a rivalry they feel is becoming established in spite of what they may do, and let them experience the torments of a jealousy which is as cruel as it is humiliating. But you must turn away your eyes from these things which would offend your sight and, pure as the Virgin, punish the offence as She does, without resenting it.

But what punishment will you impose upon me that could be more painful than the one I already feel? What could compare with the sorrow of having displeased you, with the despair of having grieved you, or with the unbearable thought that I have made myself less worthy of you? You think of punishing me while I am asking for consolation! Not that I deserve it, but because it is necessary to me, and it can come from you alone.

If you suddenly, forgetting my love and yours, and no longer setting any value on my happiness, wish to deliver me up to eternal pain, you have every right. Strike that blow. But if, with more kindness or compassion, you still recall those loving feelings which made our hearts beat as one, this voluptuousness of the soul ever reborn and ever more deeply felt, those sweet and blessed days which each owed to the other; all those blessings that love and only love procures, perhaps you would exercise your power in reviving rather than destroying them. What else can I say? I have lost everything and it is all my fault; but I may recover everything through your goodness. It is for you to decide now. I shall add only one thing. Only yesterday you assured me that my happiness was safe as long as it depended on you! Ah, Madame, will you deliver me up today to eternal despair?

Paris, 15 November 17**

LETTER 138

The Vicomte de Valmont to the Marquise de Merteuil

I insist, my love, I am not in love with her. And it is not my fault if circumstances force me to play the part. Only consent and come back. You will see yourself how sincere I am. I proved it yesterday and that cannot be disproved by what is happening today.

I was at the tender prude's, for lack of anything else to do: for the little Volanges girl, in spite of her condition, had to spend the whole night at Madame V—'s, who was giving an early ball. At first I wanted to make the evening last longer, and I had even demanded a small sacrifice in this regard. But scarcely was it granted when the pleasure I was promising myself was troubled by the thought of this love that you insist on believing I have, or at least that you blame me for. My only wish was to be able to reassure myself and convince you that it was pure slander on your part.

So I took a swift decision. On a rather slight pretext I left my lady there, surprised and undoubtedly even more hurt, while I went calmly off to join Émilie at the Opera. And she could confirm that, until this morning when we separated, not the slightest regret came to spoil our pleasure.

I should have had rather a lot to worry about, except that I was saved by my total nonchalance. For I was scarcely four houses away from the Opera with Émilie in my carriage when the austere devotee's carriage drew up right beside us, and because of a traffic obstruction we were right next to each other for between five and ten minutes. We could see each other as plainly as daylight, and there was no escape.

But that was not all. I took it into my head to confide to Émilie that it was the woman of the letter. (Perhaps you will remember that amusing little episode, and that Émilie was the desk!)* Émilie, who enjoys a laugh, had not forgotten, and was not satisfied until she had had a good look at *Lady Virtue*, as

---

* Letters 47 and 48.

she called her, with scandalous peals of laughter which made the latter take great umbrage.

And that is not all. For did the jealous creature not send me word that very evening? I was not there, but she insisted upon sending again with orders to wait for an answer. As soon as I had decided to stay with Émilie, I sent my coach home, ordering the coachman only to return for me next morning. And when he arrived at my house and found Cupid waiting, he thought the simplest thing was to say that I was not coming back that night. You can well imagine the effect of this piece of news. When I got home I found I had been given my marching orders with all the dignity required in the circumstances!

So this affair, which you think so interminable, might have been over by this morning, as you can see. That it is not is not because, as you will suppose, I attach any importance to its continuing, but because, on the one hand, I do not find it seemly to allow myself to be dismissed in this fashion, and on the other, because I wished to reserve for you the honour of this sacrifice.

So I answered her severe note with a long and sentimental epistle about my feelings. I went into the reasons in great detail, emphasizing my love, careful to make them convincing. I have already succeeded. I have just received another note, still very severe and confirming the eternal rupture, as was inevitable. But the tone is not the same. She does not wish to see me again on any account. This decision is announced four times in the most irrevocable manner. So I have concluded that there is not a moment to lose before I go and see her. I have already sent my valet to contact the porter. And in a moment I shall go myself to have my pardon signed. For with sins of this sort there is only one formula that confers total absolution, and that can only take place when one is there in person.

Farewell, my charming love. I am off to try and bring about this great event with all speed.

Paris, 15 November 17**

LETTER 139

The Présidente de Tourvel to Madame de Rosemonde

How I blame myself, my friend, for writing at such length and in such haste about my ephemeral problems! I am the reason you are suffering at the moment. You are still thinking about my sorrows while I – I am happy. Yes, all is forgiven and forgotten. Let us rather say, all is mended. Calm and delight succeeded pain and anguish. Oh, the joy in my heart, how can I express it? Valmont is innocent. No one who has so much love can be worthy of blame. He was not guilty of those serious, insulting wrongs I so bitterly accused him of. And if on one single issue I needed to be understanding, did I not also have my injustices to make reparation for?

I shall not detail the facts and arguments that excuse him. Perhaps, even, they cannot be appreciated by the intellect. It is only the heart that can understand them. Yet if you were to suspect me of weakness, I should appeal to your judgement to support mine. For, as you say yourself, infidelity for men is not inconstancy.

Not that I do not feel that this distinction, vainly sanctioned by public opinion, causes any less harm to one's finer feelings. But why should I complain when Valmont suffers even more because of it? This same wrong that I am willing to forget, do not imagine he forgives or can console himself for it. And yet, has he not mended this slight wrong many times over by his excess of love and my excess of happiness!

Either my happiness is greater than ever before or I value it more after fearing I had lost it. But what I will say to you is that if I felt the strength to bear again such cruel sorrows as I have just experienced, I should not believe I had paid too high a price for my excess of happiness since then. Oh my dear mother, scold your thoughtless daughter for hurting you by her impulsive letter. Scold her for her rash judgement, and for injuring the reputation of the man she should never have stopped loving. But while acknowledging her lack of prudence, see how happy she is, and increase her joy by sharing in it.

Paris, 16 November 17**, in the evening

LETTER 140

The Vicomte de Valmont to the Marquise de Merteuil

How is it that I have not received any reply from you, my love? And yet my last letter seemed to me to deserve one. I have been expecting a reply, and should have received it three days ago! I am rather annoyed. So I shall say nothing at all about my important affairs.

As to whether the reconciliation achieved its full effect; whether in the place of blame and mistrust it produced only a new tenderness; whether it is I who am now receiving the excuses and reparations owing to me for suspicions about my honesty. No, I shall not tell you a word about this; and without the unforeseen events of last night, I should not have written at all. But as this concerns your pupil, and she probably will not be in any fit state to tell you about it herself, at least for some time to come, I shall undertake to do that.

For reasons that you may or may not guess, Madame de Tourvel has for some days been spared my attentions. And as those reasons do not apply to the little Volanges girl, I had become more assiduous in that direction.[7] Thanks to the obliging porter I had no obstacle to overcome, and your pupil and I were leading a regular and comfortable life. But habit makes one careless. In the first days we could never take enough precautions. We were still trembling behind locked doors. Yesterday an unbelievable lack of vigilance caused the accident I have to tell you about. And if I for my part simply had a bit of a fright, the little girl has paid a higher price.

We were not asleep, but we were in the state of relaxation and abandon that follows pleasure when we heard the door of the room open suddenly. I immediately leaped to my sword, as much to defend myself as for the protection of our pupil. I advanced but saw nobody. But in fact the door had opened. As we had a light, I went in search of the person but found not a soul there. So I remembered we had forgotten our usual precautions. And no doubt the door had only been pushed to, or was not properly shut, and had reopened of its own accord.

As I went to calm my timid companion, I found her no longer in bed. She had fallen down, or had attempted to hide between the bed and the wall. Well, anyway, there she was stretched out unconscious and motionless apart from some rather violent convulsions. Imagine my predicament! However, I managed to get her back into her bed and even to bring her round. But she hurt herself when she fell, and the effect of this soon became obvious.

Pain in her back, violent sickness and more unequivocal symptoms soon enlightened me as to her condition. But in order to explain it to her, I had first to tell her what condition she had been in before. For she did not realize. Perhaps never before has anyone retained such innocence doing so expertly what was necessary to lose it! Oh, she is not one to waste time thinking about it!

But she was losing a lot of time grieving about it, and I sensed I must do something. I therefore agreed with her that I would go immediately to the family doctor and surgeon, and that when I warned them that they would be summoned, I would confide in them and bind them to secrecy. She for her part would call her chambermaid; she would let her into the secret or not, as she saw fit; but she would send for help, and above all give orders not to wake Madame de Volanges – the natural tact of a girl who is afraid of worrying her mother.

I did my two errands and made my two confessions as swiftly as I could, and then went back to my rooms where I have been ever since. But the surgeon, a previous acquaintance of mine, came at midday to report on the condition of the invalid. I was not mistaken, but he hopes that if all goes smoothly no one in the house will notice anything. The chambermaid is in the secret. The doctor has put a name to the malady, and this affair will sort itself out, just like a thousand others, unless we find it useful to have it talked about in future.

But tell me, do we still have any interests in common? Your silence makes me doubt it. I should not believe so at all if my desire to hear from you did not make me seek every means of retaining such a hope.

Farewell, my love. I send you my love, despite my resentment.

Paris, 21 November 17**

LETTER 141

The Marquise de Merteuil to the Vicomte de Valmont

Heavens, Vicomte, how your persistence annoys me! What does it matter to you if I write or no? Do you believe that if I am silent it is for lack of reasons to put forward in my defence? Would to God it were! But no, it is only that it would pain me to tell you of them.

Tell me truthfully, are you deluding yourself or are you trying to deceive me? The difference between what you say and what you do leaves me no choice but to believe either one or the other. Which is correct? What do you expect me to say when I myself do not know what to believe?

You seem to be congratulating yourself inordinately on your last encounter with the Présidente. But what does that prove in support of your views or against mine? I surely never told you that you loved this woman enough not to be unfaithful to her, that you would not seize every opportunity you could that seemed easy or agreeable. I did not even doubt that you would be quite happy to satisfy the desires she had aroused in you with someone else, the first one who came along. And I am not at all surprised that through mental licentiousness, which it would be wrong to deny you possess, you have done once quite deliberately what you have done a thousand times when the occasion presented itself. We all know that is the way of the world, and normal practice for all of you, from emperors to vagabonds. The man who abstains from such behaviour nowadays is taken for a romantic. And that is not, I may say, a fault I find in you.

But what I have said, thought and continue to think is that you are still in love with your Présidente. Not, indeed, that it is a very pure or tender love, but it is the kind that you are capable of. One, for example, that finds in a woman charms or qualities she does not have; one that puts her into a class of her own and ranks all others as second-rate. It keeps you hanging on to her even when you treat her outrageously. It is how I imagine a sultan may feel for his favourite sultana; it does not prevent him from preferring a simple odalisque from time to time. My comparison seems to me all the more exact since, like him, you are never the lover or friend of a woman, but always her tyrant or slave. So I am positive you must have humiliated and debased yourself to a degree to have become reconciled with this beautiful creature! And only too happy to have achieved this, as soon as you believed the time was ripe to obtain your forgiveness you left me for *this great challenge*.

Even in your last letter if you did not speak exclusively about this woman it is because you wish to conceal *your important affairs* from me. They seem to you so important that you think this silence is a punishment for me. And it is after these thousand proofs of your decided preference for another woman that you have the nerve to ask me whether we *still have any interests in common*! Take care, Vicomte! If I give you an answer, it will be irrevocable. And I may say that I am rather inclined to do so at this very moment. Have I said too much already? I do not wish to hear any more about it.

All I can do is recount a story to you. Perhaps you will not have time to read it or give it enough of your attention to understand it aright? Up to you. It will only be, at worst, a good story gone to waste.

A man of my acquaintance had, like you, become embroiled with a woman who did not greatly add to his reputation. At intervals he had enough sense to realize that sooner or later this affair would do him no good. But although he was ashamed of it, he did not have the courage to break it off. He was all the more embarrassed for having boasted to his friends that he was completely at liberty. And he was well aware that the more he defended himself, the more ridiculous he appeared. He thus spent his time doing stupid things and always saying afterwards: 'It is not my fault.' This man had a woman friend who was briefly tempted to expose his infatuation to the public gaze and thus permanently make him an object of ridicule. But being more generous than malicious, or again perhaps for some other reason, she wanted to try one last stratagem, so that in any event she would be in a position to say, like him: 'It is not my fault.' So, without further comment, she sent him the following letter as a remedy he might find useful for his ills.

'One tires of everything, my angel; it is a law of nature. It is not my fault.

'So if today I am tired of an affair which has preoccupied me totally for the last four boring months, it is not my fault.

'If, for example, my love was equal to your virtue,[8] which is certainly saying a lot, it is not surprising that the one has ended at exactly the same time as the other. It is not my fault.

'It follows that I have been unfaithful to you for a while now. But to some degree your relentless tenderness has forced me into it! It is not my fault!

'Today a woman I am madly in love with demands that I give you up for her sake. It is not my fault.

'I realize this is the perfect opportunity for you to accuse me of perjury. But if, where Nature has granted men only constancy she has granted women perseverance, it is not my fault.

'Believe me, and take another lover as I have another mistress. This advice is sound, very sound. If you find it bad, that is not my fault.

'Farewell, my angel. I took you with pleasure, I leave you without regrets. I shall perhaps come back to you. That is the way of the world. It is not my fault.'

It is not yet time, Vicomte, to tell you about the effect of this last attempt and what ensued. But I promise to tell you about it in my next letter. You will also find there my ultimatum on the renewal of the treaty you are proposing to me. Until then, farewell only . . .

By the way, thank you for your details about the little Volanges girl. It is an article we should reserve for the day after the wedding, for the Gossips' Gazette. In the meantime I send you my condolences on the loss of your posterity. Good night, Vicomte.

From the Chateau de —, 24 November 17**

LETTER 142

The Vicomte de Valmont to the Marquise de Merteuil

My dearest love,

I do not know whether I have read you aright or whether I have misunderstood either your letter and the story you relate or the model letter it contained. What I can tell you is that the latter seemed to me witty and likely to produce an effect. So I simply copied it out and just as simply sent it to the heavenly Présidente. I did not waste a moment, for the tender missive was already expedited last night. I preferred it this way because in the first place I had promised to write to her yesterday; and then too because I thought the whole night would not be long enough for her to gather her thoughts and ponder *this great event*, if you will forgive me using the expression a second time.

I was hoping to be in a position to send you my beloved's reply this morning. But it is almost midday and I have received nothing yet. I will wait until five. And if I do not have any news by then, I shall go and find out myself. For especially when it comes to a challenge it is only the first step that is hard.

At present, as you can imagine, I am most anxious to learn the end of the story about this man of your acquaintance, so strongly suspected of not knowing how to give up a woman if necessary. Does he not mend his ways? And does his generous friend not forgive him?

I desire just as ardently to receive your ultimatum, as you so formally call it! I am especially curious to know if you will still attribute my recent action to love. Ah, no doubt there is love, a lot of love! But for whom? However, I am not making any claims, but expecting everything from your generosity.

Farewell, my charming friend. I shall only close this letter at two, in the hope of being able to include the desired reply.

At two o'clock in the afternoon

Still nothing. Time is running out and I can write no more. But will you still refuse me love's most tender kisses?

Paris, 27 November 17**

LETTER 143

The Présidente de Tourvel to Madame de Rosemonde

The veil is torn, Madame, on which was painted the illusion of my happiness![9] The terrible truth has opened my eyes, and revealed only the path to a certain and early death, marked out by shame and remorse. I shall follow it ... I shall cherish my torments if they cut short my life. I shall send you the letter I received yesterday. I shall not add any comment for it is clear enough on its own. This is no longer a time of complaint, but only of suffering. It is not pity I need, but strength.

Please receive my adieus, Madame, the last I shall make, and hear my last prayer; which is to leave me to my fate, forget me utterly and no longer count me among the living. There is a stage in misfortune when even friendship increases our suffering and cannot cure it. When the wound is mortal, all help becomes inhumane. All other feeling but despair is strange to me. All I wish for now is darkest night in which to bury my shame. There I shall weep for my errors – if I can still weep! For since yesterday I have not shed a tear. They no longer flow from my stricken heart.

Farewell, Madame. Do not send a reply. I have sworn upon this cruel letter never to receive another.

Paris, 27 November 17**

LETTER 144

The Vicomte de Valmont to the Marquise de Merteuil

Yesterday at three o'clock in the afternoon, my love, impatient with lack of news, I went to the house of the forsaken beauty. They told me she had gone out. I understood from this expression that she was refusing to see me, but this occasioned in me neither surprise nor annoyance. And I withdrew in the hope that this action would at least compel such a polite lady to honour me with a note in reply. My desire to receive such a reply made me go home on purpose towards nine o'clock, but there was nothing. Astonished by this unexpected silence, I ordered my valet to go and make enquiries as to whether the sensitive girl was dead or dying. Well, when I got back he told me that Madame de Tourvel had in fact gone out at eleven in the morning with her maid. She had driven to the convent of —, and at seven she had sent away her carriage and her servants with a message that she was not to be expected home. That woman does everything according to the rules! The convent is the proper refuge for widows. And if she persists in such praiseworthy resolutions, I shall have to add, to all the obligations I already have towards her, the fame that this affair will attract.

As I told you some time ago, I shall reappear in society, despite your worries, shining with renewed brilliance. Let them show themselves, these severe critics who accused me of a romantic and unhappy love affair. Let them break off their own affairs in such a prompt and dazzling fashion. No, better than that, let them come and offer consolation; the way ahead is clear. Well then, let them just attempt the route that I have travelled entirely, and if one of them obtains the slightest success I shall yield pride of place to him. But they will all see that when I put myself to some trouble, the impression I leave is ineradicable. Ah, this time it certainly will be. And I shall count for nothing all my other triumphs if this woman were ever to prefer a rival to me.

This decision she has taken flatters my self-esteem, I must say. But I am angry that she has found the strength to disengage herself to this extent from me. So there will be obstacles other than the ones I have myself placed between us! So if I wished to return to her it is then possible she would no longer want me? What am I saying? Not to wish it, not to make that her supreme happiness! Is that how one loves? And do you believe, my love, that I should put up with that? Might I not be able, for example, and would it not be better, to try to bring this woman to the point where she can see the possibility of reconciliation, a thing one always desires as long as there is some hope left? I might try this course of action without attaching too much importance to it, and consequently without giving you any offence. On the contrary, it would be a simple experiment for us to make together; and were I to succeed, it would just be one more way of renewing, if you wished it, a sacrifice which has been, I think, agreeable to you. At present, my love, I am still waiting for my reward, and all I wish for is your return. So come with all speed and seek out your lover, your friends, your pleasures, back in the swing of things once more.

All is going marvellously with the little Volanges girl. Yesterday, when in my agitation I could not stay in one place, I even, in the course of my wanderings, went to visit Madame de Volanges. I found your pupil already in the salon, still in invalid's attire, but fully convalescent, and all the fresher and more interesting because of that. You women, in that situation, would have stayed a whole month on your chaise longue. Long live young ladies, say I! This one, I must say, made me wish I could find out if the cure was complete!

I have to tell you too that the child's accident has driven your *sentimentalist* Danceny almost mad, at first with sorrow and now with joy. *His Cécile* was ill! You know how one's head reels under such misfortune. He sent for news of her three times a day, and not one day went by but he went in person to see her. Finally, in a beautiful epistle to Mamma, he asked permission to go and congratulate her on the convalescence of such a very dear person, and Madame de Volanges graciously allowed it. So I found the young man ensconced, as in the past, except for a few little intimacies that he did not as yet dare to allow himself.

It is from him I have these details. For I came away at the same time as he did and got him talking. You cannot imagine the effect this visit had upon him. A joy, a desire, a delight beyond description. I, who love grand emotions, managed to make his head spin by assuring him that in a very few days I would place him in a position where he might see his love at even closer quarters.

In fact, I have decided to give her back to him once my experiment is finished. I wish to devote myself entirely to you. Besides, would it be worth your pupil also being mine merely to deceive her husband? The triumph is in deceiving her lover, and especially her first lover! As for me, I have not been guilty of uttering the word love.

Farewell, my love. Come back, then, as quickly as possible to enjoy your dominion over me, to receive my homage and give me my reward.

Paris, 28 November 17**

LETTER 145

The Marquise de Merteuil to the Vicomte de Valmont

Seriously, Vicomte, have you left the Présidente? Did you send her the letter I composed for you to give her? Really you are a delight! And you have surpassed my expectations! I freely admit that this triumph flatters me more than all I have achieved until now. You are going to think that I put a very high value on this

woman I formerly thought so little of. Not a bit of it! It is
because it is not over her that I have the advantage, it is over
you. That is what pleases me, what really delights me.

Yes, Vicomte, you did love Madame de Tourvel a great
deal and as a matter of fact you still do. You are mad about
her. But because I amused myself by making you ashamed of
it you bravely sacrificed her. You would have sacrificed a thousand more rather than be laughed at. Look where vanity leads
us! The Sage is right when he says that it is the enemy of
happiness.[10]

Where would you be now if I had wished merely to play a
trick on you? But I am incapable of deceit, as you very well
know. And were you obliged to reduce me in my turn to despair
and to the convent, I should take that risk and give myself up
to my conqueror.

However, if I capitulate, it is in truth pure weakness. For, if
I wished, what a deal of wrangling there could still be between
us! And perhaps you would deserve it? For example, I admire
your cunning – or lack of subtlety – in sweetly suggesting I
allow you to take up with the Présidente again. It would be
most convenient for you, would it not, to take the credit for
breaking it off without forgoing the pleasures of the flesh? And
since in that case this apparent sacrifice would no longer be a
sacrifice for you, you offer to renew it whenever I wish! By
this arrangement your heavenly devotee will still be under the
impression that she is your one and only love, whereas I should
flatter myself that I am the preferred rival. We should both be
deceived, but you would be happy, so what does anything else
matter?

It is a shame that with so much talent for making plans you
have so little for putting them into practice. And that by one
ill-judged action you have yourself placed an insuperable object
in the way of what you most desire.

So you were thinking of resuming relations with her, and you
sent her my letter? You must have thought me in my turn very
unskilled! Take it from me, Vicomte, when a woman strikes
into the heart of another she rarely fails to hit her where it
hurts, and the wound is incurable. While I was striking this

woman, or rather when I was directing your blows, I did not forget that this woman was my rival, that for a moment you found her preferable to me and that, in fact, you had considered me beneath her. If I made a mistake about my revenge, I will take the consequences. So I agree that you should try every means at your disposal. I invite you to do it, even, and promise I shan't get angry at your success, if you manage it. I am so easy in my mind on this subject that I do not wish to discuss it any more. Let us talk about something else.

About the little Volanges girl's health, for instance. You will tell me positive news when I get back, won't you? I shall be very happy to hear it. After that it will be up to you to judge if it suits you better to give the girl back to her lover or to make a second attempt to become the founder of a new branch of Valmont, in the name of Gercourt. That idea did seem rather amusing, and while leaving it up to you I must ask you not to take a firm decision until we have discussed it. I am not asking you to wait very long, for I shall be in Paris very shortly. I cannot tell you with certainty which day. But do not doubt that as soon as I arrive you will be the first to know.

Farewell, Vicomte. In spite of my grudges, mockery and criticism, I still love you a lot and I am preparing to prove it to you. Goodbye, my friend.

From the Chateau de —, 29 November 17**

LETTER 146

The Marquise de Merteuil to the Chevalier Danceny

I am leaving at last, my dear young friend, and tomorrow night shall be back in Paris. Amid all the upheaval that moving entails I shall not be at home to anyone. However, if you have some very pressing thing to tell me, I am happy to make an exception to my general rule. But only for you. So I am asking you to keep my arrival secret. Even Valmont shall not know when it is to be.

If someone had told me a short while ago that soon you would be the only one in my confidence, I should not have believed them, but yours has attracted mine. I am tempted to believe that you have used your arts and even your techniques of seduction upon me. That, to say the least, would be very wicked! But in any case I am in no danger at the moment. You have other things on your mind! When the heroine is on stage, one does not concern oneself with the confidante!

So you have not even found time to tell me about your recent successes? When your Cécile was absent the days were not long enough to listen to all your tender complaints. You would have shouted them aloud to the echoes themselves if I had not been there to hear them. When she was unwell you even honoured me again by telling me of your worries; you needed someone to confide in. But now that the one you love is in Paris, that she is well, and especially that you can see her from time to time, she is all you need and your friends are nothing to you any more.

I am not blaming you. It's the fault of your twenty years. Haven't we all known since the time of Alcibiades that young men never know what friendship is except when they are in trouble? Happiness sometimes provokes them to indiscretions but never to confidences. I shall soon say, with Socrates: 'I like my friends to come to me when they are unhappy,*[11] but being a philosopher he made do very well without them when they did not come. In that respect I am not quite so wise as he, and I have felt your silence with all the weakness of a woman.

But do not think I am importunate. I am very far from that! The same feeling that causes me to notice these privations helps me bear them with courage when they are the proof or the cause of my friends' happiness. So I am not counting on you for tomorrow evening unless love leaves you free and unoccupied, and I forbid you to make the least sacrifice on my account.

Adieu, Chevalier; I am so looking forward to seeing you. Shall you come?

From the Chateau de —, 29 November 17**

* Marmontel, *Conte moral d'Alcibiade*.

LETTER 147

Madame de Volanges to Madame de Rosemonde

You will surely be as distressed as I am, my dear friend, when you hear what a state Madame de Tourvel is in. She has been ill since yesterday; her malady has come on so rapidly and manifests such grave symptoms that I am really alarmed.

Burning fever, violent and almost constant delirium, a thirst that cannot be assuaged, that is what one may observe. The doctors say there is as yet no prognosis. And the treatment will be all the more difficult since the patient obstinately refuses every kind of remedy. It is so bad they had to hold her down by force to bleed her. And since then they have had to do the same twice more to put her bandages back on, which in her delirium she constantly tries to tear off.

You, who have seen her, as I have, so timid and gentle, can you imagine that four people can scarcely hold her down, and if anyone tries to reason with her she flies into an unspeakable rage? For my part, I fear it may be more than delirium, and that she is perhaps truly deranged.

What increases my anxiety is what happened the day before yesterday.

On that day, towards eleven in the morning, she went into the convent of — with her maid. As she was raised in this convent and was in the habit of going there sometimes, she was received as usual, and seemed to everyone to be quite happy and well. About two hours later she asked if the room she had occupied as a convent girl was vacant, and when she was told that it was she asked if she could see it again. The prioress and some other nuns accompanied her. It was then that she declared she was returning to live in this room, which, she said, she should never have left. And she added she would stay there *till she died*. That was how she put it.

At first they did not know what to say, but once they had recovered from their initial astonishment they told her that, because of her marital status, she could not be accepted without special permission. However, this argument and a thousand more were to no avail. From that moment on she insisted not only that she would not leave the convent, but that she would not leave her room either. Finally, at seven in the evening, they gave up the struggle and consented to let her stay the night there. They sent away her carriage and servants, and put off the decision until the next day.

They insist that during the whole evening her looks and bearing were far from distraught, but she was, on the contrary, composed and reflective, except that four or five times she fell into such deep abstraction that they did not manage to rouse her by speaking to her. And each time, before she came out of it, she raised both hands to her forehead, which she seemed to clasp with some force. Upon which one of the nuns who was present asked her if she had a headache. She gazed at her for a long time before replying, then said finally: 'That is not where my pain is!' A moment later she asked to be left alone and begged them not to question her further.

Everyone retired except her maid, who fortunately had to sleep in the same room, there being no space elsewhere.

According to this girl's report, her mistress was quite calm until eleven at night. Then she said she wished to go to bed. But before she was entirely undressed she began to walk rapidly up and down the room, gesticulating frequently. Julie, who had witnessed what had taken place during the day, dared not say anything, but waited quietly for nearly an hour. Finally Madame de Tourvel called to her twice, in quick succession. She just had time to run to her when her mistress fell into her arms, saying: 'I am exhausted.' She allowed herself to be taken to her bed, but would not take anything to eat or drink, nor let anyone go to seek help. She simply had some water put beside her and ordered Julie to bed.

Julie is positive that she stayed awake until two in the morning and that she heard neither sound nor movement during this time. But she says she was woken at five o'clock by her mistress talking in a loud, shrill voice. And then, when she had asked her if she needed anything and did not receive any reply, she took a lamp and went over to her bed. Madame de Tourvel did not recognize her, but, suddenly breaking off from the incoherent things she was saying, shouted wildly: 'Leave me alone, leave me in the dark; the darkness is where I belong.' Yesterday I noticed myself how often she uses that expression.

Well, Julie took advantage of this quasi-command to go and find someone to come and help. But Madame de Tourvel refused help from anyone, with the transports and the passion that have recurred so many times since.

The difficulties this was causing in the convent made the prioress decide to send for me yesterday at seven in the morning ... It was not yet daylight. I hurried there immediately. When I was announced Madame de Tourvel seemed to recover her senses and replied: 'Oh yes, tell her to come in.' But when I was next to her bed she stared at me, took hold of my hand and pressed it, saying in a loud, sorrowful voice: 'I am dying ... because I did not believe you.' Immediately, hiding her eyes, she reverted to her old cry of 'Leave me alone,' etc., before she lost consciousness again.

What she said to me, and a few other things that escaped from her in her delirium, make me fear that this cruel malady springs from a still more cruel cause. But let us respect our friend's secrets and content ourselves with sympathizing with her misfortunes.

The whole of yesterday was just as stormy, and divided between terrifying bouts of delirium and periods of depression and lethargy, the only times she takes or gives any respite. I did not leave her bedside until nine in the evening, and I am returning this morning to spend the whole day with her. I shall surely not abandon my unfortunate friend. But what is distressing is her obstinacy in refusing all help and attention.

I am sending you tonight's bulletin, which I have just received and is, as you will see, anything but comforting. I shall take care to pass on the bulletins faithfully.

Farewell, my dear friend. I shall go back to the invalid. My daughter, happily now almost recovered, sends you her good wishes.

Paris, 29 November 17**

LETTER 148

The Chevalier Danceny to the Marquise de Merteuil

Beloved friend, adorable mistress, my happiness began with you, is crowned by you! Dear friend, sweet love, why should the thought of your pain come to trouble my delight? Oh Madame, calm yourself in the name of friendship! Oh my darling, be happy, I implore you in the name of love.

Why reproach yourself? Believe me, your sensibilities deceive you. The regrets you feel, the wrongs you blame me for, are equally illusory. And I know in my heart that there was no other seducer but love between us. Do not then fear to deliver yourself up to the feelings you inspire, to allow yourself to burn with all the passions you kindle. Surely our hearts are no less pure for having only lately seen the light of love? No, no. It is only the seducer who never acts unless he plans in advance, co-ordinating his resources and his moves, and foreseeing events far ahead. True love does not permit meditation and reflection in this fashion. It uses our feelings to distract us from our thoughts. Its power is never stronger than when we are unaware of it. And it is in darkness and silence that it tangles us in a web equally impossible to perceive or to break.

So it was that only yesterday, in spite of the excitement which the idea of your return caused me, in spite of the pleasure I felt when I saw you, I still believed it was the serenity of friendship that beckoned, that led me on. Or rather, entirely surrendering to the sweet sentiments of my heart, I was very little concerned to unravel the origin or cause. Like me, my darling, you experienced, unknown to yourself, this powerful charm, which delivered our souls up to sweet feelings of love. And neither of us knew love until we emerged from the intoxication into which this god has plunged us.

But that in itself justifies rather than condemns us. No, you have not betrayed friendship, nor have I abused your confidence. We were both, it is true, unaware of our feelings. But, quite simply, we felt this illusion without trying to create it. Oh, far from lamenting our fate, let us think only of the happiness it has brought us. And, without spoiling it with unjust reproaches, let us try only to increase it with the delights of trust and confidence. Oh my love! How dear to my heart is this feeling! Yes, you, henceforth delivered from all fear, and entirely given over to love, will share my desires, my delirium, the wildness of my senses, the intoxication of my soul. And every instant of our blessed days will be marked by a new pleasure.

Farewell, my adored one! I shall see you tonight, but shall I find you alone? I dare not hope so. Oh, you cannot desire it as much as I do!

Paris, 1 December 17**

LETTER 149

Madame de Volanges to Madame de Rosemonde

Yesterday I hoped almost all day, my good friend, to be able to give you more encouraging news about our dear friend's condition. But last night that hope was destroyed, and all that is left is the regret that it is lost. An apparently unimportant event, but most cruel in its consequences, has made the patient's condition as grave as it was before, if not worse.

I should not have understood this reversal at all if our unfortunate friend had not yesterday taken me entirely into her confidence. As she did not leave me in any doubt that you too were apprised of all her misfortunes, I can speak to you unreservedly about her sorry situation.

Yesterday morning, when I arrived at the convent, they told me the patient had been asleep for more than three hours. And her sleep was so deep and calm that for a moment I was afraid she might be in a coma. A little while later she woke up and herself opened the curtains around her bed. She looked at us all with an air of surprise and, as I rose to go to her, she recognized me, spoke my name and asked me to draw nearer.

She did not allow me time to question her, but asked where she was, what we were doing there, if she were ill, and why she was not at home. At first I thought she must be delirious again, though she was calmer than the time before. But I observed that she could understand my replies very well. She had in fact recovered her senses, but not her memory . . .

She questioned me in the greatest detail on everything that had happened to her since she had been in the convent, to which she did not remember having come. I replied truthfully, only suppressing whatever might frighten her. And when, in my turn, I asked her how she was, she replied that she was not suffering at present, but that she had been dreadfully tormented while she was asleep, and felt tired. I enjoined her to calm herself and not talk so much. After that I partly drew her curtains, leaving them half-open, and sat down next to her bed. At the same time they offered her a *bouillon*, which she accepted and enjoyed.

She remained like that for about half an hour, during which time she spoke only in order to thank me for looking after her, and this she did with her customary grace and prettiness. Then she was absolutely silent for a while and only broke the silence to say: 'Ah yes, now I remember how I came here,' and a moment later cried out in a desolate voice: 'My friend, my friend, pity me. All my ills have come back again.' As I leaned towards her then, she caught hold of my hand and, resting her head against it, she continued: 'Great God, then can I not die?' Her expression even more than her words brought me to the point of tears; she recognized it in my tone of voice and said: 'You pity me! Ah, if you did but know! . . .' And then, interrupting herself, she said: 'Let us be alone and I will tell you everything.'

Just as I had said to you, I already had my suspicions about what might be the subject of this confidence; and fearing that our conversation, which I foresaw was going to be a long tale of woe, might perhaps have an adverse effect upon the condition of our unfortunate friend, I at first refused, on the pretext that she needed to rest. But she insisted, and I gave in to her demands. As soon as we were alone she told me everything, which you already know, and for that reason I shall not repeat it.

At length, after she told me about the cruel way in which she had been sacrificed, she added: 'I was positive I should die of it, and I had the courage to die. But what I cannot endure is to survive my misfortune and my shame.' I attempted to counter this dejection, or rather despair, with religious arguments, which until then had weighed so heavily with her. But I soon realized I was not equal to these elevated functions and I limited myself to suggesting that I call Father Anselme, whom I know to have her entire confidence. She agreed and even seemed extremely anxious to see him. He was sent for and arrived without delay. He stayed a very long time with the patient and said, as he left, that if the doctors were of the same opinion as himself, he believed the ceremony of the last rites could be postponed. He would return the next day.

It was about three in the afternoon and until five our friend was quite calm; so much so that we all took heart again. Unfortunately then they brought her a letter. When they tried to give it to her she replied at first that she did not wish to receive any, and no one insisted. But from that moment she seemed more agitated. Soon afterwards she asked whence this letter had come. It did not have a stamp. Who had brought it? No one knew. Who had sent it? The portress had not been told. Then she remained silent for some time. After that she began to speak again. But her disconnected sentences informed us only that her delirium had returned.

However, then there was another interval of quiet, until at last she asked to be given the letter that had arrived. As soon as her eyes lighted upon it she cried: 'It's from him! Oh God!' And then, in a loud but broken voice: 'Take it back, take it back!' She immediately had the curtains closed around her bed and forbade anyone to come near her. But almost straight away we were obliged to go to her. Her delirium had recurred, more violently than before, and it was accompanied by truly terrible convulsions. These symptoms continued throughout the evening, and the morning's bulletin reports that her night was no less disturbed. Well, all in all, her condition is such that I am astonished she has not already succumbed. And I don't mind telling you that I have very little hope left.

I suppose the wretched letter was from Monsieur de Valmont. But what can he possibly dare say to her still? Forgive me, my dear. I shall not allow myself to comment. But it is truly cruel to see a woman who until now has been so happy, and so worthy of that happiness, perish in such misery.

Paris, 2 December 17**

LETTER 150

The Chevalier Danceny to the Marquise de Merteuil

While anticipating the delight it will be to see you, my sweet love, I shall indulge in the pleasure of writing you a letter. It is by occupying myself with you that I beguile away my sadness at being away from you. Telling you my feelings, recalling yours, is a real joy to my heart. And because of it even this time of privation confers a thousand precious blessings on my love. However, if I am to believe you, I shall receive no reply from you. This letter is to be the last. And we shall be deprived of an exchange which, according to you, is dangerous, and *which we do not need*. Of course I have to believe you, if you insist. For what can you wish for that I, for that very reason, do not wish as well? But before you make up your mind completely, shall we not talk about it?

As far as danger is concerned, you must be the one to decide. I cannot foresee anything and I shall restrict myself to begging you to look to your safety, for I cannot be easy when you are anxious. In this regard it is not we two who are as one, but you who must act for us both.

That is not the same as *need*. In this we cannot but be of one mind. And if we differ in our opinions, it can only be for lack of explanation or understanding. So these are my feelings.

Undoubtedly a letter does not seem very necessary when we can see each other when we like. What could we say in a letter that one word, one look or even silence could not say a hundred times better? That seemed to me so true at the time you spoke to me about not writing any more that this idea slipped easily into my thoughts. It troubled them perhaps a little, but did not cause distress. It was as if, wishing to bestow a kiss upon your bosom, I encountered a piece of ribbon or gauze: I brushed it aside, and did not regard it as an obstacle.

But since then we have been separated. And as soon as you were no longer there this idea of writing letters has come back to torment me. Why, I asked myself, one more privation? We are apart, but have we then nothing more to say to one another? Let us suppose that, circumstances being favourable, we spent the whole day together. Should we waste time talking, when we might be enjoying each other? Yes, enjoying, my love. For with you even moments of repose still provide such delicious pleasures. Yet, however long we spend together, one always has to leave. And then one is so alone! It is then that a letter is precious! For if one does not read it at least one may look at it ... Oh, certainly one may look at a letter without reading it, just as, it seems to me, at night I should take some pleasure still in touching your portrait ...

Your portrait, did I say? But a letter is the portrait of the soul. It does not possess, as pictures do, that cold, static quality which is so alien to love. It reflects our every emotion. It is by turns animated, joyous, quiet. Your feelings are all so precious to me! Will you deprive me of the means of gathering them to myself?

Are you sure that you will never be tormented by the need to write to me? Suppose that in solitude your heart swells or is oppressed, a joyful feeling enters your soul, or an unwelcome sadness comes to trouble it momentarily, will it not be to your friend that you pour out your happiness or grief? Will you then have feelings that he does not share? Will you leave him then to wander far from you, brooding and alone? My love ... my dear love! But it is up to you to decide. I only wish to discuss, not to sway your feelings. I have reasoned with you. I venture to think I would have been more persuasive had I entreated you. So, if you insist, I shall try not to mind. I shall endeavour to imagine what you would have written. But you would say it better than I can. And I should certainly take more pleasure in hearing it from you.

Farewell, my charming love. The hour is finally approaching when I shall be able to see you. I leave you in haste, so that I can be with you the sooner.

Paris, 3 December 17**

LETTER 151

The Vicomte de Valmont to the Marquise de Merteuil

You must take me for a fool, Marquise, if you believe I am under any misapprehension about the tête-à-tête I interrupted this evening, or about the *astonishing coincidence* that brought Danceny to your house. Not that your practised features did not take on a wonderful expression of calm and serenity, nor that you gave yourself away with any of those phrases which sometimes escape from people who are embarrassed or contrite. I even agree that your meek glances perfectly served your purpose; and that had they been able to be believed as well as they were understood, I should not have thought or entertained the least suspicion, nor for a moment doubted, that this *importunate third party* was causing you extreme annoyance. But so as not to have exercised such great talents in vain, so as to obtain the success that you hoped for and produce the illusion that you were seeking to create, you should have trained your novice of a lover more carefully in the first place.

Since you have set yourself up as an educator, you should teach your pupils not to blush and become disconcerted at the least little joke; not to deny so vehemently about one woman things they protest so feebly with regard to all the others; teach them as well to be able to hear someone singing their mistress's praises without feeling they are obliged to pay her compliments. And if you allow them to look at you when in company, first make sure they know at least how to disguise that proprietorial look which is so easy to recognize, and which they stupidly confuse with one of love. Then you will be able to parade them in your public displays without their behaviour doing discredit to their wise teacher. And I, happy to contribute to your celebrity, promise to write you a scheme of work for this new school and have it published.

But as things are I admit I am astonished that it should be me that you have undertaken to treat like a little schoolboy. Oh, with any other woman I should soon take my revenge! I should revel in it! And it would easily surpass the pleasure she thought she was denying me! Yes, it is certainly only for you that I prefer reparation to vengeance. But do not suppose I am held back by the slightest doubt, by the least uncertainty. I know everything.

You have been in Paris for four days, and every day you have seen Danceny and no one else. Even today your door was still closed; and I was only able to reach you because your porter lacked an assurance equal to your own in preventing me. However, you told me that I would definitely be the first to be informed of your arrival – you were unable to tell me which date – while you wrote to me on the day before your departure. Will you deny these facts, or try to excuse them? Both are equally impossible. And yet I restrain myself! You see what power you have over me! But, I beg you, content yourself with having proved that power, and do not treat me like this any longer. We understand one another, Madame. One word of warning must suffice.

You will be out for the whole day tomorrow, did you say? Very well, if indeed you are going out. You may guess that I shall find out if that is true. But in any case you will be coming home in the evening. We shall not have too much time before the next day for our difficult reconciliation. So tell me if it will be in your house or *over there*,[12] that our numerous mutual expiations will take place. Above all, let there be no more Danceny. Your poor head has become full of the thought of him. I can avoid being jealous of your wild imagination, but remember that from this moment what was only a whim on your part might become a marked preference. I am not a man to suffer this humiliation, and I do not expect to receive it at your hands.

I even hope that this sacrifice will not seem a sacrifice to you. But if it were to cost you something, it seems to me that I have set you a rather fine example! A sensitive, beautiful woman who has lived only for me, and who is perhaps at this very moment dying of love and sorrow, must surely be the equal of a little schoolboy who, if you like, is not lacking in looks or wit, but is still inexperienced and unformed.

Farewell, Marquise. I shall say nothing of my feelings for you. All I can do at the moment is refrain from searching my heart. I await your reply. When you write, remember that the easier it is for you to make me forget the offence you have caused me, the more a refusal from you, or a simple delay, will engrave it indelibly upon my heart.

Paris, 3 December, 17**, in the evening

LETTER 152

The Marquise de Merteuil to the Vicomte de Valmont

Take care, Vicomte, take more account of my extreme timidity! How do you expect me to bear the overwhelming prospect of incurring your wrath and, above all, of not succumbing to the fear of your revenge? Especially since, as you know, if you did me an ill turn, it would be impossible for me to pay you back. Despite my talking about you, your life would continue, brilliant and unperturbed. In fact, what would you need to be afraid of? Of having to flee the country, if time allowed. But does one not live as well abroad as here? All in all, provided that the Court of France left you in peace at whatever foreign court you settled on, it would only be a case of changing the locus of your triumphs.[13] Now that I have tried to bring you back to your senses by these moral considerations, let us return to business.

Do you know, Vicomte, why I never remarried? It was certainly not for lack of any advantageous matches. It was purely so that no one should have the right to criticize my actions. It

was not even for fear of not being able to do what I wish, for I
should always have ended up doing that; but it was because it
would have annoyed me that anyone had the right to complain
about it. It was that in the end I wished to deceive only for my
own pleasure, and not through necessity. And there you are
writing me the most *marital* letter I could possibly receive! You
speak only of the wrongs on my side, and the favours on yours!
But how can one fall short with regard to a person to whom
one owes nothing? I cannot conceive of it!

Come now. What is all the fuss about? You found Danceny
with me and it displeased you? Fine! But what conclusions were
you able to draw from that? Either that it was coincidence, as
I said; or that I wished it, which I did not say. In the first
instance your letter would be unjust; in the second, ridiculous.
You need not have bothered writing! But you are jealous, and
jealousy will not listen to reason. So very well, I shall reason
on your behalf.

Either you have a rival or you do not. If you do, you have to
make yourself attractive to me in order to be preferred. If not,
you still have to make yourself attractive in order to avoid
having a rival. Whatever the case, you have to behave in the
same way. So why torment yourself? And, above all, why torment me? Have you forgotten how to be the most pleasing of
lovers? Are you not sure of your success? Come now, Vicomte,
you do yourself an injustice. But it is not that. The fact is that
in your eyes I am not worth you giving yourself so much trouble.
You desire my favours less than you wish to abuse your power
over me. You are an ungrateful man! See how I do have feelings!
If I continued in this vein, my letter might become most tender.
But you do not deserve it.

Nor do you deserve that I should justify myself. To punish
you for your suspicions, you can keep them. So about the time
of my return and Danceny's visits, I shall say nothing. You have
taken great pains to find out about it, have you not? Well, how
far have you advanced? I hope you took pleasure in doing so.
As for me, it made no difference to my pleasure.

So all I can say in answer to your threatening letter is that it
had neither the gift of pleasing nor the power to intimidate.

And for the moment I am not in the least disposed to grant what you ask.

In truth, if I were to accept you in your present state, it would be to be truly unfaithful to you. I should not be renewing my relationship with my former lover. I should be taking a new one, and one who was nowhere near as good as the former. I have not so forgotten the first as to deceive myself about this. The Valmont I loved was charming. I gladly even admit that I never met a more charming man. Oh, I beg you, Vicomte, if you find him, bring him to me. That man will always be most welcome.

Do warn him, however, that in any case it will not be today or tomorrow. His double has betrayed him somewhat. And if I were in too much of a hurry, I should be afraid of making a mistake. Or is it that I have promised those two days to Danceny? In your letter you said you were not joking about breaking promises. So, as you see, you must wait.

But what of that? You will still take revenge on your rival. He will not be treating your mistress any worse than you his. And, after all, is not one woman as good as the next? Those are your principles. Even the one who was *loving and sensitive and lived only for you, and died in the end for love or grief* would still be sacrificed to the first caprice, to the momentary fear that you are being made fun of. And you expect us to put ourselves out for your benefit? Ah, that is not fair.

Farewell, Vicomte; be nice to me again. Come, I ask no more than to find you charming. And, as soon as I am sure that I do, I promise to prove it. Truly, I am too kind.

Paris, 4 December 17**

LETTER 153

The Vicomte de Valmont to the Marquise de Merteuil

I am answering your letter immediately and I shall try to be clear. That is not easy with you once you have made up your mind that you are not going to understand.

It is not necessary to make lengthy speeches to establish that each of us possesses what we need to ruin the other, and that we must mutually consider each other's interests. So that is not the question. But between the dramatic option of ruining ourselves and – undoubtedly the better course – that of staying together as we always have, and becoming even closer by renewing our first liaison; between these two options, as I say, there are a thousand others. It was therefore not ridiculous of me to tell you, and it is not ridiculous to repeat, that from this very day I shall be either your lover or your enemy.

I am keenly aware that this decision will annoy you. You would find it more convenient to prevaricate. And I am not unaware that you have never liked being placed in a position where you must say yes or no. But you have to realize too that I cannot allow you a way out of this impasse without risk of being tricked myself. And you must have foreseen that I should not allow that. It is now up to you to decide. I can leave the choice to you, but I cannot remain in this state of uncertainty.

I am warning you, however, that you will not deceive me with your arguments, good or bad, nor will you seduce me with a few flattering remarks with which you might try to embellish your refusal. It is finally time to put our cards on the table. I am by all means prepared to set you an example, and I am happy to declare that I prefer peace and friendship. But if one or the other has to be broken, I believe I have the right and the means to do so.

I might add that the slightest obstacle you put in the way will be taken by me as an outright declaration of war. As you see, the answer I ask for does not demand any long or elegant phrases. One word will suffice.

Paris, 4 December 17**

The Marquise de Merteuil's reply, written at the bottom of the same letter:

Very well, then. War!

LETTER 154

Madame de Volanges to Madame de Rosemonde

You will learn more from the bulletins than from me, my dear friend, about the worrying condition of our friend. Totally occupied as I am with looking after her, I only take time out from that to write to you insofar as other things are happening apart from her illness. Here is something that I most certainly was not expecting. It is a letter I received from Monsieur de Valmont, who has been pleased to choose me as his confidante, and even as mediator between himself and Madame de Tourvel, for whom he also included a letter with mine. I sent that one back, with my reply to his letter to me. I am sending a copy of his letter on to you, and I believe you will share my opinion that I could not, nor should, do anything he asks me. Even had I wished to, our unfortunate friend would not have been in any state to listen. She is in a continual delirium. But what do you think of this despair on the part of Monsieur de Valmont? First, are we to believe it, or does he just wish to deceive everybody till the bitter end?* If for once he is sincere, he can truly say that he has brought his unhappiness upon himself. I believe he will not be very pleased with my reply. But I admit that everything I have to do with this sorry affair makes me turn more and more against its author.

Farewell, my dear friend. I return to my melancholy tasks, which become sadder still, given the small hope I have of seeing a successful outcome to them. You know how I honour you.

Paris, 5 December 17**

---

* Because nothing in the ensuing correspondence was found which could resolve this doubt, we have decided to suppress Monsieur de Valmont's letter.

LETTER 155

The Vicomte de Valmont to the Chevalier Danceny

I called on you twice, my dear Chevalier, but since you have given up your role of lover for that of adventurer you have, quite understandably, become impossible to track down. However, your valet assures me that you should be back this evening and that he had orders to expect you. But I, who am informed of your plans, understand you might only return briefly to change your costume before immediately resuming your victorious career. Well, good for you, I cannot but applaud you. But perhaps this evening you may be tempted to change direction. You only know half the story at the moment. You must be told the rest and then decide. So take the time to read my letter, not in order to distract you from your pleasures since, on the contrary, its only purpose is to give you a choice of what to do.

Had I had your entire confidence, if I had known from you the secrets that you left me to guess, I should have been informed in time and should not have held up your progress today with my inept enthusiasm. But let us start from where we are. Whatever course you take, the one you reject will always be for the good of someone else.

You have a rendez-vous tonight, have you not, with a charming woman whom you adore? For at your age what woman does one not adore, at least for the first week! The scene of the meeting must add to your pleasures still more. A delightful *petite maison that has been taken for you alone*, which will make the pleasures of the flesh even more pleasurable with the added charms of freedom and mystery. Everything is arranged; you are expected: you are longing to be there! We both know that, although you have told me nothing about it. Now this is what you do not know and what I must impart to you.

Since my return to Paris I have been busy working out ways for you to see Mademoiselle de Volanges, as promised. And the last time we spoke on the subject, I had reason to judge from what you said, I might say from your delight, that by so doing

I was working for your happiness. I could not succeed all on my own in this tricky task. But, having prepared the means, I left the rest to the zeal of your young mistress. She found, in her love for you, resources which had been wanting to my experience. Well, unfortunately for you, she has succeeded. For the last two days, she told me this evening, all obstacles have been removed, and your happiness only depends henceforth upon you.

For the last two days as well she has been hoping to tell you the news herself, and in spite of her mother's absence you would have been received at the house. But you did not even come to visit! And to tell you the whole story, our little friend, whether reasonably or unreasonably, seemed to me rather put out by this lack of attention on your part. At all events, she found a way of having me come to see her and made me promise to give you as soon as I possibly could the letter that I here enclose. To judge from the hurry she was in to do this, I should wager it is about a rendez-vous for this evening. However that may be, I have promised on my honour as a friend that you will receive this billet-doux in the course of the day and I cannot, nor will I, break my word.

So now, young man, how will you proceed? Between flirtation and love, between pleasure and happiness, what will be your choice? If I were speaking to the Danceny of three months ago, or only of a week ago, I should be quite certain of his feelings, and sure of what he would do. But the Danceny of today, the womanizer, the adventurer, who, as is often the case, has turned into a bit of a rascal – will he prefer a shy young girl, who has nothing to recommend her but her beauty, her innocence and her love, to the pleasures of a woman who is completely *experienced*?

As for myself, my dear friend, I should say that even with your new principles, which I freely admit are not unlike my own, circumstances would decide me in favour of the young girl. For one thing, she is another one to add to your list; and then there is the novelty; and, furthermore, the fear of losing the fruit of your labours if you neglect to gather it; for after all, from this point of view it would really be an opportunity lost and such opportunities do not always recur, especially with a first passion. Often in these cases one petulant mood, jealous suspicion, or even less, suffices to thwart the finest conquest. Drowning virtue may clutch at any straw; and once it has been saved, it is on its guard, and not so easily taken by surprise.

On the other hand, from a different perspective, what are you risking? Not even a rupture. A little quarrel at most, and the pleasure of a reconciliation which you would be able to buy with a few attentions. What course other than that of indulgence remains to a woman who has already given herself? What would she gain by being strict? Loss of pleasure and no increase in glory.

If, as I presume, you decide in favour of love, which seems to me also the reasonable decision, I believe it would be prudent not to apologize for the missed rendez-vous. Simply make her wait. If you risk giving your reasons, she may be tempted to check if they are true. Women are curious and obstinate; they can find anything out. I have just provided an example of this. But hope left to itself, as it is sustained by vanity, will not be lost until long after the time for making enquiries. So tomorrow you will have to choose which insurmountable obstacle has detained you; you will have been ill, dead if necessary, or there will be some other equally desperate reason for your absence, and all will be mended.

For the rest, whatever you decide, I beg you simply to let me know. Being personally disinterested, I shall always think you have done well. Farewell, my dear fellow.

What I will add is that I miss Madame de Tourvel. I am in despair at being separated from her. I should gladly give half my life to have the happiness of devoting the other half to her. Ah, believe me, only love can make one happy.

                                        Paris, 5 December 17**

LETTER 156

Cécile Volanges to the Chevalier Danceny
(Attached to the preceding letter)

How is it, my dear, that I do not see you any more when I never
cease to desire it? Do you not want to as much as I do? Oh, I
am truly unhappy now! More unhappy than when we were
completely separated. The pain I was suffering because of other
people now comes from you, and that makes me feel much
worse.

For the last few days, as you are only too well aware, Mamma
has hardly ever been at home. I was hoping that you would
take advantage of this period of freedom but the thought of me
has not so much as crossed your mind. How unhappy I am!
You so often told me that *I* was the one who did not love *you*
enough, but I knew that was not at all true and this proves it.
If you had come to visit me, you would actually have seen me.
For I am not like you; I think only of ways we may see each
other again. It would serve you right if I told you nothing of all
I have done in that respect – and it has given me so much
trouble. But I love you too much, and I am so anxious to see
you that I cannot help telling you so. And then I shall see if you
really love me!

I have contrived to have the porter on our side, and he has
promised me that every time you come he will let you in; he
will act as though he had not seen you. We can definitely trust
him, for he is a very honest man. All we shall have to do is
make sure no one sees you in the house, and that is very easy if
you just come in the evening when there is nothing else at all
to be afraid of. Since Mamma has been going out every day,
you see, she goes to bed every night at eleven. So we shall have
plenty of time.

The porter told me when you want to come in like that, all
you have to do is knock at his window instead of the door and
he will let you in straight away. Then you will soon find the
back staircase, and as there will not be any light I will leave my

bedroom door half open, and that will provide a little. You should be careful not to make a noise, especially when you go near my Mamma's door. As for my chambermaid's door, you do not need to take that into account since she has promised she will not wake up. She is such a good girl! And when you leave, you must do exactly the same. Now let us see if you will come.

Oh God, why does my heart beat so hard when I write to you? Is there some misfortune about to befall me, or is it the hope of seeing you that troubles me so? What I feel is that I have never loved you so much, and never have I wanted so much to tell you so. So come, my love, my dear love, so that I can tell you a hundred times over that I love you, adore you, that I shall never love anyone but you.

I have found a means of letting Monsieur de Valmont know that I had something to say to him. Since he is such a good friend he will certainly come tomorrow, and I shall ask him to give you my letter without delay. So I shall expect you tomorrow night, and you will come without fail if you do not wish to make your little Cécile so dreadfully unhappy.

Farewell, my dear. I send you all my love.

Paris, 4 December 17**, in the evening

LETTER 157

The Chevalier Danceny to the Vicomte de Valmont

Do not doubt, my dear Vicomte, my true feelings or my actions. How could I resist any wish my Cécile expressed? Oh, she is definitely the one, the only one, that I love and shall love for ever! Her innocence, her tenderness have charms for me from which I have been weak enough to allow myself to be distracted, but that nothing can erase. Engaged in another affair, almost, as you might say, without knowing what I was doing, the memory of Cécile has often come to trouble me during the very sweetest of my pleasures. And perhaps my heart has never rendered truer homage to her than in the very moment when I was unfaithful. However, my friend, let us be considerate of her finer feelings and hide my wrongdoing from her, not in order to be duplicitous, but in order not to hurt her. Cécile's happiness is my most ardent wish. Never shall I forgive myself for anything that might cause her to shed a tear.

I feel I deserve your jocular remark about what you call my new principles. But it is not those which guide me at the moment, believe me. And from tomorrow I am determined to prove it. I will go and make my confession to the woman who has caused me to stray and who has participated in it. I shall say to her: 'Look into my heart. It has the tenderest friendship for you. Friendship allied to desire so resembles love! ... We have both been deceived. But though susceptible to making mistakes, I am not capable of being insincere.' I know my friend. She is indulgent as well as honest. She will do more than pardon me; she will approve of what I have done. She has so often blamed herself for betraying friendship. Often her delicacy held back her love. She is wiser than I, she will fortify in my soul the salutary fears that I rashly sought to quell in hers. I shall owe it to her to be better, and to you to be happier. Oh my friends, share my gratitude. The thought that I owe my happiness to you increases its value.

Farewell, my dear Vicomte. My extreme joy does not prevent me from thinking of your sorrows and sharing in them. I wish I could help. Is Madame de Tourvel still inexorable, then? People say that she is extremely ill. My word, how I pity you! I hope her health and her kindness to you will improve and cause you eternal happiness! These things I wish as your friend. I dare hope they will be granted by love.

I should like to talk longer, but time is short and Cécile is perhaps already waiting for me.

Paris, 5 December 17**

LETTER 158

The Vicomte de Valmont to the Marquise de Merteuil
(On waking)

So now, Marquise, how are you after the pleasures of last night? A little tired, perhaps? You must admit that Danceny is charming! What a prodigy that boy is! You did not expect it of him, did you? Come now, let us be fair. A rival like that deserves that I should be sacrificed for him. Seriously, though, he has so many qualities! And, above all, what love, what constancy, what tenderness! Oh, if ever he loves you as he loves his Cécile you will not have to fear any rivals. He proved that to you last night. Perhaps if another woman were to set her cap at him she could take him away from you briefly. A young man can never resist provocative behaviour like that, but one single word from the beloved is enough, as you see, to dispel the illusion. So all you have to do is become that beloved, and you will be perfectly happy.

Surely you will not delude yourself. You have too much insight for there to be any fear of that. However, the friendship that unites us, as sincere on my part as it is acknowledged on yours, made me desire last night's proof, for your sake; you owed it to my zeal. It was a success. But do not thank me. It is not worth it. Nothing could have been easier.

In fact, what did it cost me? Some small sacrifice, a little skill. I agreed to share with the young man the favours of his mistress. Yet in the end he had as much right as me. And I cared so little! The letter the girl wrote to him of course I dictated to her, but it was only to gain time, because we had better things to do. The letter I attached was nothing at all, almost nothing. A few friendly reflections to guide the new lover in his choice, though really they were superfluous. We must tell the truth; he did not for an instant waver.

And so, in his candour, he is due to go to you today and tell you the whole tale; and surely that account will give you great pleasure! He will say: 'Look in my heart,' so he tells me, and you will see that that makes up for everything. I hope that when you find what he wishes you to find there you will also see that such young lovers have their dangers. Also that it is better to have me for a friend than for an enemy. Farewell, Marquise, until we meet again.

Paris, 6 December 17**

LETTER 159

The Marquise de Merteuil to the Vicomte de Valmont (Note)

I do not care for it when people combine bad jokes with bad behaviour. That is not my style or to my taste. When I have cause to complain of someone I do not indulge in mockery. I do better, I take my revenge. However pleased you are with yourself at the moment, do not forget it would not be the first time you have congratulated yourself too soon, in the mere hope of a triumph which escaped you at the very moment of your congratulating yourself upon it.

Adieu.

Paris, 6 December 17**

LETTER 160

Madame de Volanges to Madame de Rosemonde

I am writing to you from the bedroom of our unfortunate friend, whose condition is still more or less the same. This afternoon there is to be a consultation between four doctors. Unfortunately, as you know, that is more frequently a proof of danger than a means of help. But apparently her mind returned somewhat last night. The maid informed me this morning that towards midnight her mistress sent for her. She wished to be alone with her and dictated quite a long letter. Julie added that while she was busy sealing the envelope Madame de Tourvel became delirious again, so that the girl did not know whom to address it to. At first, I was surprised she did not know who it was from the letter itself. However, when she told me she was afraid of making a mistake but that her mistress had told her to be sure and have it sent straight away, I took it upon myself to open the packet.

There I found the letter I am sending you, which is in fact addressed to no one and everyone. I should nevertheless think that it was to Monsieur de Valmont that our unfortunate friend wished at first to write, but that she has given in unconsciously to her deranged ideas. Whatever the case, in my opinion the letter should not be sent to anyone. I am sending it to you because you will be able to understand, better than if it came from me, what thoughts are in our patient's head. As long as she is so gravely affected I shall not hold out any hope. The body has difficulty in recovering when the mind is so disturbed.

Farewell, my dear, worthy friend. I am glad you are too far away to witness the sad spectacle that I have constantly before my eyes.

Paris, 6 December 17**

LETTER 161

The Présidente de Tourvel to . . .
(Dictated by her and written by her maid)

Cruel, evil creature, will you never cease persecuting me? Is it not enough that you have tormented, debased, disgraced me? Do you wish to deprive me of my peace even in my grave? What! In this vale of shadows where shame has forced me to bury myself, are woes unceasing? Is hope unknown? I am not beseeching you for a grace I do not deserve. I will suffer without complaint if my sufferings are not to exceed my strength. But do not make my torment unbearable. Leave me my pain, but take away the cruel memory of the blessings I have lost; and when you have taken them from me, do not wave their harrowing image again before my eyes. I was innocent and at peace. Through seeing you I lost my peace of mind, by listening to you I became a criminal. What right have you, the author of my sins, to punish them?

Where are the friends who used to love me? Where are they? My misfortune frightens them away. Not one dares come near. I am crushed and they leave me helpless! I am dying and no one weeps for me. All consolation is denied me. Pity pauses on the edge of the abyss into which the criminal leaps. Remorse is tearing her apart and her cries go unheard!

And you, you whom I have offended. You whose esteem adds to my torture. You who alone in the end would have the right to take your revenge, why are you so far away? Come and punish an unfaithful wife. Let me at last suffer the torments I deserve. I should already have given myself up to your vengeance, but courage failed me to tell you of your shame. It was not that I was keeping it hidden, it was that I respected you. May this letter at least tell you of my repentance. The Almighty has taken up your cause. He is avenging you of an injury you were ignorant of. He has tied my tongue and kept back my words. He was afraid you would overlook a sin He wished to punish me for. He removed me from your indulgence, which would have harmed His justice.

Pitiless in His vengeance, He delivered me up to the one who ruined me. It is for him and through him, at the same time, that I am suffering. In vain do I try to escape. He follows me, he is there, he haunts me constantly. But how different he is from his true self! His eyes express only hatred and scorn. His mouth utters nothing but insult and reproach. His arms embrace me only to tear me to shreds. Who can save me from his barbarous fury?

But look! It is he! I am not deceived. It is him I can see again. Oh my beloved, take me into your arms, hide me on your breast. Yes, it is you, really you! What vile illusion led me not

to recognize you? How I have suffered in your absence! Let us
not be apart again, let us never be apart. Let me breathe. Feel
how my heart is beating! Ah, it is no longer fear, it is the sweet
voice of love. Why refuse me your tender kisses? Turn your
gentle eyes on me again! What are these bonds you wish to
break? Why are you preparing those instruments of death?
What can change your features like that? What are you doing?
Leave me, I am trembling! God, it is the monster again! My
friends, do not abandon me. You who were telling me to escape
from him, help me now to fight him. And you, my kind friend,
who promised to lessen my grief, come near to me. Where are
you both? If I am no longer permitted to see you again, at least
answer this letter, and I shall know if you love me still.

Leave me alone, cruel man! What new fury blazes up in you?
Do you fear some kind feeling will penetrate my soul? You
redouble my torments. You force me to hate you. Oh, how
painful hatred is! How it corrodes the heart that distils it! Why
are you persecuting me? What can you still have to say to me?
Have you not made it as impossible for me to hear you as to
answer you? Do not expect anything more from me. Farewell,
Monsieur.

Paris, 5 December

LETTER 162

The Chevalier Danceny to the Vicomte de Valmont

I am informed, Monsieur, of what you have done to me. I also
know that, not content with playing an ignoble trick on me,
you no longer fear to boast about it, to congratulate yourself
on it. I have seen the proof of your treachery written in your
own hand. I admit I am cut to the quick, and that I have felt
some shame at having myself to a large extent assisted in the
loathsome abuse you have made of my blind trust in you.
However, I do not begrudge you this shameful advantage. I

am only curious to know if you will continue to maintain all advantages over me. I shall soon find out if, as I hope, you will be tomorrow between eight and nine in the morning at the gates of the Bois de Vincennes, in the village of Saint-Mandé. I shall ensure that everything there is made ready for the explanations still necessary between us.[14]

The Chevalier Danceny

Paris, 6 December 17**, in the evening

LETTER 163

Monsieur Bertrand to Madame de Rosemonde

Madame,

It is with very great regret that I fulfil the sad duty of announcing some news which will cause you the most cruel distress. Allow me to urge you first to the pious attitude of resignation which everyone has so often admired in you and which alone can help us bear the ills which are scattered throughout our miserable lives.

Your nephew ... Oh God! Must I so distress such a good and worthy lady! Your nephew has had the misfortune to succumb in an individual combat he fought this morning with Monsieur le Chevalier Danceny. I am totally ignorant of the reason for their quarrel. But it would seem, from the note I found still in Monsieur le Vicomte's pocket and which I beg to send you, that he was not the aggressor. And yet he was the one whom God allowed to die!

I was waiting in Monsieur le Vicomte's establishment at the very moment they brought him back. Imagine my alarm on seeing your nephew being carried by two of his servants and bathed in his own blood. He had two sword wounds in his body, and was already very weak. Monsieur Danceny was there too, and was indeed in tears. Ah, and so he should be! But it is hardly the time to shed tears when one has caused irreparable harm!

As for me, I was beside myself, and though I am a poor creature I did not hesitate to give him a piece of my mind. But it was then that Monsieur de Valmont showed his true greatness. He told me to be quiet. And he took hold of the hand of the man who was his murderer, called him his friend, embraced him in front of us all, and said to us: 'I order you to have all the respect for Monsieur that is owed to a just and worthy man.' Moreover, in my presence he had delivered over to him a huge bundle of documents. I don't know what they were, but I do know he attached great importance to them. Then he asked us to leave them alone together for a while. Meanwhile I had sent for help straight away, spiritual as well as temporal; but alas, there was nothing to be done. Within less than half an hour Monsieur le Vicomte had lost consciousness. He was just able to receive extreme unction, and the ceremony was scarcely over when he breathed his last.

Oh God! When I received into my arms at his birth this precious scion of so illustrious a house, could I have foreseen that it would be in my arms that he would die, and that I should have to mourn his death? And such an early and unfortunate death! I cannot hold back my tears. I beg your pardon, Madame, that I should dare to mingle my tears with yours, but there are the same hearts and the same sensibilities in every walk of life, and I should indeed be very ungrateful if I did not for the rest of my days mourn my lord, who was so good to me and honoured me with so much trust.

Tomorrow, after the removal of the body, I shall have everything sealed and you may rely completely on me to do what is necessary. You must be aware, Madame, that this unfortunate event terminates the entail and leaves you free to dispose of the property as you wish. If I can be of any service to you, I beg you to be kind enough to give me your orders. I shall do all I can to carry them out punctually.

I am, Madame, most humbly and respectfully yours,

Bertrand

Paris, 7 December 17**

LETTER 164

Madame de Rosemonde to Monsieur Bertrand

I have just this minute received your letter, my dear Bertrand, and learned of the terrible event of which my nephew is the unfortunate victim. Yes, I shall no doubt have orders for you, and it is only in putting my mind to that that I can occupy myself with anything other than with my terrible bereavement.

Monsieur Danceny's note, which you sent me, is very convincing proof that he is the one who provoked the duel, and it is my intention that you should lodge an immediate accusation in my name. By pardoning his enemy, his murderer, my nephew may have satisfied his natural generosity. But I must avenge his death, and humanity and religion at one and the same time. One cannot do enough to invoke the severity of the law against this outdated barbaric practice still infecting our society; nor do I believe that in this case the forgiveness of injury is required of us. So I expect you to pursue this affair with all the zeal and energies I believe you to be capable of, and which you owe to the memory of my nephew. You will above all make a point of seeing the Président de —[15] on my behalf and of consulting with him. I shall not write to him, as I wish now without further delay to allow myself to grieve wholeheartedly. Please convey to him my apologies and communicate the contents of this message to him.

Farewell, my dear Bertrand; I commend you and thank you for your kind sympathy.

Yours, as ever,

From the Chateau de —, 8 December 17**

LETTER 165

Madame de Volanges to Madame de Rosemonde

I realize you already know, my dear, worthy friend, about the loss you have just sustained. I know how fond you were of Monsieur de Valmont, and I sincerely share in the distress you must be feeling. I am truly sorry to have to increase the grief you are already experiencing. But alas, you have nothing left now but your tears to offer our unfortunate friend. We lost her yesterday at eleven in the evening. Her inexorable fate, which makes a mockery of all human prudence, decreed that in the short interval she survived Monsieur de Valmont she had time to learn of his death, and, as she said herself, not to succumb beneath the weight of her misfortunes until they had gone beyond what she could bear.

In fact, as you know, for the last two days she was completely unconscious. And yesterday morning, when her doctor arrived and we drew near her bed, she recognized neither of us, and we were able to obtain from her not a word, nor the least sign. Well, we had scarcely gone back to the fireside and the doctor was just telling me about the sad event of Monsieur de Valmont's death when the poor woman recovered her senses, whether by the forces of nature alone, or because it was caused by those repeated words, 'Monsieur de Valmont' and 'death', which may have recalled to her mind the only ideas which have concerned her for so long.

Whatever the case, she opened the curtains of her bed, crying: 'What! What are you saying? Monsieur de Valmont dead?' I hoped to make her believe that she was mistaken, and assured her at first that she had misheard. But, far from allowing herself to be persuaded of this, she demanded that the doctor begin the cruel tale again. And when I tried to convince her otherwise she called me over to her and whispered: 'Why try to lie to me? Was he not already dead as far as I am concerned!' And so I had to admit it.

Our unfortunate friend listened at first quite calmly. But

soon she broke into the account, saying: 'Enough, I have heard enough.' She asked straight away that the curtains be closed, and when the doctor tried to attend to her she refused to allow him anywhere near her.

As soon as he went out she also sent away her nurse and her chambermaid. And when we were alone she asked me to help her kneel on the bed and to hold on to her. She stayed there for some time in silence, her face expressionless except for her tears, which flowed unchecked. Finally she put her hands together and raised them to Heaven, saying in a weak but fervent voice: 'Almighty God, I submit to your justice. But forgive Valmont. May my misfortunes, which I acknowledge I have deserved, not be held against him, and I shall bless your mercy!' I have allowed myself, my dear and worthy friend, to go into such detail upon a subject that I realize will be bound to renew and increase your grief, because I do not doubt that this prayer of Madame de Tourvel's will nevertheless bring great consolation to your soul.

After our friend had uttered these few words, she fell back into my arms; and scarcely was she lying on her bed again when a prolonged weakness came over her that did however yield, in the end, to ordinary remedies. As soon as she recovered consciousness she asked me to send for Father Anselme and added: 'He is at present the only doctor I need; I feel my troubles will soon be over.' She complained a great deal of a weight upon her, and spoke only with difficulty.

A short time later she gave her chambermaid a box for me, that she said contained her papers and which she charged me to give you immediately upon her death.* Then she spoke about you and your friendship for her – inasmuch as her condition allowed – with a great deal of tenderness.

Father Anselme arrived around four o'clock and stayed with her for nearly an hour. When we went back in, the patient's face was calm and serene, but it was easy to see that Father Anselme had been weeping a great deal. He stayed to administer

* This box contained all the letters relative to her affair with Monsieur de Valmont.

the last rites. This sight, always so impressive and moving, became still more so by the contrast made by the quiet resignation of the patient and the deep grief of her venerable confessor, who broke down and wept at her side. All were deeply moved, and the one that all were weeping for was the only one not weeping.

The remainder of the day passed in the customary prayers only interrupted by the frequent periods of weakness in the invalid. Finally, towards eleven in the evening, she appeared more oppressed and more in pain. I put out my hand to touch hers. She was still strong enough to take it, and placed it upon her heart. I could feel it beating no longer. And in fact our unfortunate friend passed away at that very moment.

Do you remember, my dear, that when you last came here less than a year ago, when we were talking about some people whose happiness seemed more or less assured, we paused a while to consider the fate of this same woman whose ills and whose death, both at once, we are lamenting today! So many virtues, so many qualities and so much charm! Such a sweet, gentle disposition! A husband she loved and who adored her. Friends she liked and whose society she graced. Beauty, youth, fortune. So many advantages united in one person, lost by a single imprudence! Oh Providence! No doubt we must worship your decrees, but how incomprehensible they are! I must stop. I am afraid of increasing your sadness by giving myself up to my own.

I shall leave you, and shall go and see my daughter who is somewhat out of sorts. When she heard about the death of two people of her acquaintance from me this morning, she became unwell, and I sent her to bed. However, I trust that this slight indisposition will not have any serious consequences. At her age one is not yet used to sorrow, and so it makes a stronger, deeper impression. Such lively sensibility is no doubt a praiseworthy quality, but how all we see going on in the world each day makes us fear it! Farewell, my dear, worthy friend.

Paris, 9 December 17**

LETTER 166

Monsieur Bertrand to Madame de Rosemonde

Madame,

In consequence of the orders you were pleased to give me, I had the honour of seeing Monsieur le Président de —, and I communicated your letter to him, informing him that in accordance with your wishes I would do nothing except on his advice. The worthy magistrate instructed me to call to your attention that the charge you are intending to bring against Monsieur le Chevalier Danceny would equally compromise the memory of Monsieur your nephew, and that his honour would of necessity be besmirched by the sentence of the court, which would undoubtedly be a great misfortune. His advice therefore is that one should be extremely wary of taking any action, but on the contrary try to prevent the public prosecutor from hearing about this unfortunate affair, which has already caused too much of a scandal.

These observations seemed to me full of wisdom, and I have decided to await further orders from you.

Allow me to beg, Madame, that you will let me know, when you give me the orders, about your state of health; I greatly fear the effect upon it of so much sorrow. I hope you will forgive this liberty because of my attachment to you and my zeal in your service.

I am, Madame, with respect, your etc.

Paris, 10 December 17**

LETTER 167

Anonymous letter to Monsieur le Chevalier Danceny

Monsieur,

I have the honour to inform you that this morning at the Public

Prosecutor's office the affair you had recently with Monsieur le Vicomte de Valmont was discussed, and that it is to be feared that proceedings may be taken against you. I feel this warning may be of some use to you, either so that you may instigate your defence and forestall any annoying consequences; or, in case you cannot do this, to place you in a position where you may take measures to protect yourself.

If you will even allow me a word of advice, I believe you would do well in the immediate future to be seen in public less than of late. Though usually this kind of affair is viewed with indulgence, one nevertheless needs to show respect for the law.

This precaution will be all the more necessary because it has come to my notice that a Madame de Rosemonde, who is, I believe, Monsieur de Valmont's aunt, intends to lodge a complaint against you. In this case the Public Prosecutor would not be able to refuse her demand. It would perhaps be a good idea were you to enter into communication with the lady.

Special reasons prevent me signing this letter. But I trust that, though you do not know the sender, you will nevertheless do justice to the feelings which have dictated it.

I have the honour to be, etc.

Paris, 10 December 17**

LETTER 168

Madame de Volanges to Madame de Rosemonde

The most strange and distressing rumours, my dear and worthy friend, are spreading here about Madame de Merteuil. Of course I do not believe them for one moment, and I wager it is simply a terrible slander: but I know only too well how nasty rumours, even the least plausible, may easily acquire credence, and how the impression they leave only fades with difficulty; and so I am alarmed by these, although of course they could easily be disproved. I should particularly wish to put an early stop to them before they can spread any further, but it was not until late last night that I learned of these dreadful things they have just started saying. And when I sent to Madame de Merteuil's this morning, she had just left for the country where she is to spend the next two days. No one could tell me where she had gone. Her undermaid, whom I had sent for to talk to, told me that her mistress had simply given her orders to expect her next Thursday, and not one of the servants left here knew any more than she did. I myself do not have any idea where she may be. I cannot think of anyone of her acquaintance who remains in the country as late as this.

Be that as it may, I hope you will be in a position to obtain, between now and when she returns, information which may be useful to her. For these hateful stories are based upon the circumstances of Monsieur de Valmont's death, of which obviously you will have heard, if they are true; at least it will be easy for you to ascertain the truth of them, and I am asking you if you will kindly do that. This is what people are saying, or rather, what they are whispering, but will most certainly not be slow to proclaim more loudly before long.

It is said that the quarrel which broke out between Monsieur de Valmont and the Chevalier Danceny is the work of Madame de Merteuil, who was being unfaithful to them both. As is nearly always the case, the two rivals began by fighting and only got to explanations after the event. These produced a sincere reconciliation; and in order to show Madame de Merteuil in her true colours to the Chevalier Danceny and also to clear himself completely, Monsieur de Valmont produced a pile of letters which constituted a regular correspondence he had with her, in which she recounts the most scandalous anecdotes about herself in the most libertine fashion.

They are also saying that Danceny, in his first indignation, showed these letters to whoever would look at them, and that now it is all over Paris. Two in particular are cited:* one where she tells the whole story of her life and principles, and it is said they are the very worst; the other which puts Monsieur de

---

* Letters 81 and 85 in this collection.

Prévan, whose story you will recall, entirely in the right, by proving that on the contrary he only yielded to the most obvious advances of Madame de Merteuil, and that the rendez-vous was pre-arranged with her.

Fortunately I have the strongest reasons to believe that these imputations are as false as they are odious. First we both know that Monsieur de Valmont was certainly not interested in Madame de Merteuil, and I have every reason to believe that Danceny was not either. And so it seems to me self-evident that she could have been neither the subject nor the author of this quarrel. Nor can I see why Madame de Merteuil, who is assumed to have reached an understanding with Monsieur de Prévan, would have an interest in making a scene which could never have anything but disagreeably scandalous consequences, and which might have become extremely dangerous for her, since in that way she was making an irreconcilable enemy of a man who was in possession of some of her secrets, and who had, at that time, plenty of supporters. However, it is noticeable that since this affair not a single voice has been raised in Prévan's favour, and even from him there has been no protest.

These considerations lead me to suspect him as the author of the rumours going round today, and to view these slanderous accusations as an act of hatred and revenge by a man who, seeing himself lost, hopes by this means to spread doubts, at least, and perhaps cause a useful diversion. But, whatever the origin of these wicked rumours, the most urgent necessity is to destroy them. They would subside naturally if it so turned out, as is very likely, that Messieurs de Valmont and Danceny did not speak after their unfortunate affair, and there was not any handing over of documents.

In my impatience to check the facts I sent to Monsieur de Danceny's this morning. He is not in Paris either. His servants said to my footman that he left last night after receiving a warning yesterday, and that his destination was secret. Apparently he fears the consequences of his duel. Therefore it is only through you, my dear and worthy friend, that I may have the details which interest me, and which may become so necessary to Madame de Merteuil. I beg you again to send them to me as soon as possible.

P.S. My daughter's indisposition had no ill effects. She sends you her regards.

Paris, 11 December 17**

LETTER 169

The Chevalier Danceny to Madame de Rosemonde

Madame,

Perhaps you will find the action I am taking today very odd. But I beg you to listen before you judge me, and not to take for impertinence nor temerity what is done only out of respect and trust. I do not disguise from myself the wrongs I have done to you, and I should never forgive myself for them as long as I lived if I thought for one moment that it might have been possible to avoid them. Be persuaded, Madame, that though I may be free from blame I am not free from regrets. And I might add in all sincerity that the sorrow I have caused you has a large bearing upon my own. In order to believe these feelings, of which I take the liberty of assuring you, you have only to do justice to yourself and learn that, although I do not have the honour of being known by you, I do have that of knowing you.

However, while I deplore the fate which has brought about your sorrows and my misfortune at one and the same time, there are those who would have me fear that, with revenge your only aim, you are seeking the means to achieve it, even if you have to have recourse to the severity of the law.

Allow me first to observe on this point that here you are the victim of your grief, since my interest in the matter is essentially bound up with that of Monsieur de Valmont, and he would find himself embroiled in the disgrace you call down upon me. I should therefore believe, Madame, that I might on the contrary count on you for help rather than hindrance, in the care I may be obliged to take to ensure that this unfortunate affair is consigned to oblivion.

But such complicity, the resource for both the guilty and the innocent, cannot suffice for a man of my principles. While wishing not to have you as my accuser, I claim you as my judge. The esteem of people one respects is too precious for me to allow yours to be snatched from me without my resisting, and I believe I have the means to do so.

In fact if you agree that revenge is permissible, or let us rather say a duty, when one has been betrayed in love, in friendship, and especially in trust; if you agree to that, my wrongs will vanish in your eyes. Do not take my word for this, but read, if you have the strength, the correspondence which I am placing in your hands.* The quantity of letters which may be found there in the original would seem to prove the authenticity of those which exist only in copies. For the rest, I received these papers, which I have the honour of sending to you, from Monsieur de Valmont himself. I have not added anything, and have extracted from them only two letters[16] that I permitted myself to make public.

One was necessary to the revenge of both Monsieur de Valmont and myself, to which we had a right, and with which he expressly charged me. I thought moreover that it was doing a service to society to unmask a woman as truly dangerous as Madame de Merteuil, and who as you can see is the single true cause of everything that took place between Monsieur de Valmont and myself.

My sense of justice has led me to make the second public knowledge for the justification of Monsieur de Prévan, whom I scarcely know, but who has not in any way merited the harsh treatment he has suffered lately nor the severe and even more formidable judgement of the public, under which he has been

---

* It is from this collection of letters, from the one handed over at the death of Madame de Tourvel, and from letters also entrusted to Madame de Rosemonde by Madame de Volanges that the present collection has been assembled. The originals remain in the hands of the heirs of Madame de Rosemonde.

labouring ever since then without being able to say anything in his defence.

You will find, then, only copies of these two letters, of which I must keep the originals. As to all the rest, I do not believe I can put in any safer hands papers which I consider should not be destroyed, but which I should be ashamed to make any wrongful use of. I believe, Madame, that in entrusting these papers to you I am doing as great a service to the people concerned as if I were to give the letters directly to them. And I am sparing them the embarrassment of receiving such correspondence from me, and of knowing that I am aware of affairs which they would surely wish not to be made public.

I believe I should warn you in this regard that the enclosed letters are only one part of a much more voluminous collection, from which they were selected by Monsieur de Valmont in my presence. You will find the remainder, when the seals in the house are removed, under the title *Account opened between the Marquise de Merteuil and the Vicomte de Valmont*. You will do with them whatever you, in your wisdom, decide.

I am respectfully yours, Madame, etc.

P.S. After receiving certain warnings and on the advice of friends I have decided to absent myself from Paris for a while. But the place of my retreat, which I have kept secret from everyone else, will not be so from you. If you honour me with a reply, I beg you to address it to the Commanderie de —[17] near P—and under cover to Monsieur le Commandeur de —. It is from his house that I have the honour of writing to you.

Paris, 12 December 17**

LETTER 170

Madame de Volanges to Madame de Rosemonde

My dear friend, one shock after another and one sorrow after another. You have to be a mother yourself to have any idea of what I went through the whole of yesterday morning. And if my cruel worries have been calmed since then, I am still sorely distressed and cannot see an end to it.

Yesterday, towards ten in the morning, surprised not to have yet seen my daughter, I sent my maid to learn what could be making her take so long. She came back straight away much alarmed, and frightened me a deal more by her announcement that my daughter was not in her room, and that her chambermaid had not seen her there all that morning. Imagine what a state I was in! I summoned all my servants and in particular my hall-porter. They all swore they did not know anything about it and could not tell me anything about what had happened. I went to my daughter's rooms without delay. The untidiness that reigned there told me quickly that she must have left only that morning. But there was no explanation of her behaviour as far as I could see. I looked in her cupboards, her desk. I found everything in its place together with all her clothes, except for the dress she was wearing to go out. She had not even taken the small amount of money she had.

As she had not heard until yesterday all that people have been saying about Madame de Merteuil, to whom she is very attached, even to the point where all she did was weep the whole evening, and as I remembered too that Madame de Merteuil was in the country, at first I thought she had wanted to see her friend, and had been silly enough to go there on her own. But as time passed and she did not return I became extremely anxious once more. Every moment my worry increased, and though I longed to know where she was I did not dare make enquiries for fear of making my action public knowledge, when I might wish to hide it from people afterwards. Really, I have not suffered so much in my whole life!

Well, it was not until after two o'clock that I received, at one and the same time, a letter from my daughter and one from the Mother Superior of the convent of —. My daughter's letter simply said that she feared I might thwart her vocation to become a nun, and she had not dared talk to me about it. The rest was only apologies for having taken this decision without my permission, a decision which I should certainly not disapprove of, she added, if I knew what her motives were. However, she begged me not to ask her about them.

The Mother Superior told me that when she saw a young woman on her own arrive she had at first refused to take her in. But when she had questioned her and learned who she was she had thought she was doing me a service by giving my daughter temporary asylum, to protect her from doing anything further, which was what she seemed set upon doing. The Mother Superior, while she naturally offers to return my daughter to me, if I ask, has urged me, as her profession requires, not to place any obstacle in the way of a vocation upon which she seems so decided. She tells me as well that she was not able to inform me any sooner of this event because of the trouble she had in making my daughter write to me, for her plan was that everyone should remain in ignorance of where she had gone. Children are so cruel in their thoughtlessness!

I went to the convent without delay and, after seeing the Mother Superior, I asked to see my daughter. She appeared, but only reluctantly and in fear and trembling. I spoke to her in front of the nuns and I spoke with her alone. All that I got out of her, amid much weeping, was that she could only be happy in the convent. I decided to allow her to remain there, but not as yet to be among the ranks of the postulants as she asked. I believe the death of Madame de Tourvel and that of Monsieur de Valmont may have affected her young mind too much. Much as I respect the religious vocation, I should never see my daughter embrace this calling without sorrow or fear. It is my opinion that we have plenty of duties to fulfil already without creating new ones for ourselves. Besides, it is scarcely at that age that we can know what is good for us.

What makes it twice as embarrassing is the imminent return

of Monsieur de Gercourt. Will it be necessary to break off such
an advantageous match? And how can one minister to the
happiness of one's children if it is not enough to want it and
devote all one's attention to achieving it? You will oblige me
greatly by telling me what you would do in my position. I
cannot make up my mind at all. I find nothing so frightening
as to have to decide on the fate of other people, and I am
equally fearful of behaving with the severity of a judge or the
feebleness of a mother on this occasion.

I blame myself constantly for adding to your worries by
speaking about my own. But I know your nature. The consolation you are able to give to others will be for you the greatest
consolation you can receive yourself.

Farewell my dear, worthy friend. I am impatient to receive
your two replies.

Paris, 13 December 17**

LETTER 171

Madame de Rosemonde to the Chevalier Danceny

After what you have told me, Monsieur, there is nothing to be
done but weep and be silent. One is sorry to be alive still when
one learns of such terrible doings. One is ashamed of being a
woman when one sees a woman capable of excesses like these.

For my part I should be very glad to allow everything which
could have any bearing on, or ensue from, these lamentable
events to be quietly forgotten. I even hope they will never
cause you any other sorrows than those inseparable from your
unfortunate victory over my nephew. Despite his wrongdoing,
which I am forced to acknowledge, I feel I shall never be able
to get over his loss; but my eternal affliction will be the only
revenge I shall allow myself to take upon you. It is for you in
your heart to appreciate the extent of that.

If you would allow me at my age to make a remark that one

hardly ever makes at yours, it is that if we knew what our true happiness consists in, we should never seek it outside the limits prescribed by the law and religion.

You may be sure I shall faithfully and willingly keep the documents you have entrusted to me. But I ask you to authorize me to refuse to give them to anyone else, not even you, unless they should prove necessary in your defence. I daresay you will not refuse my request, and that you now feel that one often regrets having yielded to even the most just vengeance.

I shall not stop there in my requests, persuaded as I am of your generosity and delicacy. It would be most worthy of both if you also gave me back the letters of Mademoiselle de Volanges, which you apparently have kept and which are probably no longer of any consequence to you. I know this young person has done you wrong. But I do not think you had it in mind to punish her for it. And, if only out of self-respect, you will not revile the creature you loved so much. I have therefore no need to add that the respect which the daughter does not deserve is at least certainly due to the mother, to that respectable woman with regard to whom you have considerable amends to make. For, after all, however one seeks to delude oneself by claiming a certain delicacy of feeling, it is he who first tries to seduce a simple and innocent heart who makes himself thereby the first to sin by corrupting her, and he must be the one forever accountable for the excesses and mistakes she makes thereafter.

Do not be astonished, Monsieur, at so much severity on my part. It is the greatest proof that I can give you of my perfect esteem. You will acquire new rights as well by consenting to my wish that you will preserve a secret which would harm you if it were in the public domain, and would bring death to the heart of a mother, which you have already wounded. At all events, Monsieur, I wish to do this service to my friend. And if I were afraid that you might refuse me this consolation, I would ask you to first remember that it is the only one you have left me.

I have the honour to be, etc.

From the Chateau de —, 15 December 17**

LETTER 172

Madame de Rosemonde to Madame de Volanges

Had I been obliged, my dear, to send to Paris and wait for the information you ask me for with regard to Madame de Merteuil, it would not yet be possible to give it to you. And I should certainly have received from there only vague and unconfirmed reports. But some that I was not expecting and had no reason to expect have reached my ears, and they are only too definite. Oh my dear, how that woman has deceived you!

I am loath to enter into any details in this catalogue of horrors, but whatever people are saying about it still falls far short of the truth. My dear, I hope you know me well enough to trust what I am telling you and that you will not demand any proof from me. Let it simply be said that there is plenty of that, and I have it in my hands at this very moment.

It is not without extreme reluctance that I beg you, similarly, not to make me give you a reason for the advice you have asked for concerning Mademoiselle de Volanges. I am suggesting you do not stand in the way of her vocation. Assuredly no arguments can authorize the forcing of anyone into this state when the person herself does not have a calling to it; but sometimes it is extremely fortunate when it does happen. And, as you see, your daughter has told you herself that you would not disapprove of her if you knew her reasons. He who inspires our feelings knows better than we do, in our vain wisdom, what is good for each of us. And often what seems to be an act of harshness on His part is, on the contrary, one of clemency.

So my opinion, which I know will cause you suffering, and for that very reason will persuade you that I do not give it without a great deal of reflection, is that you should leave Mademoiselle de Volanges in the convent, since that is her choice, and that you should encourage rather than oppose the plans she seems to have made. And while you wait for the outcome you should not hesitate to cancel the marriage you have arranged.

After fulfilling these painful duties of friendship, and since I am powerless to offer any consolation, all I ask, my dear, is that you will spare me further questions about anything pertaining to these sad events. Let them be forgotten, as they ought to be. And, without seeking useless and distressing explanations, let us submit to the decrees of Providence and trust in its wise ways, even when it is not given to us to understand them. Farewell, my dear friend.

From the Chateau de —, 15 December 17**

LETTER 173

Madame de Volanges to Madame de Rosemonde

Oh my dear friend, what a terrifying veil you have drawn over my daughter's fate! And you seem to be afraid of me trying to lift it! What, then, is it hiding from me that may distress this mother's heart still more than the dreadful suspicions to which you have exposed me? The more I know of your friendship and kindness, the more my terrors increase. Since yesterday I have wished to leave these cruel doubts behind a score of times and ask you to tell me everything candidly and unequivocally. Each time I have trembled with fear, thinking of your plea to me not to question you, and so I have taken a decision which leaves me still some hope. I trust that out of friendship for me you will not refuse what I am asking. That is, to let me know if I have more or less understood what you might have to tell me, and not to be afraid to reveal anything that a mother's indulgence may excuse, and for which it is not impossible to make amends. If my misfortunes go beyond this measure, then I agree to allow you in fact not to explain anything except by your silence. So this is what I know already and this is the extent of my fears.

My daughter showed some inclination for the Chevalier Danceny and I was informed that she went so far as to receive letters from him and even to reply to him. But I thought I had managed to prevent this childish mistake from having any dangerous consequences. Now, fearing the worst, I realize that it would be possible for my watchfulness to have been deceived, and I am very much afraid my daughter has been seduced and has committed the ultimate folly.

I recall several circumstances which may add weight to these fears. I told you that my daughter had been taken ill at the news of the misfortune that befell Monsieur de Valmont. It is possible she was so affected, simply because she was thinking about the risks that Monsieur de Danceny ran in fighting this duel. When later she was so upset on learning of all they were saying about Madame de Merteuil, perhaps what I supposed to be the pain of friendship was only the effect of jealousy or the regret at finding her lover unfaithful. Her latest actions may also, it seems to me, be explained in the same way. Often one believes oneself to be called to God simply because one feels revolted by mankind. So, supposing that these facts are true, and that you have full knowledge of them, you will no doubt have found them enough to justify the severe advice you have given me.

However, if that were the case, while blaming my daughter I should yet believe that I owed it to her to try all means of saving her from the torments and dangers of an illusory and passing vocation. If Monsieur Danceny has not lost all sense of how a gentleman should behave, he will not refuse to repair a wrong of which he alone is the creator. Also I do believe that marriage with my daughter is advantageous enough for him to be gratified by it, just as his family would be.

That, my dear friend, is the only hope I have left. Please confirm it quickly if possible. You can judge how much I wish for a speedy response, and what a dreadful blow your silence would deal me.*

I was about to close my letter when a gentleman of my acquaintance came to see me and told me about the cruel humiliation inflicted on Madame de Merteuil the day before yesterday. As I have seen no one in recent days I knew nothing

---

* This letter remained unanswered

about this affair. Here is the story just as I heard it from an eye-witness.

Madame de Merteuil, on arriving back from the country the day before yesterday, Thursday, was set down at the Comédie Italienne where she has her box. She was alone and, what must have seemed extraordinary to her, not a single man presented himself to her throughout the whole performance. When she left she went into the small salon, as she usually does, and it was already full. Straight away there was a buzz of conversation, but apparently she did not realize she was the object of it. She saw that there was an empty space on one of the benches and went to sit down. But immediately all the women already there rose with one accord and left her absolutely on her own. This marked display of public indignation was applauded by all the men and caused the murmurs to increase, and they say some were even jeering.

So that nothing should be lacking in her humiliation, unfortunately for her, Monsieur de Prévan, who had not been seen anywhere since his affair, entered the small salon at that very moment. As soon as he was noticed, everyone, men and women alike, crowded round and congratulated him. And he found himself carried, so to speak, towards Madame de Merteuil by the company who made a circle around them. People affirm that she maintained an expression of total indifference and that her expression did not change! But I believe they are exaggerating. Whatever the case, this situation, which was really ignominious for her, lasted until the moment when her carriage was announced. And as she was leaving, the scandalous jeering increased. It is frightful to be related to this woman. The same evening Monsieur de Prévan was welcomed most warmly by all the officers of his corps who were there, and it seems a certainty that he will soon be given back his position and his rank.

The same person who gave me these details informed me that Madame de Merteuil caught a very bad fever the following night, and at first they thought it must be the effect of the terrible situation she had been in. But since last night she has the smallpox, and it is a very virulent kind. Truly I do believe it would be a blessing if she were to die. They are also saying that this whole affair will perhaps harm her court case a great deal; they are about to reach a decision, and people claim she needed all the favour she could get.

Farewell, my dear, worthy friend. I see in all this that the wicked are punished. But I do not find any consolation for their unfortunate victims.

Paris, 18 December 17**

LETTER 174

The Chevalier Danceny to Madame de Rosemonde

You are right, Madame, and I shall surely refuse you nothing that is in my power to do, and to which you appear to attach some importance. The packet I have the honour to send you contains all Mademoiselle de Volanges's letters. If you read them, you will perhaps be surprised to see that so much ingenuousness can be combined with so much perfidy. That at least is what struck me most just now when I read them for the last time.

But, above all, can one help feeling the strongest indignation with Madame de Merteuil, when one calls to mind what fearful pleasure she must have taken in devoting all her energies to perverting so much innocence and candour?

No, I am no longer in love. I retain nothing of feelings so shamefully betrayed. And it is not that that makes me seek to justify Mademoiselle de Volanges. For this simple girl, such a gentle and uncomplicated person, would she not have been inclined towards the good more easily than she allowed herself to be borne towards evil? What young person just out of the convent, inexperienced as she was and almost devoid of ideas, and, as happens frequently in society, almost equally ignorant of what is good or evil – what young girl would have been capable of stronger resistance to such wicked schemings? Ah, to be indulgent, all one has to do is reflect upon how much circumstances independent of ourselves hold the terrifying balance between the sensitivity or the depravity of our feelings. So you were doing me justice, Madame, when you supposed that the wrongdoings of Mademoiselle de Volanges, which I have felt so keenly, do not inspire me with any thought of revenge. It is quite enough to be obliged to give up loving her! It would cost me too much to hate her.

I had no need of reflection to wish that everything that concerns her and might harm her should for ever remain a secret. If I appeared to put off fulfilling your request in this respect for some time, I think I may disclose the reason for it. I wished beforehand to be sure I should not be made anxious by the consequences of this unfortunate affair. At a time when I asked your indulgence, and when I even dared suppose I possessed some rights in this respect, I feared I might seem to be in some sense buying it by doing you a favour. And, sure of the purity of my motives, I was proud enough, I admit, to wish you not to be left in any doubt about this. I hope you will forgive this delicacy, perhaps over-fastidious, in the light of the respect in which I hold you, and the importance I attach to your esteem.

The same feelings make me ask you as a last favour to let me know if you think I have fulfilled all the obligations that may have been imposed upon me by the unfortunate circumstances in which I find myself. Once reassured on this point I have decided what to do. I am going to Malta. There I shall gladly make and religiously keep vows which will separate me from a world from which, though still so young, I have already had so much to bear. So I shall go and try to forget under foreign skies so many accumulated horrors, the memory of which would only sadden and deaden my soul.

With respect, Madame, I am your very humble, etc.

Paris, 26 December 17**

LETTER 175

Madame de Volanges to Madame de Rosemonde

The fate of Madame de Merteuil appears to be sealed, my dear and worthy friend. It is such that her worst enemies are divided between the anger she deserves and the pity she arouses. I was right to say that it would be a blessing if she died of the smallpox. She has recovered from it, it is true, but she is horribly disfigured. And in particular she has lost the sight of one eye. You will understand that I have not seen her again. But they say she is truly hideous.

The Marquis de —, who does not let slip any opportunity to say something spiteful, when he spoke about her yesterday said that 'her illness had turned her inside out and that presently her soul was in her face'. Unfortunately everyone thought the expression exact.

Another event has added to her disgrace and wrongdoing. Her court case was decided the day before yesterday, and she lost it unanimously. Costs, damages, restitution of profits, everything has been awarded to the minors. So the small amount of her fortune which was not taken up by the proceedings has been absorbed, and more than absorbed, by the costs.

As soon as she learned the news, although she was still ill, she made her arrangements and left by post-chaise alone in the night. Her domestics are saying today that not one of them wanted to follow her. They think she has taken the road to Holland.

More than anything else this departure has caused an outcry because she has taken with her diamonds which are of considerable value and which ought to have formed part of her husband's estate; her silver and jewels; in short, anything she could. And they say she has left behind nearly 50,000 *livres* of debt. It is complete bankruptcy.

The family has to meet tomorrow to see if they can make some arrangement with the creditors. Although I am a very distant relative, I had offered to go along and help. But I shall not be at this gathering, since I have to attend an even more melancholy ceremony. My daughter is becoming a postulant tomorrow. I hope you will not forget, my dear friend, that my only reason for believing I am obliged to make this great sacrifice is the silence you have maintained towards me.

Monsieur Danceny left Paris nearly two weeks ago. They say he is going to Malta and intends to settle there. Would there still be time to prevent him? My dear! Is my daughter then so very guilty? You will no doubt forgive a mother that she can only with difficulty accept such a dreadful truth.

What disasters have struck me recently, through my nearest and dearest! My daughter and my friend!

Who would not tremble to think of the ills that may be caused by one dangerous liaison! And what troubles one could spare oneself by more careful reflection! Which woman would not flee at the seducer's first approach? What mother could without trembling see anyone but herself talking to her daughter? But we are only ever wise after the event, when it is too late. And one of the most important truths, which is also perhaps one of the most universally acknowledged, remains suppressed and forgotten in the inconsequential bustle of our everyday lives.

Farewell, my dear and worthy friend. I am now discovering that our reason, already so incapable of preventing our misfortunes, is even less able to afford us consolation.*

Paris, 14 January 17**

---

* For reasons of our own, and because of other considerations that we shall always believe it our duty to respect, we are obliged to stop here.

We cannot at the moment give our readers the subsequent adventures of Mademoiselle de Volanges, nor can we give any account of the sinister events that crowned the misfortunes and completed the punishment of Madame de Merteuil.[18]

Perhaps some day we shall be permitted to finish this work, but we cannot commit ourselves on this subject. And if it were possible, we should still think ourselves obliged in the first place to consult the public taste, since the public does not have the same reasons that we do for being interested in this book.

(*Publisher's note*)

Appendix 1
Additional Letters

These two letters appear in the manuscript of the novel, but were not included in the editions published during Laclos's lifetime.

1. The following supplementary letter was placed at the end of the manuscript as a lost letter just recovered. The publishers replaced it and substituted the footnote which now ends the book.

The Présidente de Tourvel to the Vicomte de Valmont

Oh my dear, what torments I have suffered since the moment you left me! And I have so much need of calm. How can it be that I have given in to such agitation that it is paining me and causing me real alarm? Can you believe this? I feel that even to write to you I need to summon all my strength and recall my reason. I keep telling myself that you are happy; but this thought, in which my heart delights, and which you have so aptly called love's sweet solace, on the contrary has thrown me in a ferment and overwhelmed me with too violent a happiness. Yet if I try to tear myself from this delightful reverie I straight away plunge into that cruel anguish that I have so many times promised you I will avoid, which I must certainly do since it would lessen your own happiness. My friend, it has been easy for you to teach me to live only for you; now teach me to live far from you. No, that is not what I meant to say; it is rather that I should not wish to live far from you, or I should wish to forget that I lived. Left to myself I cannot bear my happiness or my pain. I feel the need for rest, but all rest is impossible. In vain have I implored sleep to come; sleep has fled far from me. I cannot occupy myself with anything, nor can I remain idle. First a burning fire devours me, then a deathly chill numbs me. Every movement tires me, and I cannot remain in one place. So, what can I say? I should suffer less in the access of the most violent fever, and though I cannot explain or understand it, I know that this state of suffering comes only from my inability to contain or direct a host of feelings, to any one of which I would happily deliver up my entire soul. The very moment you left I was less tormented. A certain agitation was mixed with my regrets, but I attributed it to the presence of my maidservants who came in at that moment, and whose service, always too lengthy for my wishes, seemed to me to be a thousand times longer than usual. Above all I wished to be alone. I did not suspect then that, surrounded by such sweet memories, I was not to find in solitude the only happiness your absence could afford me. How could I have foreseen that, strong as I was in your presence to bear the shock of so many conflicting feelings, experienced in such quick succession, I should not be able to bear even the memory of them when I was alone. I was very soon and very cruelly disabused . . . Here, my dear friend, I hesitate to tell you everything . . . However, am I not yours, all yours, and must I hide a single one of my thoughts from you? Oh, it would be impossible for me. Only I claim your indulgence for my unwitting faults which my heart has no part in. I had, as usual, sent away my women before going to bed . . .

2. The following letter, intended to be Letter 155, was crossed out by Laclos and replaced by the footnote to Letter 154.

The Vicomte de Valmont to Madame de Volanges

I know, Madame, that you do not like me; I am equally aware that you have always spoken ill of me to Madame de Tourvel, and I am just as certain now that you feel confirmed in your opinions. I even concede you may have some basis for them. None the less, it is to you I write, and I do not hesitate to ask you not only to give Madame de Tourvel the letter enclosed here, but also to make her promise to read it, by assuring her of my repentance, my apologies and, especially, my love. I realize this request may strike you as odd. I am even surprised at it myself. But despair seizes its chance and does not stop to consider. Moreover in a matter which is so important, and of interest to both of us, we must set aside all other considerations. Madame de Tourvel is dying; Madame de Tourvel is unhappy. We must give her back her life, health, happiness. That must be our goal. All means are good if they assure or hasten this outcome. If you spurn what I am offering, you will remain responsible for what happens. Her death, your sorrow, my eternal despair, all will be your doing. I know I have ignobly insulted a woman worthy of my complete adoration. I know that it is my terrible wrongdoings alone that have caused all her ills. I do not try to hide my faults nor excuse them. But, Madame, do not become my accomplice by preventing me from putting them right. I have driven a sword into your friend's heart, but I alone can draw the blade out of the wound. I alone have the means to cure her. What does it matter if I am guilty, if I can be of use! Save your friend; save her! She needs your help, not your vengeance!

Paris, 4 December 17**

Appendix 2
Selected Adaptations of
Dangerous Liaisons

1950 *Les Liaisons dangereuses*, a radio play by Paul Achard, inspired by Laclos; also staged in the theatre of Montparnasse-Gaston-Baty in 1952.

1960 *Les Liaisons dangereuses*, a film by Roger Vadim with Gérard Philipe and Jeanne Moreau.

1974 *Les Liaisons dangereuses*, an opera by Claude Prey presented in Strasbourg and re-staged in Aix-en-Provence in 1980.

1982 and 1985 *Les Liaisons dangereuses*, a televised drama by Charles Brabant.

1985 *Dangerous Liaisons*, a play by Christopher Hampton, staged by the Royal Shakespeare Company.

1985 and 1989 *Quartett*, a play by Heiner Müller, produced by Patrice Chéreau, théâtre des Amandiers de Nanterre and by Jean-Louis Martinelli, théâtre de l'Athénée-Louis Jouvet.

1988 *Dangerous Liaisons*, a film by Stephen Frears, based on Hampton's 1985 play, with Glenn Close and John Malkovich.

1989 *Valmont*, a film by Milos Forman, with screenplay by Jean-Claude Carrière.

1999 *Cruel Intentions*, a film by Roger Kumble.

2003 *Untold Scandal*, a film by Lee Je Young set in eighteenth-century Korea.

2004 *Dangerous Liaisons*, an exhibition of costumes and interiors of the period at the Metropolitan Museum of Art in New York.

2005 *Les Liaisons Dangereuses*, a ballet at Sadler's Wells, London.

Notes

EPIGRAPH

1. *Julie ... Héloïse*: Jean-Jacques Rousseau's novel, *Julie ou la Nouvelle Héloïse, Lettres de deux amants habitant d'une petite ville au pied des Alpes* (Letters of Two Lovers Living in a Small Town at the Foot of the Alps) (1761), is a frequent reference point throughout *Dangerous Liaisons*. This epistolary novel, which recounts the story of the impossible love of Saint-Preux and Julie, crystallized sentimental ideals at a time when the excesses of a cynical rationalism were starting to provoke a moral reaction in France. In *Dangerous Liaisons* a similar relationship is exemplified by that of Cécile and Danceny.

PUBLISHER'S NOTE

2. *Sixty thousand livres*: The nobility had on average an income of between forty and sixty thousand livres a year. The *livre* was an old French coin. By 1740 it had shrunk in value to such an extent that coins of a larger denomination were needed. See also *louis*, Part One, note 17.

PART ONE

1. *en grande toilette*: Dressed in her finery.
2. *secrétaire*: Writing-desk popular in France in the second part of the eighteenth century.
3. *tourière*: A nun responsible for communicating with people outside the convent.
4. *rouerie*: A cunning trick.

5. *Gercourt's cousin*: Madame de Merteuil is the cousin of Madame de Volanges.

6. *new romance*: Merteuil often sees social relationships in literary terms. See, for example, Letter 10.

7. *myrtle ... triumph*: In classical times the winner of the games at Olympia was crowned with myrtle and laurel leaves.

8. *a great poet*: Jean de La Fontaine, famous poet and writer of fables, 1621–95. The quotation is from the dedicatory epistle to the Dauphin in the first book of *Fables* (1668)

9. *a Knight of Malta*: The Knights of Malta were a religious order responsible for protecting pilgrims from the Turks. Before they took their final vows they were not obliged to be celibate. See Letter 51.

10. *his regiment in Corsica*: Corsica became French in 1768, but two military campaigns were necessary in 1768 and 1769 to impose French administration.

11. *my petite maison*: A '*petite maison*' was a discreet house in the *faubourgs* (i.e. outside the city walls) where lovers met for secret assignations of a sexual nature.

12. *Le Sopha ... La Fontaine*: *Le Sopha* (1745), a notorious novel by Crébillon *fils; Julie ou La Nouvelle Héloïse* by Rousseau; and the licentious tales of La Fontaine.

13. *the boulevard*: Only one boulevard existed at the time where the old ramparts had been, near the present-day boulevards of Bonne-Nouvelle and Saint-Martin. Most of the modern Paris boulevards were constructed in the 1850s by Baron Haussmann.

14. *High Priest ... Temple*: The *petite maison* is a temple of love. Contemporary erotic literature frequently used religious metaphor.

15. *piquet*: A card game popular at the time.

16. *I dote ... passion*: Merteuil is claiming she does not wish to seduce Cécile, but her relationship with her is not lacking in sensuality. See Letters 38, 57 and 63.

17. *ten louis*: The *louis*, so called because it bore the head of the king, was a gold coin circulating in France before the Revolution. One *louis* was worth twenty-four *livres*, so Valmont effectively pays half the tax bill.

18. *the gazette*: This was a forerunner of the modern newspaper, usually aimed at a popular audience. It contained gossip, trivia and the sensational news items of the day.

19. *the least trace ... occurred*: She does, however, keep a copy; see Letter 44.

20. *that pliability . . . spoken*: See Letter 23.
21. *Métromanie*: Alexis Piron's play was successfully performed in 1738.
22. *Scipio himself*: Scipio, in an episode recounted by Livy (XXVI, 50) famously renounced a beautiful girl after the taking of Carthage and gave her back to her husband-to-be.
23. *my ladies . . . green room*: Many women with connections in the theatre at the time were prostitutes or 'kept women'.
24. *just a head*: I.e. seal it in the usual way.
25. *The very table . . . love*: Émilie's buttocks become in turn the table and the altar of love. The whole of this letter is a masterpiece of double entendres.

PART TWO

1. *a Merveilleuse*: The *Merveilleuses* were fashionable young women of the time who adopted a classical style of dress and later, about 1797, came to characterize an anti-revolutionary and unconventional attitude in the period of the Directoire. Cf. the *Incroyables*, similar people of fashion who affected certain speech characteristics such as the dropping of the letter 'r'.
2. *a Céladon*: A respectful lover, like the character Céladon in the popular seventeenth-century novel *L'Astrée* by Honoré d'Urfé.
3. *For if one went . . . Malta*: Certain monastic orders had a very bad reputation at the time and frequently figure in eighteenth-century pornographic novels.
4. *A wise man . . . problem*: See Jean-Jacques Rousseau, *Émile, Oeuvres Complètes*, La Pléiade, vol. IV, p. 384.
5. *All is lost*: Another echo of *La Nouvelle Héloïse* where Julie's mother discovers Saint-Preux's letters (*Oeuvres Complètes*, La Pléiade, vol. II, xxvii, p. 306).
6. *'What he has said, I shall do'*: Another reference to *La Nouvelle Héloïse* (IV, ii, p. 405).
7. *Le Méchant, Comédie*: Jean-Baptiste Gresset's play was written in 1747.
8. *Magdalene . . . sinner*: A biblical reference. Mary Magdalene, a prostitute converted by Christ, came to represent penitence in western art and literature.
9. *I led her . . . entirely*: The sexual innuendoes Laclos has made so far about the relationship between Merteuil and Cécile are made more obvious in this passage.

10. *put it in the post*: An internal postal service had been functioning in Paris since 1759.

11. *Comte de B—*: See Letter 59.

12. *the Prince*: A somewhat indecent poem about Joan of Arc by Voltaire called *La Pucelle* (The Maiden) (1762), ll. 56–60.

13. *the world stage*: A recurring metaphor in the novel to designate the social scene; see Letter 81.

14. *the details . . . to me*: Valmont is not really interested in run-of-the-mill seductions. Compare the manner in which he wishes Tourvel to surrender to him, described in Letter 70.

15. *wearing . . . wear*: Néron observes Junie thus in Racine's play *Britannicus* (1669).

16. *old chestnuts about rats*: The sexual connotations of 'rat' here are obvious.

17. *nothing . . . strange to me*: An echo of a line by Terence which became the motto of the Enlightenment: 'I am a man, I count nothing human foreign to me.'

18. *one of those . . . style*: See Letter 10.

19. *the Inseparables*: 'In the second half of the eighteenth century, the concept of inseparability in female friendships helped to guide and inform the construction of gender' (C. Roolston, 'Separating the Inseparables: Female Friendship and its Discontents in Eighteenth-Century France', *Eighteenth Century Studies*, Johns Hopkins Press, 32, 2, Winter 1998–9, pp. 215–31.

20. *women rivals to contend with*: The homosexual reference is obvious here.

21. *le sept et le va*: A rare move in the card game of pharaon, or faro, which entitles the player to a sevenfold win.

22. *ten leagues*: Roughly 38 kilometres.

23. *What problems . . . overcome*: Merteuil is attacking Valmont's privileged position in society.

24. *When have you . . . created*: Merteuil here praises the methods of observation and experimentation typical of eighteenth-century rational enquiry.

25. *a truth . . . secret*: Merteuil compares herself with Delilah in the Old Testament story of Samson. When Delilah discovered Samson's secret she shaved off his hair: all his strength left him and he was subdued. See Judges 13.

26. *the victim . . . but for me*: It is likely that she means her maid had committed infanticide, a relatively common practice at that time.

27. *frotteur*: This was the servant who scrubbed and polished the floors in the castle.

28. *a fairy godmother to you*: Fairy-tales were very popular at the
time. Forty-one volumes of the *Cabinet des fées* (The Cabinet
of Fairy-tales), a collection of fairy-tales including those of the
famous seventeenth-century writer the Comtesse d'Aulnoy, were
published in Geneva between 1786 and 1789.

29. *lansquenet*: A popular gambling card game similar to faro, dating
from the fifteenth century, but much in vogue in France in the
latter half of the eighteenth century.

30. *The Bishop . . . supper*: The dining room was on the ground floor
and the sitting room on the first floor.

31. *the effect . . . produce*: Prévan's sexual excitement is easily visible
in his tight-fitting costume.

32. *Zaïre . . . weeping*: A reference to Voltaire's tragedy *Zaïre*
(1732), in which the heroine proves her love for Orosmane by
weeping.

33. *like Annette . . . in fact*: A reference to *Annette et Lubin*, a light
opera by Charles Simon Favart (1710–92). Annette and her lover
Lubin were pastoral characters of the Rousseau-esque kind much
in vogue in the literature of the 1760s.

34. *my baths . . . interrupt*: Bathing was a very fashionable therapy
at the time.

PART THREE

1. *I have never . . . lenteurs*: Valmont is referring to his taste for
proceeding slowly in his enjoyment of sexual pleasure.

2. *pretend to be a dream*: A common motif in classical mythology.

3. *Achilles' sword . . . cause*: In Homer's *Iliad*, Telephas is wounded
and then cured by Achilles' sword.

4. *I speak . . . gallantry*: Voltaire, *Nanine* (1749), I, vii.

5. *I am tricked . . . despair*: In Richardson's epistolary novel
Clarissa, or The History of a Young Lady (1748–9), the seducer
Lovelace says much the same in a similar situation. *Clarissa* was
translated (and adapted) by the Abbé Prévost into French in
1751 as *Clarissa Harlowe* and, like *La Nouvelle Héloïse*, had an
important influence on Laclos. There are many parallels between
the two novels, for example the characters of the seducers Lovelace and Valmont.

6. *the days of Madame de Sévigné*: The Marquise de Sévigné (1626–
96), belle-lettriste.

7. *Clarissa*: See note 5 above.

8. *the Feuillants*: A convent that was situated at the present numbers 229–35 in the rue Saint-Honoré in Paris.

9. *Tournebride*: A dependency whose purpose was to house the servants and the horses belonging to visitors to the chateau.

10. *I certainly . . . valet*: Azolan is typical of the Ancien Régime in that he is very aware of who is superior or inferior to himself in rank. He counts himself superior to the liveried servant, as the *noblesse d'épée* (old nobility) is superior to the *noblesse de robe* (acquired nobility).

11. *Heavenly powers . . . happiness*: Saint-Preux's hymn of happiness when Julie confesses her love for him (*La Nouvelle Héloïse*, I, v, p. 41).

12. *to make her . . . Clarissa*: In Richardson's *Clarissa*, Lovelace uses opium to put Clarissa to sleep and rape her.

13. *the pleasures . . . virtue*: Julie's words to Saint-Preux in *La Nouvelle Héloïse*, I, ix, p. 49.

14. *overcome . . . vapours*: The 'vapours' was a general term in the eighteenth century to designate any nervous or psychosomatic illness.

15. *Love . . . reason*: From Jean-François Regnard's book, *Folies amoureuses* (The Follies of Love) (1704), which had for its theme the escapades of a pupil who manages to evade the supervision of her tutor.

16. *catechism of debauchery*: The pornographic *Catéchisme à l'usage des gens mariés* (Catechism for the Use of Married People), by Father Féline, was published in 1782, and banned by the Church. Another frankly pornographic and anonymous catechism intended for the use of prostitutes, *Catéchisme libertin*, appeared in 1791.

17. *My unfortunate . . . again*: Presumably this is because of the autumnal weather.

18. *strengthen . . . her virtue*: From *On ne s'avise jamais de tout!* (One Can Never Think of Everything!), a comic opera by Sedaine (1761).

19. *to obtain . . . it is*: Valmont probably means anal intercourse.

20. *a second cycle . . . hopes*: The second menstrual cycle will confirm Cécile's pregnancy.

21. *He does . . . yourself*: Valmont is making fun of Danceny through the mouthpiece of Cécile. Cf. his letter to the Présidente (Letter 48).

22. *His wig was indeed unpowdered*: Powdered wigs were worn everywhere at the time, by servants as well as nobles.

PART FOUR

1. *a Turenne or a Friedrich*: Valmont, who has already compared himself with Alexander the Great (Letter 15), now likens himself to two other generals: the Vicomte de Turenne (1611–75) and Frederick II of Prussia (1712–86). Lovelace in Richardson's novel compares himself with Caesar and Alexander.

2. *Hannibal . . . Capua*: Having conquered the Roman army, the Carthaginian general Hannibal didn't march on Rome but camped at Capua, where his men are reputed to have indulged in the pleasures of the flesh.

3. *Sometimes . . . my person*: See Letter 10.

4. *Town*: I.e. Paris.

5. *if this is . . . over*: Compare with Merteuil's view of the 'illusion' of love in the previous letter.

6. *The more . . . home*: From the patriotic tragedy *Le Siège de Calais*, written by de Belloy in 1765, soon after France ceded Canada and India to England.

7. *For reasons . . . that direction*: Sexual relations during menstrual bleeding were taboo at the time, but Cécile is pregnant and therefore Valmont may continue to have sex with her unhindered.

8. *your virtue*: This is the first time that the familiar 'tu' form is used between the sexes in the novel, but its tone here is contemptuous and not lovingly intimate.

9. *The veil . . . happiness.* Cf. Rousseau's *La Nouvelle Héloïse*: 'the veil is torn: this long illusion has vanished', said in similar circumstances, when Julie is betrayed (III, vi, p. 317).

10. *The Sage . . . happiness*: In *La Nouvelle Héloïse*, Rousseau asserts that man's vanity is the source of his greatest troubles (V, iii, p. 574).

11. *I shall soon . . . unhappy*: An approximate reference to what Socrates apparently said, quoted by Jean-François Marmontel in his *Conte moral d'Alcibiade* (Moral Tale of Alcibiades) (1765). Alcibiades (450–424 BC) was a handsome and reckless Athenian general and politician who betrayed his homeland.

12. *over there*: That is, at the *petite maison* referred to earlier (see Part One, note 11).

13. *provided . . . triumphs*: Valmont's secret, known to Merteuil, has to do with politics.

14. *I shall ensure . . . us*: Danceny is challenging Valmont to a duel.

The practice of fighting duels, condemned by Rousseau, was still current and much debated at the time.

15. *the Président de* —: A colleague of Madame de Tourvel's husband.

16. *two letters*: Letters 81 and 85, in which Merteuil recounts 'the most scandalous anecdotes about herself in the most libertine fashion' (p. 390).

17. *the Commanderie de* —: A commanderie was a religious property belonging to the military.

18. *We cannot ... Merteuil*: This note implies that Cécile did not remain in her convent, and that Madame de Merteuil had more adventures in Holland. The suggestion has inspired many imitators of Laclos from the end of the eighteenth century right through until the present day: for example, *Les Nouvelles Liaisons dangereuses, Roman de moeurs modernes (The New Dangerous Liaisons, a Novel of Modern Morals)* by Marcel Barrière, Paris, Albin Michel, 1925; *Les Amants (The Lovers)*, by Robert Margerit, 1957, Paris, Phébus, 1990; *L'Hiver de beauté (The Winter of Beauty)* by Christiane Baroche, Paris, Gallimard, 1987, and many more. For a list of other works inspired by Laclos, and adaptations of *Dangerous Liaisons* see Appendix 2.

THE STORY OF PENGUIN CLASSICS

Before 1946 ...'Classics' are mainly the domain of academics and students, without readable editions for everyone else. This all changes when a little-known classicist, E. V. Rieu, presents Penguin founder Allen Lane with the translation of Homer's *Odyssey* that he has been working on and reading to his wife Nelly in his spare time.

1946 *The Odyssey* becomes the first Penguin Classic published, and promptly sells three million copies. Suddenly, classic books are no longer for the privileged few.

1950s Rieu, now series editor, turns to professional writers for the best modern, readable translations, including Dorothy L. Sayers's *Inferno* and Robert Graves's *The Twelve Caesars*, which revives the salacious original.

1960s The Classics are given the distinctive black jackets that have remained a constant throughout the series's various looks. Rieu retires in 1964, hailing the Penguin Classics list as 'the greatest educative force of the 20th century'.

1970s A new generation of translators arrives to swell the Penguin Classics ranks, and the list grows to encompass more philosophy, religion, science, history and politics.

1980s The Penguin American Library joins the Classics stable, with titles such as *The Last of the Mohicans* safeguarded. Penguin Classics now offers the most comprehensive library of world literature available.

1990s The launch of Penguin Audiobooks brings the classics to a listening audience for the first time, and in 1999 the launch of the Penguin Classics website takes them online to a larger global readership than ever before.

The 21st Century Penguin Classics are rejacketed for the first time in nearly twenty years. This world famous series now consists of more than 1300 titles, making the widest range of the best books ever written available to millions – and constantly redefining the meaning of what makes a 'classic'.

The Odyssey continues ...

The best books ever written

PENGUIN 🐧 CLASSICS

SINCE 1946

Find out more at www.penguinclassics.com